Rafe's voice assumed a stern tone. "I thought I made myself understood years ago, Kettie. I don't take kindly to people nagging me about my cigar smoking. A man should be able to enjoy a few of life's pleasures without some woman carping at him night and day."

"I do not carp," Caitlan rebutted petulantly and stood up.

This proved to be an unfortunate maneuver, for a pair of strong hands seized those softly curved hips and jerked her back onto the uncomfortable ledge. Caitlan sat with her backside smarting, her temper simmering, and her foot tapping out an impatient rhythm while Rafe took his sweet time about his business.

"There." Rafe concluded by tying the ribbons into a taut bow and gave Caitlan's rump a satisfying slap to indicate he had finished with her . . . for the time being.

Caitlan did not immediately relinquish her seat. Her legs were trembling with such vehemence that she did not trust her limbs to support her. Finally, she stood. Caitlan knew without looking that a smile of smug satisfaction adorned Rafe's sensuous mouth, and she resolved that he should not wear it for long. Whirling about, she snatched the controversial cigar and plunged the glowing end into the murky water . . .

Bittersweet Destiny

LUANNE WALDEN

DIAMOND BOOKS, NEW YORK

BITTERSWEET DESTINY

A Diamond Book / published by arrangement with
the author

PRINTING HISTORY
Diamond edition / March 1991

ISBN: 1-55773-473-9

Diamond Books are published by The Berkley Publishing
Group, 200 Madison Avenue, New York, New York 10016.
The name "DIAMOND" and its logo are trademarks
belonging to Charter Communications, Inc.

PRINTED IN THE UNITED STATES OF AMERICA

10 9 8 7 6 5 4 3 2 1

Dedication

In Memory . . .

Of Linda

A free spirit who touched my life for an all too fleeting space of time. I miss you, but will never forget you; I have such special memories . . . memories that echo in my heart.

ACKNOWLEDGMENTS

It goes without saying that an undertaking of this magnitude cannot be achieved without outside assistance. I would, therefore, like to extend a heartfelt "thank-you" to the following:

- Carla N. Simpson and the other ladies at the Vicksburg Book Store, who so generously gave of their time and made suggestions on appropriate reference books on Vicksburg and the period.
- The attendant at the Old Court House Museum.
- The tour guide at McRaven, whose vivid and detailed accountings of life in early-to-mid 19th-century Mississippi made me appreciate the conveniences of the 1990s all the more. The advertisement was right: If you're in Vicksburg and only have time for one historic house tour . . . make it McRaven.
- The authors of two extremely informative books on the period: *Vicksburg—A People at War, 1860–1865* by Peter F. Walker and *15 China and other tales* by Gordon A. Cotton.
- Finally, I would especially like to thank the good people of Vicksburg, who made this "Yankee Girl" feel at home in their beautiful, historic city.

Bittersweet Destiny

Chapter One

July 1860
Vicksburg, Mississippi

There it was again. It was a distinctly eerie sensation that
prickled Caitlan Webber's spine as she bent to place a folded
shirt atop a bulging laundry basket. She had experienced the
exact feeling upon climbing from her bed that morning, and
once more when she served Mr. Morgan a second helping of
pancakes and molasses at breakfast. The earlier episodes had
imbued Caitlan with a nagging sense of anticipation; almost
as if she were being warned of some portentous happening in
the offing. This time was no different.

A cynical smile spread her lips as work-worn fingers disengaged wooden clothespins from the remaining articles of
wind-dried clothing; if the truth were known, Caitlan would
cheerfully welcome a bit of diversion into her humdrum life.
With a discontented sigh, she heaved the basket onto her hip
and, turning toward the house, was confronted by the source
of all her sorrows.

Harriet Tuttle, the owner and proprietress of Tuttle's Boarding House, was leaning out an upstairs window. Her arms were
braced against the sill and a formidable expression darkened

her woefully plain features. "Katie Webber, stop dillydallying this instant!" came the shrill rebuff.

Harriet punctuated this totally unfounded indictment by stomping her foot against the pine floor that Caitlan had polished that very morning. Although she did not actually hear the thud of the leather sole, Caitlan could imagine it well enough; during her lengthy tenure at Tuttle's Boarding House, she had stood witness to this melodramatic display on more occasions than she cared to remember. Caitlan likewise understood it would be useless to refute Harriet's accusation. She could but humor her harsh taskmaster.

"I'm on my way to the kitchen now, Harriet. The irons have been warming these past thirty minutes or more, and I daresay I shall make short work of Mr. Hamilton's shirt."

"Well, mind you don't scorch it," the older woman snapped. "And have a care with Miss Crawford's powder-blue taffeta, if you please. She'll be wearin' it to afternoon tea with Mrs. Green and will want to look her best."

"Humph! If I know Penelope, she will be more concerned with what sort of refreshments Mrs. Green will be serving than if her gown is wrinkled," Caitlan muttered under her breath, carting her heavy load toward the kitchen entrance.

Satisfied that her orders would be swiftly carried out, the owner of the modest establishment made as if to abandon her lofty perch but Caitlan's suspicious-sounding mumblings prompted Harriet to inquire, "What's that you say, Katie?"

"Nothing, Harriet." Caitlan choked out a reply, quickening her step. "I'll have these garments ready in a trice."

"See that you do. And you best mind that brassy tongue of yours, missy" came Harriet's indignant warning. "That's a fine way for you to act, considerin' all I've done for you. Just remember who it was that took you in after the shameful way your papa died. Why, I gave you a roof over your head and put food in your belly when no one else would. Have you any idea where you'd be today if it wasn't for Harriet Tuttle?"

There was not so much as a twinge of acknowledgment from a certain russet-tinged downcast head, but that did not dissuade Harriet. She cackled on, wagging her bony finger at the top of Caitlan's downturned head.

"I'll tell you where. You'd be down at Mollie Bunch's place, selling yourself to the riffraff what frequents her bawdy house. Or maybe the Sisters of Mercy would have taken pity on you. But no, *I* took you in and gave you a respectable position in my house, and this is the thanks I get—backbitin' and spiteful talk. You just better mind your tongue from here on out if you know what's good for you, Katie Webber, and remember where you'd be if it wasn't for me,'' Harriet concluded on a huff, slamming the window for good measure.

''Remember!'' Caitlan scoffed, pulling a face at the recently vacated embrasure. ''With you hell-bent on reminding me at every blessed turn, it's not likely I'll soon forget.''

''She sure does ramble on, don't she, Miz Katie?'' a masculine voice commented upon rounding the corner of the house in the wake of Harriet's diatribe.

Caitlan was not startled by the intrusion, however, for the caller was well known to her. She did not so much as glance in the man's direction nor did Caitlan falter a step. Indeed, she motioned for the man to follow her, calling over her shoulder, ''After five years, one would think a body would get used to her caterwauling, Hezekiah.''

''Ain't no one, man nor beast, what could evah gets used to that.'' The big Negro shook his head doubtfully and, shifting the block of ice he carried to a more comfortable position against his shoulder, Hezekiah fell into step behind his former mistress, his progress hampered somewhat by a limp that plagued his right leg.

Caitlan no sooner crossed the threshold than she let the laundry basket drop against the stone floor with a loud thump. Then she propped the kitchen door ajar and went to ready the icebox for Hezekiah's frozen bundle. Once the block of ice had been positioned in the icebox, Caitlan swung the door closed and motioned Hezekiah to sit down at the table.

''Are you expected back at the ice company soon?'' she inquired conversationally.

''Naw, ah always makes you mah last delivry, just sose we can talk for a spell and ah can see how yer gettin' on,'' he replied kindly.

''Good. You sit yourself down, and I'll fetch you a cup of coffee and a slice of my apple-spice nut cake. I baked it fresh this morning.''

There had been a time, not so very long ago, when Hezekiah would have balked at the notion of sitting down to take refreshment at a gentlewoman's table. His concern having been for Caitlan's reputation should the town tabbies—who either did not understand, or chose to ignore, the circumstances surrounding their relationship—get wind of these Thursday-morning rituals and create a scandal. But, in time, he had come to accept Caitlan's hospitality without demur. In fact, Hezekiah had grown so accustomed to being treated thusly that he would have suspected something was awry had Caitlan not welcomed him with a promise of coffee and a sampling of one of her delicious confections.

As was typical, Caitlan did not join Hezekiah at the table. Instead, she settled the food and drink before the appreciative man and went on about her work. Hezekiah scooped up a man-size portion of the moist cake and his dark eyes narrowed thoughtfully as he observed Caitlan bustling about the small kitchen.

As Hezekiah watched, Caitlan set up a rickety ironing board, then went to the sink to pump a pan of water from the well. After sprinkling the garments from the laundry basket with a liberal dose of water, she rolled them into soft balls and returned all save one to the wicker receptacle. Finally, Caitlan spread Mr. Hamilton's promised shirt across the ironing board and lifted an iron from the hot stove.

The scene was one Hezekiah had observed on numerous occasions, yet it had an unusual effect on him this day. Swallowing a bite of the flavorful cake, he remarked, "Ah sure does hates it that you has to work so hard, Miz Katie. 'Tain't right. Your papa should've taken bettah care of you."

"I believe we have had this conversation before, Hezekiah," Caitlan began cautiously, not wanting to injure his feelings. Then with a shrug of her slender shoulders, she continued, "Papa did the best he could, I suppose. Besides, I don't mind working hard, truly I don't. Albeit, I could—and oftentimes do—wish for a more congenial employer."

"That's what ah mean. 'Tain't right for you to be workin' like a mule for the likes of Harriet Tuttle. She's no fittin' companion for you, Miz Katie. She's mean and hateful—the whole town knows it. You should've sold me to Mistah Cantrell when you had the chance right aftah your papa passed on. That's what you should've done!''

"Hezekiah! Have you taken leave of your senses? How can you say such a thing?'' Caitlan scolded and, laying the now tepid iron aside, she sat down opposite the troubled man. Without thinking, graceful fingers stretched across the table to clasp a pair of dark hands in a comforting gesture.

"Hezekiah," Caitlan repeated softly. "Just as it is senseless to blame Papa for all my woes, neither should you lament over what has come to pass. Papa was never the same after Brendan was killed in that dreadful duel—he grew distant, was easily rankled and, as you know, started squandering large sums of money. I should have taken steps to curtail his irresponsible behavior long before I did. Instead, I ignored the situation, thinking it best to let Papa's wild spirit run its course.

"By the time I realized my mistake, it was too late. Things had gone much too far. In any event, the debts Papa left behind were enormous," Caitlan explained. "I sold Grandmother's jewels in order to settle many of Papa's accounts and, although I am fairly certain you would have brought a tidy sum—bad leg and all—I'm convinced that giving you your freedom was perhaps the only decent thing to come from all this. I don't regret having done so, Hezekiah, so put your mind to rest," she concluded, giving the callused hands an affectionate pat.

Standing, Caitlan hung Mr. Hamilton's shirt aside and selected another garment from the dampened pile. "Let us talk about happier matters, shall we? How is Abigail getting on these days? Will you be going up to the Stark Plantation to see her soon?''

"As a mattah of fact, that's where ah'll be headin' when ah leaves here. Ah ain't seen her in a month or more coz ah've been takin' on extra odd jobs from the folks here 'bouts. Mr. Stark done promised he'd let Abigail go free if'n ah could raise anothah thirty dollahs.''

"And have you?" Caitlan inquired, carefully touching her finger against a freshly retrieved iron. The delicate appendage was snatched away an instant later—a sure indication that the device was of an appropriate temperature—and Caitlan proceeded with her task.

"Ah has," Hezekiah replied proudly, thumping his breast pocket in a satisfying gesture.

"What?! Then what, may I ask, are you doing whiling away the day with an old spinster like me when you could be off courting your Abigail?"

"Shucks, Miz Katie," Hezekiah protested. "You is a long way off from bein' a spinstah."

"That's neither here nor there." Caitlan dismissed the comment with an airy wave of her hand and, settling the iron on a resting plate so as not to scorch the fine material, she marched across the room to her guest. "Finish your coffee," she ordered, both her tone and manner perfunctory.

Caitlan observed as Hezekiah did as he was told, then she pointed toward the door, saying, "Off with you now. Go and fetch your bride-to-be home to Vicksburg. I'm looking forward to meeting her." When Hezekiah still did not move, Caitlan gave him a playful nudge. "Off with you, I say. You must be longing to share your good news with Abigail. Go on, Hezekiah. It will be near dark before you reach the plantation as it is," Caitlan reminded him.

This pronouncement served to spur Hezekiah to action which was evidenced by the scraping of his chair across the stone floor. Walking to the door, he paused on the threshold to say in parting, "Thank you, Miz Katie. You always was good to me. Ah'll nevah forget your kindness, and ah'll bring mah Abbie-gal by to meet you real soon."

Caitlan remained in the aperture until Hezekiah disappeared around the corner of the white-frame house. Then the faint smile that had highlighted her face during much of Hezekiah's visit withered to be supplanted with an expression of dispirited acceptance. As Caitlan turned toward the interior of the kitchen, that strange sensation which had plagued her throughout the day enveloped her once more. This occurrence coincided with a blast of sultry, summer air and a rumbling of thunder in the distance which beckoned a pair of green eyes toward the darkening sky in quizzical fascination. Thinking her qualms may have found their derivation in the approaching storm, Caitlan shook off the eerie feeling and closed the door.

The tempest came and quickly spent its fury, however, and

still the disheartened young woman could not purge herself of that haunting feeling of impending dread.

The freshly laundered clothes had been pressed and returned to their rightful owners, and supper had been cooked and the boarders served the evening repast before Caitlan was permitted the luxury of a few moments of peace and quiet. In the kitchen, the dishes had been washed and dried and safely stored in the corner hutch, and Caitlan was sitting down to enjoy a much deserved cup of chamomile tea when there came a familiar tapping at the door.

"Come in, Essie," Caitlan called without ceremony, reaching for another cup and saucer.

A steaming cup of the aromatic tea was awaiting the visitor when she sat down at the table moments later. Caitlan, who was well acquainted with her guest's sweet tooth, was preparing to slice a piece of apple-spice nut cake for Essie's gratification when a woebegone statement from that quarter made her pause.

"None for me, Katie. I fear I couldn't eat a bite, I'm that upset."

Caitlan cast a knowing look at her friend's glum face and, settling back in her chair, she took a sip of tea and said, "It's not like you to pass up a piece of my apple cake. What is wrong, Essie? What has Madame Cognaisse done this time?"

Essie—evidently undergoing a change of appetite—pulled the cake platter toward her and helped herself to a generous serving of the savory delicacy. Taking a bite, she chewed and said, "Madame Cognaisse ain't to blame, I suppose. She can't help me from being such a wretched seamstress."

"What happened?"

"I was stitchin' up Mrs. Balfour's new satin gown," Essie began to explain. "And I guess my mind wandered from my work 'cause, the next thing I know, I'm bleedin' all over Mrs. Balfour's dress. I guess I must have jabbed my finger with the needle."

"Oh, Essie, no," Caitlan lamented, mentally visualizing the couturiere's furious reaction upon discovering Essie's unfortunate blunder.

"I'm afraid so," the troubled girl mumbled, swallowing a

mouthful of the cake before revealing the worst of her tale.
"When Madame seen what I'd done, she flew into a rage—
started yellin' all sorts of things. Course I didn't understand
much of what she said, 'cause when she gets riled like that
she screams mostly in French. Anyway, she got me so flustered
with all her squallin' that, when I jumped up to see what
damage had been done to the gown, I stumbled into the table
and sent the candle tumblin' onto Mrs. Balfour's dress.

"As if the bloodstains weren't bad enough, the candle wax
spilt all over the material and the flame burnt a big hole in the
bodice before I could stomp out the fire. That's when Mrs.
Balfour came into the shop," Essie whispered ominously.

Caitlan bit back the smile that twitched at the corner of her
mouth. Not that she was unsympathetic to Essie's plight, for
she could well imagine her friend's distress. Yet Caitlan was
possessed of a keen sense of humor and, although she had
experienced little recourse to laughter as of late, she could
appreciate the absurdity of Essie's unhappy dilemma.

"Whatever happened next?" Caitlan asked, swallowing the
giggle that rippled in the back of her throat.

"I'll allow that things didn't turn out near half as bad as I
expected." Essie sighed her relief. "Mrs. Balfour—she really
is a kind lady—managed to quiet Madame Cognaisse down.
She soothed Madame's ruffled feathers by tellin' her that ac-
cidents could happen to anyone, and seein' as how she didn't
need the dress till Saturday evenin'—she's givin' a fancy ball
up at her place—we still had time to sew her a new gown.

"Course, that means I'll have to work night and day to finish
it in time, but I don't truly mind seein' as who the dress is
for. I think Madame would have fired me on the spot if Mrs.
Balfour hadn't been so understandin' and all. Not that I
could've blamed her—I'm a sorry seamstress at best. But you
know, Katie, I wouldn't mind gettin' fired if it weren't for Pa
bein' so sick. Ma would've skinned me alive if I'd lost my
job," Essie confessed ruefully, chewing the last morsel of cake
with hollow satisfaction. "I wish I could find me a job like
yours, Katie. I'm a much better cook than dressmaker."

"I know," Caitlan murmured, standing to give her friend's
shoulder a reassuring squeeze. "It would seem that fortune has

not looked kindly upon either of us, Essie. But there is little to be gained from such dismal reflection.

"Are you on your way back to the dress shop to begin your all-night vigil?" Caitlan observed Essie's dismal nod with a silent smile of understanding and, after clearing away the dirty dishes, she removed her soiled apron and turned once more to her disheartened friend. "Come along, then. I'll walk with you as far as Jackson Street. I have a dish of stew left over from supper I was planning to take to the Widow Stevens in the morning, but I may as well carry it over this evening."

A blast of steamy, July air wafted across Caitlan's face through the kitchen window as she went to collect the bowl from the counter. The smells and sounds of night gave every indication that another storm was brewing, prompting Caitlan to close the window and pluck her shawl and frayed bonnet from the peg behind the kitchen door. "Don't look so gloomy, Essie," Caitlan adjured, guiding the cheerless girl toward the doorway. "I cannot explain it, but I have a feeling our luck may soon change for the better."

Caitlan allowed the creaky gate to swing closed behind her as she stepped onto the sidewalk in front of the Widow Stevens's house. Her visit with the old woman had gone pretty much as Caitlan had expected . . . precisely as it always did in fact. The feisty octogenarian's tongue had been in rare form, making Caitlan ask herself for at least the hundredth time why she persisted with her efforts to cultivate a friendship with Delia Stevens. The irascible old woman made it clear time and again that she wanted very much to be left alone.

Caitlan knew that most of the townspeople considered Delia to be an eccentric old fool, a fact which was corroborated by many of the locals who went out of their way to avoid her. Caitlan had heard the stories and knew them for what they were, groundless tales concocted in the overactive minds of mischief-making children and worrisome town tabbies who had nothing better to do with their time. Delia Stevens was, in truth, nothing more than a lonely, reclusive old woman. A woman who, since God had not blessed with children and grandchildren to comfort her in her dotage, had grown sour

and bitter following the death of her beloved husband of more
than fifty years.

"Poor Delia," Caitlan murmured on a night breeze and,
feeling a sudden chill despite the hot evening, pulled her shawl
more tightly about her shoulders. With a sigh and a mental
promise to visit the old woman more often, Caitlan began to
walk back to the boarding house.

When she arrived at the corner of Washington Street, Caitlan
turned south out of habit. She had traveled only a few steps,
however, when she was again struck by that odd sensation that
had pestered her throughout the day and her pace gradually
slackened. With an unexpected pang, Caitlan realized that she
was in no great hurry to climb the narrow staircase which led
to the minuscule attic chamber that Harriet had allotted her.
As the tingling sensation along her spine persisted, Caitlan—
feeling strangely certain that something out of the ordinary
awaited her this night—turned about and started walking in
the opposite direction.

She lost all sense of time and place as her feet carried her—
as if of their own volition—toward some secret destination. In
fact, the seemingly possessed young woman had trudged well
beyond Vicksburg's northern boundary before she had the good
sense to take stock of her situation. Caitlan could not suppress
the mingled gasp of surprise and dismay that tumbled from her
lips when she discovered where her wayward, misguided
thoughts had led her. She was standing on a treacherous bluff,
high above the Mississippi River . . . the very precipice from
which her father had plummeted to his death some five years
earlier.

The impact of this revelation struck the bemused woman
with all the force of a mighty gale. Caitlan staggered sideways
and sank to her knees as she grappled to bring her faltering
composure under control. Her efforts proved futile, for once
the dam had been pierced the painful happenings of the past
five years, which Caitlan had heretofore tucked away in her
subconscious, flooded her being with a vengeance. There had
been occasions when her father's face had maneuvered its way
into Caitlan's head, but she had somehow managed to avoid
a confrontation with her parent's ghostly visage . . . until now.

"Papa, why?" came Caitlan's plaintive cry. "Why must

you keep popping into my head? I had hoped to have forever settled this business between us.''

In truth, there was still a great deal to be resolved between daughter and deceased father. To be sure, Caitlan had long since come to terms with her father's death. But the fact that Lawrence Webber had taken his own life was a blow that still stung Caitlan quite deeply and doubtlessly always would.

At thirty-one, Caitlan had been well schooled in the bitter realities of the world; certainly more so than most other young ladies of breeding who came from similar backgrounds. She maintained a noncommunicative tongue, however, when it came to discussing her straitened circumstances. Albeit Caitlan was reluctant to talk about her feelings, she did admit—if only to herself—that her life had not turned out as she had planned.

Caitlan had been born and raised at Thistledown, a small but thriving plantation about half-a-day's ride northwest of Baton Rouge, Louisiana. Tragedy first struck the Webber household when Caitlan was ten years old. Her mother, having grown bored with the responsibilities of caring for a home, husband, and two spirited children, had a love affair with the owner of a neighboring estate. In an almost unheard of occurrence, the pair ran away together and were never heard from again.

As may be expected, the community had buzzed for weeks when news of the scandal became common knowledge. While Caitlan and her older brother Brendan had struggled to understand their mother's disappearance, their father wrestled with the humiliation of being deserted by the wife he had cherished for more than fifteen years. Although Lawrence Webber never completely reconciled himself with his loss, the pain eventually ebbed, enabling him to get on with his life.

Lawrence had subsequently hurled himself headlong into running Thistledown and rearing his children. It is to Lawrence Webber's credit that, even though Caitlan bore a striking resemblance to her perfidious mother, he never allowed the constant reminder of his wife's infidelity to cloud his judgment when dealing with his daughter. He loved both his children with a fierce devotion; therefore, when news was brought to him one crisp, November morning in 1854 that Brendan had been killed in a duel—defending the honor of a mother who had long since forsaken him—it is little wonder that this tragedy was one from which Lawrence Webber never recovered.

Brendan's senseless death served the devastating blow to his father. Within the year, Lawrence lost Thistledown to the very scoundrel who had taken his son's life. He gambled recklessly and, as a result, was plunged deeper and deeper into a black abyss of debt from which he never emerged.

To escape his creditors and the added degradation of this latest scandal, Lawrence Webber had gathered up his daughter and their few remaining possessions and moved to Vicksburg. They took up residence at Tuttle's Boarding House where Harriet, construing Caitlan's father's well-dressed appearance and dignified air for a man of consequence, immediately set her aging cap for the onetime well-to-do planter. Thinking to ingratiate herself with the father, Harriet had doted on her would-be suitor's daughter, making certain that Caitlan wanted for nothing.

Under normal circumstances, Caitlan would have recognized Harriet's fawning ways for what they were. The sad fact of the matter was that, in addition to her brother's death and her father's self-destructive behavior, Caitlan was still mourning a memory of a very personal nature—that of a love gone sour. But with the cold reality of her father's suicide, even this private tragedy had been swept aside; Caitlan had been faced with a pressing personal dilemma . . . survival.

Lawrence Webber had accumulated tremendous debts and in the wake of his death, his creditors—both in Baton Rouge and Vicksburg—looked to his sole-surviving heir as a source of repayment. They may just as well have looked to the moon, however; Caitlan's only means of liquid assets were the jewels left to her by her grandmother. A sardonic expression found its way to Caitlan's face as this particular reflection wormed its way into her thoughts; her grandmother's legacy was to have been her dowry. Instead, she had been obliged to sell the gems in order to reckon a goodly portion of her father's outstanding accounts. The remainder had been settled by Harriet Tuttle.

At first, Caitlan thought Harriet had come to her rescue out of the kindness of her heart, but in very short order the older woman's purpose became evident. Certain that Lawrence Webber had played her for a fool and, unable to vent her spleen on him, Harriet Tuttle had determined that the daughter would pay for her father's trickery. With nowhere else to go and no family or friends to turn to, Caitlan had been left with no alternative.

She had forfeited her comfortable chamber on the second floor and took up residence in one of the boardinghouse's cramped, third-floor attic rooms. For appearance's sake, Harriet paid Caitlan a salary for the services she rendered to Tuttle's Boarding House. If the truth were told, however, Caitlan returned more than two-thirds of her meager wages to her employer in an attempt to repay the debt Harriet had incurred on Lawrence Webber's behalf. Caitlan was, in short, little more than an indentured servant—a drudge at the constant beck and call of Harriet and the boardinghouse tenants.

Blowing a beleaguered sigh, Caitlan fought off these dismal remembrances. After all, there was no use repining over that which could not be changed, and nothing would be gained by wallowing in self-pity. For although Caitlan envisioned a cheerless, lonely existence that stretched before her interminably, she knew she could never emulate her father's example.

"Oh, Papa. Yours was the easy solution," she whispered mournfully. "I have learned it is much more difficult to sort one's way through a disappointing life."

Caitlan felt a splash of water against her cheek and her hand lifted automatically to the dampened region. Having not shed a tear since the day her father had been laid to rest in the pauper's cemetery on the outskirts of town, she was not surprised to find that the source of the watery deluge was the rain that had threatened all evening. Realizing she would be properly drenched if she did not seek out some form of shelter, Caitlan cast her gloomy reminiscences aside and, pulling her shawl tightly about her shoulders, climbed to her feet.

But disaster lay lurking in the storm-riddled night; as Caitlan turned to make her way back to the roadway, her toe caught the edge of some unseen object that lay blocking the path. As she lost her balance alongside the precarious ledge, she was pitched headlong into the darkness. Terrified, her hands groped wildly for something to grasp for support, but there was nothing; only Caitlan's heart-stopping scream of terror as it echoed down the bluff.

Chapter Two

Trembling fingers groped at the slippery blades of grass and several desperate moments passed before Caitlan realized she had been spared a deadly fall. Luckily, her forward impetus was such that she had been thrown away from the edge of the cliff and had landed safely in a patch of wet grass. Her heart was still thumping wildly in her breast and her pulse pounded at her temples, however, as Caitlan dragged herself to her knees. As her equanimity was gradually regained, inquisitive hands initiated a search of the immediate area to determine what had precipitated her potentially disastrous tumble.

Fully expecting to find the culprit to have been a fallen tree branch or some such similar debris, Caitlan was understandably perplexed when her probing hands settled upon a curiously pliable object. Another moment of investigation was all that was required for Caitlan to identify the mysterious shape. With a squeal of surprise, she jerked her hands away and scrambled a safe distance from her unsettling discovery.

It was a man!

An eternity seemed to tick away as Caitlan sat perched upon her knees in the stormy darkness, the wind thrashing all about her and the rain pelting her thunderstruck face. In short, Caitlan was a bulwark of indecision, unable to do anything more than stare in gape-faced stupefaction at the hulking shadow that lay in lifeless repose just inches from her. Her head was a whirl-wind of turmoil and her stomach churned as she battled to bring her rampaging emotions under control.

Is he dead or alive?

This unspoken conjecture reeled inside Caitlan's pounding head and sent a shiver of dread rippling through her being. In spite of her distress, Caitlan realized she needed to gather her wits about her if she hoped to render assistance to the stricken man. Tamping down her fear with a burst of courage, she crept closer to the still figure. He lay on his stomach, making it impossible for her to listen to his chest for signs of a heartbeat. Swallowing a fortifying breath, Caitlan directed her fingers alongside the man's throat, and a wave of relief washed over her when she felt the pulse that thrummed there. It was weak, but he was alive.

Feeling considerably more stouthearted with the discovery that this was but a flesh and blood man and not some goblin sent to terrorize her, Caitlan set out to determine the extent of the man's injuries. Gentle fingertips wandered uncertainly through the thick strands of rain-dampened hair and found a swollen area just behind his right ear. Supposing a mere lump on the head too insignificant a malady to fell such a large man, Caitlan continued her tentative inspection. It was when she braced her hands on his shoulders, and attempted to nudge him onto his back, that Caitlan was once more imbued with a sense of urgency.

When she placed her hand along the man's left shoulder, it came into contact with a sticky, wet substance. At first, Caitlan was puzzled by the unusual texture, then with a start, she comprehended the nature of her discovery. It was blood! The front of the man's coat was completely saturated with the viscous substance.

This revelation propelled Caitlan into action. Realizing the man needed immediate medical attention, she scrambled up on wobbly legs and ran as fast as her feet would carry her back to the highway. He was too big for her to try to move by herself. Her only hope was that someone would be traveling the Yazoo Road—a faint hope indeed, considering the incle-ment weather. If not, she would have to run all the way to

Vicksburg and pray the man would still be alive when she brought help back to him.

The rain had stopped falling by the time Caitlan reached the roadway, but her worst fears were quickly realized; a frantic glance in either direction revealed no sign of activity on the Yazoo Road this night. With a little cry of frustration, she whirled toward town. As Caitlan turned, however, she caught a glimpse of a flickering light in the distance and, knowing instinctively that the beam emanated from a carriage lantern, she gathered her skirts in her hands and literally bolted toward the approaching vehicle.

"Help!" she shouted above the faltering wind, praying that her fervent plea would gain the driver's attention. "Oh, please, you *must* help me!" Caitlan's side was splitting with pain by the time she overtook the conveyance, and she was near tears as she stumbled to her knees in the middle of the muddied roadway, breathlessly beseeching the coachman's assistance.

Caitlan's spirit lifted somewhat when she heard the driver rein in the horses, and the creaking sound of the brake being applied to the wheel assured her that she would not be run over. But her heart fairly leaped when a familiar voice called out in disbelief, "Miz Katie, is that you? What are you doin' out here at this time of the night?"

"Oh, Hezekiah, never mind that now." Caitlan dismissed his question with a beleaguered sigh. "I'm just so very thankful it's you. Come. We haven't a moment to spare," she informed him as she clambered to her feet once more. "There's a man—"

"A man?" Hezekiah interrupted, taking in Caitlan's thoroughly disheveled mien and thinking the worst. "Did he hurt you, Miz Katie?"

"No, no!" Caitlan exclaimed. "He gave me quite a fright, but he's the one who is hurt, and badly so I fear. Do hurry, Hezekiah! I'm not certain there is much we can do for him, but we cannot leave him to die alone in the mud," she said, running forward to snatch the lantern from the driver's box. Turning away from the vehicle, she motioned for him to follow her. "Bring the wagon as close to the bluff as you can. I'll lead the way."

Hezekiah performed the task as instructed; however, he was unable to maneuver the team and wagon as far into the copse as Caitlan might have liked. After settling the skittish horses, Hezekiah lumbered through the dense foliage as swiftly as his crippled leg would allow. He found Caitlan moments later, kneeling beside the lifeless outline of a man, laboriously trying to pull him onto his back.

"You bettah let me do that." Hezekiah gently pushed Caitlan's ineffectual hands aside and, in one fluid motion, turned the unconscious giant onto his back.

The man's head lay in Caitlan's lap and, without hesitation, she pulled a handkerchief from the pocket of her homespun skirt and tenderly mopped up his sodden face. Hezekiah took advantage of her preoccupation by shining the lantern nearer the invalid, hoping to gain some insight as to the seriousness of the man's wounds. When the beam of light splashed across the fellow's face, however, he was given cause to feel concern for Caitlan's welfare.

Construing his former mistress's startled intake of breath as horror at the sight of the man's battered face and bloodstained clothing, the black man patted her hand in a consoling gesture. "Don't you worry none. He 'pears to be in a bad way, right enough, but they's no way knowin' how bad things are till a doctah gets a look at him. What do you wants ah should do with him, Miz Katie?"

Hezekiah looked to Caitlan for an answer and was frankly shocked by the lady's response.

"We'll take him to the boardinghouse. Put him in the wagon, Hezekiah."

"But—"

Hezekiah's startled interruption went unheeded by a stubborn Caitlan who, having obviously set her mind upon an unyielding course, continued, "After we get him situated, you may run and fetch Doctor Shannon."

"But, Miz Katie," Hezekiah protested. "Only listen to what yer sayin'. Whose gonna look aftah this man if'n we takes him to Miz Tuttle's? Bettah we should take him straightaway to the doctah's," Hezekiah wisely suggested.

"No, *I* am going to look after him, Hezekiah!" Caitlan insisted.

"But Miz Katie, you don't know nuthin' 'bout this fella. For all you knows, he might be a murderah or a thief or some such no-'count trash as that. Please reconsidah!'' Hezekiah begged.

"There is nothing to reconsider" was Caitlan's matter-of-fact reply. Pulling herself to her feet, she added, "Now, let's get this man to the wagon and into town before he bleeds to death while we dawdle about, arguing needlessly over a matter that has already been settled."

The look of sheer determination that molded Caitlan's pretty face made Hezekiah realize that further debate would be useless. He had seen that look before—Caitlan Webber had made up her mind, regardless of the consequences—and any attempt to dissuade her would be futile. Even so, Hezekiah had a feeling that nothing good would come of Caitlan's impetuous decision. Scratching the back of his head, he blew a weary sigh, after which he hoisted the unconscious man into his arms and carried him to the waiting wagon.

The wagon pulled up before the three-story, white-frame house at number thirty-seven Washington Street some twenty minutes later. The two conscious occupants of the conveyance remained firm in their convictions—Caitlan held steadfast to her notion to nurse the wounded man back to health, while Hezekiah was just as convinced that the young headstrong woman had struck upon a singularly dunderheaded idea.

"Whoa," Hezekiah cautioned the horses as he reined them in before the dimly lit boardinghouse. Setting the hand brake, he turned in his seat to stare down at Caitlan who continued to fuss over the stricken man. "Is you absolutely sure you wants to do this? Miz Tuttle ain't gonna be none too pleased to discovah the state her new boardah's in. Chances are, he can't pay a lick. Then where does that leaves you, Miz Katie?"

"I don't have time to worry about that now, Hezekiah," Caitlan replied shortly, climbing down from the wagon. "Bring him along." She jerked her head toward their disabled companion and started up the narrow sidewalk toward the main entrance to the house. "We'll put him in the empty room next to mine. I'll run ahead and prepare the chamber. And please don't worry so, Hezekiah," she called over her shoulder in an effort to calm the fretful man. "I shall deal with Harriet."

These brave words were barely from Caitlan's lips, however,

when she came face-to-face with the redoubtable boarding-house proprietress. Having heard the commotion outside, Harriet had quite naturally peered out the drawing-room window to investigate. Seeing Caitlan scurrying up the front walk, Harriet was more than a little irked to learn that her troublesome hireling was the source of the disturbance. With an angry snort, Harriet stomped to the door and flung it wide.

"What is the meaning of this, Katie Webber?" Harriet demanded, folding her arms across her small bosom in a forbidding gesture.

Caitlan came up short at the abrupt greeting; however, she promptly regained her composure. "Not now, Harriet!" she warned in a voice that plainly indicated she would brook no interference from the sour-faced woman. "As you can see, I've a bit of an emergency on my hands. I don't have time to satisfy your curiosity."

Harriet looked beyond the younger woman to the big man who trudged slowly up the walkway, laboring under the heavy burden that was draped across one broad shoulder. "You'll take time to explain *this*, missy," Harriet informed Caitlan in no uncertain terms, nodding toward the improbable spectacle that approached them. Reaffirming her stance in the doorway, Harriet made it clear that she could be just as stubborn as the upstart snippet who stood before her.

Caitlan grew uncharacteristically reticent as she considered the embittered woman in the doorway. Inside, she was seething, but Caitlan realized she must keep her head about her if she hoped to achieve her purpose. With a conciliatory shrug, she sighed, "It's a man. I found him up on the bluff just north of town. He's badly injured, Harriet. Please, move out of the way, so we may bring him inside."

"Now, why would I go and do a half-witted thing like that?" Harriet barked. "Vicksburg is fairly bursting with doctors. Take him to one of them," she said with a dismissive wave of her hand and made as if to slam the door in Caitlan's face.

The younger woman reacted quickly. Without truly considering the consequences of her actions, Caitlan shoved the dumbfounded Harriet aside and beckoned Hezekiah across the threshold. Hezekiah turned an apologetic expression on the stunned woman as he sidled by her and followed Caitlan down the corridor to the stairway. Harriet quickly gathered her wits about her, however. She was so provoked by Caitlan's wanton act of disrespect that she actually ran after the villains who had effected this unruly intrusion into her domain.

It was an odd assemblage that ascended the boardinghouse staircase on this sultry July evening. Caitlan led the procession, holding a candle high to light their way and blatantly ignoring Harriet's throaty protestations that swooped up the staircase behind her. She was immediately followed by Hezekiah, whose strength was beginning to wane under the weight of his unwieldy load. And, of course, Harriet brought up the rear, yapping at their heels like an excitable guard dog.

"You better stop and listen to me, Katie Webber," the woman screeched. "Who do you suppose is going to take care of this man? Not me, I tell you, and certainly not you. You'll not be neglectin' your regular chores and my payin' tenants to play nursemaid to this poor wretch, I'll tell you that right now. I'll not allow it. Do you hear me talkin' to you, missy? I'll not have it, I tell you."

Caitlan heard her well enough, but by this time she was preoccupied in escorting Hezekiah up the steep attic steps and did not have time to attend the agitated woman. When they arrived at the unused chamber, Caitlan threw the door open and hurried inside to make the room ready. Placing the candle on the bedside table, she tossed the bed coverings aside, then went to raise the window to allow the rain-freshened breeze to cleanse the musty room. Caitlan returned to the berth in time to assist Hezekiah as he carefully laid his cumbersome bundle upon the turned-down sheets.

Harriet bounded across the threshold at this moment as well. But before she had the opportunity to launch another verbal assault, Caitlan ushered Hezekiah to the door with the instructions that he should summon Doctor Shannon without further delay. When Caitlan wheeled from the doorway, she found an enraged Harriet entrenched between her and the ailing man.

"How dare you!" Harriet whispered between clenched teeth, her hands drawn into tight fists at her sides. "How dare you disregard my direct orders. Why, if I weren't such a compassionate woman, I'd send you packin' this very night."

"Humph!" Caitlan laughed in the woman's face, removing

her rain-soaked bonnet and tossing it aside with an impatient
motion. "You won't send me packing tonight or any other
night, Harriet, for the simple reason that you cannot find another living soul to serve as your drudge. No one else would
tolerate that which I endure from you. So, leave me be,
Harriet." Green eyes sparkled determinedly as Caitlan
wrenched the shawl from her shoulders and hurled it aside. "I
am going to look after this man and there is *nothing* you can
say or do that will prevent me from doing so. Do you understand?"

Harriet regarded the younger woman warily. This outburst
of backbone was a side of Caitlan she had not witnessed in
many a long day—since before Lawrence Webber's death, in
fact—and the boardinghouse proprietress was momentarily put
off her stride as a result. Caitlan took advantage of Harriet's
uncustomary lapse into indecision and stepped around the gape-
mouthed woman to begin her self-assumed task.

Never one to give in easily, Harriet followed her. "He's in
a bad way, Katie," she commented after glancing down at the
lifeless figure who lay sprawled upon the bedsheets. "He'll be
needin' a lot of lookin' after. What if he dies in spite of your
efforts? Who's going to pay for his room and board? And the
doctor—how is he to be paid? And who'll tend to your chores
when you've worn yourself out from takin' care of him day
and night? Have you given any thought to that, missy?"

When the explosion came, it was delivered with all the force
of an eruptive volcano that had long sat simmering. Having
endured quite enough of Harriet's trite protestations, Caitlan
lost her temper.

"I will!" she shouted her exasperation. "I'll see to him. I
will see to *everything*, Harriet. And if you had the sense you
were born with, you would be offering to help instead of
standing there, yammering like an old fool. Look at him. Can't
you tell by the cut of his coat and the make of his boots that
he is well-to-do? If he lives, you may ask him to make recom-
pense for the expenses you incurred on his behalf and—should
he die—you can always appeal to his family for compensation.
Or, if all else fails, sell his boots. They should fetch a pretty
penny. Now, get out of my way, Harriet." Caitlan's voice was
hoarse with emotion as she pushed her sleeves up to her elbows

and stomped past the argumentative woman. "There is much to be done before Doctor Shannon arrives."

Harriet did not immediately relinquish her stronghold as she watched Caitlan exit the room. Indeed, Harriet's crowlike features became shrouded in deep concentration, and she regarded the wounded man's brutalized form for several long, contemplative moments. It was a shrewdly calculating expression that eventually highlighted the woman's face, however. After giving the situation due consideration, Harriet came to an unexpected decision. But make no mistake, hers was not a judgment that was motivated through some altruistic sense of human compassion, but rather greed . . . pure and simple.

Nevertheless, when Caitlan returned moments later, her arms brimming with clean linen, she was surprised to find Harriet still loitering about the chamber. Even more amazing, however, was the older woman's ultimate inquiry, for even after hearing it uttered, Caitlan could have sworn her ears were playing tricks with her.

Lifting her gaze from the bed where the disabled man lay, Harriet met Caitlan's suspicious stare and asked simply, "What can I do to help?"

A pair of learned, work-weary hands immersed the blood-stained cloth into a bowl of lukewarm water and twisted mightily in an effort to rinse the rag clean. Then the hands returned to gently wipe at the multitude of cuts and abrasions that plagued the man who remained blessedly unconscious upon the attic bed. Caitlan, whose offers of assistance had been soundly castigated by the diligent doctor, huddled in a shadowed corner of the room and observed the proceedings in distracted silence.

As she watched, yet another porcelain bowlful of clear spring water was turned a grotesque shade of red. Growing ever fearful of this ominous sight, Caitlan allowed her eyes to drift toward the foot of the bed where the doctor had carelessly discarded the man's blood-drenched clothing. They lay in an unruly heap upon the floor and, without considering the futility of her actions, Caitlan inched out of her protective corner and soundlessly made her way toward the bed. Bending, she retrieved the ruined garments and carefully, almost lovingly, folded them into neat squares before laying them aside. Caitlan turned from this task to discover that the doctor had completed his ministrations and stood wiping his blood-covered hands on a towel, his serious gaze focused upon her.

"So, Hezekiah tells me you're determined to take on this impossible task," Doctor Joel Shannon said dubiously, the implausibility of the situation clearly registering in his tone.

"Yes, I'm going to look after him" came her straightforward reply. If the doctor had doubted Caitlan's convictions before, the unfaltering ring in her voice and the resolution that bristled in the green eyes made him think otherwise.

"Very well, then. But I think you should know you've got your work cut out for you, young lady," the doctor advised her, dropping the soiled towel onto the washstand. He continued to consider her thoughtfully and his eyes narrowed when he added, "You must know he's more than half-dead already, Katie. It'll be a miracle if he regains consciousness."

Caitlan remained undaunted by these dire monitions. Walking forward, she grasped the footboard to steady her nerves and, of its own will, her gaze wandered up the length of the disabled man to rest on his bruised face. "I'm due a miracle," she whispered reverently, then squaring her shoulders, she confronted the doctor. "Tell me what needs to be done."

The physician scratched the back of his head in a noncommittal gesture. "There's not much you can do except keep him comfortable for now. He's lost a great deal of blood from those two gunshot wounds. The shoulder injury is the more serious of the two; the other is his lower right side." He pulled back the sheet and indicated both wounds in turn.

"Luckily, the bullets passed through him without damaging any vital organs," Doctor Shannon explained. "I've patched him up as best I can, but if by some chance he wakes up, you'll want to keep him as still as possible. I'll leave you something to give him for the pain. Mind, just a drop or two every three or four hours to keep him quiet. I don't want him thrashing about and busting those wounds open again. Of course, you'll need to change the bandages every day or so." He nodded toward the stark white dressings that protected the ravaged flesh. "It's not going to be a very pleasant undertaking,'' he informed her pointedly. ''Are you certain you're up to it?''

The russet-tinged head inclined briefly before Caitlan asked, ''What about his bruises?''

''The facial swelling should go down in a day or two,'' Doctor Shannon commented as he began wiping clean the instruments he had used during the lengthy examination. ''Near as I can tell, he's got a couple of bruised ribs that will cause him considerable discomfort if he starts tossing around in bed.'' He nodded toward a distended region under the unconscious man's left arm that had begun to turn a ghastly shade of blackish purple. ''It looks as if he's been kicked in the throat, so if he does come to, he'll most likely have the devil of a time finding his voice for a spell. Oh, and that lump on his head will likely cause him some grief.''

''Is there nothing we can do for him?'' came Caitlan's plaintive appeal.

The doctor, having placed the last of his medical instruments in the black leather bag on the foot of the bed, glanced up in time to witness the truly anguished expression that darkened Caitlan's brow. His demeanor softened as he offered, ''I'll mix up one of my salves for you. Perhaps that will help ease his suffering.''

''Thank you,'' a grateful Caitlan murmured in reply. ''Is that everything then?'' she inquired, absently fingering a section of chafed skin along the stricken man's wrist.

''As if that's not enough,'' the doctor scoffed. ''There's always a chance of infection setting in.'' He retrieved his medical bag and, snapping it shut, gathered up the remainder of his belongings and prepared to take his leave. As he shrugged his shoulders into his coat, Doctor Shannon noticed Caitlan's preoccupation with the red-roughened flesh.

''Rope burns,'' he answered her unspoken question. ''Evidently, his assailants felt it necessary to bind him while they beat him senseless. Not very sporting of them,'' the doctor added offhandedly and settled his hat atop his head. As he turned to stride toward the door, Doctor Shannon became curiously aware of the tears that had welled in a pair of customarily impassive green eyes. ''Are you all right, Katie?'' he ventured.

The young woman's concerned stare never wavered from

the injured man as she nodded a response to the doctor's query.
Biting back the quiver in her voice, she said, "Forgive me,
it's just that he looks so . . . helpless."

"He's in a bad way, there's no two ways about it, but he's
big and strong. Who knows? With the good Lord's help, my
medical knowhow, and your determination to make him well,
we may just pull him through. It's the next twenty-four hours
or so that'll be the most critical, Katie" came the doctor's dire
warning. "He's going to need constant attention. Do you have
anyone to help you look after him?"

"Yes." Caitlan shook off her trancelike mien and, willing
the uncharacteristic tears not to tumble from their watery
trenches, she walked straightaway to the threshold where the
doctor prepared to take his exit. "Hezekiah will be returning
shortly, and I suspect Essie will offer to a lend a hand when
she learns what has happened. Even Harriet has offered to help
out if need be."

"Good, you're going to need them, and I urge you to take
full advantage of their support. I'll drop by tomorrow to see
how our patient fares."

Caitlan remained beside the closed portal for several moments after the doctor took his leave. Now that she was alone
with the unconscious man, the room had taken on a mysteri-
ously forbidding aura. Feeling her cheeks suddenly flushed
with heat, Caitlan made her way to the open window to allow
the night breeze to wash over her. This was the first moment
of peace she had encountered since making her startling discovery up on the bluff, and now that she had time for delib-
eration, Caitlan fell victim to an agonizing attack of self-doubt.

Her conviction that the man needed personalized attention
and not the shabby care he would receive in Vicksburg's small
and overcrowded hospital did not waver. But in the calm,
uncluttered rationalization that oftentimes follows the furor of
an emotional upheaval, Caitlan began to question her own
ability to provide the exhaustive and intimate care this man
would require. That is not to say she had grown suddenly
squeamish about the nursing duties that loomed before her . . .
quite the contrary. There were, however, other circumstances
which made Caitlan question her sanity in bringing this man
into her life.

On a hollow sigh, Caitlan turned from the window and allowed her uncertain gaze to settle on the quiescent giant. As she stared in dazed wonder at the helpless man, a small frown wrinkled her brow and, with a start, Caitlan realized the mysterious sensation that had gnawed at her being for the better part of the day had completely disappeared.

Folding her arms beneath her bosom, Caitlan's bemused mien gradually softened into an expression of benign acceptance. "So, this is what all that nonsense was about. The next time I have a *feeling* that something is going to happen, I believe I shall very well ignore it."

Caitlan's gaze remained transfixed on the man as she circled around to the opposite side of the bed. Much of his battered torso remained exposed from when Doctor Shannon had pulled back the sheet to explain the nature of the man's injuries to her. Caitlan's cheeks grew warm once more and somewhere deep inside stirred the remnants of a long dormant sensation, and she was suddenly struck with the staggering realization that beneath this mass of swollen flesh and contusions lay the body of an incredibly attractive man.

Slender fingers trembled noticeably as Caitlan carefully pulled the sheet across the man's bruised chest, and she sank down onto the edge of the bed. Without thinking, she pulled his hand onto her lap and began to gently stroke at the sun-browned flesh.

As she sat in rueful contemplation of her circumstances, her head became a whirlwind of conflicting emotions. Her heart ached for the suffering the man had endured and for that which undoubtedly lay ahead. Intermingled with Caitlan's sympathetic feelings for her patient, however, were similar thoughts of a more self-directed nature. In the midst of this inwardly focused reflection, Caitlan did something she had not done in a very long time . . . she cried.

Warm, salty tears tumbled from their boundaries and rolled down her cheeks to fall unguarded onto the man's hand. Unbeknownst to Caitlan, who was lost to her own misery, the slumbering man stirred. It was but the slightest of movements as crystal-blue eyes fluttered open for an instant, then he was still again.

Caitlan quickly brought her wayward emotions under control, but her green eyes were still misty with tears, as they drifted upward to focus on the man's face. In an impulsive gesture, she raised his hand and, laying her cheek against the bruised flesh, she gave a heart-wrenching sob and murmured, "Oh, Rafe. How will you break my heart this time?"

Chapter Three

Caitlan sat dozing in a cane-backed rocking chair, her elbow propped on the curved arm and her chin teetering precariously atop her balled-up fist. The first hazy shadows of morning had begun to flicker through the curtains, yet it was not until an ominous figure positioned itself between Caitlan and the dancing light that she stirred. The abrupt movement caused her chin to slip from its supportive platform, and she gave a little start of surprise. In the next instant, Caitlan's eyes jerked open to find Hezekiah standing over her, a thoroughly disgruntled expression highlighting his dark face.

"Hezekiah!" Caitlan blurted. "What are you—" Her spontaneous question sputtered on her tongue, as a cursory glance about the room sufficed to remind her of the previous evening's events. "Of course. How could I forget?" she mumbled to herself, then as she began to massage the kinks from her stiff neck, Caitlan lifted her sleepy gaze to his watchful eyes and asked, "What time is it?"

"Nigh on seven o'clock" came Hezekiah's terse reply.

"Seven o'clock!" Caitlan screeched and would have scampered from the chair had Hezekiah not placed a restraining hand upon her shoulder. "Let me go, Hezekiah. Breakfast is late enough as it is, and I am in no mood to suffer through another of Harriet's scoldings.''

"No need for you to go worryin' 'bout that, Miz Katie," Hezekiah assured the fretful woman, though his visage remained daunting. "Ah stopped by the kitchen already, thinkin' that's where you'd be; only ah found Miz Tuttle instead. She done gave me a message for you. She says you don't have to go fixin' no vittles this mornin'; says she'll tend to breakfast herself.''

This unprecedented announcement gave rise to an expression of pure amazement on Caitlan's weary face, but before she was given a chance to comment, Hezekiah continued, "Ah don't know what you said to Miz Tuttle to get her a flittin' 'bout that kitchen like a woman possessed, but ah does know why you was so hell-bent on takin' that no-'count scoundrel in." Hezekiah cocked his head toward the invalid who still lay motionless upon the narrow berth.

Then without warning, Hezekiah grasped the arms of the rocking chair with his big hands and slowly brought his face until it was but inches away from Caitlan's. His dark, expressive eyes were glistening with annoyance when he accused, "That's Mistah Bradrick, ain't it? Ah didn't recognize him last night, what with it bein' so dark and the hustle 'n bustle of gettin' the doctah and all. But ah got mahself a good look at him this mornin', and if'n that ain't Mistah Bradrick, ah'll eat mah hat.''

"Really, Hezekiah! There is no need for you to carry on so," Caitlan snapped, taking exception to his bold speech. Then, finding her courage withering beneath his sullen scowl, she added weakly, "Yes, you're right. It's Rafe.''

"That bein' the case, ah'd like you to tell me one thing, Miz Katie. Why'd you do it . . . bring him here? Ain't that man hurt you enough already? Bettah we should've left him up on that bluff for the buzzards," Hezekiah said, his tone bitter, and flung away in disgust.

Caitlan clambered up from the rocking chair and caught the riled man by the sleeve before he could effect a clean escape. "You don't mean that," she chided. Closing the door he had wrenched open in anger, Caitlan gave the inflexible arm a tug and coaxed Hezekiah back into the center of the room. "You worry about me needlessly, my friend. I promise you that Rafe Bradrick cannot hurt me again. He means nothing to me. He is but a poor, wretched soul who is in desperate need of help. I should like to think I would have done the same for anyone we might have found up on that ridge.''

"Ah reckon you would've," Hezekiah muttered begrudgingly, his temper having been curtailed by Caitlan's calm words. His feisty disposition remained intact, however, as he adjured, "Don't you go tellin' me not to worry 'bout you, coz ah always has—evah since that day when ah first laid eyes on you. Shucks, ah was just a young whelp mahself, but ah still remembahs. It was the very day you was born, Miz Katie."

Caitlan's lips formed a smile of fond tolerance, for this was a story that Hezekiah had recounted on numerous occasions, and he derived enormous pleasure in its telling. It was a tale that always seemed to have a soothing effect on the overprotective man. Caitlan prayed it might do so this morning.

"Your pa was out huntin' for pheasant when he came upon Mastah Johnson 'bout to take his axe to me again. Mastah Webbah didn't need no more darkies, but he was in such high spirits—seein' as how you'd just been born—that he offahed the mastah five-hundred dollahs for me right there on the spot. Well, you knows that Mastah Johnson was always a right greedy old cuss, and ah suppose he figgered he'd eventually have to chop mah whole foot off to keep me from runnin' away. Seein' as how ah'd be no good to him then, he up and sold me to your pa." As always, when Hezekiah became embroiled in telling his story, a wistful expression fashioned his black face and there was a telltale misting of tears in his deep brown eyes.

"Mastah Webbah brung me back to Thistledown that very aftahnoon," Hezekiah said proudly. "Ah figgered he meant to have me work in the fields like ah did for Mastah Johnson, but no, your pa led me straight on up to the big house. He took me into his private office and settled hisself in that big ole leathah chair behind his desk. As ah recollects, he lit up one of them fancy cigars he was partial to, then he took a dollah out of the strongbox he kept in the bottom drawah.

"He gives me that dollah and says to me, 'Hezekiah, there's no need for you to go runnin' off every whipstitch, lad. So long as you mind your mannahs and does as yer told, ah'll gives you one of these every week. Mind you keep them safe, and when you has saved the five-hundred dollahs ah just spent savin' your ahnrey hide, you'll have earned your freedom.'

"Ah had just asked your pa what was expected of me when the door opened and one of the maids come bustlin' in carryin' you in her arms. There you was, all pink and wrinkledlike, squallin' your head off. You sure was a sight." Hezekiah chuckled and gave his head a fond shake. "And the mastah sure was proud of you. He told me ah was to help out with the chores whenevah the housekeepah needed me, but more important, ah was to look aftah his brand new baby girl and young Mastah Webbah.

"Your pa kept Mastah Johnson from lashin' out at me again that day, Miz Katie and, ah suppose in a way, so did you. Ah've watched you grow from a tiny mite of a thing into a fine young woman, and—in some ways—ah knows you bettah than you knows yourself," he informed her with a pointed look. "Now, ah've seen this man come and go, and every time he comes back, you welcome him with open arms. And every time he just hurts you more.

"So, don't go thinkin' you can bamboozle me with them brave words. Of course this man *means* somethin' to you; he always has. Ah still remembah the othah times is all, and ah can't bear to watch him hurt you again, Miz Katie."

From the resolved look on Hezekiah's face, Caitlan realized it was useless to try to convince the man that his fears were groundless. Her green gaze found its way back to the subject of their conversation, and Caitlan's eyes momentarily clouded over with self-doubt as her mind became a flurry of long-suppressed images. These carefree memories of Caitlan's youth were quickly supplanted, however, with reflections of less happier times—Brendan's death, her father's suicide, and Rafe leaving . . . always leaving.

As she continued to stare at the lifeless figure, Caitlan was herself amazed that she did not so much as feel a twinge of the old, familiar stirrings in the vicinity of her heart. This total absence of emotion made her feel with a certainty that she could withstand the rigors of playing nursemaid to this man who had, conversely, been the source of so much joy and sorrow in her life. She was dead inside . . . nothing and no one could ever hurt her again.

Squaring her shoulders, Caitlan faced Hezekiah once more. "Am I to assume from your outburst that you intend to have no part of this?"

"Yer to assume no such thing!" Hezekiah countered. "He's just ahnrey enough to pull through and, if by some miracle he does, you'll be needin' someone to look aftah you . . . someone whose head ain't cluttahed with no nonsense and who knows what's best for you."

It goes without saying that Hezekiah fully intended to cast himself in the role of watchdog. Blowing a reluctant, albeit acquiescent sigh, he lumbered over to the rocking chair Caitlan had momentarily vacated and plopped himself down. "What do you want ah should do?" he asked with all the enthusiasm of one being requested to carry out a particularly repugnant task.

"Just sit with him. Doctor Shannon said he would stop by to check on Rafe today, but do call me if he begins to stir. We can't have him squirming about and reopening those wounds. I'll be back later to change his bandages."

"Don't you worry 'bout him none," Hezekiah assured a doubtful Caitlan. "Ah'll looks aftah him like ah promised. You get yourself some rest."

"Rest!" Caitlan scoffed. "I'll rest later. I'm going down to the kitchen to prepare a nourishing broth for our incapacitated guest. As for you, my surly friend, shall I send breakfast up to you, or will you make good on your threat to make a meal of that shabby hat of yours?" she offered with a good-natured chuckle.

"Truth told, ah'd soonah have a thick slice of your baked ham and a chunk of bread" came Hezekiah's hungry admission.

"And so you shall." With that, Caitlan turned toward the door, but before she let herself from the room, her attention was once again commanded by the object that had preoccupied much of the morning's discussion. For the first time since awakening, Caitlan truly looked at her slumbering patient.

The even breathing motion of his chest beneath the sheet assured her that he had indeed survived the night. With a little sigh of relief, she pulled the door open and, catching an askance glimpse of Hezekiah, was compelled to say, "You know, Hezekiah, I must have heard you and Papa rehash that story of how he rescued you from Mr. Johnson's axe at least a hundred times. I must confess that there is a part of your tale that has always puzzled me."

"What's that, Miz Katie?"

"Well, if Papa gave you a dollar a week since the time you came to live at Thistledown, you must have earned your freedom nearly three times over by the time I presented you with your papers of manumission following Papa's death. How is it that you never left before then?" she asked, a thoughtful frown turning down the corners of her mouth.

"Ah suppose ah was happy enough where ah was, and there weren't no need for me to go elsewhere," Hezekiah answered truthfully. "Besides, ah knew ah could leaves anytime ah took the notion to and that made all the dif'rence for me. Can you undahstand that?"

"Yes, I believe I can," she murmured, a grateful smile highlighting her tired face. Many had been the time through the years when Caitlan had found herself thankful for the friendship of this big, gentle man.

"Do you evah miss the times we had at Thistledown, Miz Katie?" Hezekiah continued, his thoughts turning once more to heartwarming remembrances from the past.

"Of course I do, but, I try not to dwell overmuch on the past. Nothing good can come of it, for the past is over and done. We must look to the future" came Caitlan's sensible reply. "Speaking of family and future; what has become of your Abigail? I want very much to meet her. I find myself ashamed to admit this, but I quite forgot her in last night's furor. You obviously returned from the Stark Plantation alone. What happened, Hezekiah?" Her question was innocent enough, but Caitlan grew full of concern when Hezekiah did not favor her with an immediate reply.

The peaceful man's voice trembled with angry emotion when at last he said, "She weren't there, Miz Katie. Mistah Stark done went and sold mah Abbie-gal to Mistah Cantrell down at Church Hill, down Natchez way."

*   *   *

The aromas that emanated from the Tuttle Boarding House kitchen the following afternoon were an unusual mixture to say the least. The mouth-watering odors of fresh baked, hot bread and crispy fried chicken mingled most unappetizingly with the more pungent scent of a medicinal concoction that simmered unassumingly on the stove. Next to the foul-smelling container rested a large pot in which bubbled a hearty beef stock. The contents of both of these vessels were earmarked for the stricken house guest who inhabited the attic chamber opposite Caitlan's.

The young woman responsible for the preparation of these victuals presently stood at the kitchen sink, peeling potatoes and washing a variety of vegetables that would shortly become a part of the evening's menu. The unrelenting force of the July, Mississippi sun combined with the sweltering heat of the kitchen to create unbearable working conditions. Caitlan, however, was absorbed in her work and did not appear to be affected by the stifling temperatures. As she labored, little beads of perspiration formed on her brow and gradually trickled downward, thereby threatening to impair her vision. Only then did Caitlan show the slightest indication that she was plagued by the annoying heat as she reacted by wiping her sleeve across her brow. Her concentration was destined to be interrupted it would seem; as she turned to carry the now skinless tubers to the stove, Caitlan was startled by a solemn figure who stood in the kitchen doorway.

Caitlan jumped at the unexpected sight and the potatoes that she cradled in her apron skirt went tumbling to the floor. "Essie!" she exclaimed and fell instantly to her knees to begin gathering up the errant vegetables. "You gave me such a start! You should have said something!"

"I did," Essie countered, "but I guess your thoughts must have been otherwise engaged," she added meaningfully, screwing up her face and directing her eyes toward the ceiling as if to indicate a particular room in the upper regions of the house. "I didn't mean to frighten you, Katie," she said apologetically, coming full into the room and bending down to help her friend collect the scattered vegetables. "Will you have to peel fresh ones? I'll help," Essie offered with a guilty grimace. "It's the least I can do, seein' as how it's kinda my fault you spilt them."

"No, that . . . won't be . . . necessary," Caitlan grunted, as she pressed her cheek against the base of a kitchen cabinet and stretched her arm as far as she could to reach a potato that had rolled underneath. Gathering in the last of the runaway tubers, she sat back on her haunches with satisfaction and smiled at her friend. "I'll just wash these. No one will know the difference." Balancing the potatoes in her apron once more, Caitlan made her way back to the sink.

The soiled potatoes clattered noisily in the basin and a steady flow of cool, refreshing water was streaming from the sink pump before Caitlan thought to question her friend. "What brings you here today? I was certain you would be sewing Mrs. Balfour's gown right up until the last possible moment."

"I finished it this morning. I came here straightaway just as soon as the madame checked out my handiwork and told me I was free to leave, and this is the thanks I get for my trouble," the girl grumbled as she made her way to the counter and proceeded to help herself to a gingersnap from the cookie canister. She took a bite of the flavorful morsel, chewed, and appropriated a second helping before replacing the lid.

The caustic tone of her friend's voice caused Caitlan to throw a quizzical look over her shoulder, prompting her to inquire, "Why the sour face, Essie?"

"Well, I just think it's a pretty sad day, Katie Webber, when somethin' as excitin' as this happens and you don't even bother to tell me—your very best friend in the whole world—about it, that's all."

Caitlan felt rather than heard the "humph" of disappointment as Essie flung herself onto a kitchen chair. Caitlan repressed the pixieish impulse to poke fun at her friend's frustration; one glance was all she needed to realize that Essie was suffering from genuinely bruised feelings. Knowing that she would derive no pleasure in prolonging the girl's unhappiness, Caitlan stepped to the stove and dropped the potatoes one by one into the simmering beef stock.

Caitlan assumed a casual air as she proceeded with her kitchen chores and there was but the slightest hint of amusement in her voice when she said, "Really, Essie, I had no idea you would take offense. But you must realize that it's been ever so hectic around here since our guest's arrival. Why, I've barely had time to think for myself. Besides, you were frantically trying to finish Mrs. Balfour's dress. I knew you would come around just as soon as you could when you heard the news.'' A frown deepened at the corner of Caitlan's eyes as a thought occurred to her, and she was persuaded to ask, ''How did you hear about it?''

Essie hunched her shoulders in a noncommittal gesture and leaned forward to rest her arms on the table. ''I must have heard it from a dozen different customers. You know how fast gossip spreads in this town. I can't remember which one told me first. I only remember thinkin' how romantic it was . . .'' Essie's voice took on a wistful timbre and an expression of pure rapture transformed her young face '' . . . you findin' this man—hurt and all—out of the blue and bringin' him back to Tuttle's to tend to. I'll wager old Harriet was fit to be tied when she seen what you had on your mind.''

''Yes, you might say that,'' Caitlan admitted. ''I had to do some fast talking to convince Harriet that taking him in was in her best interest. But I fear you have sadly misjudged the situation, Essie. I assure you there is absolutely nothing *romantic* about tending festering wounds, applying unctuous salves, brewing smelly restoratives, òr changing soiled sheets,'' Caitlan informed her moonstruck friend. ''If anything, it is backbreaking, tedious work.''

''Humph!'' Essie pouted. ''Well, I should think that, if you had any imagination, it *could* be romantic. Do you have any notion as to who he might be?''

''Uh, no. Uh . . . that is—'' Caitlan stammered, reluctant to tell her friend an out-and-out falsehood, but even more disinclined to reveal the truth. Turning her back on Essie, lest the girl glean the facts from her expression, Caitlan added, ''I searched his clothing, but could find no identification. His assailants apparently felt obliged to relieve him of his personal belongings.''

''You mean he hasn't spoken a word since you brung him here!'' Essie blurted, aghast.

''No. He has yet to regain consciousness,'' Caitlan returned with a weary sigh.

Caitlan stepped across the threshold onto the back porch where she retrieved a basket of freshly harvested garden peas and, setting them on the table, went to take down a pan from the pot rack beside the stove. Plopping the empty pot onto the table, she settled herself on a straight-backed chair opposite her friend. The frown that wrinkled Essie's brow deepened as she watched Caitlan heap a pile of the tiny green vegetables onto the scratched surface in front of her. Caitlan plucked a pod from the green mountain before her and, as she began to shell the peas, she wisely decided the time had come to assuage Essie's near-bursting curiosity.

Green eyes never wavered from their task as Caitlan began to fill Essie in on the status of the boardinghouse's infamous new resident. "Doctor Shannon comes by at least once a day, and he seems to think our patient is improving. At least, he hasn't died yet, and that is something when one considers the severity of his injuries."

"Hmm." Essie mulled this piece of information and reached for a legume. Splitting the shell open, she dumped the seeds into the near-empty pot and discarded the useless skin with a careless motion. Instinctively, Essie selected another pea pod, but she did not immediately shuck this one. Instead, she balanced the legume between the tips of her forefingers and leveled a thoughtful stare across the top of the narrow shaft at her preoccupied companion. "It appears as if you've been pitched headlong into a regular whirlwind around here."

"We've been busy, that's for certain," Caitlan agreed.

"We?"

Caitlan repressed the urge to smile. It was obvious that Essie wanted very much to be a part of the goings on at Tuttle's. Caitlan was, however, acquainted with her friend's personality quirks and knew full well that it would be useless for her to merely ask Essie if she would like to help care for the injured man in her spare time. No, Essie would not feel truly needed until she had been given the opportunity to make Caitlan understand that the situation was in desperate need of her assistance.

"Hezekiah has been lending a hand now and again," Caitlan advised her. "Why, even Harriet has assumed many of my duties so that I may spend most of my time caring for him."

"Even so, I expect you could use another pair of hands. You're lookin' mighty peaked already" came Essie's blunt rejoinder. Paying no attention to Caitlan's indignant gasp at this offhand assessment of her somewhat haggard appearance, Essie pressed on, "As you well know, I'm no stranger to sickrooms. Did I ever tell you about the time I—"

"Yes, Essie." Caitlan interrupted and threw up her hands in mock surrender. "You have often regaled me with tales of your exploits in caring for your brothers and sisters. Now, if all this roundaboutness is your way of persuading me to ask you to help take care of our wounded stranger then consider yourself asked. You're quite right; another pair of hands will be a blessing in the days to come." Caitlan had her answer by way of the smile that instantly brightened Essie's freckled face.

A jubilant Essie plunged her fingers into the bulging basket of garden peas and tossed a handful onto the table. She began to shell the legumes in earnest this time, however, her visage grew suddenly somber once more when she said, "Now that we've settled that, what do you intend to do about Hezekiah's problem?"

A visibly shocked Caitlan came erect in her chair. "What?!"

"I've heard all about how he went up to the Stark Plantation to fetch his Abigail back to Vicksburg, only to discover that old man Stark had sold her to Jeremy Cantrell" came Essie's matter-of-fact reply.

"The news does spread through this town quickly," Caitlan muttered beneath her breath. To Essie, she said, "Who told you about Hezekiah?"

Essie shook her head. "I don't know; a wife of one of the men Hezekiah works with at the ice factory, I suppose. Like I said, people talk. The thing is, I'm wonderin' what you intend to do about it."

"Me?!" shrieked a thoroughly bumfuzzled Caitlan. One dark eyebrow shot upward as she demanded, "What do you expect me to do?"

"Everyone from Natchez to Memphis knows how Jeremy Cantrell feels about you," Essie countered with a pointed look at her friend. "I was just thinkin' you might be able to help

Mr. Cantrell see what an unjust thing he did, that's all. You don't have to snap at me like an old turtle."

"Jeremy drives me home from Sunday services now and again, but that hardly constitutes a romantic entanglement," Caitlan said with a huff. "Besides, his last wife—he's gone through three, you must know—is barely cold in the family cemetery."

"You could do worse."

"I'm not looking to *do* anything!" Caitlan exclaimed in exasperation.

Standing, she went to ready a tray to carry above stairs to the stricken house guest. Dishes rattled precariously as they were flung haphazardly onto the wicker platter. Then, having held in her say long enough, Caitlan whirled around to confront an enormously amused Essie.

With one hand planted firmly on her hip and her foot tapping out an impatient rhythm on the stone floor, Caitlan blurted, "And another thing, you know as well as I that the only reason Jer—" Caitlan's animated tirade ended abruptly when she sensed a movement in the doorway and, glancing up, she found Harriet about to enter the kitchen.

The two occupants of the chamber watched as the boarding-house proprietress dumped an armful of soiled linens into the laundry basket that sat just inside the door then walked straightaway to the kitchen sink. "Don't stand there gawking at me, Katie Webber," Harriet barked, wiping her dripping hands on her apron. "As for you," Harriet turned her acerbic stare on Essie, "I'm fairly certain you're needed elsewhere," she said in a dismissive tone.

Helping herself to a cup of coffee from the pot that sat simmering on the stove, Harriet directed the remainder of her irascible speech at Caitlan. "How like you to tittle-tattle the day away while I toil in a sweltering sickroom. You best get on up them stairs and start looking after that man you foisted off on me. He came to not more than ten minutes ago—looked me square in the eye, he did—then drifted off again. It's my guess he'll be waking up for good any minute now, so you best be there when he does."

Totally oblivious to the conflicting emotions this revelation stirred in the breast of the one at which the lecture was aimed,

Harriet's tongue wagged on, "He'll be needing you and your fancy concoctions then."

Expectant green eyes warily regarded the sleeping giant of a man as Caitlan pushed the door open and let herself into the attic chamber. Her breathing was slightly labored as a result of her recent ascent of two flights of stairs, a feat which had been rendered more difficult by Caitlan's struggle to maneuver the heavy tray without upsetting its contents. With a grateful sigh, she relieved herself of the unwieldy burden and, almost immediately, was struck full force by the suffocating heat that pervaded the room.

"What were you thinking, Harriet?" Caitlan asked of no one in particular. "As if things aren't bad enough. Must you smother him as well?"

An agitated Caitlan scurried about the room, flinging open the windows in the hopes that an afternoon breeze might find its way inside the stuffy room. As an afterthought, she pulled the chamber door ajar to allow for more cross ventilation. The sound of raised voices from the floor below—inquiring of Harriet as to her whereabouts—gave Caitlan sufficient reason to reconsider her actions, and she promptly closed the door. After all, she did not have time to brush Miss Crawford's hair into a becoming style, or help Mr. Hamilton search the house over for the pocket watch he had misplaced . . . again. There were more important matters at hand.

Caitlan pressed her ear against the door and braced herself for the sharp clamoring of footsteps on the staircase. Instead, it was Harriet's composed, though nonetheless commanding, voice that wafted up from the second floor. Harriet's words were muffled as they filtered through the wooden portal, but Caitlan encountered no difficulty deciphering them.

"Katie's tending to her chores and can't be bothered with you now. Besides, your hair is as lovely as always, Penelope." Caitlan appreciated what it had cost Harriet's pride to pay the woman a compliment, for it always pained her to do so. "As for your pocket watch, Mr. Hamilton, you know it will turn up sooner or later just in time for you to lose it again. Now, go on about your business, the both of you."

A feeling of relief washed over Caitlan when she realized

that Harriet had successfully shooed the pesky tenants away. Giving her head a bemused shake at having been rescued from such an unlikely quarter, she pushed away from the door and turned her attention on her slumbering patient once more. Taking a seat on the edge of the bed, Caitlan lifted a spoonful of the now lukewarm beef broth from the bowl on the wicker tray. Cupping her free hand beneath the utensil to prevent any errant drops from spilling onto the sheets, she carefully positioned the spoon at the corner of the unconscious man's mouth.

"Come, Rafe," she whispered soothingly. "I know this is somewhat awkward, but you need to eat something or you'll never get your strength back. Just a few spoonsful, I promise." As she spoke, Caitlan poked her index finger between his teeth and forced his mouth open just wide enough to allow her to tip the spoonful of broth inside.

As the liquid trickled to the back of Rafe's tongue, Caitlan began to stroke his throat in slow, languid motions. She had happened upon this technique the previous evening when her first attempt to coax a few drops of nourishment down his throat had very nearly choked him. Caitlan had reacted by gently massaging his ravaged neck. The constricted muscles had been persuaded to relax as a result of her quick thinking, thereby allowing the liquid safe passage.

Caitlan repeated the procedure until she was satisfied that her patient had ingested more of the hearty broth than had managed to dribble down his chin. She concluded the unusual feeding ritual by encouraging him to drink a sizable dose of the medicinal bitters she had brewed especially for him earlier that day. A grin flitted across Caitlan's face when she heard a small groan of protest from the invalid when the pungent taste enveloped his tongue.

"That's a good sign," she murmured, dabbing at his lips with a napkin. "Now, let me get a look at you."

Caitlan was pleased to note that the facial swelling was showing definite signs of improvement since the previous evening. With a nod of approval, she pulled the sheet back in order to observe the distended rib area. Despite her efforts, Caitlan could not suppress the tingle of excitement that rippled throughout her being when she was presented an unobscured view of Rafe's muscular chest. Fascinated by the tufts of dark, curly hair that embellished the expanse of sinewy flesh, a graceful hand unwittingly reached toward the enticing sight.

This impromptu adventure would end as abruptly as it had begun, however. Before inquisitive fingertips had the opportunity to conduct an examination of a purely nonmedical nature, Caitlan came to her senses and snatched her hand away. Giving herself a mental—if not frustrated—shake, she directed herself to the matter at hand.

Deciding she would tend to Rafe's minor wounds first and change the dressings later, Caitlan plucked a jar of salve from the bedside commode. She administered the soothing ointment to the bruised area just beneath his left arm, covered the tortured region with a piece of bandaging cloth, and pulled the bedsheet over him once more. Caitlan repeated this gesture by dabbing the healing unguent onto his scarred wrists, then dipping her fingers into the container one last time, she withdrew a small dollop of the cooling lubricant.

With featherlike strokes, Caitlan began to spread the salve along Rafe's swollen and bruised throat. She was engrossed in her nursing duties and was taken by complete surprise when, without warning, a hand sprang from nowhere to imprison her fingers in an agonizing grip.

Startled, Caitlan gave a frightened squeal and would have run for the door were it not for the fact that her hand was entrapped in a bone-crushing vise. Her shocked expression gradually gave way to one of genuine pain and, with some effort, Caitlan lifted her gaze to confront a pair of crystal-blue eyes for the first time in seven long, lonely years.

Chapter Four

Rafe wondered if the pain would ever go away. Fortunately, he had not been awake for any length of time since Caitlan had found him on that bluff outside of Vicksburg. Even in those rare moments when reality had pierced his consciousness, he had been suffused with such agonizing discomfort that he had been content to seek refuge in a pain-free dreamworld. Rafe remembered little of the circumstances that had led him to this excruciating predicament. He had only vague recollections.

His fuzzy memory thought it recalled having been hoisted from a wet patch of earth in the darkness. Through the haze, Rafe relived the nauseating sensation that one often experiences when bounced about on the floor of a moving vehicle. Less painfully, he remembered the voices. Rafe's taut muscles relaxed as his being reflected on the soft, soothing whispers of one voice in particular that encouraged him to try and get better. Then there was the other voice—this one harsh and shrill—that commanded him not to die. Even in his debilitated state, Rafe had the distinct impression that this discordant decree had been issued with selfish intent rather than any great concern for his personal welfare.

The singular nagging aspect to this situation was the fact

that the gentle voice always seemed to be the one that inflicted the most pain. Even as the unknown speaker cooed her comforting refrains, inquisitive fingers forced foul-tasting potions down his protesting gullet, then poked and prodded his throbbing limbs with unbearable persistence until Rafe thought he might be driven mad from it all. In fact, it was during a particularly grueling session that he found himself provoked beyond endurance.

Damn the woman! was his unspoken epithet. *Will she not be satisfied until she's strangled me to death?* In the next instant, a surprisingly strong hand, spurred on by sheer determination, shot upward to seize the offensive appendage and force it into submission.

He would have chuckled outright at the woman's terrified squeal had the impulse not aroused a most disagreeable reaction in his throat. Thus compelled to forgo his small taunt of revenge, Rafe contented himself by increasing the pressure on that despised instrument of torture that he held steadfast in a relentless grip. His emotions underwent a dramatic transformation, however, when smug, blue eyes focused on the anguished face of the woman bent over him.

Kettie! his mind screamed, though no sound was forthcoming. Taken aback by the unexpected vision above him, Rafe's hold faltered and Caitlan pulled her hand free. Completely ignorant of the turmoil raging inside the semiconscious man, she retreated to a straight-backed chair beside the bed and watched with growing trepidation the gamut of conflicting emotions that ravaged an otherwise handsome face. What began as a painful grimace gradually dissolved into an expression of horrified disbelief, then mercifully, the bewildered blue eyes closed once more.

The distraught man did not immediately lapse into a restful slumber, however. Indeed, his brain verily raced with the implications of his impossible discovery.

Kettie? his mind reverberated the inconceivable thought. *I must be out of my mind with pain. It can't be Kettie. My Kettie is dead.*

It is understandable that, given his muddled state of mind, Rafe had lost all concept of time. He, therefore, had no way of knowing that nearly thirty-six hours had lapsed before he awakened again. The room was encased in virtual darkness, lighted only by the flickering flame of a single candle. A solitary figure sat in a rocking chair beside the open window and, from her slumped posture, Rafe surmised that his diligent nursemaid had forsaken her lonely vigil for a much-deserved respite. The woman's face was turned from him, thereby denying him an uninhibited view of her features.

As the cobwebs gradually cleared from his confused head, Rafe struggled to sort out the perplexing situation into which he had unwittingly stumbled. One might think the dazed man would attempt to reconstruct the events that had transpired to leave him in his present bedridden state. Instead, his brain verily whirled with an altogether different conundrum . . . Kettie.

All this exercise in thought served to do, however, was set his head to aching. With a beleaguered sigh, Rafe conceded there was but one plausible explanation to this puzzling mystery—his eyes must have been playing tricks with him. Caitlan Webber had perished seven years ago in a riverboat explosion on the Mississippi. It was simply not possible that it was Kettie he had seen before, unless—

God, this heat is unbearable, Rafe swore to himself. *Perhaps I'm dead, for this surely must be what hell is like . . . insufferably hot and excruciatingly painful.* He grimaced as his effort to shift to a more comfortable position inspired a torturous response from every fiber of his being.

Rafe's facial expression took on the appearance of one engrossed in serious thought and eventually—in deference to the impending pain—he shook his head. *I'm not dead,* he decided. *This might be a fitting end for me, considering the wasted life I've led, but it's not for Kettie,* he reasoned.

Rafe's opinion of the lady in question had not always been quite so charitable. In fact, there had been a time when Rafe might have been inclined to condemn Caitlan's soul to the very place he had but moments earlier presumed himself to be. Oh, she deserved it right enough, considering the heartbreaking hell she had put him through. The hurt had mellowed with time, however, leaving Rafe with nothing more than an occasional bittersweet yearning for that which might have been.

No, his sweet Kettie would not be found wallowing amid the hounds of hell, but rather frolicking with the angels in heaven.

Then, who is this angel of mercy that fate has so generously sent to look after me? Rafe struggled to boost himself up onto his elbows in order to get a better glimpse of his slumbering attendant. But the exertion proved too great an effort for him in his weakened condition, and he fell back against the sweaty sheets.

The sound of the bed ropes creaking out a noisy protest jarred Caitlan from the depths of a serene sleep. Realizing that Rafe had begun to stir, she took a moment to gather her wits about her before approaching the sickbed. Sweeping aside an errant strand of brown-and-russet hair, Caitlan gave a little moan as tired, aching limbs found the strength to push her up from the chair. The smile that parted her lips was a mixture of guarded expectancy and sympathy as she stepped around the foot of the bed and gazed down at him.

Thusly positioned above Rafe in the dimly lit room, the light from the candle illuminated Caitlan's soft features, giving her an almost ethereal presence. For one heartstopping moment, he feared his earlier suppositions must have been correct. Instead of hell, however, he was now given every reason to believe he had somehow managed to gain entrance to heaven's pearly gates. Caitlan's subsequent words quickly allayed Rafe's spiraling fears.

"So, it would seem you have finally decided to rejoin the world of the living." Caitlan's cheerful greeting penetrated his bewildered thoughts. "That's a good sign, however, you mustn't move around just yet, lest you reopen your wounds," she cautioned and, perching on the edge of the narrow berth, Caitlan placed a reassuring hand on his arm. "And for heaven's sake, try not to look so apprehensive. Goodness, from the expression on your face, one would think you had just seen a ghost."

"I thought I had" was Rafe's frank rejoinder, however, the sound that emerged from his throat was little more than a hoarse croak.

"Oh, dear," she lamented. "I was afraid of that. The doctor said you might experience some difficulty in talking at first. But not to worry, I have prepared an herb elixir which should hasten your recovery." As she spoke, Caitlan extended her arm toward the bedside commode where she retrieved an amber-colored bottle.

Her reluctant patient observed these actions with a sense of resigned acceptance, sprinkled with a liberal dose of distrust. After all, he had recourse to a hazy memory of a singularly foul substance being forced down his throat and was in no hurry to repeat the experience. With a sinking heart, Rafe heard the "thwoop" of the cork being extracted from the bottle, and he realized the moment of truth was at hand. Knowing he could do nothing to forestall the imminent happening, Rafe met the challenge bravely.

Conscious of the suspicions her patient harbored in his breast—they registered plainly on his distrustful face—Caitlan made ready to administer the dreaded elixir. Leveling a table-spoonful of the curative beneath Rafe's nose, she said in a voice that one might use to coddle a child, "There, there, I promise you it isn't so very awful as you might think. Now, take a sip, hold it on the back of your tongue, then allow the medicine to trickle slowly down your throat. That cooling sensation you should feel just about now is from a hint of checkerberries," she explained.

Setting the medicinal articles aside, Caitlan took a moment to straighten the other items on the tray, then devoted her attention to Rafe once more. Her expression was circumspect when she asked, "Better?"

Surprisingly enough, Rafe had to allow that the soothing potion had indeed contrived to still the relentless throbbing in his neck. Frankly, Rafe was impressed by Caitlan's ingenuity, and he found himself wondering if she might possess another magic remedy that could be applied toward alleviating the distress he seemed to be experiencing everywhere else. He was, however, soundly discouraged from voicing such an inquiry when Caitlan pressed her index finger against his mouth.

"No, you mustn't try to speak just yet" came her stern reprimand. Then in a gentler tone, she whispered, "Poor Rafe. So much has happened to you. Doctor Shannon said your memory might be a little blurred when you first came to. Do you have any recollection at all as to how you came to be here?"

Rather than risk aggravating the demons that had taken up residence in his aching head by shaking them about, Rafe mouthed a silent "no" in response to her query.

"I feared as much. Perhaps your memory might be stimulated if I told you what the doctor has surmised from your injuries," Caitlan offered. "To begin, you were found three nights ago a few yards off the Yazoo Road just north of town, and mere inches from a deadly bluff, I might add. You had been badly beaten and left for dead." As Caitlan elaborated on the full extent of his injuries, she dipped a cloth into the washbasin and began to mop up the perspiration that dotted his brow.

These soothing ministrations, coupled with the soft inflection of Caitlan's voice, soon encouraged Rafe to relax and let his mind ramble back to that fateful night. He remembered being astride his horse, Wanderer, and looking forward to a bed and a hot meal when he arrived at the Washington Hotel in Vicksburg. Then there had been a sudden rustling noise in the underbrush to his left, followed by a glancing blow to his head, and then . . . nothing.

As he lay there, Caitlan's soft purrings floating above him, Rafe closed his eyes and began to piece together the events of that grisly night. His face grew hard with unbridled emotion as the memory washed over him in glaring detail. He had been ambushed by two men. Rafe knew them well enough; he had been tracking the pair for several months. But in one unguarded moment, he had become the victim of a depraved attack.

The bile rose in his throat as he remembered how his assailants had rendered him helpless by trussing him up like a roped calf. He recalled with vivid clarity the countless blows that had pummeled his face and chest, then having wriggled free of his bonds, the smell of burning flesh—his flesh—that had been punctured with hot lead. Finally, he relived the horrifying sensation of being dumped over a precipice and his frantic attempt to hang onto a clump of earth heedless of the boot heel that his attacker dug into his knuckles. It was here his memory grew foggy; Rafe had no recollection as to what occurred up on that ridge to prevent his adversaries from achieving their dastardly purpose. His final conscious remembrance of that night was that of commanding every ounce of strength in his broken body and, in one last desperate effort, somehow managing to drag himself back onto the grassy bluff to safety.

Oh, yes. I'll not soon forget what those two bastards did to me, was Rafe's unspoken vow.

"I cannot imagine how anyone could do such unspeakable things to another human being," Caitlan was saying when Rafe next focused his attention on her. Having long since concluded bathing Rafe's brow, Caitlan appeared content to sit beside him, her hands folded primly in her lap. "We suspect you were set upon for any valuables you might have been carrying with you. Since you arrived here with no personal belongings, I can only assume—"

Caitlan was induced to silence when, for the second time that night, Rafe's hand flew upward with lightning quickness to grasp her hand in a surprisingly strong grip. Until this moment, Rafe had every reason to believe he had been successful in keeping his assailants from obtaining the information they sought from him. But upon hearing Caitlan's candid discourse, Rafe was no longer certain. He had to be sure.

Sensing Rafe was about to make some profound announcement, Caitlan allowed herself to be coaxed forward, so he would not have to strain his crippled voice. The hand that held hers abruptly relinquished its fierce grip and blue eyes darkened to a stormy shade as he lifted his hand to her cheek. The intensity of the expression that contorted Rafe's bruised face was such that, for one incredible moment, Caitlan feared— hoped—he might be about to kiss her.

As the pulse pounded at her temples, Caitlan became acutely aware of the gentle pressure of Rafe's fingers as they caressed her cheek, and she shivered in spite of the sweltering heat of the chamber. Despite her resolve that she was well beyond feeling any such fanciful emotions, Caitlan discovered herself nonetheless fascinated by the titillating idea. Years of self-denial prevailed, however.

Forcing herself to effect a nonchalant air, Caitlan merely said, "Yes, Rafe. What is it?"

With considerable effort, Rafe commandeered the use of his swollen larynx and somehow contrived to rasp out a single, hollow-sounding word.

"Boots."

"Boots?" Caitlan echoed, a quizzical pout crinkling her forehead. Then, drawing erect, her expression deepened into an out-and-out frown, and she repeated incredulously, "*Boots*?!"

To be sure, Caitlan had no idea what Rafe's first words might be, but she had most certainly not anticipated being quizzed about the status of his footwear. After all, they had neither seen nor had word of each other's well-being for seven years. All things considered, Caitlan was more than a little miffed by the fact that Rafe displayed more regard for his boots than for her. Thus thrust into the throes of a flaming temper— the first she had experienced in a very long time—Caitlan reacted impetuously.

Telling herself that if the man wanted his boots, then he must surely have them, she bolted up from the bed. Her fingers trembled with angry emotion as she dragged the black leather boots from underneath the bed and, in a fit of ill humor, let them fly against the wall behind Rafe's head. The footgear subsequently fell to the floor with a lame thud. Caitlan's fury, however, remained effusive.

"There, sir, are your boots," Caitlan fairly shouted. Without another word, she whirled and stormed from the room, slamming the door behind her. Her agitated departure caused the candle flame to flutter violently, then fizzle altogether, thereby plunging the chamber into total darkness.

Rafe lay in the dusky room in the wake of Caitlan's acrimonious leave taking, an expression of shocked bemusement adorning his handsome face. Slowly, a smile began to spread his sensuous mouth and a deep chuckle reverberated in his muscular chest; given the lady's outburst, he considered himself fortunate for not having inquired after his horse.

The echoing refrains of a door banging against its casing was immediately followed by a second deafening clamor as an embittered young woman gained entrance to her chamber with all the fanfare she had displayed upon exiting the sickroom. The uproarious commotion rambled down the attic stairway to the second floor and caused at least one boardinghouse resident to lift his head from his pillow in drowsy confusion. There being no further disturbing noises forthcoming, however, Mr. Morgan merely gave a sleepy yawn, nestled his balding head in his downy-soft pillow, and promptly returned to his dreams.

Caitlan was not to be so readily mollified. She stood in the middle of her cramped room, hands fairly embedded in her sides, and grappled with her burgeoning temper. Green eyes darted angrily about the sparsely decorated room as Caitlan contemplated what she should do next. One thing was certain; she would not cry. Caitlan had vowed a long time ago that she would never again shed a tear over Rafe Bradrick. Never mind the few tears she had shed the night she had brought him back to the boardinghouse; they were to be forgiven, considering her rattled state of mind that evening.

As she stood there, silently fuming over her recent encounter with the insufferable man, Caitlan's gaze fell on the chest of drawers that rested against the wall beside the door. On impulse, she lighted the candle atop the sturdy piece of furniture and dropped to her knees. Grasping the brass handles, Caitlan trembled visibly as she pulled the bottom drawer open. Without further hesitation, slender fingers delved beneath the layers of folded undergarments and extracted a small box.

Inside the mahogany container were various keepsakes from Caitlan's childhood, but there was one of particular interest she sought this sultry predawn morn. She did not waver, but lifted the smooth lid to find—as she knew she would—a stack of letters all neatly tied up with a pink satin ribbon. Taking a deep breath, Caitlan removed the missive that rested on top of the thin pile and glanced at the bold, masculine script on the face of the envelope. The aged paper made a distinctive crinkling sound as Caitlan unfolded the missive and spread it out in front of her. Squaring her shoulders, she began to read the words she had—in reality—committed to memory many years ago.

Caitlan read the letter three times before returning it to its protective pouch and, by the time she climbed to her feet several moments later, she was once again in control of her tempestuous emotions. To say the least, Caitlan thought it peculiar to discover that the very words, which had at one time been the source of such heartbreaking tidings, could now instill within her this sense of utter tranquillity.

Having already resettled the mahogany box among her personal belongings, Caitlan tapped the missive in the palm of her hand as if contemplating what should be done with it. She was of half a mind to rip the despised thing to shreds, but more rational thoughts triumphed and, with a shrug, she slid the yellowing envelope beneath the edge of the hand-crocheted doily that lay draped across the chest of drawers. Now that her anger had dissipated, Caitlan felt suddenly tired and listless.

Stretching her arms above her head, she gave nary a thought to changing into her night-shift. Instead, she extinguished the candle and walked straightaway to the bed in the hopes of gaining an hour or two of sleep before the sun rose. As she settled herself atop the bedclothes, Caitlan felt at peace with her newfound sense of self-confidence. Rafe had caught her off guard with his seemingly affectionate display, but Caitlan was wise to his ways now.

Rafe Bradrick would not play her for a fool this time.

"He's askin' for you again, Miz Katie," said a matter-of-fact voice from the drawing-room aperture.

"Is he?" droned an obviously unimpressed Caitlan in reply.

"Uh huh. He says you ain't been to see him in two days." Hezekiah crossed his arms in front of him and leaned into the doorjamb. His tone was accusing when he speculated, "Mah guess is you ain't been back since you lost your tempah and flung his boots at him."

"He *told* you about that?!" Caitlan blurted and nearly toppled from the step ladder on which she stood.

"Naw. It didn't take no expert to figger out what happened. Any fool could see he was in no shape to fetch 'em himself, and ah knows them boots didn't walk ovah to that cornah on their own. They's only one othah explanation," Hezekiah concluded. "You let that Bradrick fella get you all riled up like you always does. Ah told you so, didn't ah?"

Caitlan heaved her shoulders, reaffirming her indifference to the situation. "Well, you are quite mistaken. I have simply been busy with other household duties as you can plainly see. Besides, Essie adores doting on him."

"Essie has a job—a payin' job, mind you—to see to, as do some of the rest of us" came Hezekiah's pointed jibe.

Ignoring this chastisement, Caitlan concluded polishing the drawing-room window. Climbing down from the precarious perch, she threw Hezekiah a look, then went to collect the freshly laundered curtains that lay draped across the back of the sofa. Before one dainty foot found its way onto the bottom slat, however, Caitlan's purpose was thwarted by the gentle black giant who presently towered over her.

"You bettah let me do that. It'd be just mah luck for you to go and break your dang fool neck," Hezekiah grumbled as he trudged up the ladder, the curtains fluttering about him like a billowy cloud. "And where would that leaves me, ah ask you? Granted, ah can't say that Mistah Bradrick don't deserve Harriet lookin' aftah him, but ah sure don't see how the rest of us deserves him. He's been whinin' all mornin' 'bout this, that, and the othah.

"Ah told you we should takes that man somewheres else when we found him, but you was set on bringin' him here. Well, you had your way, Miz Katie, so don't go thinkin' you can leave the rest of us holdin' the bag now that you done gone and got your feathahs ruffled. Get yourself on up them stairs and tend to the man." He indicated the door with an impatient gesture. "The doctah's here, besides, and he wants a word with you afore he leaves."

Feeling very much like the fabled dog who retreats from an embarrassing situation with its tail tucked firmly between its legs, Caitlan turned to creep from the drawing-room before Hezekiah found reason to continue lambasting her actions. What he said was true; she had not faced Rafe since that night when she allowed her temper to get the better of her, and she was not looking forward to the forthcoming reunion.

Caitlan was granted a small reprieve as she emerged from the downstairs chamber; she encountered a number of boardinghouse tenants, all of whom appeared intent on inquiring after the status of her patient. Eventually, Caitlan was left with no recourse, and she swiftly mounted the steps to the third floor. She paused outside the door to compose herself . . . Rafe must never suspect just how much she dreaded this meeting. Then exhaling a long breath, she pushed the door ajar.

"Here she is now," Doctor Shannon said as Caitlan waltzed into the room. Having just concluded a thorough examination of Rafe's wounds, the physician had returned his instruments to his medical bag and was snapping it closed when the door opened. "Our patient has been telling me all about your famous elixir, Katie" came his sunny greeting. "It appears to have served the purpose. He's still a bit hoarse, but he's definitely on the mend.

"I checked both gunshot wounds for any sign of infection, and they seem to be healing nicely. Oh, and I bound his chest to keep him from jostling those ribs about and causing him more misery. I expect he'll be uncomfortable for a spell, but it's better than the alternative. As far as I can tell, you've done a mighty fine job, Katie," he complimented her. "Keep up the good work. Make sure Mr. Bradrick gets complete rest for the next couple of days, then get him up on his feet. Nothing too strenuous, mind you, just a turn or two around the room. And you might want to let him sit up in a chair for a while every morning and evening, so he can start building his strength back.

"I'll be back in a few days to see how things are going. You know where to reach me if you need me for anything in the meantime. Any questions?" he asked, as he rolled down his shirtsleeves and shrugged into his coat.

"Uh, yes," Caitlan began, then glancing at Rafe, her voice faltered.

"Well, be quick about it, Katie," Doctor Shannon advised. Settling his hat atop his head, he gave all the appearances of a man ready to take his leave. "I'm due out at the Shively Plantation. Constance is about to begin her fifth confinement. I sure hope she manages to give that husband of hers a son this time," he said more to himself than anyone. "Now, what is it you'd like to know?" He smiled down at Caitlan.

She wanted very much to inquire as to when the doctor thought Rafe might be fit enough to go his merry way. Caitlan was, however, keenly aware of a curious blue gaze that scrutinized her every move. Although she was not intimidated by that unswerving stare, years of experience had taught Caitlan that if one wanted Rafe Bradrick to do a particular thing, it was more probable that he would do the opposite for mischief's sake. Therefore, Caitlan realized that, if Rafe thought she was eager to be rid of him, he would be only that much more determined to stay and torment her.

Consequently, Caitlan choked back her original question and inquired instead, "Shall I continue to feed him broth?"

"For a day or two. Use your own judgment, or consult your patient." The doctor nodded toward Rafe. "If anyone, he should be able to tell you what sort of vittles he can stomach. Anything else?"

"No, that's all," Caitlan said, walking with the physician to the door. "Thank you for coming, Doctor. I'll send Hezekiah round if we need you for anything."

"No thanks needed, Katie. You've done all the work. I just hope this young fella appreciates all you've done for him," Doctor Shannon commented in parting and, giving Caitlan's shoulder an affectionate pat, he was gone.

Caitlan stepped across the threshold and watched until the physician had descended the steep staircase, then suppressing the urge to follow his example, she reentered the room. "Decided to stay and brave the lion in his lair, have you?" came Rafe's gravelly taunt.

Caitlan did not rise to the bait, however. Sniffing the air, she wrinkled her nose in disgust and walked over to the foot of the bed. A smile of sublime complacency pinned back her lips when she said, "Rather more like a smelly, old bear, don't you think?"

Rafe was momentarily taken aback by Caitlan's candor. It would seem his Kettie was full of surprises these days. Not only had she spurned death, but she had grown bold in both manner and speech. The Kettie he had known before—albeit she had been a spunky lass—would have shrunk away from his intimidating demeanor, but this Kettie appeared undaunted. Rafe found himself struck with a nagging sense of ambivalence by this revelation. On the one hand, he found her newfound show of spirit to be refreshing and even somewhat alluring. Yet, on the other hand, he was saddened by her loss of naïveté.

What had happened to the innocent girl of his youth; the guileless young miss who had charmed him with her beauty and her unfettered love for life, and to whom he had quite hopelessly lost his heart nearly fifteen years before? What horrors had she suffered over the past seven years to leave her such an embittered, distrustful woman? But, more importantly, why had Caitlan preferred him to think her dead all these years rather than consent to be his wife? Intrigued by the veritable plethora of questions that whirled about his head, Rafe promptly determined that he would have the answer to each and every one before he departed Vicksburg.

"Humph!" Rafe snorted in reply to Caitlan's sally. "It's little wonder I stink, what with you smearing me all over with those abominable ointments every chance you get." Then his voice grew serious as he asked, "Why didn't you tell them who I was, Kettie—that we know each other?"

Here it was—the long-awaited and much-dreaded inquisition to which Caitlan knew she would be subjected when Rafe awakened. Cloaked in the steely armor of cold resilience that had gotten her through the difficult times since her father's suicide, Caitlan resolved to emerge from this encounter unscathed.

"Hezekiah knows," she reminded him. Stepping to the window, Caitlan drew the curtain aside and peered outside as she added a most humbling postscript, "And perhaps I thought it best that Doctor Shannon and the others not know I was acquainted with such a black-hearted rogue as you."

"If you truly feel that way, Kettie, why did you bring me here? Why didn't you just leave me to die?" came Rafe's forthright query. He discerned from Caitlan's grimace—though she tried to mask it—that she was not aware that he was privy to so much information about the night he had been brought to Tuttle's.

"Hezekiah told me." Rafe answered the question Caitlan refused to voice. "For the most part, the man is downright uncommunicative where you are concerned, but he did admit it was you who found me and insisted on bringing me here. Since you obviously find me so completely undeserving, I cannot help but wonder why you would take it upon yourself to single-handedly save my worthless hide."

There was a long pause, then he added, "Why did you, Kettie?" Rafe's lengthy discourse had taken its toll on his beleaguered larynx, causing this final question to emerge as little more than a coarse whisper. Allowing the curtain to fall back into place, Caitlan approached the bed.

"You're talking too much," she scolded in a motherly tone. Retrieving the medicine bottle from the stand, she prepared to administer another dose of the now-infamous elixir. "Perhaps this will help."

Rafe dutifully swallowed a spoonful of the soothing potion, but when Caitlan would have moved away from the bed, he caught her hand in his and persuaded her to sit beside him. "Why?" he demanded.

Knowing she would not have another moment's peace until she offered the irritating man some sort of explanation, Caitlan blew a conciliatory sigh and said, "To be completely honest, Rafe, I don't know. I cannot explain my motives, not even to myself. But when I realized it was you I had stumbled upon, I never considered any other course of action.

"Perhaps I should have," she mumbled under her breath, "for I would not presently be suffering through this interminable interview." Assuming a disinterested mien once more, Caitlan continued, "At any rate, I would not place undue significance on the matter if I were you. I very likely would have done as much for any other wretched creature who was so foolhardy as to go and get himself all shot up."

Having grown weary of trying to satisfy Rafe's curiosity when, in fact, she had no logical explanation for him, Caitlan took it upon herself to change the subject. "Now, sir, I shall have the answers to a few questions of my own" came her blunt pronouncement. "I have known you for a long time, Rafe. How is it that you allowed yourself to get caught in a situation like this? Why would anyone want to do these horrible things to you? How could something like this happen to a man like you?"

Now it was Rafe's turn to be evasive. Not that he distrusted Caitlan, but he had come too far and waited too long to chance jeopardizing his mission now. His carelessness had nearly cost him his life. He would have to execute considerable more discretion in his future endeavors if he hoped to achieve his purpose.

For all Rafe knew, the men who had reduced him to his present helpless state were still lurking about the city, questioning the locals to determine if they had seen a man of his description, and if they knew what had become of him. If

someone should mention how Kettie had taken in a badly
wounded stranger—

Rafe's worrisome gaze found its way back to Caitlan's face,
her green eyes glittering—though he knew full well she would
deny it—with concern for him. Before he answered, Rafe allowed his gaze to wander downward to the soft, pouting lips
that had so long ago experienced the passion of his caress.
Even though these memories were but hollow glimmers in a
tempestuous past, Rafe promised himself that one day soon he
would again know the taste of those wondrous lips against his
own.

Thus avowed, he came to a decision. With his jaw firmly
set, Rafe concluded that everyone's interests would be better
served if he kept his secrets to himself for the time being. He
resolved to do this even though he realized that Caitlan would
"raise the devil of a fuss" when she discovered—as she undoubtedly would—that she had been deceived. But Rafe would
sooner withstand one of Caitlan's tirades than risk placing her
in danger. Consequently, he offered the following vague explanation.

"Ambushed. Two men."

"I suspected as much. You cannot be bested in a fair fight"
was Caitlan's offhand comment. Apparently oblivious to the
smile that these words of praise had planted on the face of her
former sweetheart, Caitlan chewed a finger thoughtfully and
asked, "What were they after?"

"Money," he rasped. A self-satisfied smirk peeled back
Rafe's lips when he added, "But they soon discovered they
were barking up the wrong tree." His manner grew grim, and
he watched Caitlan's face for her reaction as he concluded with
a wholly unexpected revelation, "You see, Kettie, I don't have
anything worth stealing . . . well, besides my horse. Fact is,
I've lost everything. I'm as poor as a church mouse."

Chapter Five

❧❧❦❧❧

"I told you this would happen, Katie Webber. I knew nothin' good would come of bringin' that no-account scoundrel into my boardinghouse. But would you listen to reason? No. 'He'll pay you if he don't die—' '' Harriet flung Caitlan's words back in her face,—'' 'or his family will.' Well, that was a pretty speech you made on his behalf that night when you brung him here. Now we come to find out that, not only is he little more than a penniless wretch, his family won't so much as give him the time of day, let alone pay for his keep.''

Under normal circumstances, the less than flattering mimicry of her impassioned plea for Rafe's life might have rankled Caitlan's temper. The fact was, for all that Caitlan gave the impression of a rapt, sympathetic listener, her thoughts were otherwise preoccupied. Incredible as it may sound, Harriet's face would have grown a shade redder, and she would have given vent to an even greater rage had she been privy to the younger woman's musings.

As Caitlan peered across the rug-draped clothesline and observed Harriet's hysterical ravings, she was put in mind of a chicken. Not a young pullet, mind you. The vision she had conjured was rather more that of a tough, old bird, but a chicken nonetheless. Even though the severe style in which

Harriet dressed her dull, gray-streaked hair served to accentuate her pointed beaklike nose and wattled neck, Caitlan conceded that it was Harriet's mannerisms more so than her actual physical appearance that brought these comical images to mind.

Harriet strutted about the backyard, cackling like a freshly laid hen, with her arms flapping wildly at her sides. Just when Caitlan thought the agitated woman might actually take flight, she was rousted from these amusing reflections by Harriet who marched over to Caitlan and slapped her soundly across the cheek.

"Don't you laugh at me, missy!" squawked an embittered Harriet. "You better mind what I'm saying, do you hear?"

Caitlan, whose bewildered gaze was focused on the bony finger that Harriet had thrust beneath her nose, blinked back the painful tears that had sprung to her eyes. Pressing a consoling hand to the insulted cheek, she silently berated herself for her carelessness in allowing Harriet to catch her daydreaming. Assuming a stony mien, Caitlan met and returned the angry woman's glare in full, but her tone was far from apologetic when she said, "My thoughts were elsewhere, Harriet. What did you say that was of such importance?"

"I want to know how that Bradrick fella came to be such a pauper. Why won't his family have anything to do with him?" Harriet demanded, crossing her arms across her next-to-nothing bosom in a huff.

"I have already explained," Caitlan said with a pointed look at her employer.

"Well, explain it again" came Harriet's irascible reply.

Bending to retrieve the paddle that had slipped from her fingers during Harriet's unwarranted assault, Caitlan gave the rug a self-satisfying swat. The ensuing cloud of dust that wafted up from the carpet irritated Harriet's nose, prompting a resounding sneeze from the fractious woman. Feeling somewhat vindicated, Caitlan steeled herself against the urge to giggle, but before Harriet could seize the opportunity to castigate her for this latest mishap, she said, "Very well then. He gambled away all his possessions.

"Mr. Bradrick has always been a bit of a rounder . . . uh . . . or so he says," Caitlan corrected, her gaze fixed on her task lest Harriet interpret the duplicity in her eyes. Caitlan was still of a mind to keep her prior association with Rafe a secret. "As for his family, he told me that his father passed away a few years ago. The only family he has left is a sister near Baton Rouge, and she is so scandalized by his reckless behavior that she refuses to have anything to do with him."

"Serves him right," Harriet grumbled. Brushing the dust particles from her skirt, she turned away from Caitlan, calling out a dire warning as she made her way to the house. "Well, missy, all I can say is you better pray that man finds some way of settling his debt, else I'll be obliged to tack his account onto what you already owe me."

"Cackle, cackle, you hateful old biddy," Caitlan mumbled under her breath in defiance to the bitter woman's intimidating words. Her gaze fell to the idle rug beater she balanced on her fingertips, and she was just envisioning Harriet's furious reaction to having the paddle whacked across her backside when Hezekiah appeared on the back porch.

"Aftahnoon, ladies." He doffed his hat and nodded to each of them in turn. Hezekiah looked beyond the angry thundercloud that blew in his direction to find Caitlan's pleasing face and, smiling, said, "Ah just come from Mistah Bradrick's room and was wonderin' if'n ah might have a word with you, Miz Katie."

"Out with it, man!" Harriet fairly screeched, more than a little out of patience with everyone's preoccupation with her poverty-stricken tenant. "Whatever you have to say to her can be said in front of me. Go ahead."

Hezekiah worked his hat between deliberate fingers—much as an accordionist might when coaxing a tune from his instrument—and fought back the overwhelming desire to replace his tattered headgear with Harriet's scrawny neck. His expression never changed, however, as he addressed his comments directly to Caitlan.

"Ah was up yondah by the Ffolkes's homestead this mornin'. Jim invited me in for a cup of coffee. Well, we gets to jawin' 'bout this and that, and he tells me 'bout a horse he found runnin' loose up at his place a few nights back.."

"Humph!" Harriet snorted—indeed, no other word can better describe the hideous sound—finding nothing remarkable about Hezekiah's disclosure. Having grown impatient with the proceedings, she snapped, "Is that what this is about—a stupid horse? Get back to work, Katie. And you," Harriet glared dagger eyes at Hezekiah "get on about your business." She dismissed Hezekiah with a sharp gesture and stomped past him to the doorway. His subsequent remarks, however, made Harriet reconsider her hasty actions, and she paused on the threshold to listen.

Hezekiah shook his head and sighed, then continued, "Like ah was sayin', Jim told me 'bout a horse he found. He asked me if'n ah'd heard tell of anyone inquirin' aftah some such animal. Mah first inclination was to say no, but then ah gets to thinkin' 'bout Mistah Bradrick. The Ffolkes lives a ways off the Yazoo Road not too far from where we found him the othah night. So, ah figgered that, if'n the men what bushwhacked Mistah Bradrick didn't bothah themselves with his horse, it might've wandahed ovah to Jim's place."

"And?" Caitlan prompted.

"Well, ah follows Jim out to the barn to take a look and, sure enough, it's his horse all right. Mistah Bradrick's name is carved plain as day on the undahside of the saddle; that's how ah could tell," he explained. "Anyways, ah brung the animal back to mah place. Ah suppose ah'll stable it till Mistah Bradrick is on his feet again. His saddlebags was still intact, so ah brung them to him just now. That's what ah come to tell you, Miz Katie," Hezekiah said kindly. "If'n you don't need me to do nothin' for you, ah'll just get on 'bout mah business like Miz Tuttle said."

Caitlan was about to thank him for his trouble when she was preempted by an excitable Harriet who clapped her hands together and squealed, "Saddlebags! Maybe he's got some valuables after all, Katie, somethin' that he neglected to tell you about. I think I'll just go and have myself a look at Mr. Bradrick's saddlebags." With that ominous pronouncement, Harriet bolted inside the house.

Hezekiah and Caitlan exchanged knowing looks, then he asked, "Ain't you goin' aftah her? It's likely to get ugly up there if'n she commences to badgerin' him. And you know she will. Miz Tuttle don't know no othah way to be," Hezekiah said, his tone more matter-of-fact than accusing.

Squinting against the glare of the hot, Mississippi sun, Caitlan allowed her gaze to meander up the side of the house to a third floor window behind which a curtain fluttered gently in the afternoon breeze. Chuckling to herself, she gave the rug a final whack and replied, "In a minute. Rafe has been cooped up in that stuffy attic room for days now. He deserves a bit of diversion, don't you think, Hezekiah?" she asked with a prankish quirk of her brow.

Hezekiah thought Caitlan's smile was positively wicked, and he told her as much. The chastisement was not meant to offend as was evidenced by the playful wink that accompanied it. Hezekiah glanced up at the attic window, then stuffing his hat under his arm, he trotted down the porch steps. Waving farewell to Caitlan, he began to whistle an airy little ditty as his limp-impaired gait took him to the corner of the house.

Caitlan listened to the lighthearted melody until Hezekiah disappeared from view. Then giving herself a shake—the day's chores were hardly finished—she hauled the rug from the clothesline and made her way back inside.

Caitlan rearranged the flowers in the vase to her liking and stepped back to view her handiwork with a critical eye. Satisfied that she had returned the drawing-room to its original state and that Harriet could find no fault with the room, Caitlan used her apron to polish a smudge from the cherry whatnot table in a final, sweeping gesture. Nodding her approval, she turned to exit the chamber, only to come up short when a brilliant ray of sunshine, reflecting off a metallic object, caught her eye.

Her curiosity aroused, alert green eyes scanned the room in search of the source of the mirrored light. Caitlan fully expected the culprit to be nothing more than a coin dropped and long forgotten by one of the boardinghouse tenants. She was, therefore, genuinely surprised when a second glittering led her to the laminated rosewood sofa where a length of gold chain protruded from between the cushions and twinkled invitingly in the bright sunlight. Sliding her hand behind the cushion, Caitlan withdrew a watch.

Realizing in an instant that she had unwittingly located Mr.

Hamilton's missing pocket watch, Caitlan deposited the time-piece in her apron pocket with a mental reminder to return the watch to its owner at the earliest opportunity. At the moment, there were other matters that required her immediate attention, such as the surly patient who occupied an upstairs chamber. With her thoughts otherwise engaged, it is little wonder that Caitlan nearly toppled a boardinghouse tenant who awaited her in the open doorway.

"Good afternoon, Miss Crawford," Caitlan greeted the woman. "I hope you will excuse me, but I haven't time to chat now. I am just on my way upstairs to change Mr. Bradrick's bandages."

The blond beauty measured Caitlan up and down with a pair of cool, blue eyes and replied, "It seems that your Mr. Bradrick consumes a great deal of your time these days, Katie dear. Why, you'll likely wear yourself to a frazzle if you don't let someone help you. I'd be more than happy to sit with Mr. Bradrick so you can tend to your other chores," Penelope offered in her sweetest, softest voice.

I just bet you would, was Caitlan's resentful thought, though her countenance did not betray her. To the woman, she said, "He is hardly *my* Mr. Bradrick, Penelope. And I do thank you for your kind offer, but I fear there is little sitting to be done around that one. He would wear you ragged in a matter of minutes, and we cannot have that. Whatever would Harriet say?"

"But—" A visibly disappointed Penelope pouted, only to have her protest ruthlessly interrupted by an ear-piercing scream that echoed down the stairway and verily exploded in Caitlan's ears.

"Oh, dear Lord!" Caitlan wailed. "What has he done now?" Without giving Penelope a second thought, Caitlan picked up her skirts and bolted down the hallway to the staircase.

Thus distracted, Caitlan did not witness the childish behavior of the young miss she left standing in her wake. It was generally understood by Miss Crawford's acquaintances that she did not fancy being dismissed in such a—as she considered it—blatantly discourteous fashion. Feeling very much affronted and, silently vowing to get even with the upstart housekeeper, Pe-

nelope pulled a face at Caitlan's back. Then swinging her wide
skirts about, she flounced off in a fit of pique.

Caitlan's side was splitting with pain, and she was gasping
for breath when she arrived at the third floor. Since Rafe had
regained consciousness, she always made a point of rapping
on the door before intruding on his privacy, but Caitlan did
not waste time with such mundane niceties this day. Rather,
she hurled the portal wide and scurried across the threshold.
For the second time in the space of but a few fleeting moments, Caitlan was persuaded to stop dead in her tracks. It
was not the reflection of a shimmering bauble that garnered
her attention this time, however. Instead, she found herself
staring down the barrel of a deadly looking Colt revolver.

Instinctively, Caitlan started to fall back into the corridor
when her disbelieving eyes fell upon a heap of crumpled
brown muslin at the foot of Rafe's bed. "Good God! Have
you taken leave of your senses? Tell me you haven't shot
Harriet!" Caitlan exclaimed and scampered across the floor to
kneel beside the stricken boardinghouse proprietress.

When no disclaimer was forthcoming, a russet-tinged head
popped up from just beyond the footboard and favored the
bed's occupant with her most fulminating glare. "Rafe! Put
down that ridiculous gun and answer me," Caitlan shouted at
him.

"Aw hell, Kettie. Of course I didn't shoot her," he
snapped. "Although I ought to have shot her. She *deserves* to
be shot. And I may bloody well do just that if the old hag
ever tries to steal my boots again."

"Your boots," Caitlan spat in disgust. "I might have
known." Standing, she put her hands on her hips and allowed
her gaze to wander across the unconscious woman. She was
not surprised when her cursory inspection revealed a patch of
black leather that jutted out from beneath Harriet's torso.
Shaking her head, Caitlan mumbled, "I have never in all my
born days known a man to be so prodigiously fond of his
footwear." To Rafe, she said, "Well, if you didn't shoot her,
what happened?"

Rafe hunched his shoulders and instantly came to regret his
impetuous gesture. Wincing at the pain, he gasped, "I took

my gun out of my saddlebags to keep Harriet from abscond-ing with my boots and, when she saw it, she let out that aw-ful yell—you must have heard it, Kettie—and fainted dead away. That's all.''

"That's all?'' she repeated incredulously. "I assure you, Rafe, that is quite enough.''

Hands still on her hips, Caitlan released a long, low breath and surveyed the situation. Shaking her head again, for in-deed she could think of nothing else to do, she stepped to the washstand. Selecting a small bottle from the medicine tray, Caitlan slipped it into her pocket, then she dipped a wash-cloth into the basin and said, "We'll be lucky if Harriet doesn't toss the both of us out on our ears.''

"From where I'm sitting, I'm not so sure that would be such a terrible thing'' was Rafe's candid reply.

"Perhaps not . . . at least, not for you,'' Caitlan murmured, her soft refrain barely audible above the splashing of water in the porcelain bowl. "My situation is vastly different, however. Therefore, if I am successful in convincing Harriet that you are not some crazed gunman who will attack her at every whim, I want your promise that you will conduct yourself in a gentle-manly fashion for the duration of your stay here at Tuttle's.''

Rafe was tempted to counter with some flippant remark, but Caitlan's troubled countenance made him reconsider. Instead, his tone grew as somber as the look on Caitlan's face when he said, "You have my word on it, Kettie.''

There was a lengthy pause as Caitlan appeared to mull his response. Eventually, she made a cynical grunting sound in the back of her throat and said, "I suppose that will have to do. Although, I doubt seriously that Harriet will place much stock in your word.''

Rafe took exception at this blatant assault on his character and directed a challenging glare at Caitlan's rigid back. "It sounds more like you're the one who doubts my word,'' he accused.

Caitlan could almost feel the heat of a pair of crystal-blue eyes boring into her shoulder blades. Willing herself to remain undaunted by Rafe's intimidating demeanor, she wrung the washcloth dry and turned to face him, green eyes staring unwaveringly into blue. "Perhaps you have given me reason to distrust you" came her blunt reply.

Before he could rally a response, Caitlan hurried on, "But that is neither here nor there." She dismissed the issue with a wave of the dampened washcloth and promptly squelched Rafe's attempt to salvage the conversation by saying in a voice that brooked no argument, "And I have no intention of engaging in a discussion on the subject. I must see to Harriet without delay."

Dropping to her knees beside the dazed woman, Caitlan gently rolled Harriet onto her back and began to dab at her temples with the cool washcloth. This brought about marginal results as the unconscious woman began to stir. But when Caitlan pulled the cork from the bottle of smelling salts and waved the restorative beneath Harriet's nose, the woman's eyes snapped open.

Harriet clambered to a sitting position, coughing and gasping all the while in protest of the pungent aroma that permeated her nostrils. Caitlan observed cautiously as a pair of black, befuddled eyes struggled to focus on their surroundings and, thinking it for the best, she treated Harriet to a second whiff of the malodorous remedy. Any misgivings Caitlan might have been harboring about the woman's well-being were swept away as a testy Harriet slapped the offensive bottle aside.

"Stop it, you stupid girl. Stop it!" Harriet cried. "What are you trying to do to me?" As her head cleared, she demanded, "What happened?"

Caitlan glanced up the length of bed to observe Rafe's smug face. With a shrug, she turned back to Harriet and said simply, "You fainted."

"Fainted? Impossible." The older woman dismissed the explanation out of hand. "I've never fainted in my life," she proclaimed, then her black gaze settled on Rafe and comprehension flooded her muddled brain. "You!" she seethed. Refusing the helpful hand that Caitlan proffered, Harriet scrambled to her feet and pointed an accusatory finger at Rafe's head. "It was you. You tried to shoot me."

"Hardly, ma'am," droned Rafe, unaffected by the serious charges Harriet leveled at him. "I seldom *try* anything. When I set my mind on a thing, I usually do it. Therefore, I assure you that, had it been my intention to shoot you, I would have done so . . . cheerfully.''

''Oooh, you arrogant—'' The darkling look that Rafe presently cast in Harriet's direction persuaded her to forgo the remainder of her uncharitable comments. Instead, she whirled in frustration to confront a less formidable adversary. ''This is all your fault,'' she barked at Caitlan.

Caitlan, who knew invariably that the blame for these latest contretemps—as was the case when anything disrupted the humdrum way of life at Tuttle's—would be laid at her feet, did not react. Consequently, an untethered Harriet was permitted to vent her fury.

''I want him out of my boardinghouse, do you hear?'' she railed. Her eyes narrowed into angry slits as she added a most disagreeable postscript. ''And you just better pray to the good Lord above that I don't throw you out with him, missy.''

Feeling somewhat more courageous, Harriet turned to Rafe again and continued ranting, ''I've never heard the like, assaulted in my own home by an ungrateful, good-for-nothing excuse of a man, and me lettin' you stay here out of the kindness of my heart. You had no call to go treatin' me the way you did, mister. Why, I have half-a-mind to get Sheriff Bodeker,'' she said, her tone threatening.

Rafe, whose pensive gaze had been focused on Caitlan throughout Harriet's diatribe, turned a chilling expression on the boardinghouse proprietress. An astute observer—which, of course, Harriet was not—would have surmised that such a frigid countenance could not possibly bode harmonious tidings for the one responsible for provoking it. Harriet, however, appeared unmoved by Rafe's frosty glower.

Unconsciously fingering the revolver's handle, Rafe chose his rebuttal deliberately. Calling Harriet's bluff, he said, ''Go ahead. Fetch the sheriff. I would welcome the opportunity to tell him how I was set upon—without provocation, mind you— by a money-grabbing old hag who forced me to resort to extreme measures in order to keep her from stealing my belongings.''

Harriet's pallor changed from ashen white to bright scarlet in the span of a few seconds as Rafe delivered his valid litany of complaints, but she did not speak a word. Indeed, the woman was so completely enraged with the man's complacent air that her tongue refused to deliver a parting blistering retort. In the end, Harriet responded in her own indelible way.

Thumping her foot against the floor, she whirled about and stomped to the door where the use of that rapierlike organ returned long enough for her to shout at Caitlan, "Get him out of here! I don't care where he goes or how you do it, but I want him gone from my house by sunup. Do I make myself clear, missy?"

A visibly distraught Caitlan stood staring at the portal long after Harriet had slammed it shut, unwittingly twisting the washcloth into pretzellike shapes. Then as the rapid thrumming at her temples began to subside, and she discovered that she could once again think with an uncluttered, rational mind, Caitlan flew into action. Flinging the useless washcloth aside, she sprinted to the door and jerked it open.

"Kettie," Rafe called after her. "You mustn't worry so. I'll wager Harriet didn't mean half of what she said. Come here." He extended his hand toward Caitlan in a beckoning gesture. "You're upset. Stay with me and take a moment to gather your wits, then go fetch the old crow back here. I fancy I can make amends once she's calmed down. Assuming, of course, she can be persuaded to keep her mouth shut long enough to listen to reason."

Caitlan faltered on the threshold as if mesmerized by Rafe's invitation. She stared blankly at the hand that stretched out to her and, of their own will, her feet took a tentative step toward the bed. Then something akin to the ferocious slap that Harriet had inflicted upon her that very afternoon snapped inside Caitlan's memory, and she backed instinctively toward the door.

"No!" she said, giving her head a determined toss. "You'll not talk yourself out of this situation quite so easily, Rafe Bradrick. I fear it will take a good deal more than a handsome face and a speech laced with pretty promises to sway Harriet's cold heart," Caitlan informed him with a smug quirk of her brow. Not trusting herself to deny him should he persist in asking her to remain, Caitlan promptly quit the room.

*   *   *

It was a decidedly skeptical expression that dressed Caitlan's face when she reentered the tiny attic chamber later that evening carrying Rafe's supper tray. If she was surprised to see that her unruly patient had somehow managed to pull himself to an erect position against the headboard, and that there was an expectant twinkle in the cool, blue gaze that regarded her, Caitlan gave no indication. Instead, she settled the tray on the side table. Then no longer able to control the curiosity that burned in her breast, she marched straightaway to the bed to ask a question of its occupant.

"How did you do it?" she demanded without demur.

One dark eyebrow shot heavenward in feigned surprise and Rafe affected a nonchalant mien as he drawled, "Whatever are you talking about, Kettie, my dear?"

"I am not your dear," Caitlan snapped irritably. "And don't play coy with me, Rafe. It won't wash. I know you, remember?" She gave him a pointed look and, grabbing a napkin from the dinner tray, thrust it under his chin. "I want you to tell me, if you please, what you said to Harriet. She waltzed into my kitchen not more than five minutes ago—singing your praises, mind you—and informed me that she had undergone a change of heart and had decided that, 'the darling man'— she actually called *you* that—'could remain until he had fully recovered from his injuries.'" Caitlan screwed up her face in a fair mimicry of the older woman.

"What is so remarkable about that?"

"Harriet doesn't have a heart," Caitlan grumbled and threw herself onto the bedside chair.

Rafe suppressed the urge to laugh at Caitlan's woebegone countenance and his voice was soft and cajoling when he said, "Even the blackest of souls has a heart, Kettie. Sometimes, one just has to care enough to dig a little deeper to find it is all."

Caitlan, knowing full well that Rafe was attempting to lead the conversation onto a more personal course, refused to be steered down that disquieting path. Shrugging aside his high-minded observation, she said, "Be that as it may, I still maintain that Harriet cannot change that which she does not possess. So, what did you do, Rafe Bradrick, to convince that old shrew that you could make good on your account?"

Rafe, who could be just as stubborn as the next man, determined that Caitlan would not easily wriggle out of this discussion. Blue eyes did not falter as they stared into green, and he answered, "I gave her Grandmother's diamond-and-emerald ring. You remember the one, Kettie," he goaded her, but when Caitlan did not rise to the bait, Rafe smiled knowingly and continued, "That ring is the one thing of value I somehow managed not to fritter away . . . sentimental reasons, I guess. Grandmother was always partial to it, and she meant a lot to me. I suppose I didn't want to risk losing something the old girl held so dear.

"Granted, I had always intended that my bride should have the trinket." He paused to allow the significance of this statement to sink in . . . he needn't have bothered. "But since I've attained the ripe old age of thirty-six without succumbing to the charms of a member of your wilier sex, I don't foresee myself ever having need of it." Rafe could not swear to it, but he thought he detected a glimmer of tears in the green gaze that remained unswerving.

In the end, it was Rafe who, feeling very much at odds with himself for having broached this delicate subject, averted his eyes to the window. As his fingers toyed with the edge of the sheet, he explained, "I kept the ring tucked inside a pair of socks in my saddlebags. I suppose that would account for why the highwaymen didn't make off with it.

"Anyway, old Harriet's eyes lit up as bright as a beacon on a moonless night when she saw it. So, I decided that if the silly gewgaw would serve to pacify her bruised feelings, then she should have it. Leastways, she won't be badgering you about leaving, and I am free to stay as long as I like." Rafe recounted the terms of his agreement with Harriet. His warm gaze returned to peruse Caitlan's unreadable face as he murmured, "I would say that Grandmother's ring served a worthwhile purpose, wouldn't you, Kettie?"

"It seems a rather high price to pay for your keep, sacrificing something that was so near and dear to your heart" came her matter-of-fact retort. "I daresay I could have smoothed Harriet's ruffled feathers if you had given me half a chance, but there is no use crying over spilled milk. What's done is done." She sighed her indifference and hunched her shoulders in an aloof gesture that made Rafe long to throttle her.

His brusque mien would have softened, however, had he known that, despite Caitlan's crusty exterior, inside her heart was breaking. She had not thought the disposition of a mere trifle could have such a staggering effect on her. In truth, it galled her to the very core to know that Harriet Tuttle would presently be flaunting the ring that—by rights—should have been hers. Vowing that Rafe would never know how deeply his actions had hurt her, Caitlan stood up.

"Your supper has most likely grown cold by now," she announced without ceremony. "Shall I take it back to the kitchen and warm it for you?"

Rafe cast a wary eye over the dinner tray and asked, "Broth again?"

"Yes, and tea."

"Then it hardly matters," he said sulkily. "Hot or cold, they taste the same. The only thing that could make this meal more palatable is if you served it up with a thick beefsteak."

"I'm only following the doctor's instructions, Rafe," Caitlan scolded. "You heard what Doctor Shannon said; that I should use my judgment in preparing your meals."

"As I recall," Rafe bickered, "he also said you should consult me as to what I might fancy. I'll tell you right now, Kettie, I cannot stomach much more of that bilge water." He jerked his head toward the bowl that Caitlan lifted from the tray. Rafe sensed her bristle with hurt pride and hastened to add, "I don't mean to sound ungrateful, because I know you've gone to a lot of trouble for me, but a man needs more than gruel and watered-down tea to get by on."

Caitlan considered the earthenware dish for several long moments while she battled to maintain her composure. Winning the inner struggle, she said, "You're right, of course. I'll see that your breakfast consists of a heartier fare . . . perhaps a poached egg and toast . . . but certainly no beefsteak, at least not yet." Taking a seat on the edge of the bed, Caitlan proffered a spoon and asked, "Do you feel up to feeding yourself or shall I help you?"

"I think I can manage," he said with just a hint of haughtiness creeping into his voice.

"Suit yourself." Caitlan handed him the utensils, then busied herself by tidying the messy chamber. As she scuttled about the room, Caitlan was very much aware that her every move was monitored closely by a pair of observant blue eyes. Therefore, she was not surprised when she straightened from returning his sacred boots to their honored place beneath the foot of the bed to find that unnerving cerulean stare focused squarely upon her.

"All finished?" Caitlan asked, reaching for the empty bowl and spoon.

"Every drop, ma'am," Rafe proclaimed, licking his lips in mock exaggeration and holding up the dish for her inspection.

Caitlan rolled her eyes in response to his sarcastic antics and, depositing the used utensils on the dinner tray, she turned to him and said, "I will change your bandages now, if you like. Afterward, if you're feeling up to it, perhaps you would care to sit up in the chair for a while."

"That sounds like a mighty fine suggestion, Kettie." Rafe nodded his concurrence. "Hezekiah helped me take a turn around the room earlier today and it almost got the better of me. I suspect I will grow a little stronger with each try."

Caitlan brought the tray of medical supplies with her as she reclaimed her seat on the edge of the bed. Always before, Rafe had been unconscious when she undertook this particular task, therefore, she felt herself grow a little self-conscious as she began to conduct her routine inspection of his injuries.

She lightly ran her fingers through the thick strands of hair behind his right ear and was happy to discover that the nasty bump had almost vanished entirely. Next, Caitlan took his chin between her thumb and forefinger, and turned his head this way and that in order to get a thorough look at his battered face. Once again, she was pleased to note that the swelling and discoloration had shown a marked improvement.

"I know you don't much care for my ointments, but I'm going to apply just a dab here at the corner of your mouth." Gentle fingertips accomplished their goal under the vigilant scrutiny of a very interested patient. Further examination revealed that the swelling along his neck had diminished, prompting Caitlan to ask, "How is your throat? Does it still grieve you when you talk? I can brew another batch of my elixir if you need it."

"It scratches every now and then, but nothing to speak of," Rafe assured his compassionate nurse. "I daresay you needn't go to the bother of mixing up more medicine. My throat will heal with time."

Caitlan gladly conceded this point; it would spare her the aggravation of wheedling Hezekiah into making another excursion into the woods to gather the necessary herbs and roots that went into the making of her special recipe. Thus having tended to Rafe's less serious afflictions, she directed her attention to his shoulder wound. Hoping to spare him any undue discomfort, Caitlan carefully peeled back the soiled bandage, but she felt him flinch despite her painstaking efforts.

"I'm sorry, Rafe," Caitlan blurted. Snatching her hands away, her anxious eyes searched his pain-riddled face. "I'll try to be more careful."

"Don't worry about me, Kettie." Rafe exhaled a haggard breath and Caitlan could almost visualize him steeling himself against another sudden onslaught of pain. "It has to be done. Just—"

Caitlan paused as she felt the touch of his hand upon her arm. Looking into his eyes, she could appreciate the monumental effort it took for him to withstand her probing—however gentle—into the torn flesh.

"Just be quick about it" came Rafe's throaty appeal.

Caitlan nodded, then set about to honor his simple request. A cursory inspection of the tormented region revealed that, like his other injuries, this one also appeared to be healing nicely. The area immediately surrounding the wound was a healthy shade of pink and the sutured flesh was cool to the touch and showed nary a sign of swelling. Thankful that none of the dreaded signs of an impending infection were apparent, Caitlan quickly redressed the wound.

A glance at Rafe's face revealed that he was holding up under the strain. Thus reassured of his stamina, she pressed on. Caitlan decided against removing the bandages that held his bruised ribs in check. Instead, she stepped around to the opposite side of the bed and prepared to carry out the last of her nursing duties; that of rebandaging the bullet wound that ravaged his lower right side. But as slender fingers reached out to grasp the edge of the white sheet, Caitlan suddenly faltered.

After all, it was one thing to reveal a sizable portion of this virile man's naked flesh when he was oblivious to her actions, but it was quite another to do so under his watchful eye. Caitlan realized full well that the longer she tarried, the more likely Rafe was to notice her hesitation and presume the reason for her missish behavior. Having no desire to undergo a lengthy interrogation from the gentleman in question, she gulped down her anxieties and plucked the edge of the sheet from where it nestled against his chest.

Caitlan avoided Rafe's eyes as she slowly dragged the cloth down across that broad expanse of distracting hard flesh to reveal a bandaged area just above his right thigh. Laying the sheet across Rafe's lean stomach, she promptly set about her work. Caitlan soon discovered that the soiled bandage would present a small dilemma in that it had stuck to the wound, thereby preventing a swift and painless removal. She would presently find herself plagued with a far more disconcerting problem, however. When Caitlan stripped the dressing away, Rafe gave an involuntary jerk that provoked the unfortunate displacement of her carefully arranged drapery.

Though Caitlan kept her eyes trained on the immediate crisis—the forced removal of the bandage had caused the wound to seep—her cheeks flushed scarlet. Pressing a clean compress against the torn flesh, she held it steadfast to stanch the flow of blood. Once this had been accomplished, she applied an emollient to the region, then swiftly bound the wound.

Blowing a relieved sigh at having completed the tedious chore, Caitlan set about restoring the sheet to its former position. She hoped to accomplish this ticklish feat without causing undue embarrassment for either of them, especially herself. Caitlan dared not look at Rafe's face; she did not trust her temper should she encounter one of his smug looks. Neither could she bring herself to cast an eye over the exposed area lest her maidenly senses be thrown into a state of confusion by a spectacle of an altogether different ilk. Knowing that she could not deliberate the situation forever, Caitlan acted.

Without looking, she stretched out her hand and began a tentative exploration of the area where she hoped the displaced sheet was situated. Surprisingly, Caitlan managed to locate the crumpled cloth in this haphazard fashion, but as her elated fingers enclosed on the edge of the fabric, Rafe shifted his leg. The unexpected movement caused Caitlan's fingertips to brush—ever so fleetingly—along his lower abdomen, a mere whisker's space from the very personal part of his anatomy that she had desperately tried to avoid from the outset. Her inadvertent fondling provoked an involuntary groan from Rafe which, in turn, inspired Caitlan to drop the sheet as if it were aflame and snatch her hand away.

"For Christ's sake, Kettie," Rafe gasped out a little breathlessly, "it won't bite you! Will you just take hold of the damn thing and jerk it this way?" came his brusque, not to mention thoroughly ambiguous, command.

Already flustered by the awkward situation, Caitlan misinterpreted Rafe's meaning. Utterly scandalized by his suggestion, she jumped up from the bed and shrieked, *"What?!* I'll do no such thing!"

Caitlan's ample bosom, heaving in righteous indignation beneath the thin lines of her faded blouse, served as a momentary distraction to a completely befuddled, albeit much-appreciative, Rafe. Sounding more gruff than was his intent, he raised himself up from the pillow and said, "The sheet, goddammit! Stop acting like a giddy schoolgirl and pull the blasted thing back over me."

His frustration spent and winded by his efforts, Rafe fell back, adding an apologetic afterthought. "I cannot reach it, Kettie, or I'd spare you the embarrassment and do it myself."

Feeling prodigiously sheepish for having overreacted to his innocent proposition, Caitlan swallowed a generous helping of her pride and promptly covered Rafe with the linen. Thinking this an opportune time to execute a clean escape, she gathered up the bandaging materials and prepared to take her leave without further ado.

Rafe observed Caitlan's frantic movements with a puzzled eye. Determined that she would not run away without explaining her perplexing behavior, he placed a staying hand against her arm. This gesture caught a visibly shaken young lady off guard, and Caitlan nearly spilled the contents of her tray onto Rafe's lap.

"Whoa there. Calm down, Kettie," Rafe said, stroking her hand in a cajoling manner that succeeded in coaxing her back down beside him. Then more to the point, he demanded, "Just what the devil did you think I meant?"

Caitlan, her cheeks flaming a bright red, shook her head and muttered, "Never mind."

Realizing it was unlikely that he would learn anything from his close-mouthed companion, Rafe took a moment to reconstruct their conversation in his mind. Presently, a deep chuckle was heard reverberating in that wide, muscular chest and he said, "Good heavens Kettie! Is that what you thought?" he guffawed. "Well, I must say you flatter me, darlin', but man that I am . . . and as much as I might want to . . . I fear I wouldn't be much good for you in my present state. I'm not quite ready to undertake anything quite so strenuous, however pleasurable it may prove to be."

Caitlan, her embarrassed blush having grown hot with anger, opened her mouth to deliver a scathing setdown to this overly presumptuous and thoroughly impossible man. Just as abruptly, she closed it again, deciding that little could be gained from exchanging insults with Rafe. Standing, she returned the tray to the bedside table and, summoning her courage, faced him once more.

Thinking it wise to ignore his risqué comments, Caitlan said, "All things considered, I think it best if we postponed getting you up until morning. Hezekiah will be here, and he can help you into your trousers. That way, you'll be free to move about whenever you like, and I will be able to change your dressings without—" She faltered and looked away, then said sharply, "Well, it will just be better for all concerned."

When she did not receive an argument from her roguish patient, Caitlan turned toward the door. A parting glimpse at Rafe persuaded her to forgo her departure once again; she noticed his forehead was literally drenched with perspiration. Realizing that her ministrations had taken a toll on even Rafe's stalwart constitution, Caitlan dunked a washcloth in the basin and, leaning over, she began to mop up his brow with the cool cloth. In the midst of this soothing application, she was taken by surprise when Rafe lifted his hand to tenderly stroke at the cheek that bore the imprint of Harriet's punishing hand.

"Might this be that old troll's handiwork?" came his compassionate conjecture.

Caitlan, unable to look at him, merely nodded in reply.

"Oh, no. You'll not get off that easily," he said, cupping her chin in his hand and obliging her to meet his steady blue gaze. "What is it? What are you doing in a place like this anyway? What has happened to you, Kettie? Why do you let that woman treat you like this? Why don't you just leave?" As Rafe gave voice to the questions that had been gnawing at him for days, he slid his unoccupied hand around Caitlan's waist.

Caitlan, who had been anticipating this conversation ever since the night he had regained consciousness, hunched her shoulders and said "I cannot leave, Rafe. I . . . I have nowhere else to go."

His curiosity duly piqued by Caitlan's forlorn admission, Rafe prepared to pursue this discussion. He was prevented from doing so, however, by an excited Essie, who chose that inopportune moment to enter the chamber.

Essie, who did not seem to think it extraordinary to find her friend thus entwined in a virtual stranger's arms, began chattering away the moment she crossed the threshold. "Katie, Harriet said I'd most likely find you here. I'm sorry for bein' so late and all, but Madame asked me to run an errand for her, and on my way back to the dress shop I happened by the Widow Stevens's house. There was a big commotion goin' on, what with the doctor leavin' and the housekeeper wailin' at the top of her lungs.

"Anyway," Essie removed her bonnet and tossed it onto the rocking chair, "I'm here now. What would you like me to do?"

Caitlan, who had pulled away from Rafe the moment she heard the chamber door open, turned toward her friend and, wearing her most tolerant expression, asked, "Essie, what's wrong? Has something happened to Delia?"

Essie did not immediately reply, for the ever-hungry young lady had become engaged in scanning the supper tray for signs of any uneaten delicacies. When her search rendered but a lonely cup of cold tea, she turned up her nose and said, "They say she's dyin', Katie. In fact, the doctor don't expect her to make it through the night."

Chapter Six

Delia Stevens did not die that night. The craggy old woman's condition stabilized near dawn, thereby granting her a small reprieve. In fact, an entire fortnight came and went without Essie's dire prediction coming to pass. By the end of the third week, Delia had improved so much that she was able to sit up in bed and grudgingly accept a few spoonsful of the same nutritious broth that Caitlan had used in coaxing the life back into Rafe's battered body.

The townsfolk who knew of Delia's near critical state were of mixed opinions when news of her miraculous recovery buzzed through the city. There were those who smiled and said that the good Lord obviously was not ready to call the widow to her heavenly home. There was, however, an equal contingent that theorized it was the devil himself who, being disinclined to accept Delia's soul into his fiery domain, had intervened and spared the crotchety old woman's life. Still another faction's speculations were blunt and to the point; they maintained that Delia Stevens was simply too stubborn to die.

And then there was that one devoted individual who presently sat at the aged widow's bedside, doggedly scolding her patient until Delia opened her mouth and swallowed a dram of the rejuvenating liquid. Caitlan had heard the talk on the street regarding Delia's revival, but dismissed it for what it was . . . idle chitchat. The truth was, Caitlan did not concern herself with the whys and wherefores of Delia's recovery, she was merely glad the dear, old girl was still alive. She admired Delia's resilience and the courage the woman displayed in her determination to experience every precious breath she had coming to her.

Even the heartiest of constitutions weakens with age, however. Caitlan knew it was just a matter of time—perhaps days or even hours—before she would bid farewell to the eccentric lady she had come to regard as friend. All the foreboding signs were present; Delia's pasty visage and clammy skin, her eyes that had sunk back in their sockets and were ringed in black circles. But what was perhaps most disarming to Caitlan was the haunting sound of an ever-present deathlike rattle that rumbled inside the woman's chest.

Resolving that Delia should not know the essence of her dismal contemplations, Caitlan shook off her troubled mien and smiled down at the ailing woman. "Care for another spoonful, Delia?" Caitlan leveled the utensil at the woman's lips as if to tempt her. "You've not eaten much. You will never get your strength back if you don't eat properly."

"You call that swill proper?" snorted a grumpy Delia. "I'd find a beefsteak a sight more appetizing, I tell you."

This pronouncement prompted a chuckle from Caitlan as she recalled that Rafe had expressed those exact sentiments following a week of being spoon-fed her soup. Giving Delia's wrinkled hand an understanding pat, Caitlan cleared away the dirty dishes and said, "Perhaps in a day or two, Delia. Until then, you will just have to reconcile yourself to choking down my swill at mealtime. Granted, my soup may not have much bite to it, but it is chock-full of herbs and other good things to make you strong again."

"Stuff and nonsense!" came Delia's blunt retort. "Just who are you trying to bamboozle with such talk? You're old enough to know by now, Katie Webber, that you can't fool an old fool like me. You and I both know that I'll most likely be with my sweet Gus in heaven before week's end. So, I'll thank you not to go patronizing me with talk of herbs and miracle-soup that will make me strong again."

Setting the tray of dishes atop the marble top bureau, Caitlan turned and, with her hands behind her, gripped that sturdy piece of furniture as she murmured, "I do wish you would not talk like that, Delia. It's most upsetting to hear you dismiss your own death in such a flippant manner."

"Well now, how do you suppose I feel? After all, I'm the one who's dying," Delia grumbled and lapsed into a fit of coughing.

Caitlan held the woman until the spasms subsided, then gently settled her against the pillows. Sitting on the edge of the bed, Caitlan selected a brush from the bedside table and began to pull it through Delia's hair in slow, soothing strokes until the elderly woman's eyes closed and her breathing became regular once more.

"I'm going to miss your cantankerous ways more than you can ever imagine, Delia Stevens" was Caitlan's reverent whisper.

Caitlan had thought Delia to be sleeping; consequently, she was taken aback when an age-spotted, wrinkled hand enclosed around hers and Delia said, "I know that, Katie dear. But you mustn't fret over an old crow like me. I'm near seventy years of age, and I've had a good, long life. I can't complain. Fact is, these old bones have earned a long, peaceful rest."

The old widow opened her eyes then and, looking up, discovered Caitlan with a visage that was fraught with despair. Giving the younger woman's hand a consoling pat, Delia murmured, "I know, I know, lovey. It's hard to watch someone— even an old witch like me—slip away. Would it be any easier for you if I told you I'm ready to meet my maker?"

"Delia, please," Caitlan interrupted, only to have her entreaty ignored.

"I know it's hard for you to understand now, Katie, but some day a big, strapping man will walk into your life." Delia's eyes sparkled with some secret memory. "And then you'll know. Make no mistake, lovey. There will be times when you believe you could die from such a headstrong man, but then he'll up and leave you all alone one day and your heart will know such an ache—" Her voice trailed off and the twinkling eyes now glimmered with unshed tears. "And then . . ." she sighed, " . . . well, then you'll be just as certain you'll die without him," came Delia's sorrowful confession.

"My Gus had his faults right enough, but I came to love each and every one just as much I adored him for his sweet, caring ways. When he passed on five years ago, a part of me died with him. Why, I've not known a single moment of happiness since that terrible day. Now the time is drawing near when I'll get to be with my Gus again, so rest easy in your heart, Katie dear, and know that I'm ready." Delia stroked Caitlan's hand once more and, closing her eyes, her withered lips echoed, "I'm ready."

A moment later, the tired, old eyes fluttered open to find Caitlan still sitting on the edge of the bed, her countenance even more disheartened than before. "For pity's sake, Katie," Delia said testily. "Stop looking so down in the mouth. I haven't died yet! And stop hovering over me as if you expect every breath I take to be my last."

"I'm sorry, Delia," Caitlan apologized. Returning the brush to the bedside table, she stood up, clasped her hands in front of her, and said, "I don't mean to be a nuisance. I . . . I only want to help."

"I know that, child." Delia's aged face softened with a smile. "Before you go back to that rickety shack that Harriet Tuttle calls a boardinghouse, would you be willing to honor an ungrateful, outspoken old woman's silly request?"

"You are neither of those things," Caitlan promptly chided the ailing widow. "What is it you would have me do?"

"It would please me to have you tell me what's going on outside that window yonder." Delia pointed to the embrasure on the opposite wall where the starch white curtains did not so much as flutter in the sweltering August heat.

Nodding her understanding, Caitlan stepped to the opening and pulled the curtains aside. She took a moment to scrutinize the city streets below her before commenting, "It seems that little Petey Wilson is up to his usual antics. There is a group of young girls just making their way up the hill from Morrison's grocery. From the looks of them, it appears as if they have squandered their pennies on candy or some such treat, and Petey is hunkered down behind the Taylor's fence post waiting to waylay them." Even as she spoke, the young lad leaped up from his place of concealment to frighten the unsuspecting quintet.

He then stretched out his hands in front of himself and proceeded to taunt the startled girls with a rather large and vociferous bullfrog. This provocative act prompted the young misses to scream and scatter in a variety of directions. All, that is, save one. Little Prissy Simpkins was so terrified by Petey's prank that she dropped her coveted bag of sweets. With the candy strewn about her feet and her arms rigid at her side, Prissy could do nothing more than stand transfixed on the sidewalk, shrieking at the top of her lungs.

Even as Caitlan described this raucous scene, a number of passersby came to Prissy's assistance. While these Good Samaritans made every effort to appease the distraught child, a thoroughly satisfied Petey roared with laughter. In blatant defiance of the adults in his midst, the trouble-making youngster continued to taunt poor Prissy with the repugnant frog. It was then that Mrs. Taylor—who had been sweeping her front stoop—marched down the sidewalk and through the gate to grab Petey by the ear.

The unanticipated seizure caused Petey to lose hold of the wily frog. As the playful animal slipped from his owner's hand and hopped gleefully across the street—creating mayhem for the driver of a skittish team of horses—its throaty refrains could be heard echoing behind him. Petey immediately tried to give chase only to have his efforts steadfastly denied by Mrs. Taylor. That determined lady held firmly to Petey's ear and, heedless to his howls of protest, the matronly woman dragged the boy down the street toward his home where a suitable punishment would be sought.

"Poor Amy Wilson," Caitlan lamented with a sorry shake of her head. "She certainly has her hands full with the raising of that hellish child."

"Oh, Petey will turn out all right. He was just having some fun." Delia laughed. "You mark my words, Katie. That boy will grow up to become mayor of this town, or a state senator. And the young miss that was screeching the loudest will no doubt become his wife. What else do you see?"

Green eyes returned to scan the city thoroughfares, then Caitlan gave a nonchalant shrug and said, "Not much of anything really. Penelope Crawford is sashaying back and forth in front of White's barbershop, trying to look inconspicuous—and failing miserably, I might add—hoping to attract the notice of some poor man.

"And I suppose one of the riverboats must have docked to take on supplies because there is a group of men making their way toward Mollie Bunch's place or one of the other houses in that shameless district." Caitlan turned up her nose and her haughty intonation reflected her feelings on the subject of bawdy houses and the men who frequented them. "One would think a man could find something better to do with his hard-earned money than waste it on the likes of those women. Why must men insist on frittering away their wages on such wicked acts? Disgraceful!" She clucked her tongue and continued to watch the men as they ambled up the street.

"Hah!" Delia barked. "How old are you, Katie?"

"Hmm?" Caitlan muttered, momentarily diverting her attention from the window. "Thirty-one. Why?"

"Because you sound like one of those sour old biddies that stops by now and again to ease her conscience and conduct her churchly duties. You shouldn't go judging people just because you don't understand their reasons, Katie."

Caitlan watched as the men disappeared inside a popular house on China Street, and a thoughtful expression crinkled her brow when she looked at Delia and said, "Did Gus ever—"

"Only once that I know of." Delia interpolated Caitlan's half-asked question. "And what a night we had after he confessed his little transgression to me. As I recall, we did some fighting, some yelling, and a whole lot of loving that night, and I never gave him reason to go looking elsewhere again." She chuckled and her eyes narrowed in shrewd contemplation of the young lady who stood by the window. "Suppose you tell me about that young fella you've been looking after. Has he poked you yet?"

Caitlan, visibly shocked by Delia's bold and wholly unexpected query, dropped the edge of the curtain and whirled toward the bed. "No! Of course not!" came her affronted reply.

With a ponderous shake of her head, Delia muttered to herself, "No, I didn't think so." Then with a cantankerous grunt, she demanded, "What's wrong with him?"

"Nothing, he's—"

But Delia would not hear Caitlan's explanation, charging instead, "Well, what's wrong with you then, Katie? You're not getting any younger. For all you know, this man might be your last chance for happiness."

"I am happy enough, thank you," Caitlan returned tersely and walked straightaway to the chamber door. "If you have nothing else for me to do, I believe I'll just be going. I'm certain Harriet must be wondering if I am ever coming back." Then her temper waning, she paused with her hand on the knob and said, "I will come back tomorrow, Delia. Shall I send Mrs. Burke to you now?"

"Bother my housekeeper!" Delia snapped. "Think about what I'm saying to you, Katie. It ain't natural for a woman to go so long without a man. You need a man to snuggle up against in bed at night, a man you can tell your troubles to and who will kiss your fears away. From what that Campbell girl tells old Burke, I'd wager you would be good for him, too."

"Essie should mind her tongue," Caitlan muttered and opened the door.

"And you should mind what I'm telling you," Delia countered, but her words went unheeded; Caitlan had already slipped into the corridor.

Caitlan's composure had returned by the time she emerged from the front door a few moments later, albeit her head still reeled from Delia's outrageous suggestions. Her anger flared again, however, when she found the ignominious Petey Wilson—looking none the worse from his recent confrontation with Mrs. Taylor—perched on the gatepost, carelessly pelting the front of Delia's white-frame house with pebbles.

"You stop that this instant, Petey!" Caitlan shouted at the bothersome youth.

The boy did not immediately respond to Caitlan's outcry. Indeed, his subsequent actions suggested that he had not heard her at all, for he launched another missile toward the structure that came precariously close to striking Caitlan. She was naturally annoyed by the boy's brazen act of disrespect, but it was the child's ensuing taunting statement that prompted Caitlan to lose her temper.

Petey screwed up his face and sneered, ''Make me stop, you ugly old maid.''

''Oooh! You horrid little boy!'' Caitlan gasped and sprinted down the walkway toward the impudent child.

Petey, like all lads of dubious wit, miscalculated the speed with which Caitlan could reach him. In less time than it took him to jump down from his roost—granted his escape was hampered by the fact that his britches became entangled on the gatepost—Caitlan descended on him. For the second time that day, Petey Wilson's ear became the target of a pair of enraged fingers.

''How dare you say such things to me!'' Caitlan seethed at the lad. ''Why can't you just leave decent, respectable folk be? You run along home before I forget I'm a lady and take a switch to your backside.'' Caitlan bent forward and, wagging a finger beneath the child's nose, she looked him in the eye and vowed, ''And if I ever catch you skulking about Mrs. Stevens's house again, I'll do just that. Now, go on home, Petey.'' She released his reddened ear and was relieved when the boy did not attempt some measure of retaliation but rather turned tail and scampered off in the opposite direction as fast as his legs would carry him.

Caitlan, who had been so embroiled in the fracas, was completely oblivious to the fact that her encounter with the young ruffian had been witnessed by a number of fascinated passersby. She was, therefore, duly surprised when Petey's departure was immediately heralded by the sound of thunderous applause.

''Bravo, Katie! Well done, indeed,'' cheered one voice in particular.

Glancing at the driver of a buggy that had stopped in the middle of the street, Caitlan found herself staring up into Jeremy Cantrell's engaging face.

''Hello, Jeremy,'' she mumbled, embarrassed to discover that her shrewish outburst had been witnessed by someone of Jeremy's standing in the community. ''I guess I must have lost my temper.''

''The whole town knows that Petey Wilson is little more

than a common bully. I'm certain the lad provoked you, and you were well within your rights to reprimand him." Jeremy, as would any southern gentleman worth his salt, defended his— as he considered Caitlan—lady's actions.

"Delia says that Petey will grow up to be a great statesman. I, on the other hand, contend it is more probable he will grow into a murdering, thieving wastrel unless someone takes him in hand soon," Caitlan said, frowning.

"Let's forget about that troublesome urchin, shall we? He's none of our concern." Jeremy dismissed the boy and proffered his hand to Caitlan. "Come, Katie. Climb aboard and let me drive you back to the boardinghouse."

Caitlan stared at that hand for a full thirty seconds before reaching a decision. In fact, she was about to decline Jeremy's invitation when Hezekiah's mournful face swam into her thoughts. Remembering fragments of a conversation she had once had with Essie, Caitlan swallowed her reservations and allowed her would-be suitor to assist her onto the seat beside him.

As her gallant driver maneuvered the buggy along the busy thoroughfare, Caitlan broached a touchy subject by saying, "Thank you, Jeremy. As a matter of fact, there is an important matter I've been wanting to discuss with you."

Had any of the bystanders, who had witnessed Caitlan's ascent into Cantrell's buggy, been on hand to observe her grim countenance when she climbed down from the conveyance mere moments later, they would have been curious—and justifiably so—to know what Jeremy had said to thrust Caitlan headlong into an uncontrollable rage. As the vehicle rolled to a stop before the boardinghouse, Caitlan ignored the helping hand Jeremy extended and flounced out of the buggy unassisted. Then, without so much as a by-your-leave, she turned her back on the befuddled man and, with head held high, stomped up the narrow sidewalk to the house.

Caitlan's anger showed nary a sign of waning as she jerked open the front door and charged across the threshold. By the time she swooped down the corridor to exit the rear of the house and find her way to the kitchen door, Caitlan's temper was nearing the boiling point, a fact which was evidenced by her ruthless treatment of that heavy portal upon her entrance to the cooking chamber. As the rattling of the mishandled entry subsided, Caitlan yanked aside her bedraggled bonnet and whirled to hang it upon the hook on the back of the door.

"Men!" she spat as she exchanged her headgear for the apron that rested upon the hook. Work-worn fingers trembled with irritation as she endeavored to tie the garment's strings about her waist and, in the end, succeeded in tangling the ribbons in an unyielding knot. Frustrated, Caitlan flung herself onto a kitchen chair. Burying her head in her hands, she acted completely out of character by swearing, "Damn it all! Damn *him!*"

"Now, Kettie girl. It's not like you to say such things," scolded a masculine voice from across the room. "Get hold of yourself and tell me what I've done to get your dander up this time," Rafe said, assuming himself to be the one responsible for Caitlan's foul disposition.

"What the—" Caitlan started, snatching her hands from her face and jerking to a ramrod-straight position on the chair. Caitlan's exclamation sputtered on her tongue, however, and her expression grew even more aghast when green eyes latched onto the wholly unexpected spectacle of Rafe lounging in a tub of bath water, a cloud of cigar smoke swirling lazily above his dark head.

An instant later, her chair scraped noisily against the stone flaggings as Caitlan jumped up to confront her guest. "What are you doing in my kitchen?" she demanded.

"Taking a bath" came Rafe's roguish, albeit truthful, answer. "Hezekiah said you had gone over to the Widow Stevens's house for the afternoon, so I thought I'd take advantage of your absence and wash away some of this grime. Besides, I would have gone stock raving mad if I'd been forced to spend another minute in that sweltering, matchbox excuse of a room. Not that the heat is any better down here, but the scenery is a damn sight prettier," he said, his warm gaze sweeping over her.

Caitlan disregarded Rafe's attempt at artful flirtation and asked instead, "Are you certain you are ready to go traipsing up and down the stairs? After all, you have been through quite an ordeal. You mustn't exert yourself too soon."

"I'm fine, Kettie, fit as the proverbial fiddle," Rafe assured her. His eyes narrowed in shrewd contemplation of her face and he asked, "What about you? You haven't answered my question. What have I done to make you so angry?"

"Oh, that." Caitlan shrugged and looked away. "You have done nothing, Rafe. I fear I am at war with someone else today."

"Who?"

Caitlan shook her head to indicate she did not care to discuss the matter and murmured, "No one you know." Glancing about, she put her hands on her hips and said, "Are you finished with your bath? I don't mean to rush you, but I do have to get supper started. Mr. Morgan grows positively peevish if his mealtime is put off by more than five minutes."

"I've scrubbed everything I can reach," he announced with a mischievous wink and admitted, "My shoulder is stiff and my side still pains me somewhat. I could use a hand washing my back. Would you mind?" He extended washcloth and soap toward a reluctant wash maid and delighted in the embarrassed flush that dotted Caitlan's cheeks.

Determined that Rafe should not get the better of her, Caitlan swallowed her missish pride and accepted the proffered articles. After all, in recent weeks she had conducted acts of a far more intimate nature for this insufferable man. Kneeling at the head of the bathtub, she nudged him forward and began to scour his back and shoulders with the lathered washcloth. Had Rafe been secretly harboring notions of a sensual prelude to a more romantic interlude, his hopes were promptly dashed; Caitlan attacked this chore with all the vigor of a laundrywoman scrubbing a dirty shirt against a washboard.

Although Rafe tried to conceal his discomfort, observant green eyes caught his telltale flinch when the edge of the soapy rag flitted across his exposed shoulder wound. A knowing grimace sprang to Caitlan's lips and, when she completed these personal ablutions, she encouraged him to lie back while she inspected the healing region. With her arm draped across Rafe's right shoulder in a careless gesture and his head resting in the crook of her arm, Caitlan leaned closer to examine the scarred flesh. As she did so, her fingers fleetingly brushed along his chest, causing him to shudder again—this time with contentment.

Taking hold of her hand, Rafe stroked the slender digits fondly with his thumb and said, "You have a gentle touch, Kettie."

"And you have a smelly cigar" was her waspish reply.

"Ever the flatterer," Rafe chortled, inhaling a fortifying draft of the offensive tobacco.

Turning back toward Caitlan, he found himself consumed with the overpowering desire to bury his face in her neck. He suppressed his baser urges, however. Instead, he pressed a playful kiss against her cheek. When Caitlan wheeled toward him furiously—as Rafe knew she would—he exhaled a puff of the aromatic smoke in her gloriously livid face.

The verbal admonishment Caitlan had been prepared to unleash on him, consequently emerged as a helpless choking spasm. Caitlan, her eyes red and shimmering with involuntary tears, wrenched away the hand he still cuddled and scrambled to her feet. She managed only a stumbling step or two toward the door when a determined hand reached up to grasp the apron strings that fluttered behind her.

Stopping Caitlan dead in her tracks, Rafe gave the gnarled ribbons a firm tug, thereby forcing her down onto the edge of the tub. Gripping his cigar between his teeth, purposeful masculine hands set about the diverting task of untangling the hopelessly knotted strips of cloth.

As he worked, Rafe's voice assumed a stern tone when he said, "I thought I made myself understood years ago, Kettie. I don't take kindly to people nagging me about my cigar smoking. Christ, a man should be able to enjoy a few of life's pleasures without some woman carping at him night and day," he editorialized.

"I do not carp," Caitlan rebutted petulantly and stood up.

This proved to be an unfortunate maneuver, for a pair of strong hands merely seized those softly curved hips in their relentless grip and jerked her back onto the uncomfortable ledge. Left with no recourse, Caitlan sat with her backside smarting, her temper simmering, and her foot tapping out an impatient rhythm while Rafe took his sweet time about his business.

"There," he said eventually. Rafe concluded by tying the ribbons into a taut bow and gave Caitlan's rump a satisfying slap to indicate that he had finished with her . . . for the time being.

Caitlan did not immediately relinquish her seat. Indeed, her legs were trembling with such vehemence that she did not yet trust her limbs to support her. Finally, she willed her tempestuous emotions under control and stood up. Caitlan knew without looking that it was a smile of smug satisfaction that presently adorned Rafe's sensuous mouth, and she promptly resolved that he should not wear it for long. Whirling about, she snatched the controversial cigar from his surprised lips and plunged the glowing end into the murky water.

As Rafe scrambled to avoid being burned by the red-hot cigar, Caitlan dropped the repellent cylinder into the water and brushed her hands together as if to wash them of the matter. Impervious to the sound of splashing water behind her, Caitlan made her way to the kitchen sink, intending to devote her attention to preparing the evening repast. Her fingers were within inches of the paring knife when she felt her shoulder gripped by a wet hand. Before Caitlan understood what was happening, Rafe twirled her about to face him.

Caitlan was relieved to note that it was not a truly angry face that glared into hers. There was, however, something she could not quite explain burning in those crystal-blue eyes that made her feel ill at ease. She was very much aware of the burly arm that crept about her waist and, as Rafe dragged her forward, Caitlan stiffened and unthinkingly braced her hand against his dripping-wet chest.

Despite her attempts to remain calm, her voice quivered when she said, "Rafe, don't." She squirmed and tried to wriggle—unsuccessfully—from his embrace. "I . . . I'm sorry I lost my temper, but you must know that you provoked me."

"Yes, I know," Rafe breathed, leaning close to cuddle her ear with his lips. "You always did rile easily," he commented, nipping at the tempting lobe. Rafe chuckled when he felt Caitlan bristle in his arms and, to further torment her, he nuzzled her crimson cheek with his.

Had Caitlan known that Rafe was but seconds away from seizing her pouting mouth in a feverish kiss, it is highly probable that she would have forgone her churlish comment. She was, in truth—for all her thirty-one years—very much a novice insofar as men and their worldly ways were concerned. Ultimately, it was Caitlan's own credulous naïveté that spared her from becoming a helpless victim of Rafe's passionate plunderings.

Touching her fingertips to the area that his stubbled face had momentarily caressed, she grumbled, "You need a shave."

"Argh!" Rafe groaned, burrowing his disbelieving forehead in Caitlan's shoulder. Realizing that the romantic moment had fizzled beneath his very lips, he pressed a disappointed kiss on the tip of her nose and sighed. "And you, my dear, need to develop a better sense of timing."

Caitlan's brow crinkled into a becoming frown, and she asked, "What is that supposed to mean?"

"Never mind, Kettie," Rafe said, smiling to himself. Tweaking her chin, he turned toward the chair upon which a clean, albeit sadly crumpled, suit of clothes was draped.

Caitlan, who was gratified to note that Rafe had possessed the decency to wrap a towel about his waist when he emerged from his bath, was chagrined when she saw the woeful state of his personal attire. Correctly assuming that the garments had been stored for weeks on end in his saddlebags, she stepped forward.

"You cannot wear those clothes, Rafe," Caitlan announced summarily, taking the shirt from his hands even as he endeavored to struggle into it.

"Oh?" One dark eyebrow lifted to a querulous angle. "Far be it from me to contradict you, Kettie. But I am fairly certain that even old Harriet might be persuaded to blush were I to appear at her supper table wearing this get-up." He indicated the towel that fit snugly about his waist.

Caitlan, despite her efforts to the contrary, found her green gaze wandering down Rafe's muscular chest to that narrow strip of damp cloth that clung provocatively to him. She could not help but notice that the towel barely covered his powerful physique. This was evidenced by the fact that a wide slit fell open from his waist where he had tucked the ends of the cloth together, leaving one brawny thigh clearly exposed.

Caitlan was at a loss to account for the sudden emotional

upheaval that swept over her. Her skin tingled with prickly gooseflesh, her heart pounded so hard in her chest that she was fairly certain Rafe could see it beating against her blouse, and her mouth was as dry as a desert. Cognizant of the awkward silence that filled the spacious kitchen, Caitlan pressed her fingertips to her temples to massage the relentless thrumming that threatened to mushroom into a full-fledged headache.

Turning back to the sink, Caitlan drew a glass of cool spring water from the well and, gulping it down, said, "No, silly. I meant if you give me a moment, I'll iron your things for you. Sit down while I get the fire going. Afterward, I'll tend to those pesky whiskers."

Rafe settled himself in a chair as Caitlan suggested and rubbed his chin thoughtfully. "I don't know" came his rueful reply. "I'm not exactly crazy about the notion of letting you have at my neck with a razor."

Rafe sipped at the glass of freshly squeezed lemonade Caitlan placed on the table before him and watched as she made short work of pressing the wrinkles from his clothes. He was not overly surprised when the first article of neatly ironed clothing she presented him was his trousers. Understanding her unspoken meaning, Rafe began the arduous task of dressing himself while Caitlan turned her attention to the remainder of his wardrobe.

His efforts met with a conflicting reaction moments later when Caitlan completed her task. She was mollified to see that he was at least partially clothed, but one glance at his painful expression induced Caitlan to rush to his side with concern. The sound of his labored breathing and the little beads of sweat that dotted his forehead verified her fears; Rafe had not fully recovered his strength. Adjuring him to lean back against the chair, Caitlan held the glass of lemonade to his lips and ordered him to drink.

"I told you not to overdo," she scolded.

"Damn it, Kettie!" Rafe swore, though his frustration was aimed at himself, not Caitlan. "I hardly consider dressing myself a taxing activity."

"Under normal circumstances, no," Caitlan said in a soothing voice, smoothing back a thick strand of hair that had toppled over his brow. "You're still quite weak. Only consider that you have done little more than lie abed for a month now. In a single afternoon, you have climbed down two flights of stairs, bathed yourself and persecuted me with your silly schoolboy shenanigans. Is it little wonder your strength has flagged, I ask you?'' She smiled into his aggravated eyes and received a begrudging grin for her efforts. ''That's better. Now, sit back and drink your lemonade while I put supper on.''

Rafe's mood underwent a sobering transformation in the following minutes as he observed Caitlan embrace her scullery duties with an enthusiasm that one would hardly expect from the onetime belle of a Louisiana parish. He watched in subdued silence as Caitlan pulled two plump roasting hens from the icebox and readied them for baking. In less time than he could imagine, a variety of fresh vegetables had been washed and prepared for cooking and Caitlan was sitting in the chair opposite him to take a well-deserved rest before embarking upon the next phase of her culinary chores.

Without warning, Rafe reached across the table and gathered her hands in his. Caitlan's normal reaction would have been to pull away from such a courtly gesture, but there was something about this brooding man's countenance that gave her pause. The couple sat in companionable silence for a time, Caitlan regarding the studious set of his jaw with rapt curiosity while Rafe tenderly caressed her work-roughened hands.

Caitlan was on the verge of asking him what he could possibly be thinking to provoke such a serious frown when Rafe stirred and said, his voice low, ''Your beautiful hands. They were not, *you* were not made for this kind of life, Kettie. Tell me, sweet pea.'' Rafe unthinkingly reverted to the use of the nickname he had called her by so many years ago. ''I must know how you came to be here in Vicksburg, living like this, serving as that woman's drudge. It galls me to see how she orders you about.'' He gripped her hand and his tone was full of urgency when he repeated, ''Tell me!''

The explanation that Rafe had demanded was destined to be put off again, however, for his plea was no sooner from his lips than the kitchen door burst open and Essie bolted across the threshold.

''Damn it to hell!'' Rafe muttered under his breath and yanked his hands away in a frustrated gesture.

Caitlan was considerably more hospitable in her greeting, even though her disposition would undergo a dramatic change when she learned the basis for her friend's visit. "Come in, Essie. Have a seat while I fetch you a cold glass of lemonade."

"Thank you, Katie," Essie said, taking off her bonnet and sitting in the chair that Caitlan had indicated. Essie's forthcoming statement caused her hostess to flinch and regret she had invited the chatterbox to stay, however. "I've been wantin' to talk to you ever since I seen you climb out of Jeremy Cantrell's buggy this afternoon" came her blunt announcement and, heedless of the meaningful look that Caitlan threw at her, she prattled on, "I would have stopped by to talk to you sooner, but Madame insisted I run a few errands for her. But now I'm here, and I'm simply dying to know what happened."

Caitlan clutched the lemonade pitcher so tightly that her knuckles turned white and, through taut lips, she whispered, "Not now, Essie."

As was her way, the girl simply brushed Caitlan's protests aside, saying, "You're just actin' shy cause you don't want to discuss your beau in front of strangers. I'm sure he won't mind, will you, Mr. Bradrick?"

"Not at all," murmured that thoroughly intrigued gentleman, his blue gaze fastened on Caitlan's exasperated face.

"See." Essie pursed her lips in an 'I told you so' moue and chatted on, "Madame Cognaisse is expectin' me back at the shop, Katie, so I don't have a moment to spare. Tell me everything," she begged.

Caitlan slammed the glass of refreshment onto the table in front of Essie and, pulling a face at the girl's masculine conspirator, plopped down onto her chair in complete frustration. "Essie," Caitlan warned between gritted teeth, "I said, *not now*!"

"Okay." Essie pouted. "You don't have to tell me if you don't want to, but I bet I can guess what it was that Jeremy said that got you so upset. You should've seen the way she came tearin' out of that buggy." Essie directed this comment to Rafe. "Why, it's a miracle she didn't break her neck."

"You may not be so fortunate," Caitlan muttered, smiling sweetly at Essie's credulous face.

"Well, the way I figure it, the two of you got to discussin' that slave girl Jeremy bought off of Mr. Stark. And," Essie continued, heedless of Caitlan's beseeching expression, "unless I miss my guess, I'd say Jeremy told you he'd be willin' to let Hezekiah have his Abbie if you agreed to marry him. Am I right?"

When Caitlan did not immediately respond to this impertinent query, a grim voice demanded from the open doorway, "Well, ansah the gal, Miz Katie. Is she right? Is that what Mistah Cantrell said to you?"

Startled by the unexpected outburst, Caitlan lifted her eyes to gaze into Hezekiah's embittered face as he stood on the threshold directly behind Essie. "Oh, Essie," Caitlan lamented. "Will you never learn to keep quiet?"

"Nevah minds that. Ansah me, Miz Katie," Hezekiah said, his tone harsh.

"Hezekiah," Rafe interrupted, thinking he might reason with the agitated man.

"Stay out of this, Mistah Bradrick" came Hezekiah's stern warning. "It ain't none of your affair." To Caitlan, he said, his mien ominous, "Miz Katie, ah'm waitin'."

Caitlan shivered as she stared into that cold face; she had never before witnessed Hezekiah with such a forbidding countenance, and she was more than a little frightened by his uncharacteristic behavior. In her heart, Caitlan knew that Hezekiah would never do anything to harm her, but she could not extend the same guarantee to anyone who was foolhardy enough to threaten her happiness or that of his beloved Abbie. Willing her quaking legs to hold her, Caitlan stood up.

Before she could speak, Hezekiah shouted, "Is that what the man done said to you?"

"Yes!" Caitlan blurted an involuntary response to his badgering. "But—" She tried to explain, but Hezekiah was having none of it.

Lifting a hand to silence her, a hauntingly peaceful expression settled on Hezekiah's face as he said, "Well, then, you don't have to worry none, Miz Katie. You ain't gonna have to marry that man. Why, ah'll kill the bastard afore ah'd let you do that."

Chapter Seven

❧❦❧

The clock on the drawing-room mantelshelf was just chiming midnight when Caitlan entered the boardinghouse through the back door, having concluded her kitchen chores for the night. It was not her custom to keep such grueling hours, but Hezekiah's portentous threat had prompted Caitlan to forgo her normal routine. Immediately following the serving of the evening repast—a meal that was hastily flung together in the wake of Hezekiah's pronouncement—Caitlan had cast off her apron and gone in search of the brooding Hezekiah.

She had returned home shortly after ten o'clock to be greeted by a most disheartening sight. The dining-room table still bore the accoutrements of the evening meal. The table lay strewn with food-encrusted place settings, half-empty wineglasses, and the paltry remains of the evening's fare which now lay cold and congealed in their serving dishes. Fighting back tears of weary frustration, Caitlan had pushed up her sleeves and tackled the monumental chore without demur, deciding it was better to get the job over and done rather than be faced with the task first thing in the morning.

Caitlan presently made her way toward the staircase along the darkened hallway with the aid of a lighted candle. With her index finger curled around the candlestick stem, she blew a tired sigh and, grasping the banister with her free hand, began to climb the steps. Her slender shoulders were slumping noticeably with fatigue by the time she arrived at the base of the attic steps and, unbeknownst to Caitlan, an observant eye at the top of the landing saw that she did not ascend the stairs with her usual briskness.

In a word, Caitlan was exhausted. She longed only for the comfort of her bed. She was, therefore, more than a little chagrined to find Rafe lounging negligently against his closed door, his unnerving blue stare watching her with subdued interest as she made her way slowly up the narrow staircase.

When Caitlan gave every indication of breezing into her own chamber without acknowledging Rafe's presence, he thwarted any such plan by asking, "Did you find Hezekiah?"

"Yes," she mumbled and would have entered her room without further comment had Rafe not placed a staying hand on her wrist.

"And did you convince him that this jackass you've somehow got yourself mixed-up with is not worth hanging over?" came his ensuing smug question.

Caitlan took umbrage at Rafe's condescending attitude, although she contrived to maintain an aloof mien when she replied, "I managed to persuade Hezekiah to have done with his ridiculous notion. Only imagine, killing a man because of some stupid remark he made to me in passing."

"Wars have been fought for less, Kettie," Rafe informed her, adding, "Besides, the situation is more serious than you realize. This blackguard is attempting to blackmail you into marriage by playing on your attachment to Hezekiah. Why, if he doesn't murder the bastard, I just might," Rafe growled.

"No! You mustn't say such things!" Caitlan exclaimed, whirling toward Rafe with such urgency that the candle wax spilled onto the fingers that persisted in delaying her entrance into her chamber. Mindful of the hand he snatched away, yet heedless of the pain she had inadvertently caused him, she demanded, "Promise me you will not undertake this foolish act of revenge."

Rafe, his scorched hand forgotten, gazed searchingly into her upturned face. Bracing himself for the worst possible news, he asked, "Does this Jeremy Cantrell mean that much to you then?"

"I don't love him, if that is your question." A cynical smile pursed her lips and, leaning back against the opposite wall, she said, "If the truth were told, I doubt very much that Jeremy loves me either. He is simply looking for a wife to play nurse-maid to the passel of children his previous wives have left behind. He has lost three to childbirth," Caitlan explained when she observed Rafe's bemused expression. "I do not intend to be the fourth."

Noticing the dried tallow on the back of Rafe's hand, Caitlan settled the offending taper on the candle stand in the corner of the landing and took his sun-bronzed appendage in hers. As she began to gently peel away the hardened wax, she said as if scolding a naughty child, "Just because I am vexed at Jeremy for the unorthodox manner in which he has chosen to court me, does not mean I countenance this fool notion you and Hezekiah have taken into your heads. Jeremy is not a truly bad man, Rafe, however like other headstrong men of my acquaintance," she looked him squarely in the eye, "he is accustomed to having his way in all things. When a matter does not proceed to his liking, he simply plots to turn the situation to his advantage. I'm certain I can persuade Jeremy to do the right thing by Abbie and Hezekiah, and I will not have to marry him in the bargain. I need a little time to do so is all."

Caitlan finished fussing over his singed hand. Lifting her eyes to his face, she unthinkingly reached up to brush her fingers along his stubbled cheek. "I never did give you that shave," she muttered. Turning toward her chamber door, she said, "Perhaps tomorrow. At the moment, I fear I'm quite dead on my feet and want only to fall upon my bed and sleep for days."

Opening the door, her gaze fell upon the uncomfortable cot in the opposite corner and her wry chuckle filled the small entranceway. "Of course, I will have to settle for this lumpy mattress and the four or five hours left to me, but that is better than nothing, I suppose." Before entering the dreary chamber, she said to Rafe, "I thank you for your concern about Jeremy, but you worry needlessly. I shall deal with him when the time is right. Hezekiah trusts my judgment. I wish you would do the same." On this parting note, she bid Rafe a good night and entered her chamber before he could invent some reason to detain her further.

Rafe remained standing in the narrow hallway long after Caitlan left. His thoughtful gaze fixed on the portal that she had—for all intents and purposes—closed in his face. Eventually it was an expression of cold indifference that wafted his handsome features as he stared at that hard, unyielding barrier. She was right; her problems were none of his concern. In effect, Caitlan's elusive actions merely reaffirmed the position she had taken years before; she had no desire to include him in any part of her life.

"So be it," Rafe mumbled, reaching inside his breast pocket to retrieve a cigar.

Lighting the aromatic rod from the candle that Caitlan had left on the stand, he turned to enter his room. Rafe's hand had barely encircled the doorknob when he wheeled around again, his eyes ablaze with rekindled determination.

"No, by God! You're not going to get off that easily, Caitlan Webber," Rafe breathed between taut lips. "You were my betrothed, my true love—my only love. You vowed to be mine forever, that *nothing* would ever keep us apart. Yet, for the past seven years you let me believe you were dead. So much for true love," he spat, his sarcastic laugh echoing down the steep staircase.

There was nothing amusing, however, about Rafe's menacing glare or the spiraling rage he felt for the unsuspecting lady just beyond the bedchamber door.

"Now I come to find out you've been wallowing in this cesspool for years, a veritable slave to the spiteful bitch who owns this place and snipes at you at every turn. I deserve—no, goddammit—I *demand* to know why you chose to live in squalor when I could have—and would have—gladly given you everything." The flaming blue eyes flickered with some deeply felt emotion, but an embittered Rafe persevered, determined not to succumb to his sentimental reflections. Instead, he reacted by walking back across the narrow landing to Caitlan's door.

"By damn!" he swore. "I shall have my explanation now."

Realizing that Caitlan would merely try to put him off until morning once she learned his purpose, Rafe did not announce himself but pushed the door ajar slightly. His intent had been to march into the room and confront his wily adversary head-long, but as inquisitive blue eyes conducted a cursory inspection of the diminutive chamber, he was given every reason to forestall his impetuous plan. Indeed, Rafe's vitriolic speech sputtered on his tongue and gathered in the back of his throat as a choking gasp when his searching eyes beheld the exquisite sight awaiting them.

Caitlan sat at her dressing table, meticulously brushing the day's accumulation of tangles from her waist-length, russet-tinged hair. The light from a solitary bedside lamp cast a shadow along the wall behind the length of bed in which Caitlan's silhouette was clearly reflected. It was this shadowy apparition that caught Rafe's attention and, thus mesmerized, he continued his silent vigil from the threshold unobserved.

Caitlan, with her back to the door and completely unaware that her nighttime ablutions were being monitored by an appreciative eye, stood and began to shed her clothes. Slender fingers directed their attention to unbuttoning her blouse and skirt which Caitlan summarily discarded upon the hardwood floor at her feet. Rafe could not suppress a grin when he heard her groan with contentment when she relieved herself of the binding corset and promptly added it to the growing pile of rumpled garments. The reality of the intimate moment struck Rafe full force once more when he heard the soft, ruffling sound of her chemise as Caitlan slid it from her shoulders and allowed the undergarment to flutter to the floor.

Realizing that she must be nearly—if not already totally—naked, a parched Rafe swallowed hard and continued to stare at the enchanting silhouette. Thoroughly fascinated, he watched while Caitlan balanced her foot on the edge of the dressing table chair and leaned forward to carefully roll her stocking down one shapely leg, then to Rafe's supreme gratification, repeated the gesture in order to dispense with the remaining hosiery.

Rafe would find his Peeping Tom antics severely frustrated in the subsequent moments, however. When Caitlan bent over to pluck her clothes from the floor, a cascade of long satiny tresses tumbled all about her, thereby concealing her more feminine attributes from a pair of pesky masculine eyes. A less tenacious man might have forsaken his station at this point; Rafe knew that he would be hard-pressed indeed to explain his presence should Caitlan turn and find him gawking at her in the semidarkness.

His persistence paid off in the next moment when Caitlan straightened and, lifting her arms behind her head, began to gather in the wayward tendrils in order to secure them with a ribbon before retiring for the night. Thus positioned, a pair of perfectly shaped breasts were clearly reflected on the shadowed wall. Rosebud tips sat proudly atop those alluring mounds of flesh that jiggled invitingly with Caitlan's every movement. Rafe inhaled a throaty breath and even went so far as to take an involuntary step toward the bewitching vision.

Fortunately, he possessed the good sense not to proceed any farther, but Rafe had no control over the unruly direction his thoughts took in response to such a provocative display. As Caitlan carried on with her bedtime rituals, Rafe indulged himself with any number of diverting contemplations. He wondered what it would be like to clasp Caitlan roughly against him, to experience the glorious sensation of the crimson, stiffened tips of her breasts boring into his chest.

Once they took root, it became difficult for Rafe to shake off these intoxicating reflections, although to be truthful, he did little to dissuade the flood of erotic visions his active imagination conjured up. Rafe imagined how it would feel to run his hands over the silky smoothness of her back, on downward across her gently curving hips, and down farther still to caress her thigh. He could almost hear Caitlan's soft whimperings when his lips enclosed around the proud crowning summits of her breasts and her outright exclamation of surprise when his fingers became engaged in some playful shenanigans of their own, lost—as they inevitably would become—amid the velvety triangle of her femininity.

As Rafe stood in the doorway, grappling with the overwhelming urge to drag Caitlan into his arms and suit his actions to his very amorous thoughts, the curtain crashed down abruptly on his fanciful aspirations. His expression underwent a radical transformation in the following moments, changing from one of hopeful anticipation to outright frustration. As Rafe watched, Caitlan pulled a nightgown over her head, and the linen garment had no sooner slithered down the length of her well-proportioned figure than she extinguished the lamplight and climbed into bed.

Rafe noted with some chagrin that his shoulder had begun to ache again and, as he lifted a hand to massage the thrumming region, his lips parted in a wry smile. He considered it ironic that the throbbing in his shoulder in no way compared with the nagging pressure that had begun to build in his loins. Realizing his passions would not find satisfaction this night and, deciding that his inquisition could wait, he cast a parting wistful glance at Caitlan's back and started to withdraw into the corridor.

As he backed across the threshold and reached to pull the door closed, his gaze fell on the exposed corner of an envelope barely peeking out from under the edge of a lace doily atop the chest of drawers. Even as inquisitive fingers plucked the yellowed epistle from its hiding place, Rafe knew in his heart that he had no right to meddle in Caitlan's private affairs, and that it certainly was not his place to read her personal correspondence. Still, there was something about the missive that taunted him and, glancing down at the letter, Rafe understood the basis for his intuitive curiosity. The bold script that was sprawled across the face of the envelope had been written by his own hand.

Rafe frowned at the aged piece of paper, then casting an even more quizzical glance at Caitlan, he retreated into the hallway and carefully pulled the door closed behind him. Once he had gained the privacy of his own chamber, Rafe sat down in the rocking chair beside the window. Drawing a rejuvenating draft on his cigar, he examined the letter more closely.

Scrawled across the front of the yellowing envelope was a solitary word: *Kettie*. Curious to know what he had written that had prompted Caitlan to keep his letter all these years, Rafe unfolded the missive and began to read.

December 29, 1853

My Dearest Friend,
A matter has come to my attention that has caused me some

concern. It would seem that you have come to expect more from our friendship than I am willing to give in return. The truth is, my heart belongs to another. In fact, if the lady will have me, I intend to make her my bride by summer's end.

It saddens me to learn that I have in any way caused you grief, but you must know that, while I consider you—and hope you will always be—a dear friend, I cannot love you. I am not a magician; so please do not believe I can conjure up feelings that simply do not exist.

I feel obliged to tell you that the kiss you gave me at my sister's Christmas Ball, though very sweet, did not inspire any great passion in my heart. If anything, it only served to reaffirm what I have known for months now . . . I love someone else. Perhaps, knowing this, you will give up your silly schoolgirl notions and start searching for your own true love. I've already found mine.

In parting, please accept my apologies. I never meant to hurt you. I will always consider you to be my friend and hope that, in time, you may forgive me for the hurt I have caused you. Indeed, my greatest wish is that you will one day know the kind of happiness I have found with my own dear love.

Always,
Rafe

Rafe sat in a state of bewildered silence as he read and reread the incredible letter. Oh, he had written it right enough, but he had contrived these words to discourage the husband-hunting exploits of one of his sister's forward friends. Rafe had never intended for Caitlan to know of the letter's existence, much less think the heartless contents were meant for her.

"How could this have happened?" Rafe groaned, shaking his head in stunned disbelief.

Thinking back, Rafe remembered that an urgent family matter had called him away prematurely from a holiday visit to his sister's plantation near Baton Rouge. There had been no time to ride over to Thistledown and tell Kettie the news himself, and there was that unfinished business with Caroline Foster that she had instigated at the Christmas Ball. Hoping to appease both ladies' sensibilities, Rafe had penned two separate missives which he subsequently entrusted to his sister's safe-keeping. Now after seven long, lonely years, he discovered that somewhere between his writing and the delivery of those letters a horrible mistake had occurred.

"Oh, Josie," Rafe mumbled his sister's name aloud, pounding his fist against the arm of the rocking chair. "How could this have happened?"

A heavyhearted Rafe scanned the dreaded letter once more and he gave a lugubrious moan. "My poor sweet pea. You must have been devastated when you read this. For you to think that I could have forsaken you again. . . . How you must have hated me." The blue eyes filled with tears of remorse as he imagined Caitlan's pretty face alive with animation as she ripped open the letter, expecting it to contain the heartfelt expressions of an ardent admirer. And then, to have all her hopes and dreams shattered with the reading of a few hastily scrawled sentences.

"By God, this should never have happened!" Rafe cried, hurling himself from the chair with such vengeance that he provoked a painful response from the partially healed wound in his side.

Ignoring the hurtful summons, Rafe began to pace about the room as he endeavored to make some sense of the confounding situation. He was of half a mind to march straightaway into Caitlan's room and confront her with his startling discovery. Indeed, he had taken two steps toward the door before a sobering thought occurred to him. For seven years Caitlan had believed the words contained in this missive, had thought him to be a faithless, heartless jilt—by God, he held the proof in his very hands. Why should she believe otherwise now simply because he said so?

Backing away from the door, Rafe ambled over to the rocking chair and sat down. He returned the crinkled epistle to its protective pouch and tucked it inside his coat pocket. Then, leaning back, he inhaled another long draft on the sweet-smelling cigar, wishing all the while it was a decanter of whiskey. God, but he needed a drink.

It was a pensive frown that wrinkled his brow as he began to think. "At least now I understand why you wanted me to believe you were dead all this time. I know your game, Kettie."

He chuckled, a fond smile turning up the corners of his sensual mouth. "You didn't want to take the chance that I'd waltz back into your life and make you fall head over heels in love with me—just like I always do. And yet, you plucked me off that ledge when I was more dead than alive and literally spoon-fed the life back into me.

"Women!" Rafe scoffed and scratched the back of his head. "If I live to be a hundred, I'll never figure them out."

He stood then and, bracing his hands against the windowsill, his mood became somber once more as he stared up at the starlit sky. "My God, Kettie!" His mournful wail floated out the window on the night breeze. "I nearly gave up living myself when Josie sent word about your death. Don't you know that you have haunted my thoughts for years? I've never met another woman like you, never wanted to. The fact is, sweet pea, I *am* back—thanks to you—and I'm in no hurry to make myself scarce. My problem, darlin', will be getting you to admit that you would be none too pleased to have me gone either."

Rafe extinguished both candle and cigar, then stretching his tall frame atop the bedclothes, he folded his arms behind his head and focused his contemplative gaze on the ceiling. The task that loomed before him was not an easy one, to be sure. After all, for seven years Caitlan had nursed her wounded pride, had made herself hate and distrust him.

Then there was Kettie herself. Rafe could not deny she had undergone many changes over the years. This was an independent, willful young lady; the meek lass of his youth was gone. Oddly enough, Rafe found he rather preferred this version better.

Rafe had changed in many ways as well, however, the past few weeks with Caitlan had made him realize one important thing—he still cared for her. He must somehow convince Caitlan that for now and always, she could trust her heart to him. Fate had—though at times fickle—brought them together and kept them apart for much of their lives. It was ludicrous that she had not yet realized they were destined to be together. Thus resolved, Rafe vowed to think of a way to show Caitlan once and for all that, bittersweet though it had often proved to be, their love was inevitable.

* * *

Delia Stevens died the following night. Death came peacefully to the elderly widow. After Mrs. Burke administered her nightly dose of medicine, the old woman simply closed her eyes and went to sleep, never to awaken in this world again.

Caitlan was just putting off her shawl, having returned from her daily trip to the market, when Harriet came into the kitchen to bring her the news of Delia's demise. Though she had long since resigned herself to the inevitability of this dreadful moment, Caitlan was still saddened to learn of her friend's death. She did not have all that many friends, and to lose one—even a feisty old curmudgeon like Delia—made her heart ache with loneliness. Lost as she was in her own sorrow, Caitlan barely paid heed to Harriet's inane chatter.

"It's about time that woman passed on. If you ask me, that old widow outlived her usefulness years ago" was Harriet's insensitive and wholly inappropriate pronouncement. "I've had my eye on her house for some time now. I've been thinkin' about openin' up another boardinghouse and that piece of property would be an ideal location. See if you can find out what they're asking for it, Katie." Harriet delegated this task to an unresponsive Caitlan.

Turning to exit the kitchen, Harriet noticed Caitlan's sad countenance and her own expression soured as she grumbled, "I suppose you'll be wantin' time off to attend the funeral."

Caitlan nodded. "If it will not be too much trouble."

"Oh, I'll be troubled right enough, missy, but not near as much as you." Harriet laughed. "No, I'm fairly certain it's you who'll be troubled when you receive this month's pay envelope and find I've deducted a suitable amount from your wages. But don't mind me, go ahead and waste your time on that eccentric old fool. It makes me no never mind."

The day of the funeral dawned hot and muggy. Despite Harriet's vow to withhold a portion of her woefully meager salary, Caitlan attended the ceremony. As she stood in reverent silence at the grave site and listened to the comforting passages the minister read from the scriptures, Caitlan began to contemplate her own mortality. Glancing about, she thought it a sad testimony to Delia that, besides herself, the minister, and Mrs. Burke, only two other mourners had come to pay their final respects while the old woman was laid to rest.

Caitlan's sensibilities received a staggering jolt when her morbid ramblings made her realize that if she died tomorrow, she would be in much the same situation as her dearly departed friend. For she could count on the fingers of one hand the number of good friends she named among her acquaintance. The thought was not a comforting one, to be sure. Consumed by these woebegone reflections of her ill-fated, lonely existence, Caitlan very nearly sought emotional release in tears.

Giving her head a stern shake, she regained control of her impetuous senses. Nothing was ever gained by indulging one's self in such maudlin histrionics and Caitlan was not about to make a spectacle of herself by blubbering in public. Delia would expect better from her.

The observer who had arrived late and come to stand beside Caitlan evidently did not hold such high standards; he slipped his arm about her waist and whispered, "Go ahead and cry, sweet pea."

Caitlan flinched at the sound and recoiled instinctively from Rafe's intrusive touch, although she did resist the urge to slap the offensive appendage aside. Thankfully, she noted that the minister had concluded the service and that he and the other mourners were making their way toward the cemetery gate. Relieved that Rafe's familiar overtures had not been witnessed by the others, Caitlan promptly disengaged herself from his unwanted embrace.

"I never cry," she said tersely.

"Never, Kettie?" Rafe questioned, one dark eyebrow arching at a skeptical angle. "Why, even a hardened rogue like me is moved to tears now and again when something touches my heart."

Caitlan wanted desperately to inform him that, although she thought his confession very sweet, she doubted its veracity since it was a foregone conclusion that Rafe Bradrick was not in possession of that tender organ. But knowing that little would be accomplished from bantering words with the quick-witted man, Caitlan bit back the sarcastic retort, saying instead, "What are you doing here, Rafe?"

The hairs on Rafe's neck bristled at the grating sound in Caitlan's voice, making him yearn to take those stubborn shoulders between his hands and shake some sense into her. To ensure that he did not embark upon such a foolhardy course, Rafe shoved his fists in his pockets and said, "I came to walk you back to the boardinghouse. Fool that I am, I thought you might welcome a friendly ear after all you've been through lately. I guess I was mistaken," he said. Wheeling around in disgust, he started to walk away.

The thoughts that had tormented Caitlan throughout the funeral service—those of her painfully solitary existence—flooded her memory and, on impulse, she whirled and shouted after Rafe, "Wait! Don't go. I . . . I," she stammered helplessly and looked away when his blue gaze settled on her face. Feeling the heat rise in her cheeks, Caitlan damned herself for her missish reaction and said without demur, "I would like very much to walk with you. Just give me a moment alone with Delia."

Turning her back to him, Caitlan kneeled down beside the narrow trench and lovingly placed a bouquet of daisies atop the casket. Touching her fingers to her lips, she pressed the moistened fingertips against the wooden coffin in a parting kiss and whispered softly, "Good-bye, my dear friend. I shall miss you, but I will not be sad because I know you are at peace, for you are with your Gus. Be happy," she breathed sorrowfully.

Caitlan stumbled a little as she started to climb to her feet, but a steadying hand upon her arm prevented her from taking an awkward tumble.

"Are you all right?"

"Yes, Rafe," she assured him. "I'm fine, although I admit I'm not quite ready to face Harriet. Do you think we might stop in at Bailey's café for a glass of lemonade?"

"I can do better than that," he announced, swinging the gate wide and standing aside so Caitlan could exit in front of him. "How does lunch at the Washington Hotel sound?"

"Lovely, but—" Caitlan faltered, not wishing to cause him undue embarrassment. Finally, she said, "Are you certain you can afford such an extravagance? I know you haven't any money."

"My pockets are not quite to let yet, Kettie. I have a little money stashed away for emergencies." Rafe smiled down at

Caitlan . . . that mischievous boyish grin that always did strange things to her heart.

Caitlan was well-acquainted with Rafe's flirtatious ways. Steeling herself against his practiced charms, she commented, "I hardly think lunch is an emergency."

"It is when one is trying to cheer up an old friend," Rafe said, stepping onto the grassy path and latching the cemetery gate behind him.

Caitlan did not cavil when Rafe entwined his arm with hers and escorted her across the dusty street. She even went so far as to relax her guard enough to engage in casual discourse as they walked the several blocks to the Washington Hotel. They chatted familiarly about mundane things; the ownership of a stray dog, the stifling heat, the dilapidated condition of a one-time Vicksburg showplace. Caitlan was willing to discuss anything that would keep the conversation from turning to a more intimate footing.

In fact, such was Caitlan's preoccupation that she was unaware that her entrance into the Washington Hotel dining-room on Rafe's arm did not go unnoticed. As the couple was directed to a secluded table by the headwaiter, the owner of a pair of cold, calculating blue eyes stomped off in a rage to plot her revenge.

After their luncheon order had been taken, Rafe took a lengthy draft from his mug of beer. Signaling the waiter to bring him another, he settled back in his chair and leveled his purposeful gaze at Caitlan. Their brisk walk had caused a luster to brighten her cheeks and a few carefully arranged brown-and-russet curls had fallen loose of their confines to flutter in charming disarray about her face. As Caitlan sat across from him, sipping at her glass of iced lemonade and fanning her flushed cheeks with her handkerchief, Rafe was reminded of the carefree days of his youth, many of which he had whiled away with Caitlan in just such a fashion.

It was perhaps his unnerving stare, more so than the prolonged silence, that made Caitlan feel increasingly uncomfortable. Fearing that she must have grown a wart on the end of her nose to warrant such an unrelenting scrutiny, Caitlan blurted, "What?!"

Thus shaken from his reverie, Rafe leaned forward to say,

"It's nothing, I suppose. I was just remembering something. I wonder—" he hesitated, then deciding he had nothing to lose, forged ahead, "do you recall the first time we met?"

"Rafe!" Caitlan scolded, glancing about to see if anyone had overheard his comment. "Keep your voice down. No one in Vicksburg knows of our previous association. Besides, I thought I made myself clear, I do not care to discuss this topic with you."

"Kettie, be reasonable," Rafe cajoled, stretching his arm across the table to encircle her hand with his. Stroking the shapely digits with his thumb, he said, "You misunderstand my intent, sweet pea. I don't mean to hurt you by bringing up the past. But it's impossible for me to look at you and not think of the times we shared together."

"No, it is you who misunderstand, Rafe," Caitlan said coolly, pulling her hand free. "I feel nothing for you now, therefore, it is unlikely that you could ever say anything that will hurt me."

Rafe stiffened at the insult, but his expression showed nary a sign that Caitlan's blunt speech had stung him. Folding his arms across his broad chest, he returned her dispassionate gaze in full, saying, "Well, if that truly be the case, I shouldn't think it would pain you overmuch to answer my question."

Caitlan could not withstand that harsh glare for any length of time. Lowering her green gaze, she took another sip of the tart beverage to appease her dry throat, then heaving a sigh of acquiescence, she mumbled, "Yes, I remember."

Obviously gratified by his minor victory, Rafe leaned back. Draping his arm around the back rail of the chair, he said, "Ah, but I wonder if you recall that memorable day as clearly as I do. As I recollect, it was my family's first visit to the Carter plantation. Josie and Wesley had just become engaged and, while they tended to more romantic endeavors, I rode out to survey the countryside. That's when I first saw you," he murmured throatily, a wistful memory flickering in the brilliant blue eyes. "Yes, I remember perfectly. You were wearing that tawny-brown riding frock that fit you so delightfully."

"It was green," Caitlan immediately corrected him. Taking a bite of the braised chicken the waiter had placed in front of her, she favored him with her most disinterested expression, but to no avail.

Rafe was determined not to be put off by Caitlan's nonchalant demeanor. Slicing off a chunk of the thick pork chop he had ordered, he chatted on, "You were galloping hell-bent for leather across the meadow between Foxborough Hall and Thistledown when that behemoth you were riding refused to top a hedge and hurled you headlong into a bramble bush."

"Ajax always did have a mind of his own," Caitlan muttered.

"Nonsense." Rafe dismissed her paltry excuse. "He was simply too much horse for a young girl to handle. You were only sixteen, as I recall."

"And you were twenty-one," Caitlan whispered, being drawn into the telling of the story despite her convictions to the contrary.

"God, you were a sight to behold." Rafe chuckled, giving her a sidelong glance. "I thought you had broken your damn fool neck the way you were lying there in a crumpled heap, all limp and listless, that little trickle of blood flowing from the corner of your mouth where a thorn had scratched you. I was all set to haul you from that thicket when you said—"

"Well, don't just stand there gawking at me, mister. Give me a hand up out of these brambles," Caitlan quoted perfectly from memory.

"You always were a caution, Kettie." Rafe smiled, pleased by her impromptu recitation. "Most girls would have succumbed to a fit of the vapors or, at the very least, pitched a holy tantrum over mussing their finery, but not you. You bewitched me that day. I thought you were the most beautiful, enchanting vision I had ever encountered and, if memory serves, you liked me, too," he reminded her, a haughty grin curling up the corner of his sensual mouth.

"Oh, and just what makes you so sure of yourself?" Caitlan demanded, pushing her half-eaten plate of food away and folding her arms atop the table in a confrontational gesture.

Soulful blue eyes gazed deeply into Caitlan's composed face and Rafe's voice was thick with emotion when he whispered, "Don't you remember? You let me kiss you that day, sweet pea."

Caitlan's cheekbones flamed scarlet and it was all she could do to keep from hurling her napkin at his pompous head. Tossing the linen cloth onto the table, she snapped, "It was disgraceful of me to have done so then, and you are a shameless scoundrel for reminding me of it now."

"Now, Kettie," Rafe scolded, his voice playful, "don't poker up at me over something that happened fifteen years ago. Besides, it was not just the hope of coaxing more kisses from those wondrously pouting lips of yours that prompted me to make so many visits to my sister's home the following two years. Nor was it Wesley's boorish conversation that drew me to Foxborough Hall, I assure you." He laughed. Then the glimmer in his eyes grew serious once more and he said, "It was you I came to see, Kettie. I could not bear to be away from you."

"A malady from which you happily recovered," Caitlan said in a voice completely devoid of emotion. "Let me think." She laid her forefinger aside her chin in a thoughtful gesture; meeting his direct gaze, she said, "Yes, I believe all the local speculation of an impending marriage proposal proved instrumental in your recuperation."

A military strategist could not have contrived a more ingenious assault. Although Rafe was prepared to defend himself against an embittered outburst, Caitlan's insouciant attitude baffled him. It was almost as if those dispassionate green eyes were communicating some unspoken message, warning him not to delve deeper, for he would find nothing. The owner of those once magical pools of shimmering green had grown stone cold inside, and she would not allow anyone or anything to touch her heart again. Rafe shivered as this disheartening thought enveloped him and for the first time in his life, he found himself at a loss for words.

"Then one day you left for good," Caitlan said shortly, her face expressionless.

"I came back" was his hoarse whisper.

"Yes, you did." Caitlan laughed . . . a hollow, empty sound. "And you left again."

No longer able to endure her cold and indifferent air, Rafe thrust his hand across the table and seized her wrist. Thinking that physical pain might evoke a passionate response from her where calm reasoning had failed, he squeezed hard.

"Kettie, please! I can explain—"

"No, I rather doubt you can," Caitlan returned curtly. Shaking off the hurtful appendage, she stood up. When Rafe attempted to make his speech in spite of her denunciation, Caitlan threw up a restraining hand to deter him. "No, I have had enough of your reminiscences for one day, Rafe," she told him in plain terms. "I do thank you for your concern over Delia and for the lovely dinner, but I really must be getting back to the boardinghouse. You know how Harriet can be."

This comment required no further elaboration and, tucking her handkerchief in the cuff of her blouse, Caitlan stepped around the edge of the table. The sound of a chair leg scraping across the restaurant floor made her realize that Rafe was preparing to accompany her. Wanting very much to be alone, she blurted a little more harshly than was her intent, "No, thank you. I can manage on my own."

With that, Caitlan swept from the room. Thus abandoned, a rueful gentleman was left to contemplate all that had transpired between them. Shoving aside the plate of food in disgust, Rafe reached for the lukewarm mug of beer. With the glass poised at his lips, however, Caitlan's image swam before his eyes. Knowing full well that a tasteless glass of beer would do little toward assuaging his tempestuous thoughts, he ordered a whiskey.

Caitlan arrived at Tuttle's Boarding House a few moments later to find its proprietress in a virtual uproar. Fully expecting Harriet's ill humor to have come about because of her lengthy sojourn at Delia's funeral, Caitlan was at first surprised, then dismayed when she learned the reason for her employer's foul mood.

Harriet was entering the house from the back entrance, balancing a platter of fried chicken in one hand and a bowl of parsley potatoes in the other, when Caitlan stepped through the front door. Espying her prey at the opposite end of the narrow corridor, Harriet wasted little time in accosting the unsuspecting woman. "Well, it's about time you got back. Now, you can serve dinner while I start lookin' again."

"Looking?" Caitlan repeated, a quizzical frown deepening

her eyes. "What are you searching for, Harriet?"

"My ring. The one that Bradrick fella gave me for letting him stay here," Harriet said grouchily, bustling across the dining-room threshold amid the hungry glances of the chamber's occupants. "Mrs. Wheeler stopped by for a visit. She's always flauntin' every gewgaw her husband buys her, so I thought I'd show off my ring, only it was nowhere to be found when I went to fetch it" came Harriet's forlorn whine.

"Calm down, Harriet," Caitlan adjured, following the distraught woman into the dining-room. "The ring will turn up somewhere. Do you remember where you left it?"

"Well, if that ain't the silliest thing I ever heard," Harriet snapped. "If I knew where I left the ring, I wouldn't be turnin' this house upside down lookin' for it, now would I, Katie?"

The boardinghouse tenants had all gathered in the dining-room to partake of the midday meal before returning to their respective jobs. Considerate of his landlady's distress, and even more sympathetic to the beleaguered young woman who always seemed to be the target of Harriet's irascible tongue, a normally reticent Mr. Morgan interrupted his perusal of the *Daily Sun* to say on Caitlan's behalf, "I believe Miss Webber meant well, Miss Tuttle. If you can remember where you last saw the ring, then perhaps a mental rehashing of your activities since then will lead you to your misplaced bauble" was his logical suggestion. Suddenly cognizant of the attention his unexpected speech had warranted—every eye in the room had turned to watch him—Mr. Morgan buried his reddening face in the paper once more.

Frustrated, Harriet plunked the bowl of potatoes onto the table. Thrusting the plate of chicken into Caitlan's hands, she screwed her face into a pensive frown. Eventually, she said, "Near as I recollect, I left the ring in the trinket box on my bureau."

"Do you remember when that was, Harriet?" Penelope Crawford inquired with an innocence that did not match the malicious glare of her frosty blue eyes.

"This mornin', I think. Why?"

Penelope, noting with satisfaction that a curious observer had taken up a stance in the doorway, shrugged and said, "It's probably not worth mentioning, but I do recall seeing Katie enter your room this morning.''

Caitlan, who had just rewarded Mr. Morgan with a plump piece of chicken for his kindness, glanced up, the backhanded accusation taking her completely by surprise. "There is nothing remarkable about that, Penelope," Caitlan said, her voice trembling with irritation. "I clean Harriet's chamber every Friday morning.''

"And do you make a habit of rifling through the things on her dresser?" was Penelope's blunt inquiry. Her tone grew taunting when she added, "You really should refrain from leaving the door ajar, dear. You see, I was passing by and saw you take the ring from the trinket box. I would have said something sooner, but I had no idea you meant to keep it.''

"I didn't!" Caitlan shouted and somehow resisted the urge to dump the greasy contents of the meat tray on Penelope's smug head.

Instead, the platter fell with a noisy rattle upon the sideboard as Caitlan dispensed with it and whirled toward a red-faced Harriet. As she turned, Caitlan caught a glimpse of the daunting figure who loitered on the threshold. She was further dismayed to know that Rafe would be a witness to her latest humiliation, but she did not have time to worry about her wounded ego now.

Knowing what must be done, Caitlan took a deep breath and said, "I apologize, Harriet. What Penelope says is true. I did take the ring, but only to admire it," she said with a rush. "It . . . it is so pretty. I simply wanted to try it on for a moment,'' Caitlan whispered, her voice trailing off.

Possessed of a will of their own, her eyes lifted to Rafe's face. His expression was unreadable, but there was no denying the intense passion that flamed in the cerulean gaze that watched her. Uncertain if that fire burned from disgust or desire, Caitlan gave an involuntary shiver and looked away.

"I know it was presumptuous of me to do such a thing," Caitlan murmured, lowering her head in sincere penance. Her voice held a near-desperate ring when she added, "But I swear to you, Harriet. I did not steal your ring.''

"Oh, and I suppose you were merely admiring Mr. Hamilton's pocket watch that day I saw you in the drawing-room,''

Penelope offered casually. It was a smile of immeasurable satisfaction that spread the conniving woman's mouth as she leaned back in her chair and observed Caitlan's growing discomfiture. To worsen an already impossible situation, she said, "How many weeks ago has that been now, Katie?"

Mr. Hamilton did not usually bother himself with other people's affairs, but Penelope's offhand comment about his lost timepiece garnered his attention. Cupping his left ear with his hand so that he might hear better, he asked, "What's that you say about my pocket watch, Miss Crawford?"

It was Caitlan, however—determined that Penelope would not have the chance to level any more false charges against her—who answered. "My God! I completely forgot," she exclaimed, clasping her hands to her face. "I did find your watch, Mr. Hamilton. It had fallen between the cushions of the drawing-room sofa. I meant to restore it to you that very day, but Delia became so frightfully ill that . . . well . . . I guess it must have slipped my mind.

"Your pocket watch is quite safe," Caitlan assured the bespectacled man, who—in truth—had heard very little of her impassioned speech. "It's just upstairs in my chamber. I'll run and fetch it for you now."

Favoring the one responsible for making her suffer through this humiliating explanation with a parting scathing look, Caitlan bolted for the door. She did not falter when she came upon the formidable obstacle blocking her path, but merely pushed past him. And Rafe, sensing Caitlan's hostility, wisely made no attempt to deter her.

Without a backward glance, Caitlan stomped down the hallway, muttering, "Why that backbiting little . . . "

" . . . Bitch?" Rafe suggested, falling into step behind her.

Completely out of patience with the unjust situation, Caitlan came up short and, jamming her hands against her hips, whirled to confront Rafe. "I've never given Penelope cause to hold me in such dislike. Why would she do such a thing to me?"

Rafe grimaced and, scratching his bearded cheek in a pensive gesture, said, "I can't be certain, honey, but I believe it might have something to do with me."

"You?"

"Uh huh. Unless I miss my guess, I suspect your Miss Crawford has set her cap for me."

"What?!" Caitlan choked out, finding his theory difficult to swallow. "You could not possibly be interested in that . . . that *shrew*."

"Precisely," Rafe agreed. "In fact, I have demonstrated considerable more regard for my nurse and, accordingly, Penelope has grown jealous and decided to teach you a lesson. I understand you find this hard to believe, sweet pea, but I seem to have that effect on my women," he informed her, a roguish smile highlighting his rugged features.

Caitlan was of a mind to tell her incorrigible companion exactly what she thought about him *and* his women. Indeed, she had opened her mouth to do just that when Harriet stormed into the corridor.

"You come back here, missy. I'm not finished with you yet," Harriet barked. Shoving Rafe aside, she marched up to Caitlan and, thrusting a bony finger beneath the younger woman's nose, demanded, "What about my ring?"

"I told you, Harriet," Caitlan said between gritted teeth. "I don't have your ring."

"That's not good enough," Harriet told her point-blank. Then a cunning smile spread her thin lips as she said, "I think I'll just march myself on up them stairs and search your room. But first," she took a purposeful step toward Caitlan, "I'll just have a look at what you've got hidden about your clothes."

Caitlan bristled at the coarse implication and took a defensive step backward, but it was Rafe's intervention that ultimately spared her further embarrassment.

"Over my dead body" came his throaty growl.

The hoarse threat was barely above a whisper, but it served to make Harriet reconsider her actions.

"Excuse me?" an unfamiliar voice called from just inside the doorway. "I knocked but no one came to the door. I heard voices—"

"Rooms are eight dollars a week," Harriet interrupted the man's explanation, "twelve, if you take your vittles here. And it's payable in advance," she said. Adopting a businesslike pose, she stuck out her greedy hand to accept the specified payment.

"I fear you misunderstand me, ma'am. I'm not here to inquire after a room. My name is Harold Underwood. I'm an attorney, representing the estate of the late Mrs. Delia Stevens. I have been told that a . . . '' he paused to scan the legal parchment he held in his hand, " . . . Miss Caitlan Webber resides here. Might I have a word with her?"

"I am Miss Webber," Caitlan introduced herself, extending her hand toward the lawyer.

Harriet, impatient as always, slapped Caitlan's hand aside and stepped in front of her, saying, "Pleased to meet you, Mr. Underwood. I'm glad you dropped by. My name is Harriet Tuttle, and I've been wantin' to talk with someone about buyin' that old woman's estate. Now, I'm prepared to offer a fair price, mind you. How much are you askin' for the house?"

Mr. Underwood, thoroughly confused by this unexpected development glanced from Harriet to Rafe to Caitlan, then clearing his throat, he cloaked himself in a professional demeanor, saying, "I'm not at liberty to discuss the terms of Mrs. Stevens's will with you, ma'am. You'll have to take that up with the new owner."

"Oh, and who might that be?" came Harriet's haughty query.

Having assumed much from his brief encounter with the encroaching female, Mr. Underwood gave Caitlan a sympathetic look. A smile lightened his usually somber visage and it was obvious the man derived great pleasure in saying, "Why, you're looking at her, Miss Tuttle. My client bequeathed all her worldly goods and possessions to Miss Caitlan Webber."

Chapter Eight

✶⟋ↂ⟍✶

"There goes another one!" Essie squealed, letting mop and bucket fall where they may.

Essie's terrified scream, which was accompanied by the sound of splashing water and the mop clattering against the stone flaggings, induced Caitlan to glance away from her own work in time to see her friend clamber atop the nearest kitchen counter. Smiling inwardly at Essie's distress, Caitlan put aside the vinegar-soaked rag she had been using to polish the kitchen window and walked over to the cleaning tools that Essie had hastily discarded.

Bending over to retrieve the mop, Caitlan draped her arm over the handle and looked at Essie. It was an amused grin that twitched at the corner of her mouth when she warned, "I doubt you'll be much safer there, Essie. I discovered one of our furry friends playing atop that very counter when I arrived this morning."

"What?!" Essie screeched and would have jumped down from her perch had another of the pesky critters not chosen that particular moment to dart out from beneath a cabinet and skitter across the floor. Retreating once more into her corner, Essie drew her knees up to her chest, exclaiming, "Lord, I hate mice! And this house is overrun with them, Katie. However will you get rid of them all?''

"I've not quite figured that out yet," Caitlan admitted, a rueful frown wrinkling her brow. Eyeing one of the despised vermin beside the ice box—boldly gnawing on a piece of cheese in full view of its human predators—she gripped the mop handle and began to carefully stalk her prey. "I've set any number of traps, but to no avail. They appear to be clever little beggars," she said, plopping the mop down in front of the mouse that had grown plump·from the kitchen's coffers.

Caitlan had hoped she might trap the animal until she could put her hands on a container in which to imprison it. But as it is a well-known fact that the 'best laid schemes' oftentimes go awry, so did this one. Even as she beseeched Essie to fetch her the bucket, the cornered mouse reacted by scampering across the drenched mophead to disappear beneath Caitlan's skirt-tails. In the next instant, the ill-used mop could be heard clanking against the kitchen floor once more, as the would-be huntress was caught off guard by the rodent's offensive maneuver.

Not realizing that the animal was as—if not more—frightened of her than she was of it and had long since wriggled between a crack in the baseboard beside the sink, Caitlan screamed and promptly scrambled atop a chair. Terrified by the thought that the disgusting mouse was at that very moment climbing about the folds of her petticoats, Caitlan began shaking out her skirts with violent, jerking motions.

This chaotic scene was still being enacted when Rafe pushed open the kitchen door mere seconds later. The initial impact of the spectacle in progress made him pause on the threshold to survey the situation. Sensing Caitlan's real distress, he was compelled to action. Thinking she must have brushed against the stove and caught her skirts on fire, Rafe rushed into the room.

"Kettie, honey!" he blurted, the concern in his voice reflected in his blue gaze. "What is it?" Rafe, who fully expected to see flames spurting all about Caitlan at any moment, was thoroughly dumbfounded by her response.

"M-m-m-m-mouse!"

Rafe blinked in surprise. Though only seconds before he

had nearly panicked with the thought that Caitlan might be about to expire before his very eyes, this preposterous revelation brought a chortle to his lips.

"Mouse?" he repeated incredulously, forcing back the bark of laughter that rose in his throat.

A russet-tinged head bobbed up and down in answer to his inquiry and, though Rafe might find the situation amusing, it was obvious that Caitlan's fear was very real. "Help me get my skirt off!" she pleaded, her voice reaching an hysterical pitch. Even as the bold pronouncement reached his ears, Caitlan's quivering fingers groped at the waistband as she endeavored to loosen the buttons that held the garment fast.

"Kettie, darlin'." Rafe blew a long sigh and placed his hands atop hers to quell their frenzied motion. "You have no idea just how tempting that sounds, but I doubt we'll have to resort to such extreme—not to mention—potentially compromising measures." Giving his head a regretful shake, Rafe gathered Caitlan's waist in his strong hands and lifted her from the chair.

Draping a protective arm about her shoulder, he held Caitlan to him, stroking her hair and murmuring, "Calm down, honey." Then unable to contain his mirth, he scolded, "My God, woman! Why make such a to-do over a silly little mouse? Considering the ruckus you kicked up, I'd wager you scared him a damn sight more than he scared you."

"Don't be so sure," she mumbled against his broad chest.

Rafe laughed outright at Caitlan's continued squeamishness and, tilting her head back so that he could look into her face, he smiled into a pair of petulant green eyes. "Better, sweet pea?" came his solicitous inquiry.

Caitlan thought it strange indeed that she should feel comforted by this scoundrel's embrace. But instead of flinging away from Rafe—as her every self-preserving instinct shouted at her to do—she merely nodded and snuggled more closely against him.

"Is that coffee I smell?" he asked, tenderly rubbing her arm up and down.

"Yes."

"Good. Sit down here and gather your wits about you, and I'll pour us a cup." He lowered Caitlan onto the very chair she had but moments earlier used as refuge from the dreaded mouse, then recalling this was his first visit to her newly inherited residence, he was obliged to ask, "Where do you keep your dishes?"

Caitlan made a nonspecific gesture toward the row of cabinets behind him and, turning, Rafe was greeted by yet another surprise. Essie still cowered atop the kitchen counter. Shaking his head in wonder that a tiny mouse could wreak such havoc, he proffered his hand to the frightened girl.

"Climb on down from there, Essie," Rafe ordered. Taking the girl by the hand, he led her to the table. "I suppose this means I need to rustle up three cups," he mumbled and turned to rummage through the cabinets.

"Do you suppose you could make that four, Mistah Bradrick?" asked a familiar voice from the open doorway. "Ah sure could stands a cup of Miz Katie's coffee."

"Certainly Hezekiah. Come on in." Rafe greeted him with a cheerful smile. "You'll have to forgive Kettie; she's not feeling overly talkative this morning. It seems she and Essie have been under attack by some pesky vermin."

"What?" Hezekiah asked, taking a seat at the table opposite Caitlan. "Is them mice still givin' you trouble, Miz Katie?"

With his back to the group, no one noticed the wounded expression that Hezekiah's innocent question brought to Rafe's handsome face. The simple truth was, though Rafe harbored no ill feelings toward him, he was resentful that Caitlan still presumed that Hezekiah was the only man who took an interest in—or could help her solve—her problems.

While Rafe wrestled with these nagging thoughts, Caitlan began to relax. In fact, she was feeling considerably more at ease now that she was surrounded by so many friendly faces. Confident that there was sufficient activity to discourage any unwanted intrusions from the rodent population for a while, she smiled at Hezekiah.

"Yes, Hezekiah," Caitlan said presently. "I fear the mice dilemma will be mine until I can find a buyer for the house. Then, happily, it shall become the new owner's problem."

"Is you sure you wants to sell the place, Miz Katie?" Hezekiah asked, his brown eyes searching Caitlan's face. "Aftah all, this is the first home you've had to call your own in quite a spell. Ah hates for you to let it go if'n there's a chance you can keep it.''

Caitlan, aware that Rafe was taking an inordinate amount of time in preparing the promised coffee, went to assist him. Motioning for him to bring the coffeepot, she gathered cups and saucers from the cupboard and carried them to the table. Finally, she collected the cream from the ice box and, sitting down again, said, ''I hate to sell the house, too, Hezekiah. But don't you see? This is my chance to be free of Harriet once and for all. If I can fix the place up a bit and sell it, I will be able to pay Harriet all that I owe her. As things presently stand, I shall have to continue working at the boardinghouse just to make ends meet.''

''Why is that?'' Hezekiah asked. ''Ah thought Miz Stevens done left you sittin' pretty.''

''No, there was very little money in her account at the bank and most of that went to pay the attorney's fees. And I thought it only fitting that Mrs. Burke receive some token for the loyalty she had shown Delia all these years, so I gave her enough money to get to California to be with her son. I have a little left over, but mainly there is this house and the furnishings,'' Caitlan explained.

''But what will you do if you sell the house, Katie?'' Essie asked, saddened by the thought of losing her dear friend. ''Where will you go?''

''I'm not sure.'' Caitlan stirred a heaping teaspoon of sugar into her coffee. Lifting the cup to her lips, she took a contemplative sip and said, ''Perhaps I shall go to California, too.''

Essie, horrified by this conjecture, cried, ''No!''

''I don't understand, Kettie,'' Rafe said, sitting down at the table. ''Why don't you just stay here?''

''I explained that already, Rafe,'' she chided. ''I cannot afford to maintain this house on the piddling salary that Harriet pays me.''

Rafe mulled her reply for a moment, then certain he had found the perfect solution to her problem, said simply, ''Then quit.''

Caitlan very nearly choked on the mouthful of coffee she had just imbibed. ''And do what?'' she sputtered.

"Open your own place," Rafe stated, as if that was the most natural thing she could do.

"That takes money," Caitlan informed him.

"Aw hell, Kettie!" he snapped at her, jumping up from his chair. "Stop throwing up fences at everything I say. You don't have to open a fancy hotel or a boardinghouse. You can start with a small restaurant or tearoom, or even a dress shop. You can do anything you put your mind to, Caitlan Webber, and don't let anyone tell you different," Rafe said, striding to the door.

Before taking his leave, he paused on the threshold to impart a final thought-provoking comment, "Don't reject the idea out of hand, sweet pea. Look around. You have three friends in this very room who would be willing to help you get started. All you have to do is ask," he baited her. Smiling that roguish grin that always made Caitlan feel all giddy inside, he departed by saying, "Think about it."

Caitlan thought of little else in the following days. In the end, it was the ever hateful Harriet who proved instrumental in helping her reach a decision. The last straw was hoisted upon an already overburdened Caitlan as she served the midday meal. She had just ladled a portion of rabbit stew onto Penelope's plate, and was turning to do the same for Harriet, when her slipper became hopelessly entangled with an obstacle which caused Caitlan to lose her balance. The culprit proved to be a foot which had been purposefully thrust in Caitlan's path by a vengeful Penelope. It is unlikely, however, that the scheming young miss gave much thought to the possible repercussions of her spiteful deed, else she might not have acted so impulsively.

In that frightening moment when a hapless Caitlan was pitched headlong toward certain disaster, she had the forethought to wheel away from Harriet's daunting countenance. Caitlan put forth a valiant effort as she struggled to regain her footing, all the while fighting to keep the tureen from toppling to the floor. She very nearly won the battle in spite of these insurmountable odds, but as Caitlan whirled away from her surly employer, Penelope—sensing misfortune was at hand—bolted from her chair.

Rather than escaping the unhappy situation that she herself had brought about, Penelope made matters worse. As she leaped to her feet, she collided with Caitlan and upset the tray. Whereas the nimble woman had only moments earlier managed to spare Harriet an untimely meeting with the laden serving dish, Penelope would not be as fortunate. Helpless to prevent that which appeared destined, Caitlan watched in horror as the contents of the porcelain tureen sloshed all over the front of Penelope's fashionable dress. Her bemused demeanor would presently undergo an uncharacteristic transformation, however, as an embittered Penelope vented her hostility on Caitlan.

"You stupid, clumsy fool!" Penelope shrieked, wiping at her soiled dress with hysterical gyrations. "Look! Just look what you've done to my new gown. I swear you'll pay for this."

"Stop your squallin', Penelope." Harriet hushed the distraught woman. Standing, she said, "There's no need fussin' over what's happened. It's true it was Katie's fault—what with her bein' so clumsy and all—but she'll see that your dress is properly laundered, never fear. Now, run along and change while Katie cleans up this mess and fetches another bowl of stew from the kitchen. We'll wait for you."

"No," Penelope spewed, blue eyes boring into Caitlan's unusually expressionless face. "She did this on purpose to get back at me for accusing her of stealing your ring and Mr. Hamilton's pocket watch. I'm not going anywhere until she apologizes."

"Very well then." Harriet blew a weary sigh, very much put out with the entire proceedings. Sitting down, she made an offhand gesture at Caitlan, saying, "Apologize, Katie."

Caitlan made no immediate effort to comply with Harriet's command. Instead, her aloof gaze measured the faces of the other tenants seated around the table. She looked from Mr. Hamilton's disinterested face to Mr. Morgan who, having had his efforts to mollify Penelope's insulted sensibilities ruthlessly rejected by the ungrateful woman, sat in dejected silence. Finally, her unswerving gaze fell upon Rafe. Though Caitlan had expected to be greeted by an expression filled with loathing or—worse—pity, she was duly surprised by the smile of unholy merriment she observed dancing in those glorious blue eyes.

Following the direction of his cerulean stare, Caitlan soon came to understand the reason for Rafe's blithe disposition.

Penelope looked prodigiously silly, standing with her arms dangling at her sides in helpless confusion and her mouth agape in stupendous wonder, helpless to prevent the ever-widening circles of brown juice from staining the folds of her skirt. Glancing down, Caitlan discovered another amusing sight. The stew drippings trickled from the hem of Penelope's gown to create a puddle among the chunks of meat, potatoes and other vegetables that lay strewn at her feet. Under normal circumstances, such a preposterous spectacle would have brought a laugh to Caitlan's lips, but she was very much aware that this was a situation that required delicate handling, and therefore, wisely held her tongue.

Turning to Harriet, Caitlan maintained her poise and, in a voice that was remarkably composed, said, "No."

"What!" Harriet bristled at her hireling's defiant air. "What do you mean?"

"Simply that I have no intention of apologizing to Penelope," Caitlan replied. "It was her fault, not mine. Penelope tripped me to make me look foolish in front of everyone. She only got what was coming to her."

Harriet barely had time to make herself comfortable on the dining-room chair before Caitlan's wholly unexpected rebuttal stung her ears. The irascible woman was on her feet in a flash, her vindictive tongue at the ready. "How dare you? I'll teach you to say such things to me, missy" came her ominous threat.

As was typical of Harriet, her method of instruction invariably involved some disciplinary action. Over the years, Caitlan had been the unfortunate victim of any number of her employer's painful lessons, but on this day, she vowed that she would never again play the docile scapegoat for Harriet.

"I would think twice if I were you, Harriet," Caitlan whispered, returning her employer's scathing glare in full.

Harriet's bosom heaved mightily at this wanton act of rebellion and, overwhelmed by the sudden urge to put this upstart in her place, she drew back her hand.

Even the reserved Mr. Hamilton, sensing that the situation that had begun by the innocuous spilling of a dish of stew had grown into something far more profound, put aside his daily tabloid to watch the proceedings with newfound interest. The gentleman sitting beside Mr. Hamilton, however, did not share his table companion's morbid curiosity. Blue eyes no longer danced with unbridled merriment; indeed, it was a darkling look that molded the ruggedly handsome face. Rafe felt the anger rise in his throat as he observed Harriet whip her arm back, and he was on his feet in an instant, intent upon wrenching the despised hand from Harriet's arm before she had the chance to defile Caitlan's cheek.

In the end, Caitlan proved to be her own salvation. With blinding swiftness, she threw her hand up to deflect the glancing blow. Catching Harriet by the wrist, she twisted the wrinkled flesh until Harriet—her pride bruised rather more than her arm—flopped back down upon the chair.

"You've struck me for the last time, Harriet," Caitlan seethed between clenched teeth. "Never again, Harriet! Never again," she cried. "Do you hear me?"

"I'll hit you whenever I like, missy. And I owe you double for what you done today." Harriet wagged her throbbing arm in Caitlan's face.

"No, you won't, you old witch," Caitlan spat. "And do you know why?"

Harriet, completely dumbfounded by Caitlan's display of backbone, could not readily find her tongue.

"Because . . . " Caitlan faltered and, gulping back her indecision, she looked to Rafe for reassurance. Blue and green gazes mated for a fleeting moment in the sunlit dining-room, but in that brief glimpse, Caitlan found the encouragement she sought. With renewed determination, she faced Harriet and her tone left little doubt when she said, " . . . Because, I'm no longer in your employ, Harriet. I quit."

"*What?!*" Harriet screeched, as only she could and tried to scramble from the chair.

Caitlan felt suddenly vindicated, as if a heavy weight had been lifted from her shoulders. Smiling broadly, she untied— literally as well as figuratively—her apron strings and flung the stained garment in Harriet's face, thereby postponing that agitated woman's flight.

Wheeling about, Caitlan marched to the dining-room door, calling over her shoulder, "You heard me."

"But . . . but you can't leave. What will you do?" Harriet squawked.

"Open my own place" came Caitlan's prompt and thoroughly unexpected reply.

"*What?!*" If possible, Harriet's incredulous shriek grew even more shrill. "What about the money you owe me?" she cried.

"You shall have it."

"But . . . but who will I get to take your place? You can't just up and quit without givin' me notice," Harriet shouted at Caitlan's rigid back.

When Caitlan did not honor this objection with a reply, an outraged Harriet leaped to her feet, prepared to chase after her disgruntled housekeeper and continue their argument. Before she could take a single step toward the aperture, however, Harriet found her shoulder gripped by an unyielding hand and, with a whimper, she meekly returned to her seat.

"It appears to me as if Kettie just turned in her notice, Mrs. Tuttle," Rafe drawled and jerked the chair backward with such force that Harriet nearly tumbled from it sideways. Stepping around in front of the disconcerted woman, Rafe brought his face until his nose was nearly touching hers. In a tone that was bone-chillingly intimidating, he said, "I've got two things to say to you, you old battle-ax, so you best listen.

"First, you leave Kettie be," he told her in no uncertain terms. "She's got a right to make her own life. Kettie's a fine woman and God knows she deserves better than the hell you've put her through." Rafe straightened and walked to the door and Harriet, thinking the demoralizing interview was over, breathed a sigh of relief.

Her reprieve proved short-lived, however, for Rafe paused on the threshold to deliver a parting caution. "And secondly, have a care, Harriet. I've never struck a woman in my life, but if you ever raise a hand to Kettie again, I could very well be persuaded to forget that I'm a gentleman. You take my meaning, Harriet?" Those cold blue eyes searched the woman's white face and when he observed her stiff nod, Rafe grunted, "Good," and quit the room.

Rafe did not go immediately to Caitlan's room; he wanted to give her time alone to consider all that had taken place during those heat-filled moments in the dining-room. He knew Caitlan well enough to realize that she was having second thoughts by now. Rafe could appreciate her hesitancy to embark upon a chancy proposition such as opening her own business, but he was resolved to make her stand by her decision.

Rafe paced about his own chamber for nearly three-quarters of an hour before deciding that he had given Caitlan enough time to contemplate her uncertain future. Stepping across the narrow corridor to Caitlan's door, he rapped his knuckles against the hard panel. Black eyebrows knitted into a puzzled frown when no voice bid him entrance into the room. For a moment, he thought Caitlan might have slipped out without him taking notice but as quickly as the thought came, Rafe dismissed it. Pushing the door ajar, he saw her.

She was sitting on the bed with her head downcast, a flowered carpetbag at her feet and a shabby leather portmanteau perched beside her. Rafe knew without asking that these bags contained all of Caitlan's worldly possessions, and a lump welled in his throat as he thought this a sad testament to the lonely life she had led for so many years. Shaking off his melancholy mien—lest Caitlan misconstrue his concern for pity—Rafe came into the room. Without waiting for an invitation he sat down beside her.

"I see you've finished packing," he said and made himself comfortable by crossing one long, muscular leg over the other. When all he received was a glum sigh for his efforts, Rafe took her chin between his forefinger and thumb and obliged Caitlan to look at him. "You mustn't fret over this, sweet pea. You'll only work yourself into a state if you think on it too much, and you need to be strong now and keep your wits about you. Come on," he said, his tone gentle as he patted her arm. "Let's get you settled in your new house before nightfall."

With that, he stood and gathered the larger case in his hand, but when he bent to retrieve the carpetbag from the floor, he was surprised when Caitlan lifted her hand to his cheek. "You don't think I'm crazy then?"

"No, Kettie." Rafe coughed, feeling suddenly very much aware of her nearness. The scent of her hair, the hand that had moved from his cheek to rest upon his shoulder, and the vulnerable look in those wondrous green eyes all contrived to set his pulse racing. Knowing full well that he was treading in dangerous waters, Rafe plucked the carpetbag from the floor and straightened. "It took a lot of nerve to stand up to that old cow. So, what is it to be then . . . a dress shop?" he inquired, affecting a casual air.

Caitlan shook her head and replied, "I think I'm better suited to run a tearoom."

"That you are," Rafe agreed, turning to stride toward the door. "Come on, Kettie. Let's get away from here before Harriet gets her second wind and comes to pick a quarrel."

"Rafe?"

Caitlan spoke but a single syllable, but it was the serious inflection of her voice that caught Rafe's ear. Not quite knowing what to expect, he faced her. "Yes?"

"Do . . . do you recall that day at the house when Essie and I were . . . vexed by the mice?" Caitlan asked haltingly, her head lowered as though she was reluctant to proceed.

"Yes?" His brow puckered into an amused frown.

"You said . . . well, that is . . . you *implied* that, should I decide to open a business in Delia's house, you would be willing to . . . to help me. Did you mean that?" Caitlan looked him squarely in the eye now, and her heart felt considerably lighter when she saw the expression that lit up his face.

"Aw hell, Kettie. Of course I did," Rafe said, smiling. Then jerking his head toward the door, he grew suddenly somber and his voice lowered to a mere whisper as he added, "I know I've given you reason to believe otherwise, Kettie, but I never go back on a promise to a friend." His smile returned and he chuckled. "Hell, I guarantee you'll be plumb sick of the sight of my mangy hide before the month is out."

Rafe passed through the gate and swaggered up the walkway, making a mental note that the hinges needed oiling and the picket fence could use a fresh coat of whitewash. His saddlebags made a small thudding sound as he let them fall against the porch planks. He gave the lid of the basket he carried beneath his arm a playful "thunk" with his knuckles and reached for the door. Without knocking, he pulled the portal open, but one polished boot had barely scraped the threshold when the sound of voices floating out the open sitting-room window gave him pause. A roguish grin fashioned Rafe's lips when he detected Caitlan's gay laughter, but an annoying frown took its place seconds later when he heard a man's answering chortle.

Rafe backed slowly away from the door, resisting all the while the urge to barge straightaway into the house and interrupt this cozy tête-à-tête. After all, Caitlan was not a nun. She had every right to entertain a gentleman in her parlor if she so desired. The fact that the gentleman in question was not "his truly" was the thing that stuck in Rafe's craw. Fighting back his baser instincts, Rafe assumed a nonchalant air as he stepped across the threshold and took up an observational stance in the sitting-room doorway.

From his vantage, propped against the door casing, Rafe had the upper hand insofar that he could take the man's measure before making his own presence known. The couple sat opposite one another, the gentleman balancing a cup and saucer on his knee while Caitlan proffered a plateful of confections for his consideration. Rafe had never seen the man before, but he had a fair guess as to his identity. Jeremy Cantrell looked harmless enough, Rafe supposed, but he was vying for Caitlan's attention and this fact alone made Rafe dislike him.

Cantrell was dressed out in his Sunday best and had put on his courting manners, but a cursory glance was all Rafe needed to know that this was not the man for Caitlan. In the first place, he was much too old for her. Why, he was forty-five if he was a day, as was evidenced by his receding hairline and the telltale hint of gray that highlighted his brownish mane. Cantrell was of medium build and, from all accounts, seemed to be a biddable fellow. Even so, Rafe reaffirmed his original assessment, the man was no match for his Kettie.

Caitlan, for all that she had been browbeaten into submission by that domineering Tuttle creature, was a woman of passion. Rafe had realized that the moment he laid eyes on her all those years ago. Knowing her as he did, the docile—almost subservient—mien she had displayed since his arrival in Vicksburg had proved a nagging mystery to Rafe. He had, however, witnessed a resurgence of that spirit when she walked out on Harriet, and by damn, he was not about to let her stroll blindly into a like situation with this Cantrell fellow.

Rafe knew the type. Oh, Cantrell affected the airs of an ardent suitor, but should he prove successful in his efforts to win Caitlan's hand, she would be miserable. The man would mold her into his preconceived notion of wife and mother, make her a mere shadow of himself rather than encourage her to be her own woman. Caitlan would go mad within a week. His Kettie did not need that. She needed a man . . . a man who would help her rediscover life, someone to teach her about living and loving, a man who wanted her for his helpmate . . . a man who would love her for herself. She should be doting on her own children, not looking after this man's whelps.

This last thought brought Rafe's attention back to the matter at hand full tilt. In fact, he was just about to announce himself when the occupant of the basket—having grown impatient with its lengthy incarceration—forced the lid open far enough to extend one furry paw and claw at Rafe's exposed forearm. The unexpected attack brought an oath to his lips. Slapping the offensive paw back inside the container, he turned a sheepish grin on Caitlan who had leaped to her feet at the discordant sound.

"Rafe!" The exclamation was a mixture of surprise at finding him lurking in the aperture and censure for his coarse language.

Doffing his hat, Rafe murmured a hasty, "Beg pardon, ma'am."

Pushing away from the doorjamb, he entered the room.

Caitlan made the appropriate introductions and Rafe noticed with some perplexity that an expression of understanding spread across the man's face. Extending his hand toward Rafe, the man said, "Oh my, yes. You must be that unfortunate fellow that Miss Webber has been looking after all this time. She has told me all about you."

"Has she now?" Rafe drawled. As he shook Jeremy's hand, his aloof gaze settled on Caitlan's face.

"Yes. It would appear you are a very lucky man."

"Indeed?"

"Oh my, yes. It isn't like our Miss Webber to go wandering—unescorted, mind you—along the Yazoo Road after dark," Jeremy explained. "I, for one, am more than a little shocked by such unseemly conduct in a woman of Miss Webber's years, but she has assured me that she will not act so foolhardily in the future.''

"She has?" Rafe offered, his jaw beginning to twitch.

His gaze returned to Caitlan's face, and he had to fend off the impulsive desire to grab her by the shoulders and shake some sense into her. Had she gone completely mad? The Kettie he knew could not possibly be interested in this pompous jack-ass.

Rafe ran an agitated hand along his neck and, as he grappled to bring his emotions under control, Jeremy said, ''But then, everything has worked out for the best, has it not? For had Miss Webber not taken that unprecedented jaunt in the night, you would not be here, Mr. Bradrick.''

Rafe gained new respect for the man in that fleeting moment; although his words had been sincerely tendered, Rafe took his implied meaning. Realizing that, despite Jeremy's meek appearance, this was a man to be reckoned with, Rafe nodded a silent ''touché.'' Ignoring the hand that Caitlan extended toward the chair beside Jeremy, he sat down on the sofa next to her. He declined Caitlan's offer of refreshment and devoted his efforts to a more thorough scrutiny of his adversary's—for that is surely what Cantrell was—countenance.

He was about to make some offhand comment when Caitlan said, ''I was just telling Mr. Cantrell about my plans to open a tearoom.''

"Really?" Rafe said, stretching his arm along the sofa behind her and crossing his legs.

Glancing away from Cantrell, he settled his knowing gaze on Caitlan. By her disheveled appearance, Rafe surmised that her visitor must have arrived as she was in the midst of cleaning that very chamber. He attributed his assumption to the fact that a pile of soiled rags and a bucket sat just beneath the windowsill. Also, there was the unruly smudge that adorned Caitlan's cheek, the blouse sleeves that still bore the wrinkles from where they had been hastily rolled down from her elbows, and the wisps of brown-and-russet hair that had fallen free to curl about her face in charming disorder. He thought she looked delightful, but Rafe doubted that a poker-faced buffoon like Jeremy Cantrell could truly appreciate Caitlan's guileless beauty.

"She speaks the truth, Bradrick," Jeremy was saying. "Perhaps I can prevail upon you to join me in my efforts to dissuade Miss Webber from going forward with this ridiculous notion she has taken into her head. Running a business is, after all, a man's job. What do you think, Mr. Bradrick?"

Rafe would have been more than happy to give the man his considered opinion on the subject, but it was Caitlan who surprised both men with her candor. "I fear I cannot agree with you on that point, Jeremy. Why, only look at the success Madame Cognaisse has achieved with her dress shop. I cannot think that a man could have done better. Then there is Mrs. Flannery's bakery and—"

"You mistook my meaning," Jeremy interrupted. "I simply meant that *you* are not suited to run a business. You have no experience in that area, after all. Wouldn't you agree, Mr. Bradrick?"

"On the contrary. I gave Kettie the idea of opening a business in the first place." Rafe could have sworn that Cantrell actually flinched at his familiar use of Caitlan's name. Wallowing for a moment in his self-proclaimed triumph, Rafe eventually added, "In fact, Kettie knows that my services are at her disposal." *Night and day, if need be,* Rafe wanted desperately to add, but out of deference to Caitlan, he bit back the scandalous taunt.

"Oh?" Jeremy remarked and fidgeted on his chair. Feeling suddenly ill at ease, he pulled his watch from his pocket and, flipping open the lid, glanced down at the time. Standing, he said, "My, my, where has the morning gone, I wonder? I had no idea it had grown so late. I really must be on my way."

"Must you go, Jeremy?" Caitlan asked, genuinely dismayed by his early departure. Glancing aside at Rafe, she continued, "I was hoping we would have a moment to chat about Abbie before you left."

"Another time perhaps, Katie" came his dismissive response.

Thus put off, Caitlan had little choice but to walk with Jeremy to the door. She accompanied him out onto the porch and, crossing her arms in front of her, watched in disappointed silence as Jeremy climbed atop his horse and rode away. Caitlan sensed that Rafe had followed her outside and, jamming her hands against her hips, she turned on him.

" 'My services are at her disposal,' " she mimicked him. "Whatever possessed you to say such a thing?"

Rafe made an impatient gesture at the now empty thoroughfare in front of the house, saying, "Aw hell, Kettie. It was that Cantrell fella and his highfalutin airs that started everything, what with his Miss Webber this and Miss Webber that. He's no better than the rest of us, and I thought he should know what he was dealing with. Besides, I can talk hoity-toity with the best of men when I'm of a mind to. And then for him to say you had no business opening up a tearoom. Well, dammit, he went too far."

Caitlan bit back the grin that twittered on her lips and said, "He isn't so very awful, you know. A woman could do a lot worse."

"And you could do a damn sight better" came Rafe's surly retort.

Knowing they had reached an impasse insofar as the qualities of the recently departed Jeremy Cantrell were concerned, Caitlan wisely changed the subject. Noting with some curiosity the basket that Rafe carried under his arm, she asked, "What's in the basket?"

As eager as Caitlan to put the topic of her erstwhile visitor behind them, Rafe said, "A present."

"A present? For me?"

A broad smile fashioned his mouth as Rafe situated the container in front of him. Extending it toward her, he said, "Go ahead. Open it."

Caitlan's expression remained circumspect as she flicked open the lid. Glancing downward, she was more than a little surprised to find her own curious green stare returned in full by a rather large striped tabby.

"Meow," said the cat.

"Miss Webber," Rafe began, reaching inside and lifting the heavy feline from its comfortable, albeit cramped, quarters. "Allow me to present Mr. Beauregard Jackson Lee." He made a grand bow before her and concluded by dumping the cat into her arms.

"Rafe!" Caitlan protested. She was fighting a lost cause,

however; Beauregard, having found her scent to his liking, had already snuggled into a comfortable position in her arms and was purring contentedly. "But . . . why? Where?"

"The why is simple, Kettie," Rafe said, then proceeded to explain, "You cannot run a proper tearoom if you are forever in fear that your customers will be pestered by mice. Just imagine the chaos should one of Vicksburg's respectable ladies be sipping tea at your table, only to have one of those furry critters scurry across her feet. Why, they would close you down within a week, and then Jeremy Cantrell would be proved right—you have no head for business—and we cannot have that," he informed her in no uncertain terms. "Now, I'm the first to admit that Beauregard Jackson Lee has a bit of an attitude, and he can be contrary when he wants to, but aside from that he's a fine mouser, or so I'm told."

"Oh? And who told you that? Where did you happen to find Mr. Beauregard Jackson Lee. And where did you get the money to buy him, Rafe?" she asked, her eyes narrowing in shrewd contemplation as she petted the animal. "And don't try to pass him off as a stray. He has been well-fed and well-cared for. Now, fess up. Where did you get him?"

Rafe had hoped he might be able to avoid divulging the cat's prior ownership, but a glance at Caitlan's dogmatic mien sufficed to tell him that his hopes had been in vain. Running a finger between his neck and the collar of his shirt that had grown unbearably tight, he coughed and mumbled, "Sadie."

"Sadie?"

"Yes." Rafe faltered and looked to where a group of young boys were actively engaged in kicking a tin can up the middle of the street. Vaguely, he wished that he might join in their frolicking rather than make a full and true confession, but Caitlan was not to be so obliging.

"And this Sadie . . . she just gave her pet to you?"

"Uh huh."

"Why?" came Caitlan's relentless query.

Rafe hemmed and hawed for as long as he could. Deciding he might as well get it over and done with, he gave those broad shoulders a shrug and said, "It seems that the little fella made her . . . ahem . . . *patrons* nervous."

"Patrons?" Caitlan repeated. She mulled this disclosure,

then taking his meaning, her face grew a fiery shade of red and her voice an octave higher when she next addressed her gift-bearing visitor. "Do you mean to tell me that you *procured* this animal from one of those . . . those—"

"Mind what you say now, Kettie," Rafe cautioned, his expression not nearly as serious as his tone indicated.

" . . . fancy women on China Street?" she concluded with an indignant huff.

"Not exactly." Rafe scratched the back of his head and wished that Kettie would just take the damn cat and leave go with all the infernal questions. "Like I said, Beauregard here proved to be a source of intimidation while Sadie was . . . uh . . . entertaining her customers. I guess he liked to sit on the bed and watch—"

"Rafe!" Caitlan fairly shouted at him.

"Well, to answer your question, there was no charge for the cat." And now Rafe smiled broadly and winked. "Trust me, Sadie was glad to be rid of him."

Caitlan, thoroughly scandalized by Rafe's admission, tried to thrust the animal back into his arms. Mr. Beauregard Jackson Lee, however, was not taken with the notion that he was to be uprooted from his comfortable niche. Consequently, he dug his claws into Caitlan's bodice as a means of stating his displeasure with the proceedings.

Thus ensnared, Caitlan pleaded, "Do something, Rafe! Take him."

"Now, Kettie, don't get your back up, and don't go taking that holier-than-thou attitude with me. It's just a cat. What harm can there be?"

Caitlan did not dare tell him that it was not the idea of where he found the animal so much as the fact that he obviously frequented the place that troubled her. By rights, Caitlan knew she had no cause to be upset with him; men would be men, after all. The truth was, the mere thought of Rafe sneaking off to be with *that woman* in the dark of night bothered her very much indeed.

"No, there is no harm, I suppose," she mumbled.

"Good. You'll keep him then?"

Caitlan nodded. Glancing down at his feet, she saw something there that was even more startling to her than the knowl-

edge by which Beauregard's former owner earned a living . . .
Rafe's saddlebags. Tearing her gaze from the alarming sight,
she willed herself to remain calm. After all, it was of no
consequence to her whether he stayed or went, Caitlan told
herself over and over. Yet, despite her efforts, she could not
quell the desperate hammering in her chest.

At the same moment Caitlan had taken note of his saddlebags, Rafe's attention had been captured by the "Help
Wanted" sign that was tacked to the window frame. Puzzled
by their respective discoveries, the couple asked of each other
in unison, "What's that?"

Rafe, glancing away from the notice that had proved to be
the source of considerable concern, was the first to reply, "Oh,
those?" He nodded toward his saddlebags. "Harriet threw me
out. I guess she didn't cotton to the way I took up for you
when you stood up to her the other day, so she suggested I
find other lodgings."

"Where will you go?"

"I'm not sure, but never mind that." He thumbed at the
paperboard sign. "What's that all about? I thought Essie had
agreed to come work for you and help with the cooking and
the serving."

"She has, but I need someone else. Someone to fix the place
up a bit," Caitlan explained. "You know, mend the roof, paint
the house and fence, see to the upkeep and general repairs. I
fear I'm no good when it comes to that sort of thing."

"There's no reason on this earth why you should be," Rafe
said flatly, then trying not to appear overzealous, he added,
"I could do all that for you, Kettie."

"Really?"

"Sure. I'm not one to boast, but I'm pretty handy with a
hammer and paint brush."

Caitlan was of a mind to readily accept his offer, but her
expression led him to believe otherwise. Frowning, she asked,
"What about your wounds? Are you fully recovered, Rafe?
Do you truly believe you can undertake something this strenuous?"

Pulling a handkerchief from his breast pocket, Rafe dampened the edge with his tongue before applying it to the dirty

smudge that blemished her cheek. It is little wonder then that Caitlan barely took note of his reply.

"I'm fine, Kettie," he whispered. "Just a twinge now and again, but I'm fairly certain I can perform most any task you care to send my way." He repocketed his handkerchief and stood staring down at her.

Caitlan considered his ambiguous statement for a moment before saying, "The pay isn't much, just five dollars a week to start. But there is a room over the carriage house out back where you can stay, and I will provide all your meals."

"That sounds fair. When do I start?"

"Now, if you like. I'll just take a moment to acquaint this chubby fellow with his new living quarters and the vermin that inhabit it. Then I'll help you get settled in." Looking down at the cat that snuggled against her breast, she chuckled and said, "However did that woman decide upon such a ridiculous name for you?" Realizing she had voiced her thoughts aloud and that Rafe was only too eager to relate the details of what would doubtlessly be a ribald story, Caitlan waved a cautionary finger at his nose and stepped inside the house. Scratching the striped tabby behind his ear, she said, "I shall call you Beau and have done with it. Now, Beau, come along while I prepare you a nice saucer of cream. Then you may start earning your keep."

Rafe loitered behind on the porch for a moment to ponder the morning's happenings and suddenly he began to laugh. It started as a soft chuckle in the back of his throat but by the time it reached his lips, it emerged as a hearty guffaw. He doubled over from the force of it. Then knowing he must have his wits about him before he encountered Caitlan again, Rafe wiped the tears of mirth from his eyes. He shook his head in wonder, thinking that—all things considered—the day's events could not have turned out any better if he had planned them himself. Smiling that secret smile that—had Caitlan seen it— would have driven her mad with curiosity, he hoisted his sad-dlebags over his shoulder and, ripping the paperboard "Help Wanted" sign from its nesting place, followed Caitlan inside the house.

Chapter Nine

※※◦◦※※

By the first week in October, Caitlan's new house had undergone such an amazing transformation that she doubted if Delia herself would have recognized the place. Going forward with her plans to open a tearoom, Caitlan had decided to utilize the four downstairs rooms for dining areas while maintaining the upstairs chambers as her personal living quarters; a sitting-room, sewing-room, and two bedrooms. Consequently, while Caitlan—with considerable help from Hezekiah and Essie—had devoted her efforts toward remodeling the interior, Rafe had seen to the repairs needed to the exterior of the house.

Thus far Rafe's skillful hands had completed any number of tasks; patching the roof, mending the shutters, whitewashing the fence, and repainting the entire house to mention but a few. In addition, he and Hezekiah had carted furniture up and down the stairs until Rafe thought his back would surely break. They had positioned sofas, tables, chairs, bedsteads, and what nots in any number of perfectly acceptable places, only to have their efforts reviewed by a pair of critical green eyes. Invariably, that brown-and-russet head would give an abrupt shake and, with a sigh, the two men would heave their burdens back into their hands and dutifully follow their guide to the next destination.

With the tearoom scheduled to open in less than a week, Caitlan still did not know how she was going to manage. After all, opening a business required a great deal of capital; money that she did not have on hand. And what with Harriet hounding her night and day for the money that was due her . . . well, Caitlan simply did not know how she was going to carry it off. Still, Rafe and Hezekiah kept assuring her that she could do it, therefore, she was determined to try.

Caitlan presently stood high upon a stepladder in the former downstairs sitting-room, preparing to hang the freshly ironed curtains she had carried in from the kitchen. As she stretched to secure the curtain rod onto the brass bracket, Caitlan was distracted by a movement outside. Glancing down, she saw Rafe stride around the corner of the house carrying a large, rectangular-shaped piece of wood which she had never seen before. Her curiosity aroused, she polished the glass with her sleeve and peered more closely out the windowpane.

As she watched, Rafe leaned the wooden piece against the porch railing. Thumbing his hat back from his forehead, he took a step backward and folded his arms across his chest, his studious blue gaze trained on the unknown object. Caitlan, more intrigued than ever, all but climbed through the window as she strained to get a glimpse of the mysterious item. Then a soft padding sound on the rug drew Caitlan's attention away from the window. Looking down, she was not surprised to discover the identity of the intruder . . . Beau.

The big striped tabby, who gave the air of a feline that was very much pleased with himself, trotted happily across the floor to the ladder where he proceeded to present Caitlan with his latest "catch" of the day. Then he plopped himself down under the ladder and, stretching his front paws out before him, yawned lazily as if to say he was completely worn out from all this mouse chasing. Caitlan gave a little shiver of disgust when she saw the plump brown carcass. One would think she would have grown accustomed to this particular ceremony; she had been the recipient of many such offerings in recent weeks. Rafe had been right about one thing—Beau certainly was a good mouser.

With a rueful grin, Caitlan turned back to the window to find that Rafe was nowhere to be seen. Hunching her shoulders, she extended the curtain rod toward the bracket once more. Realizing that she could not quite reach it with her outstretched fingers, Caitlan lifted her foot up to the next step. As she did so, the toe of her shoe became entangled in her skirt and thus jolted, she was thrown off balance. Caitlan teetered precariously on the high rung, one hand groping furtively for the window frame, the other clutching the useless curtains. A terrified scream froze in her throat and, in that awful moment when certain disaster seemed imminent, Caitlan was luckily rescued.

Rafe, who had come in search of her to show off his latest bit of handiwork, stepped inside the chamber just as Caitlan swayed backward. Within seconds, he scrambled up the ladder to catch her in his strong embrace. Even though he stood one rung below Caitlan, Rafe towered over her and, with one arm wrapped snugly about her waist, his other arm came around to grab hold of the curtain rod. Caitlan's jumbled brain had barely comprehended the fact that she had been spared a horrible accident when it was pitched headlong into another emotional quandary. She was to be forgiven this mental lapse, however. Indeed, what woman's sensibilities would not be affected by a pair of hard, muscular thighs thrust intimately against her backside? For Caitlan the sensation was—in a word—dizzying.

She did manage to effect some semblance of composure by the time Rafe fitted the cylindrical-shaped rod onto the brass holder. Thankful that the task had been completed and—more importantly—there was no reason for Rafe to continue to caress her in that . . . familiar way; that he could, in fact, peel his very intimidating body away from her more feminine curves, Caitlan breathed a sigh of relief. The hand that snuggled beneath her breasts and his warm breath that tickled the back of her neck indicated otherwise, however. Plainly, Rafe was in no great hurry to relinquish his cozy perch.

Clearing her throat, Caitlan said, in a voice that trembled ever so slightly, "Thank you, Rafe. It would seem you have come to my rescue yet again."

Rafe, whose hand—positioned as it was just beneath the curve of one voluptuous breast—could feel the frantic reverberation of her heart, smiled knowingly. Caitlan's agitation

was not the result of her near mishap, he correctly surmised.
Rafe recognized the symptoms of a woman in the throes of a
passionate denial when he saw one, and it pleased him to no
end to know that he could provoke this response from her.
Indeed, Rafe was gratified to find that a flame still flickered
beneath Caitlan's frosty facade. Oh, she did her best to conceal
it—that was true enough—but with the proper motivation, Rafe
was confident that those smoldering embers of hers could be
banked into an out and out conflagration.

*And heaven help the man who unleashes all that pent-up
passion,* came his silent thought.

Suddenly aware that the object of his lusty musings was
trying to wriggle from his grasp, Rafe chuckled and said, ''You
all right, Kettie? You didn't wrench your back or anything?''
He slid one hand along her arm and brought the other up to
her chin, forcing her to turn sideways to look at him.

''No, no, I'm . . . I'm fine,'' she gasped and, feeling suddenly flushed, pressed her fingers to her hot cheeks.

Caitlan was just thinking it very peculiar that Rafe always
seemed to turn the simplest of situations into a sensual encounter when a noise from the street commanded her attention.
The embarrassment she had momentarily experienced flared
into outright rage when she peered through the glass to observe
one red-headed, freckle-faced, Petey Wilson—the very same
who had tormented the girls with his frog and called her an
ugly old maid—hopping from foot to foot, howling with laughter and pointing his grimy finger at their image through the
window. Caitlan's initial reaction was to run the little monster
to ground and give him a sound thrashing, but realizing that
any such response would only encourage him all the more, she
wisely curtailed her vengeful urges. Though she willed herself
to ignore Petey's taunting gestures, Caitlan's nonchalant demeanor belied her underlying perturbation to which her subsequent blasphemous mutterings attested.

Rafe, at once shocked and amused by Caitlan's reaction to
the gangling lad, pinched her arm. ''Kettie! Mind your tongue,
young lady.''

''I cannot help myself where that . . . that *boy* is concerned.
I would dearly love to box his ears. He would try the patience
of a dozen saints,'' Caitlan defended her outburst. Pushing his

hand aside, she motioned him down the ladder.

Rafe obliged her, but by the time his boot struck the bottom rung, he paused and directed his pensive gaze toward the now-deserted street. "Do you think people gossip about us? That is, the fact that you're a single woman—alone and all—with me living in the room out back? I mean, people are bound to have noticed."

Caitlan, noticing the serious frown that deepened the blue eyes, said, "Don't give Petey or the residents of this town a second thought. Besides, why would anyone waste time gossiping about me? I'm just a dreary old maid, after all . . . no one of consequence."

Rafe was thinking that it was Caitlan—and not the nefarious Petey Wilson—who needed her ears boxed for making such a halfwitted statement when an apathetic meow from beneath the ladder caught his ear. The interruption served to remind Caitlan of the nauseating gift Beau had deposited on the rug she had just cleaned. Shaking a mental finger at the disinterested cat, she released the hand that Rafe had offered in helping her down the last remaining steps and turned straightaway toward the door.

"Whoa!" he called, catching her by the arm. "Just where in blue blazes are you running off to?"

"To fetch the dustpan." Caitlan inclined her head at the tiny brown corpse that lay just inches from Rafe's dust-covered boots. Bending down to scratch Beau behind the ear, she said, "He is everything you said he was . . . and more." She nodded toward the pathetic-looking mouse. "He brings me at least two of those a day, plus an occasional bird or rabbit—for which he receives a stern scolding, I might add." She straightened and leveled an accusing eye at the bored cat who merely "meowed" and looked away. "And when I came down to the kitchen this morning, I found Beau standing guard over his latest quarry . . . a garter snake. But, as it turns out, this wily victim was only playing possum. When Beau ran over to greet me, the snake flopped onto its belly and slithered away.

"Poor fella," she purred at the cat. "I suppose there is little else for him to do. He must find life with me woefully unexciting as compared to his previous owner's. I mean, all I do in *my* bed is sleep." Caitlan gave a startled gasp following this last statement; she could not believe she had said that aloud. But she must have, for her cheeks were growing hot with embarrassment and there was Rafe, regarding her with the most bemused expression.

He did not have to say a word; Caitlan could read his thoughts as clearly as if they were front-page headlines on the *Vicksburg Daily Whig*. Thinking to escape before Rafe had the opportunity to put a voice to his scandalous thoughts, she bolted for the door.

"Wait, Kettie!" Rafe shouted. He overtook her in the corridor and, when she would have turned toward the kitchen, he grabbed her and whirled her about. Rafe pressed his hands against her shoulder blades and pushed her toward the front entrance.

"Dustpan," Caitlan mumbled, pointing a lame finger behind her and twisting her head about to gaze over her shoulder with longing at the shrinking portal at the opposite end of the hallway.

Taking her by the hand, Rafe stepped around in front of Caitlan and tugged her toward the door. "Do that later. I've got something to show you." He pulled . . . rather . . . dragged her along behind him. When they were outside, standing on the porch, he startled her by saying, "Close your eyes."

"What?!"

"You heard me. Close your eyes."

Reluctantly, Caitlan complied with his unusual request. Clutching his hand with both of hers, she allowed him to lead her down the steps. Once Rafe had positioned her to his satisfaction, he said, "Okay, open them."

Caitlan—suspicious of his motives, and rightly so—hesitated for a moment, then with a shrug opened her eyes. To be honest, she had not known what to expect, but her expression indicated that she was pleasantly surprised with her discovery. The mysterious object she had viewed earlier from the window proved to be a sign. From the looks of it, considerable thought and skill had gone into its making . . . from the elaborate fleur-de-lis crown, to the less intricate—albeit ornate—carved edges, to the elegantly scripted, "Katie's Tearoom," that was boldly emblazoned in black across a starch-white background. All in all, it was an impressive piece. Without asking, Caitlan knew who had been responsible for its design and craftsmanship.

"I . . . I don't know what to say, Rafe," she murmured, touched by his thoughtful gesture.

"Well, you needed a sign. Otherwise, the good people of Vicksburg would have no way of knowing that this is—or soon will be—the finest dining establishment in the city," Rafe informed her. Digging his hands in his pockets, as he was wont to do when he had been a lad forced to deal with an awkward situation, he asked, "Do you like it? I mean, the name and all. I was of half a mind to put 'Kettie's Tearoom' instead, but I kind of like knowing that I'm the only one who calls you that. But if you had your heart set on some other name, I can always change it."

"No. The sign is perfectly lovely as it is, Rafe," Caitlan assured him. She lifted her hand to his cheek and, as her fingers gently stroked at his beard, she murmured a grateful, "Thank you."

Rafe reached up to clasp the slender hand that still hovered along his cheek and their eyes met. Feeling more sure of himself, he stepped closer and his gaze never faltered when he brought her hand up to his lips. "You're welcome, Kettie" came his husky whisper.

Surprisingly, Caitlan did not wrench her hand away when Rafe pressed his lips against the sensitive flesh, nor did she appear disgusted by his impulsive act. In truth—though she was loath to admit it—Caitlan's resistance was beginning to crumble. In fact, seeing Rafe day in and day out for nearly three months had begun to take its toll on even her staunch resolve. Despite her efforts to ignore him, she realized that the old charm was working.

For example, Caitlan knew that Rafe was about to kiss her; all the telltale signs were in evidence. He had pulled her so close that their bodies were touching and, while his hand gently played with a wisp of hair alongside her ear, his arm encircled her waist in a purposeful gesture. Oh, yes, he most certainly was going to kiss her; right there where they stood on the lawn, where any passerby could plainly see. The rational-thinking Caitlan had the decency to be scandalized by Rafe's rakish intentions. She resisted the urge to pull away, however, for her whimsical musings prevailed.

In a daze, Caitlan became aware of some imp inside her head silently cheering Rafe on, shouting, *Go ahead, Rafe. Let Petey Wilson gawk . . . bother, let the whole town see. Give them something to talk about!*

Caitlan heard his throaty chuckle and, fearful that—as before—she had blurted her thoughts aloud, she glanced up. She worried needlessly; there was a look of fond reassurance on the face that drew near hers. Sensing that something portentous was about to happen, Caitlan closed her eyes and waited. She tingled with anticipation of Rafe's mouth gently caressing her own; indeed, even though any number of years had passed since she had last experienced that marvelous sensation with him, she could still remember how it was . . . could almost taste the sweet memory.

Rafe's lips were but a hairsbreadth from giving Caitlan a somewhat more tempestuous memory when Hezekiah's excited shout startled them, causing the couple to spring apart. "Miz Katie, Miz Katie!" Hezekiah's voice rambled down the hallway from the dining-room and echoed out the front door to mingle with Rafe's frustrated oath. "Miz Katie? Come quick! Come, look at what ah found."

Caitlan stared down in wonder at the strongbox full of paper currency and gold and silver coins and asked for the tenth time, "Are you absolutely certain you found all this under the dining-room floor?"

"Yes, ma'am." Hezekiah nodded. "Like ah done tolds you, I was fixin' to replace that section of warped floor yondah. But, when ah sticks the crowbar undah the plank and starts to pry it free, ah notices somethin' funnylike. It turns out the board was already loose. When ah lifts it up, ah founds this here strongbox sittin' in that hole just as pretty as you please."

Caitlan looked at the strongbox, at Hezekiah, at Rafe, before her stupefied gaze eventually resettled on the pile of money. She unconsciously licked her lips and said, "There must be at least a thousand dollars here."

"At least," Rafe drawled, his circumspect gaze finding its way to Hezekiah's face.

"But . . . but where did it come from?"

"Ah'd guess Miz Delia done hid it here for safekeepin'."

You know, in case she evah had an emergency and needed some money quicklike" came Hezekiah's plausible explanation.

Caitlan, nervously fingering a gold coin, asked, "What should I do with it, do you think? Should I make Delia's attorney aware of this?" These questions were directed at Rafe, however, it was Hezekiah who was quick to respond.

"Naw, Miz Katie!" he exclaimed. "Ah mean . . . that is . . . well, it appeahs to me that, since Miz Delia done left everythin' she had to you, this here money rightfully belongs to you. If you go talkin' to one of them fancy mouthpieces, he'll most likely find a way to swindle you out of some of it, callin' it a fee or some such. Wouldn't you say so, Mistah Bradrick?"

Rafe, who had taken up a stance near the fireplace, leaned his imposing form against the mantelpiece. His expression ever thoughtful, he said, "Yes. Yes, Hezekiah, I do believe you're most likely right."

"See, Miz Katie." He smiled broadly. "Even Mistah Bradrick agrees with me, and you knows it ain't often that the two of us sees eye to eye on anythin'. Now, you got enough money here to get that Tuttle woman off'n your back and still have a tidy sum left ovah to keep you comfaht'ble until your tearoom gets on its feet," Hezekiah said patiently, as if explaining an important detail to a small child. "But ah don't recommends you follah Miz Delia's example of hidin' your valuables in a hole in the floor. Aftah all, ah'm gettin' ready to fix it up good as new. Mebbee you ought to take yourself on ovah to Mistah Cord's bank and open up an account afore he closes for the day," he suggested, avoiding the discerning gaze that Rafe continued to level at him.

Caitlan, thinking that a very wise suggestion, snapped the lid closed on the metal container and stood up from the floor where she had been kneeling. Glancing down at the pendant watch pinned to her blouse, she murmured, "I should have just enough time if I leave now." With the coveted box tucked under her arm, she bobbed up on her toes and pecked Hezekiah on the cheek. "Thank you," she whispered. "To be honest, I've been having doubts about going forward with my plans to open a business. This should make things easier for a while."

"Shucks, Miz Katie." Hezekiah blushed. "All ah did was

dig up your floor like you done asked me to. If'n anyone deserves thankin', it's the good Lord for givin' us this crazy Vicksburg weather what caused that piece of flooring to warp so, else ah nevah would've found the strongbox. Now, get on ovah to the bank, sose ah can finish this here chore afore nightfall. You don't want me leavin' anothah openin' for them mice to skitter through, does you?''

"No, I should say not.'' Caitlan laughed, turning to the door. She took a step toward the open portal, then on impulse, wheeled and ran over to Rafe. Before he could comprehend her purpose, she stood on tiptoe and bussed his cheek. ''And thank you, too. For my beautiful new sign, for helping me put this house in order and . . . well, just for being my friend these past few weeks. I could never have done this without you.''

Rafe, his arms aching for want of holding Caitlan against him and kissing her the way those tempting lips of hers were begging to be kissed, had to content himself with watching her walk away. As she stepped across the threshold, he heard himself say, ''Hold on a minute, Kettie. What are you thinking about? You can't go traipsing through the streets by yourself.''

''Of course I can,'' she countered. ''I do it all the time.''

''Not carrying a strongbox full of money, you don't,'' Rafe reminded her. Observing her lips form a silent ''oh'' of understanding, he said, ''I'll walk with you, if you like.''

Caitlan nodded her acquiescence and said, ''I won't be but a moment,'' before darting up the stairs to tidy her appearance.

Rafe smiled to himself, flattered at the hidden inference behind Caitlan's actions—if she was going to be seen with him, she wanted to look her best. Shaking his head, he walked over to the door. Keeping an eye on the staircase, lest Caitlan reappear and overhear his comments, he said to Hezekiah, ''Why?''

''Why what?''

''Let's have done with the charade, shall we?'' Rafe said, though not unkindly. His voice softened and there was a hint of admiration flickering in the blue eyes when he said, ''Why didn't you just give Kettie the money? Why go to all this trouble?''

Hezekiah, who had knelt down to measure a length of pine flooring, slowly climbed to his feet, his brown stare never wavering from Rafe's face. His countenance was pensive as he thumped the crowbar against the palm of his hand. Hunching his shoulders, he said, ''You ought to know Miz Katie by now. She's as stubborn as the day is long. She nevah would've taken the money if'n she'd knowed it was from me.''

Rafe considered this and said, ''That must have been your life savings, Hezekiah.''

''Most of it.''

''What about Abbie? I thought you were saving your money, so you could buy her freedom from Cantrell.''

''Mistah Cantrell ain't nevah gonna let mah Abbie-gal go, Mistah Bradrick. Leastways, he'll nevah agree to me havin' her, not so long as Miz Katie keeps tellin' him no.'' Rafe noticed the lethal grip by which Hezekiah clutched the crowbar and imagined he was wishing it was Cantrell's neck instead. ''But don't you worry none. Ah'll gets mah Abbie-gal someday. One way or the othah, we'll be togethah. And Miz Katie won't be hurt none in the bargain neithah.''

The closing of a chamber door above stairs alerted Rafe to the fact that Caitlan would presently rejoin them. His eyes never leaving the staircase, Rafe's tone held a note of sympathy when he said, ''I know firsthand what it's like to be separated from the one you love. You feel empty inside, like there's no reason to keep on living. But you do . . . and you keep hoping, too. Never lose hope, Hezekiah. I'm certain you'll be reunited with your Abbie soon.

''You're a fine man, Hezekiah. Kettie is lucky to have had you to look after her all these years.'' He wanted very much to tell Hezekiah that looking after Caitlan was a task he fully intended to assume henceforth, but her arrival in the foyer prevented him from making any such presumptuous announcement.

Hezekiah heard the closing of the front door and, confident that he was alone, devoted his attention to the task at hand once more. It was a somber frown that twisted the brown face, however, as he bent down, muttering to himself, ''Ah do thanks you for your kind words, Mistah Bradrick. Ah might be a fine man like you says, but ah'm a damn lonely one, too.'' His expression akin to that of one who was privy to some grave secret, Hezekiah added, ''But not for long.'' He fitted the piece of pine flooring into place and gave it a satisfying jab with the hammer. "No, suh. Not for long."

The day of the grand opening of Katie's Tearoom arrived. As one might suspect, Caitlan could be found rushing madly through the house making certain that all was in readiness in anticipation of her first customers. A cursory inspection of the dining-rooms revealed her worries to be groundless; Essie had been faultless in carrying out Caitlan's instructions. Each table had been laid out to her specifications; complete with table-cloth, table setting, and linen napkins. A copy of the menu—fresh from the printer and listing the tearoom's standard offerings—lay on each table. An easel supporting a blackboard upon which was written the tearoom's hours of operation, as well as the day's special fare, stood on the porch just outside the door to welcome visitors.

Satisfied that they were indeed ready to do business, Caitlan smiled to herself as she made her way back to the kitchen. Her establishment might not be as elegant as some of Vicksburg's more fashionable restaurants, she conceded, but she was proud of it just the same. In fact, Caitlan thought that her mix-and-match assortment of tables and chairs and casual decor lent a homey atmosphere to the place, and she was certain her patrons would be put instantly at ease in the quaint setting.

The smell of tansy wafted across the room to envelop Caitlan's nostrils as she entered the kitchen. She had hung a cluster of the smelly weeds in the window as a deterrent to flies, however, she would presently lament that the plant's powers did not extend to troublesome urchins. The pungent aroma reminded Caitlan that she had placed two cherry pies on the window ledge to cool upon taking them from the oven. Thinking that she would go ahead and slice the pies for serving later, Caitlan turned toward the window.

Her whimsical smile was destined to be replaced by a dis-believing frown and then an outright scowl; as Caitlan approached the embrasure, a pair of grubby hands appeared from nowhere to snatch one of the pies from the windowsill. She did not have to see the culprit's freckled face to recognize his identity, however.

The tearoom's opening forgotten and, in complete disregard

'or the spectacle she created, Caitlan bolted from the kitchen. Clutching her skirt in her hand, she emerged from the house, shouting, ''Petey Wilson, you odious child! Come back here this instant!''

She rounded the corner of the kitchen in time to see a pair of gangly legs scramble over the fence and disappear behind the carriage house. Calculating the young thief's escape route, Caitlan wheeled and ran toward the front of the house. Impervious to the curious stares of an elderly couple who stood on the porch perusing the blackboard, she barreled through the gate in hot pursuit of the infamous Petey Wilson. At the corner of Walnut and Grove, Caitlan paused to glance up and down the thoroughfare, hoping to catch sight of the fleeing youngster, and was nearly knocked over by the larcenist himself.

Momentarily caught off guard by the unexpected collision, Caitlan promptly recovered her wits and reached out to grasp Petey's ever-tempting ear. She was persuaded to relinquish that appendage in the very next instant, however, when the quick-thinking Petey—who was by no means a novice when it came to eluding outraged crime victims—reacted by stomping on Caitlan's foot. When she jerked away from him, wincing with pain, Petey darted away. Despite her painfully throbbing toes, Caitlan gave chase, running for all she was worth. In fact, she found that her persistence was paying off; she was gaining slightly on the speedy youth . . . that was until he turned the corner from Walnut onto China Street.

About halfway up the block, Caitlan witnessed another sight that proved to be far more distressing than a mere pilfered pie. For she caught a glimpse of a tall, bearded gentleman trotting up the steps of one of the bordellos that littered China Street. There was no mistaking that muscular physique or those darkly handsome features. Forgetting Petey Wilson and the stolen pie, Caitlan stopped in her tracks and observed as a scantily clad woman flung wide the brothel house door and stepped out onto the porch to greet Rafe.

Caitlan felt a sudden tightening in her chest as the painted-up woman entwined her lily white arms about Rafe's neck and pulled him inside. For a moment, as she stood holding a hand to her aching side and gasping for breath, Caitlan thought she might be physically ill. But a loud whoop of laughter brought

her attention back to the matter that had—fatefully—brough
her to this place and, lifting her eyes toward the sound, sh
saw Petey scampering off in the distance. Conceding the pi
as a lost cause and, with a parting, hurtful look at the despisec
house, Caitlan turned toward home.

By the time she arrived at the tearoom, however, her hur
had blossomed into full-blown anger. This was made apparen
by her ruthless slamming of the kitchen door.

"Whoa there, Miz Katie," Hezekiah scolded as Caitlar
threw herself onto a kitchen chair. "You don't want to scares
your customahs away, does you?"

"What customers?" she asked sulkily.

"What customahs?" Hezekiah repeated. "Is you blind"
Them rooms of yours is plumb full of folks just waitin' to have
themselves a taste of your cookin'. Poor Essie's been flittin
around here tryin' to wait on customahs and dish up vittles
too. Why, she was near to tears when ah happened by. Where
you been anyways?" he asked, his thoughtful gaze scanning
her gloomy face. "It ain't likes you to run off when you is
needed."

"Never mind that now," Caitlan snapped, jerking her apror
from the hook behind the door. "What does Essie need?"

Hezekiah, who had just ladled a helping of stew onto a plate
gladly relinquished the stove to its worthy mistress. Pluckin₃
a fluffy biscuit from the pan that sat warming in the oven, he
dropped it onto the plate and said, "She needs anothah disl
of stew and a helpin' of fried chicken. Oh, and Mistah Morgar
is here from the boardin' house. He says for you to fry hin
up one of your steaks likes you used to do when you workec
for Miz Tuttle."

As Hezekiah talked, Caitlan bustled about the kitchen, preparing the requested orders. "Here. Take these into Essie,"
she said abruptly, thrusting the plates of hot food into Hezekiah's surprised hands. "And tell Mr. Morgan I'll have his steak
ready in a trice," she called over her shoulder, reaching inside
the icebox to select a thick beefsteak and tossing it into the
hot frying pan.

Thus the dinner hour proceeded. Caitlan no sooner filled
one order than a breathless Essie appeared at the door with
another. By midafternoon, however, the crowd had petered

out, leaving Essie with but a smattering of customers to attend. While the tired, but exhilarated, young woman saw to these straggler's needs and tidied the dining areas, an exhausted Caitlan began preparing for the evening patrons. Hezekiah was sitting at the table, counting out the afternoon's earnings and Caitlan was standing at the sink with her hands immersed in dish water when a familiar voice made her stiffen with rage.

"It appears that Katie's Tearoom is a resounding success. At least that's the word on the street," Rafe said from the doorway, his tone jovial. "And I overheard one man say to another as he was just leaving that he had never tasted anything so scrumptious in his life, after which his wife promptly boxed his ears." Rafe laughed and stepped into the room, doffing his hat as he did so. "So, what do you think, Kettie? Are you pleased with how the day turned out?"

Caitlan did not offer an immediate answer; it took her a moment to unclench her hands from the side of the sink. Eventually, she did turn to face the lecherous swine. However, Rafe was understandably confused by her subsequent actions.

"Get out!" she seethed between taut lips.

Rafe, who had been about to take a seat at the table, paused in midstride. His expression was incredulous when he asked, "What?"

"You heard me!" she shrieked.

When Rafe continued to demonstrate an annoying reluctance to comply with her wishes, Caitlan—now beside herself with unleashed anger—grabbed the first weapon she could get her hands on . . . a mop. Wrapping determined fingers about the long handle, she wrenched it from the bucket of dirty mop water and aimed the dripping mophead at Rafe in a menacing gesture.

"Kettie?" Rafe drawled, eyeing the mop with foreboding.

"Shut up!" she snapped and jabbed him in the chest with the wet mop.

The punch caught Rafe unawares and caused him to stumble backward. Regaining his balance, Rafe swore, "Dammit, Kettie! What the hell is wrong with you?"

"What is wrong with *me*?" Caitlan all but screamed at him. "I'll tell you what . . . *you!*" she shouted and punched him again, prodding him toward the door. "You're what is wrong with me. I cannot stand to look at you. Get out!''

''Kettie,'' Rafe rasped, his voice gravelly. Looking down at the blotchy stain that spread across his shirt, Rafe's jaw began to twitch . . . a sure indication that he was but seconds away from losing his temper.

Whatever Rafe might have been about to say would remain forever an enigma, however. Caitlan, having grown sick of the sight of him, lunged forward and shoved the drenched mophead into his face. Thus disoriented by the watery deluge, she was able to push him toward the door. Rafe was not done for yet, however. Though he sputtered uncontrollably, he was determined not to be dismissed without having his say. Groping blindly, he wrenched the mop from Caitlan's hands.

He looked prodigiously silly, Caitlan thought, dripping from head to toe as he was with filthy water. Though these were her private thoughts, she did not voice them aloud. Rafe also looked frightfully dangerous, glaring at her with those eyes of cold blue steel, eyes that looked for all the world as if he could murder her where she stood.

Flinging the mop aside, Rafe took a faltering step toward her and growled, ''Goddammit, Kettie! What the devil has got into you?''

Though Caitlan stood her ground, she clenched her lips together, refusing to answer him.

''Kettie!'' Rafe repeated, his tone threatening.

''Go ask your precious Sadie,'' Caitlan spewed.

''What?!''

''You heard me'' came her embittered reply.

''For Christ's sake, Kettie. You don't have any idea what you're talking about. Let me explain,'' Rafe said and took another step forward.

Snatching a butcher knife from the counter, Caitlan waved the ugly-looking weapon at Rafe in a manner that indicated she would not hesitate to use it. ''You don't have to explain anything, just *get out*!''

Hezekiah, who had been drinking all this in with rapt interest, suddenly decided that matters were treacherously close to getting out of hand. Standing, he crept up behind Caitlan and plucked the knife from her hand. Wrapping his arms about her waist to keep her from charging full tilt at her onetime sweetheart, he looked across the top of her russet-tinged curls to a thoroughly bewildered Rafe and said, "You best do as Miz Katie says, Mistah Bradrick."

"But—" Rafe started to protest.

"Go on now . . . get," Hezekiah said, motioning toward the door with the knife. "Ah'll do mah best to settle her down, but ah ain't got no chance of doin' that lessen you takes yourself off." Hezekiah, who witnessed Rafe's tortured countenance as he continued to stare at Caitlan, felt a pang of remorse for the younger man and added softly, "Please, Mistah Bradrick."

Rafe, still distraught by Caitlan's unprecedented outburst, cast a parting look over her before turning to take his leave. The door had no sooner closed behind his slumped shoulders than Hezekiah exhaled a sigh of relief and pushed Caitlan— none too gently—onto a chair. Taking a seat opposite her, he tossed the knife onto the table and said as if adjuring a small child, "Now Miz Katie, suppose you go and tell old Hezekiah just what bee it is you've taken into your bonnet this time."

Later that night, long after the "Closed" sign had been hung in the window and the last dish had been dried and put in the cupboard, Caitlan climbed the stairs to her bedchamber. She presently sat on the stool before her dressing table mirror, brushing her brown-and-russet curls into a silky luster. The measured strokes gradually subsided and, laying the brush aside, Caitlan's moody gaze studied her reflection in the polished looking glass. Though her temper of the afternoon had waned, Caitlan pinkened when she recalled the irrational words she had screeched at Rafe. Even now, she could hardly believe that she had conducted herself in that wholly shrewish manner.

She had acted despicably, but had she the opportunity to do things over, Caitlan knew that—given the exact circumstances—she would behave the same way . . . with one exception. If the opportunity presented itself again, Caitlan would take that knife and plunge it squarely into Rafe's black heart. Her thoughts now riveted on that terrible scene with Rafe, she allowed her musings to drift to the afternoon's conversation she had with Hezekiah. In spite of the comforting words her old friend had offered after Rafe departed, Caitlan remained skeptical of Rafe's association with that . . . painted woman.

Caitlan had confessed the whole story to Hezekiah, how she had chased Petey Wilson onto China Street and her subsequent scandalous discovery. But rather than being upset—or even the slightest bit shocked—by Rafe's debauchery, Hezekiah had merely mulled these findings for a moment and said, "Don't you think it's obvious what the man is doin', Miz Katie? He's protectin' you."

"Protecting me?" Caitlan had laughed, unconvinced. "From what?"

"Idle chitchat. The town gossip mongers who ain't got nothin' bettah to do than sit around and talk 'bout decent folk. And from hisself most likely" had been Hezekiah's candid answer. "You see, Miz Katie," Hezekiah had gone on to explain, "men has . . . uh . . . certain *needs*. And a big, strappin' fella like Mistah Bradrick . . . well, that is to say, you can't 'spect him to go without a woman forevah. Ah suspects he has taken up Miz Sadie's acquaintance sose people round town won't speculate 'bout what might be goin' on in this here house betweens the two of you."

Caitlan knew that Hezekiah had told her these things in an effort to appease her troubled spirit. But the mere idea of Rafe entwined in that woman's arms doing . . . oh . . . unspeakable things, only made her feel more depressed than ever.

"Then it could very well be that nothin' goes on once Mistah Bradrick gets inside. Mebbee he only wants people to *think* he's goin' there for . . . well," he coughed awkwardly, "you know," Hezekiah had said. Even to Caitlan's gullible ears, his words had sounded doubtful. "Ah means, you only seen him step inside. You don't know what went on aftah that door closed behind him."

Albeit Caitlan had made a small groaning sound in the back of her throat, her musings had remained her own. *Oh, Hezekiah*, had been her silent rumination, *you have no idea just how right you are*. Caitlan could only guess at what went on behind the closed doors of those houses in which Sadie—and women like her—lived, or even in the bedchambers of decent married couples for that matter. She had no firsthand knowledge of the intimacy that men and women shared; only a nagging, compelling desire to know.

Hezekiah had concluded by adding a ruthlessly frank observation that had the effect of a stake being driven through her heart. "Besides," he had said, watching her closely, "what the man does with his time ain't really none of your concern, now is it, Miz Katie? Ah mean, like you done told me the mornin' aftah you brung him to Miz Tuttle's . . . he don't mean nothin' to you no more, does he? Does he, Miz Katie?"

Caitlan had avoided her faithful friend's eyes and given her head a halfhearted shake. Though she might lie to Hezekiah and even to Rafe himself, there was no denying it to herself. Rafe had—just as he always did—somehow managed to worm his way inside her heart. He had, in truth, come to mean more to her than she had ever thought was again possible. And it hurt—oh, how it hurt—to know that he preferred the arms of his sultry Sadie to hers.

Caitlan, her ponderings now ensconced in the present, allowed her gaze to drift to the mirror once more and felt only disgust for the lonely, desolate image that stared back at her. But before she could lose herself in a fit of the sulks, there came a pounding at the front door. Fearful that it was Rafe come to have it out with her for her totally unwarranted behavior—and in no mood to deal with him at the moment—Caitlan decided to let him wait until the morning.

The pounding persisted, however, until unable to endure the earsplitting sound a moment longer, Caitlan stood up and pulled her dressing gown tightly about her. On impulse, she collected the derringer she had recently purchased—a woman living alone needed to be able to protect herself—from the bedside table and slipped it into her pocket. Then squaring her shoulders, she went to greet her late-night caller.

Chapter Ten

❦❧

The relentless hammering at the door continued until an exasperated voice was obliged to call out tersely, "All right, all right! I'm coming. Hold on just a blessed minute." An agitated hand grasped the door latch and wrenched the barrier open. The annoyed look that had momentarily twisted the troubled face vanished straightaway, however, upon finding a thoroughly distraught visitor on the doorstep.

"Kettie?!" Rafe blurted. His surprise at finding Caitlan knocking on his door at such a late hour was surpassed only by the concern that sluiced through him when he observed her disquieted mien. "Kettie," he repeated, his voice low and comforting, and stepped out onto the narrow landing beside her.

The stairway leading up to the small apartment was located just inside the carriage house and was encased in complete darkness. Silently, Rafe wondered how Caitlan had managed to scramble up those treacherous steps without breaking her neck. Peering behind her into the black abyss, he strained his eyes to see if by chance she was being chased by some sinister being. When the searching blue eyes detected no imminent threat, Rafe draped a sinewy arm about Caitlan's shoulders and nudged her inside.

"My God, you're trembling!" Rafe exclaimed. Turning Caitlan to face him, he gripped her upper arms and shook her roughly, saying, "What is it? What's happened?"

Caitlan barely took note of the little shards of pain darting out from where the steely fingers dug into the soft flesh. She could think of only one thing, the single purpose that had driven her to Rafe in the middle of the night.

"Oh, R-R-afe." Caitlan shook her head in despair and her voice quivered despite her efforts to regain her composure. Then, willing herself to be calm, she cried, "Oh, Rafe! Something terrible has happened. I . . . I need your help. Please, say you'll help me!"

"Of course I will, darlin'," Rafe purred at her, his hand stroking her arm with a tender, soothing motion. Closing the door, he guided her into the room, saying, "I'll do anything you ask, you know that. But first you have to tell me what it is that has you so stirred up. What is it, honey?" His bemusement having subsided, he allowed his gaze to sweep over her, truly taking in her appearance, and he was startled by what he saw.

Caitlan stood before him in a state of virtual dishabille. From the mass of brown-and-russet tendrils that tumbled down her back in wild confusion, to the fist that clutched at the splayed opening of her dressing gown just beneath her heaving breasts, to the dainty bare toes that peeked out at him from beneath the frayed hem of her nightgown, she was in a word . . . disheveled. In fact, under different circumstances, Rafe would have found her attire to be charming, perhaps even alluring. At the present, however, he could think of only one reason for her distress and the bile rose in his throat as he leaped to the worst possible conclusion.

Growing purple with rage, Rafe gave Caitlan's slender shoulders another merciless shake and demanded hoarsely, "Who was it? Was it Cantrell? Did that bastard—"

"*No!*" Caitlan cried out, as if warding off some vicious blow. Frightened by the primitive rage that flared in those brilliant blue eyes, she could only stare at Rafe in stunned silence. Then reading his anguished face more clearly than the lines in a book, she suddenly understood. On impulse, Caitlan reached up to smooth his worried brow and whispered, "No, Rafe. It's nothing like that."

Rafe, clearly relieved by her statement—yet understandably confused—directed Caitlan toward a chair, asking, "Then what?"

Vaguely, Caitlan became aware of the dimly lit surroundings. Though Rafe had lived in the carriage house apartment for some weeks, this was the first time she had ever visited it. A cursory glance about the room served as a glum reminder of the cramped chamber that Harriet had so "graciously" provided for her all those years. Momentarily forgetting her reason for beating down Rafe's door at such a late hour, Caitlan clung to his arm as she absorbed the room's stark plainness.

A narrow bed with its dull iron rails and sagging mattress, whose lumps were plainly visible beneath a thin blanket, was shoved up against one drab wall. A single window provided the room's only source of ventilation from which hung a pair of dirty, tattered curtains. Besides the bed, the chamber's other meager furnishings consisted of a corner stand upon which reposed a porcelain pitcher and bowl—the bowl bearing an ugly hairline crack from which water presently seeped—above which hung a cockeyed picture of some faraway seascape. A leather, upholstered wing chair—that had seen better days considering the amount of stuffing that protruded from its myriad cracks and holes—sat beside the open window. Next to that stood a small table and reading lamp, with the final piece of furniture being an uncomfortable straight-backed chair onto which Rafe presently settled her.

Caitlan felt a tremor of shame creep up her rigid spine. After all that Rafe had done for her, it was unconscionable that he should be forced to live like this. Then the realization struck her like a glancing blow to the face; *she was no better than Harriet*. True, Caitlan reasoned, she had been caught up with all the hubbub and the excitement of opening her own business. Still, green eyes glistening with self-recrimination swept the dreary room once more, she should have done better by him . . . Rafe deserved better than this.

"I'm so sorry," she muttered, her blank stare focused on the dingy plaster-cracked walls above the rumpled bedclothes.

Rafe, unaware of Caitlan's rueful reflections, noticed the

direction of her gaze and immediately misconstrued her ambiguous mumblings. Thinking she was apologizing for keeping him from his bed, he dropped into the wing chair opposite her. Dismissing her concerns with a wave of his hand, he said, "Never mind that now. Tell me what it is that's troubling you, sweet pea."

Sweet pea, Caitlan thought with a wrenching heart. After those hateful, despicable things she had said and done to him, Rafe could still call her that. A lump gathered in her throat, making it impossible for her to speak and, as her eyes filled with unbidden tears, Caitlan proffered a wrinkled piece of paper to him, managing to croak out a raspy, "Hezekiah."

"What?" Rafe asked. Snatching the paper from her trembling fingers, he glanced down at Hezekiah's crude penmanship.

While most men would have been surprised to discover that the Negro could both read and write, Rafe was not. He recalled the stories that Caitlan had told him long ago of how Hezekiah—with her father's blessing—had learned these rudimentary skills right alongside her in the Thistledown nursery. Even now he was persuaded to smile at the thought of a strapping young man seated beside a scrawny lass of seven or so, their heads bent in rapt concentration over a slate or primary reader.

Dashing these fond recollections away with the blink of an eye, Rafe said, "What's happened to Hezekiah?"

"He . . . he is . . . gone" came Caitlan's sorrowful whisper.

"What do you mean . . . *gone*?"

"To get Abbie. He has gone to steal her away from Jeremy and run away to Canada," she said with restored equanimity, her manner as blithe as if she had just told Rafe that Hezekiah had run down to the corner market to fetch her a sack of flour rather than off into the night to commit a serious felony.

"Goddammit!" Rafe swore and raked his hand through his hair, adding a wretched, "I should have seen this coming."

"But how could you have known?" Those great pools of shimmering green, only moments earlier bright with unshed tears, now clear and questioning, looked at him.

"The money." Rafe shrugged. "Delia didn't put that money in the strongbox and bury it under the dining-room floor. Hezekiah did. I figure he must have wanted to make sure you were financially set before he took off. Fool!'' he hissed, leaving Caitlan unsure as to whom he meant; Hezekiah or himself. ''He's no doubt been planning this for weeks,'' Rafe theorized. Looking at Caitlan, he asked, ''How long have you known?''

''Only a moment ago,'' she explained. ''Essie brought me Hezekiah's note. He gave it to her when he left the tearoom this afternoon and told Essie to give it to me when we closed this evening. But you know Essie—how flighty she is—she forgot all about the note until she was getting ready for bed. Luckily, she thought it might be too important to wait until morning and brought it right over. . . . '' Her voice trailed off and her brow twisted into a maze of thoughtful lines.

The next moment, Caitlan's face sprang alive with emotion and, hugging her arms to herself, she wailed, ''Oh God, oh God! *I* should have known. I should have suspected he might attempt something like this. I knew how upset Hezekiah was about Abbie. I should have tried to stop him.''

Rafe, his tone soft, placed a consoling hand on Caitlan's knee and said, ''How could you have stopped him? No one knew that the big fella had taken this foolhardy notion into his head.''

''No, you don't understand. How could you? You were not there. You did not see the way Hezekiah looked at me when he said good-bye this afternoon . . . as if . . . as if—'' Caitlan remembered the haunted, infinitely sad expression that had clouded those big, brown eyes and her shoulders sagged as she said, ''As if that was indeed good-bye . . . forever.''

''No it isn't,'' Rafe said, his voice laced with grim determination. Standing, he plucked his coat from the back of the chair and shrugged it on. Then, striding across the floor, he knelt and pulled a rifle and gun-and-holster from beneath the bed.

''What . . . what are you doing?'' Caitlan's voice cracked with fear. ''What do you need those for?''

''You never know. I may need these where I'm going'' came his vague explanation. ''A man never knows what he may stumble upon on a darkened roadway, Kettie.''

''You mean, you mean . . . you're going after Hezekiah?''

''Of course. That's what you came to ask me, isn't it?''

Rafe straightened from buckling the holster about his trim waist.

"Yes, but—" She faltered and, turning her embarrassed face from his, mumbled, "I thought . . . well, after today, you would never want to see me again."

In a fraction of a moment, Rafe was stooping before her, balancing the deadly rifle across his muscular thighs and caressing her cheek with his knuckles. Smiling, he said, "Not bloody likely. No, ma'am, it will take more than a face full of dirty mop water to scare *me* off, Kettie Webber. And don't you forget it." Giving her chin a playful tweak, he walked to the door, saying, "Don't fret that pretty head of yours. I'll no doubt return—with Hezekiah in tow, mind you—in time for breakfast."

"Ah ain't goin' back, Mistah Bradrick," the black man growled between clenched teeth, his voice barely audible in the cool night air. "Ah ain't nevah goin' back . . . not without mah Abbie."

Rafe cast a wary eye over the club that Hezekiah wielded threateningly in one hand and blew a disheartened sigh. This was not going to be easy.

"Hezekiah," Rafe pleaded, his voice little more than a hoarse whisper. "You must listen to reason. I tracked you straight here, and in the dark no less. That wagon of yours leaves a trail a blind man could follow."

"Cantrell ain't half the trackah that you is" came Hezekiah's blunt retort. "Ah means, just coz he's got a face like a bloodhound, don't mean he's got the makin's of one. Ah can outrun him right enough."

"Not with that bum leg of yours, you can't," Rafe reminded him. "Listen, Hezekiah. Do you truly believe that you can just waltz onto Cantrell's plantation, find Abbie, then breeze out of Jefferson County unnoticed? He'll have his hounds on you by daybreak," Rafe scoffed. "You must have a plan, man!"

"Ah does," Hezekiah grunted. "Ah plans to go in there," he thumbed over his shoulder, "fetch mah Abbie-gal and gets the hell outta here."

Without dropping his guard, Rafe looked beyond Hezekiah

through the thick stand of trees and woodland foliage to the rows of tiny cottages where the slaves were quartered. Through the darkness, he could just make out a thin stream of smoke fluttering from the top of one of the chimneys. As he watched, the flow of smoke abruptly halted to be followed by two quick puffs, then three, then two, then the steady flowing stream of curling smoke returned.

Hezekiah, noticing the direction of Rafe's gaze, said, "That's Abbie. That's the signal she said she'd give when she was ready and all was clear. Ah has got to go now, Mistah Bradrick," Hezekiah hissed, the urgency registering plainly in his voice.

"I *am* sorry, Hezekiah," Rafe murmured, leveling his revolver at the Negro's chest. "But I cannot in good conscience permit you to go through with this half-baked scheme of yours. Cantrell and his men will have tracked you down by noon tomorrow and strung you up by nightfall. Besides, I promised Kettie I would bring you back."

"Don't go pointin' that gun at me lessen you intends to use it, Mistah Bradrick," Hezekiah warned, his expression grim. "And don't go toutin' Miz Katie at me neithah. Ah'm gonna miss her somethin' terr'ble, but sometimes a man's just gotta do what a man's gotta do. Do you remembah what you said to me when you found out it was me what put the money in the strongbox? You said that ah should nevah lose hope of bein' with mah Abbie, that you knows what it's like to be kept apart from the one you loves. Ah assumed then that you was talkin' 'bout Miz Katie.

"Well, ah don't know what it was that kept you from her all these years, but ah knows what's keepin' me from mah Abbie-gal, and Mistah Cantrell ain't gonna keep me from bein' with her no longah." Hezekiah put his hands on his hips and looked Rafe squarely in the eye. "So, if'n yer gonna shoot me, you might as well does it now, coz ah don't intends to leave without her."

Rafe returned Hezekiah's menacing scowl in full, carefully mulling the man's thought-provoking words. Eventually, the hoot of an owl pierced Rafe's thoughts, bringing him back to reality. With a careless shrug, he holstered the revolver and an impish grin fashioned his lips when he said, "Aw hell,

Hezekiah. You know damn good and well that I could no more shoot you than I could my own flesh and blood.''

Hezekiah's lips parted in a wide smile and, tipping his hat at Rafe, he said, "Thanks, Mistah Bradrick. Ah owes you one. You be sure and takes good care of Miz Katie now, you hear? Else ah may have to come back and gives you what for." He ducked his head and started to dart through the underbrush toward the cabin when a hand gripped his shoulder.

"Mistah Bradrick?!" Hezekiah protested.

"Shh! Do you want to wake the whole bloody plantation?" Rafe cautioned by putting a finger to his lips. Jerking his head toward the end cottage, he motioned for Hezekiah to follow him.

Hezekiah blinked in surprise. "What?! Does you mean to help me?" he whispered his disbelief.

"Don't let me stop to think about this, or I may very well change my mind." Rafe shook his head in wonder and chuckled to himself, saying, "Kettie will most likely rail and pout at me for a month if she finds out. But come on, Hezekiah." Rafe thumped him on the back and, crouching down low, said, "Time's a wasting and so is your Abbie." Then with blue eyes twinkling in the darkness, he lowered his voice to a conspiratorial whisper and mumbled, "I've got a plan."

Rafe folded down the edge of the newspaper he was reading and focused a surreptitious eye on Caitlan. The object of this covert surveillance sat on the sofa opposite him, glumly putting the finishing touches on a pair of curtains she was sewing for his room. Sighing, Rafe allowed his gaze to wander across the columned print once more.

Three weeks, he thought.

Three long, miserable weeks had passed since that fateful night Rafe had gone in search of Hezekiah. Thinking back, he still found it hard to believe that, rather than thwarting Hezekiah's scheme and bringing him back to Vicksburg, he had instead helped him secure his sweetheart's release. To make matters worse—if possible—he had then assisted the pair in their escape to freedom. Even now, Rafe did not know what had possessed him to change his mind and aid Hezekiah in the perpetration of—what was by all accounts—a flagrant criminal act. There was one thing, however, of which Rafe was certain. Caitlan was not aware of the role he had played in assisting Hezekiah, and he was determined that it should stay that way.

Oh, he supposed he would break over and tell her one day. Lord, there were so many things he longed to tell her, share with her. But for now, he would bide his time and wait. Perhaps when she had two or three children clinging to her skirt and another at her breast, when the most dangerous thing she could put her hands on was a pillow from the drawing-room settee. Then, and only then, would he tell her about Hezekiah.

A wistful gleam, put there by the thought of Caitlan snuggling a child—his child—to her breast, sparkled in the soulful blue eyes. In fact, it was a prodigiously winsome expression that settled on Rafe's handsome face. Smiling to himself, he returned to the reading of his evening tabloid in earnest.

In contrast, Caitlan's countenance was far from winsome. It was rather more morose. There was a simple explanation for her gloomy disposition, however. She was homesick for Hezekiah.

Hezekiah had been the one constant force in her life. Ever since she had been a little girl, growing up at Thistledown, he had always been there for her. Why, his had been the first name—"Mama" and "Papa" notwithstanding—that had tumbled from her lips as a baby. Hezekiah had taught her how to ride her first pony, then had been there to nurse her bloodied knee and dry her tears when that very same pony dumped her headlong into the creek bed. Hezekiah had been the one who protected her from local bullies like little Johnny Perkins, who had teased her with snakes and frogs and . . . worse . . . taunted her about the mother who deserted her.

It was Hezekiah who had brought her the news of Brendan's death in a bloody duel and—years later—her father's suicide. Both times, Hezekiah's broad shoulders had weathered her hysterical sobs, and he had comforted her until she fell unconscious in his arms from sheer exhaustion.

Caitlan had not truly wept in years, but she had come oh so close to blubbering out loud when Rafe—battered and weary from riding all night—had stumbled into her kitchen that fateful morning three weeks ago with the news. He had been too late. By the time he arrived at the Cantrell plantation, Hezekiah had already taken Abbie and fled. He had tracked them for a while, but a storm had blown up and washed away any visible signs of their tracks.

Caitlan blew a sad sigh. Hezekiah was gone. She would always hold a special place in her heart for him, that much was true. But who could she turn to now when she needed help? Who would look after her now that Hezekiah was gone?

Caitlan, having finished hemming the white ruffled curtain, bit the thread in two and returned needle and thimble to the sewing basket that sat upon the cushion next to her. Closing the lid, she folded the drapery and unthinkingly fondled the soft material as it lay upon her lap. *Who could she turn to now?* The unbidden thought haunted her and, without truly realizing it, Caitlan's gaze lifted to the gentleman who sat directly opposite her, casually perusing the *Daily Whig*.

Caitlan's melancholy ponderings vanished upon seeing his face, however. Indeed, she very nearly laughed out loud when she observed Rafe's moonstruck mien, prompting her to blurt, "For goodness sake, Rafe. Whatever are you reading?"

The paper made a distinctive rustling sound as Rafe, startled by Caitlan's outburst, jerked his head back to meet her twinkling gaze. "What?"

"Your face. You should see it," she tittered. "It's positively *glowing*. What *are* you reading?"

Rafe did his best to disguise the sheepish expression he felt creeping across his face. Just as he had been reluctant to give her a full and true confession about Hezekiah, Rafe was not about to reveal the details of his very amorous musings.

"Nothing," he said a little too quickly and none too convincingly. Seeing Caitlan's circumspect look, he added offhandedly, "The usual. Editorial upon editorial about secession. Those in favor, those against, not to mention the endless pratings from those yahoos who advocate outright war.

"Oh, here's something interesting," Rafe continued, glancing down at a headline that suddenly caught his eye. "It seems that the Ladies Auxiliary of the Vicksburg Preservation Society is sponsoring an autumn carnival to raise money to—" and here Rafe quoted, " 'aid in the restoration of the rustic Horne house and its beautiful rose garden.' Hmm," he droned and scratched his chin, the article having truly taken hold of his curiosity. "It says here that it's rumored George Washington once spent the night with the Hornes during his travels. I didn't know old George ever traveled this far west," he muttered to himself. Looking over at Caitlan, Rafe said, "What do you think, Kettie?"

"About George Washington?" Caitlan returned, her nose wrinkling with indifference. "I have no idea."

"No, silly," Rafe chided. "About the carnival. Would you care to go? It is Saturday next and the whole town is invited. The Millers, up on Jackson Road, have donated the use of their farm for the festivities. There will be games and prizes for the children, ice cream, a quilting bee and pie-judging contest for the ladies and, of course, more intrepid contests of skill for the men. No doubt the politicians will be out in droves, trying to win their adversaries over to their way of thinking," he mused, his expression sour. With a philosophical tilt of his head, Rafe conceded that one must often endure the bad with the good. Thus, he said, "Even so, it sounds like fun, don't you think, Kettie?"

Caitlan, who—in truth—had paid very little heed to Rafe's accounting of the upcoming event, hunched her shoulders and said, "I suppose."

The clock on the mantelshelf chose that moment to remind Caitlan of the lateness of the hour. Feeling suddenly tired, she stood up. "Is everything satisfactory with your room now?" She made reference to the thorough refurbishing his chamber had undergone in recent days.

Rafe nodded a reply and felt a pang of frustration as he watched Caitlan stride toward the door. He had come to look forward to these peaceful moments they spent together in the evenings in the quiet comfort of her sitting-room. But tonight, as always, the evening had ended long before he was ready to bid her a good night. Sitting there, biting back his disappointment, Rafe became aware of her soft fragrance wafting across the room to taunt his already strained sensibilities.

"Good. I'll hang these curtains in the morning. Good night, Rafe. Don't forget to lock-up downstairs," Caitlan called from the threshold. "Oh, and Rafe. About the carnival—" she added with a demure smile. "We'll see."

*   *   *

Caitlan stood atop the crudely crafted makeshift stage and grimaced as she felt the beads of nervous perspiration gather on her lip and in the hollow between her breasts. She resisted the compelling urge to pull the lace-edged handkerchief from her skirt pocket and dab at the annoying moisture on her face lest the watchful crowd was persuaded to place undue significance upon her actions. Caitlan did, however, fold her arms across her indignant bosom. Absently she fingered the top button of her blouse, and offered up a desperate prayer that she be swiftly delivered from this impossible situation. As she stood there, glaring alternately at the two men who were responsible for her embarrassing predicament, Caitlan found herself wishing—for at least the hundredth time in the past ten minutes alone—that she had never agreed to accompany Rafe to this wretched carnival.

That was not entirely true, she grudgingly admitted to herself. Caitlan had been having a perfectly lovely time, milling about the booths filled with homebaked goods and handcrafted items, eating the delicious ice cream, and bubbling with uncontrollable laughter as she watched Rafe manfully try to outlast the rapacious Billy Merritt in the much-touted pie-eating contest. Then Rafe had seen the sign about the auction.

ENJOY A PICNIC WITH YOUR FAVORITE GIRL. AUCTION AT 4:00, the notice had read.

"Come on," Rafe had cajoled. "It will be fun."

Caitlan's protests to the contrary had consequently fallen upon deaf ears as a determined Rafe literally dragged her through the group of spectators. Finally, she had managed to wrest her arm free of his domineering grip and hissed, "What will everyone think . . . Katie Webber—acting like a giddy schoolgirl! No, I tell you. I won't do it. This auction is meant for young sweethearts, not old spinsters like me."

If she lived to be a thousand, Caitlan would never forget how the carefree expression had withered from Rafe's handsome face. The heavy basket of food had landed against the stage floor with a loud "thunk" and Rafe, propping one shoulder against the pillar that supported the canvas roof and from which was tied a rainbow of gaily colored streamers, had turned to level a stony gaze at Caitlan.

"What's wrong with you?" he had demanded, his manner

terse. "You used to be a free spirit, willing to try or do most anything? Hell, I never knew what you might say or do next. Now look at you; all closed-up as tight as a tortoise in its shell, afraid to let life touch you." Rafe had shaken his head in utter frustration. "I don't know what to make of you anymore. What's happened to you, Kettie?"

Caitlan had stiffened at his harsh criticism. Pulling herself up proudly before him, she said, "Let's just say I have suffered a disappointment or two in my day that has somehow soured my perspective on life."

Her words scored a direct hit and Rafe—his countenance grim—had to forcefully repel the urge to drag her across his knee right there in front of the whole town and beat some sense into her stubborn hide. Instead, he had satisfied his primal desires by taking hold of Caitlan's elbow and propelling her toward the stage.

"Now, you listen to me, Caitlan Webber," Rafe had growled between tightly gritted teeth. "You are not the only person on whom life has played a cruel trick. Hell, woman," had come his cynical chuckle, "life is full of disappointments. I, myself, have experienced a few setbacks along life's fickle highway. Someday I'll tell you about them. At the moment, however, I want you to stop wallowing in self-pity. Now, get up on that stage and at least pretend to have a good time," he had ordered, giving her rump a push up the platform steps for good measure.

At first, Caitlan did not have to pretend; indeed, she became caught up in the spirit of the occasion. She had watched with knowing compassion as a shy, freckle-faced lad of eighteen or so had manfully outlasted those who bid against him for the right to dine with the not-so-bashful Sissy Prichard. Caitlan's interest had turned to outright mirth, however, as she observed the stout Mrs. Butler openly badger her henpecked husband into paying for the same privilege that—in all likelihood—he would have cheerfully relinquished to some other hapless soul for one evening.

All too soon it was Caitlan's turn to stand center stage before the attentive crowd.

"All right, gents," Max Olsen had bellowed, plunking Caitlan's bulging wicker basket down in front of her. Max, a longtime resident and merchant of Vicksburg, had agreed to serve as auctioneer for the event. With a reassuring smile toward Caitlan, he had addressed the onlookers. "You all know Miss Webber, proprietress of Katie's Tearoom—Vicksburg's newest eatery. Now, I just had myself a peek at what she's got packed underneath that checkered napkin and all I can say is one of you lucky fellas is in for a special treat. She's gone and prepared a feast fit for a king. The question is, which of you will it be? Now, who will start the bidding at one dollar?" Max had barked.

"Fifty cents," offered a ruddy-complected gentleman in the first row.

"Fifty cents?" Mr. Olsen had repeated, incredulous, pushing his hat back to reveal a silver-white head of hair. With hands on hips, he had trudged to the front of the stage and glowered at the man who dared to voice such a piddling bid. "Have you taken leave of your senses, Mr. Van Dorn? I'm talking fried chicken, glazed ham, and homebaked beans, with biscuits so light and fluffy they melt clean away in your mouth. And I'm fairly certain I caught a glimpse of a jar of Miss Katie's prize-winning pickled corn, a jug of sparkling apple cider, and there's a blackberry cobbler for dessert. Besides which, you get to pass an hour or so in the company of a mighty fine lady. Shucks, I'll bid a dollar for all that myself," Max Olsen had proclaimed.

"A dollar twenty-five cents," shouted another masculine voice nearer the back.

"That's the spirit," Max had cheered. Snapping his suspenders against his shirt, he had cocked his ear toward the crowd and asked, "Do I hear a dollar fifty cents?"

Thus the bidding had started. But what had begun as innocent fun, suddenly took an unfortunate turn.

Jeremy Cantrell, who had been lounging against his closed carriage door, listened with an amused ear as half-a-dozen men or more—most of them regular patrons of the tearoom—progressively increased their bids for the coveted honor. Their shouts ricocheted all around the auction site like a sudden barrage of bullets off a flat rock, but Jeremy had shocked them all to silence with his first bid.

"Twenty-five dollars," he had called from just outside the circle of activity.

As if one, the crowd had turned in unison to stare at the dignified gentleman, dressed in his Sunday best, who stood with his arms crossed, leaning against an impressive conveyance and smiling a crooked grin at the lady atop the platform. They all recognized him, of course. In fact, many of them knew of Jeremy's quest to woo Caitlan away from Vicksburg and into his spacious mansion near Cotton Hill. Jeremy, in turn, was acquainted with several of the auction participants and likewise knew that they lacked both the mettle and financial wherewithal to continue bidding. With a smug quirk of his brow, Jeremy had stuffed his thumbs inside his vest pockets and pushed away from the carriage to shoulder his way into the buzzing assemblage to collect his winnings.

Jeremy's haughty smile had momentarily withered into an embittered scowl, however. For when he curled his hand around the basket handle, a lazy voice behind him had drawled, "Twenty-five dollars, fifty cents."

Once again, the crowd had turned their collective heads toward the unexpected voice. This time, they had seen a man— who, though less smartly dressed, carried himself with a marked distinguished air—push away from the trunk of a towering oak tree and swagger toward the stage, an adversarial sparkle deepening a pair of crystal-blue eyes.

"Isn't that the man Miss Webber rescued up on the north bluff and nursed back to health?" Caitlan had overheard the hushed whisper from a lady seated behind her. "Perhaps what they're saying is true," had countered the soon-to-be auctioned miss to her right, and yet a third had hissed, "Well, Penelope Crawford says—"

But Caitlan had been unable to overhear the spiteful biddies' gossip; her attention had been commanded elsewhere. The buzz of the crowd had warned Caitlan that the onlookers were as curious as the ladies behind her as to the reason for Rafe's sudden interest in the proceedings. The gathering's quizzical murmurings had ultimately proved to be the least of Caitlan's worries, however. As she had watched, Jeremy released the basket and slowly turned to face Rafe.

Without batting an eye, he had promptly upped his offer.

"Twenty-six dollars."

As speculation ran rampant among the growing horde of intrigued spectators, the two men had entered into a feverish bidding war. There had been an underlying current of animosity that whiffled back and forth between the two men, and they— if not the others—had been aware that more than a mere picnic with Caitlan was at stake. Even Max Olsen had seemed nonplussed by the goings-on; indeed, it rapidly became apparent that his services were not needed. He no longer had to ask for bids; following every offer that Jeremy made, Rafe had issued an immediate counteroffer.

Thus the bidding had progressed for several nerve-racking minutes until Caitlan, perspiring freely and her cheeks as scarlet as the red-checkered napkin that lay draped atop the wicker basket, felt she could gleefully strangle the pair of them and not suffer a moment's compunction for her actions. How could they do this . . . make a laughingstock of her *and* themselves in front of the whole town? Yet, there they stood—two grown men—haggling over her like she was some prize Thoroughbred they had each taken a fancy to. Green eyes smoldered vengefully at the mere notion and, regardless of the victor in this ridiculous charade, Caitlan vowed to give him a tongue-lashing he would not soon forget.

Then Caitlan, suddenly aware that a hush had fallen over the assemblage, blinked in confusion and took a faltering step backward. Somewhere through the haze, Rafe's deep voice had penetrated her thoughts. "One hundred dollars."

One hundred dollars! was Caitlan's frantic thought. Gulping for the breath that had gushed from her lungs as though someone had struck her full in the stomach, Caitlan turned a near-hysterical glare on Rafe. *What could he be thinking? Had he lost his mind?! He didn't have that kind of money. And even if he did, what would everyone think?* A cursory glance at the stunned faces along the front row alone sufficed to answer this last unspoken question.

With a groan, Caitlan directed a beseeching look at Jeremy. She need not have bothered; that gentleman—whether in deference to Caitlan's sensibilities or perhaps he simply felt the price was too dear to pay just for the pleasure of her company—

made a conciliatory bow toward Rafe and stepped away from the platform.

Caitlan, however, would not swallow her anger quite so easily. As Rafe stepped forward to pay the auctioneer his due, amid raucous applause and much shoulder slapping, she gathered her skirt in her fists and swept down the steps to march off in a fit of pique. By the time Rafe had collected the picnic basket and worked his way through the boisterous crowd, Caitlan was but an indignant spot on the horizon.

"Kettie," Rafe called, smiling knowingly—not to mention appreciatively—at the glorious sway of her hips as she hurried away from him. "Kettie!" He all but shouted her name. When Caitlan still did not acknowledge his summons, Rafe blew a frustrated sigh and gave chase.

When Rafe caught up with Caitlan, he was out of both breath and patience. That would account for the rough way in which he grabbed her arm and twirled her around to face him.

"Dammit, woman!" he panted. "What's wrong *now?* Where are you going so all-fired mad?"

Caitlan instinctively tried to jerk her arm free, but Rafe held her steadfast. Anger swarmed in her throat with all the force of a summer thunderstorm as she blurted a single, scathing word, "Home!"

"Home? What on earth for? You cannot seriously mean to leave now, Kettie. There's still dancing and fireworks."

Rafe had no idea just how right he was about the fireworks. A more observant man would have been wary of the unbridled rage that burned in the smoldering green eyes. But Rafe was to be forgiven his oversight. After all, it appeared he had just spent a vast sum of money on a lady who had no desire to be seen with him.

With smarting pride and, heedless of the gathering tempest, Rafe said, "Besides, you're going the wrong way."

"What?"

"Vicksburg is about ten miles in the other direction," Rafe informed her, a lopsided grin twitching at his lips.

Rafe had not meant to taunt her, but the reality of the day's emotionally upsetting event seemed to overwhelm Caitlan all at once, causing her to lash out at him. Before either of them could comprehend her intent, Caitlan's hand shot upward to land a vicious blow across his cheek.

"How dare you humiliate me like that? I hate you. I *hate* you!" she cried. Caitlan regretted instantly her rash outburst and, horrified by what she had said and done, she bolted from the roadway to disappear into a stand of trees.

Rafe, staggered more so by the vehemence of Caitlan's words than from the force of the blow, took a moment to collect his rattled senses. Then letting the basket fall where it may, he too ran into the forest, calling out for Caitlan to wait for him, but to no avail. For some unfathomable reason, she had worked herself into a frenzy and nothing he could say or do would pacify her.

Rafe caught up with Caitlan just as she was about to crest a gently sloping knoll and, determined that she would hear him out, he lunged forward, catching her just below the knees. Caitlan cried out as she felt her legs buckle beneath her. In the next instant, she and Rafe were tumbling over and over down the grassy slope. When they finally came to rest alongside a rippling brook, Caitlan lay gasping for air on her back, with a disconcerted Rafe sprawled atop her.

When Caitlan realized what had happened and tried to wriggle out from underneath him, Rafe soundly squelched any such plan with a glaring look. In truth, he had not quite known what he might do when he finally put his hands on his quick-tempered minx. He supposed he would deliver a much-deserved thundering scold, but upon seeing Caitlan's thoroughly disheveled and vulnerable mien, Rafe did what he had been longing to do for ages . . . he kissed her.

Again, Rafe had no idea how Caitlan would react to his presumptuous behavior. Frankly, he did not truly care. He could concentrate only on the wondrous sensation of her breasts boring into his chest and the intoxicating nectar of her lips blending with his. One may imagine Rafe's surprise then, when having anticipated a full-scale resistance, Caitlan coiled her arms about his neck and returned the caress with yearning. In that incredible instant, as lips trembled hungrily—then, languidly—upon each other, seven interminable years of separation were obliterated to come crashing together in one, undefinable moment of perfect bliss.

With a sigh, Rafe lifted his mouth from hers. Brushing back the wayward russet-tinged tendrils that had broken free of their pins, he said throatily, "Humiliate you? I would never wantonly cause you grief, Kettie. Don't you know that?"

Caitlan nodded haltingly, left breathless from the passion of his kiss. Lifting a tentative finger to his cheek, she tenderly stroked the red welt that rose above the dark line of his beard. Her tone was sincerely penitent when she said, "I'm sorry, Rafe."

"Forget it."

"No, I cannot forget that easily. I . . . I don't know what possessed me to do and . . . and say such hurtful things to you. I . . . I don't hate you," she stammered and looked away at the myriad colors of the setting sun shimmering off the gurgling stream. "It's just that . . . well—" Caitlan pushed herself up on her elbows and looked Rafe squarely in the eye. "Where did you get a hundred dollars? And why on earth would you fritter away all that money on a stupid auction when you knew perfectly well that I had intended from the outset that you should share the contents of that basket with me?" With renewed pique, she pushed away from him and rolled onto her side.

Men, was Caitlan's wretched thought. *I shall never understand them.*

Frowning petulantly, she accused, "I'll have you know that this is all your fault, Rafe Bradrick. *I* was not the one who insisted on participating in that silly auction. Whatever possessed you to offer a hundred dollars for me?"

Rafe followed Caitlan's example by rolling onto his side. He propped himself up on one elbow and rested his head in the palm of his hand while he allowed his other hand to trace imaginary lines down Caitlan's arm. Her back was to him, making it impossible for Rafe to see her facial reaction to his answer. Plucking a blade of grass, he chewed thoughtfully on the sweet-tasting shoot while he carefully chose his reply.

Eventually, he hunched his broad shoulders and said, "I'm not sure. I only know that I would have gladly conceded my supper to the gluttonous Mr. Van Dorn, or any of the other young, pimply faced lads who were vying for the privilege of dining with you and your overflowing picnic basket. But you see, those gents had only one thing on their collective minds . . . food.'' His tone grew somber and there was a calculating glint flashing in the blue eyes that stared off in the distance as he added, "The same cannot be said, however, of your Mr. Cantrell.''

Caitlan smiled to herself when she detected the jealous inflection in his voice and, shifting onto her back, she stared up into Rafe's rugged face. "I do not love Jeremy,'' she whispered, lifting a hand to brush aside a clump of dirt that clung to his shoulder.

"I know that,'' Rafe grunted. "But the man is *always* around. He comes into the tearoom at least three times a week, and he's constantly asking you to accompany him to parties, or nagging after you to let him drive you to church on Sunday. The man grates on my nerves, Kettie. He came begging for a lesson today, and I was more than happy to teach it to him.'' Then a sheepish grin spread his lips and, looking down at her, he asked, "Still mad at me?''

"No,'' she admitted. "But I am famished. Where is the picnic basket?''

"Up on the road,'' he said, standing. Proffering his hand, he pulled Caitlan to her feet, urging, "Come on, we better go fetch it before Mr. Van Dorn or one of the others notices it. All this damsel-chasing has given me quite an appetite.''

They located the basket intact and found a quiet spot where they could dine in peace. Following their meal, they clapped along in time with the music while adults and children alike stamped about to the lively tunes. Rafe naturally invited Caitlan to dance, but her tumble down the hillside had left her with a slightly twisted ankle. Not wishing to aggravate it, she declined, but did agree to remain and watch the fireworks display. They sat upon a blanket and oohed and ahed along with the rest of the crowd as each rocket was launched into the heavens and exploded in all its splendor, lighting up the sky above them with little bursts of vibrant colors. They stayed until the last rocket had fizzled into oblivion, then a weary couple climbed into their buckboard and headed for home.

The witching hour was almost upon them by the time Rafe

maneuvered the vehicle into the carriage house. Caitlan, the memory of Rafe's kiss still sweet upon her lips, did not retire immediately to her chamber but rather contented herself with watching Rafe as he unhitched and brushed down the aged workhorse—also a part of her inheritance from Delia—and stabled him in the stall next to Wanderer. Rafe, in turn, murmured a friendly greeting to his own animal before turning to Caitlan.

She felt a shiver of anticipation race down her spine when she beheld his fiery, brooding gaze. From his expression, Caitlan sensed that he, too, had been remembering that tempestuous embrace alongside the stream. Knowing that, and fully aware of what could happen if she allowed Rafe to escort her inside, Caitlan did not cavil when he walked up to her.

Taking her hand in his, Rafe led her toward the house. They walked in companionable silence to the back door and, without saying a word, Rafe pulled Caitlan into his arms to give her a good-night kiss. Graceful arms lifted automatically to grasp onto a pair of sturdy shoulders as Rafe's head lowered with purpose toward her lips. But his mouth had barely settled upon the sweet tasting flesh when he heard a twig snap.

Rafe instinctively made a move for the pistol that bulged just inside his jacket. But upon hearing Caitlan's soft whimper of disappointment, he shrugged the noise aside, thinking it was more than likely just Beau out scavenging up game in the night. The subsequent ominous-sounding click of a revolver's chamber being rotated into position against his right ear, however, soon gave Rafe reason to regret his nonchalance.

Chapter Eleven

꧁ᳫ꧂

Caitlan had experienced all manner of fears during her life; the fear of being punished as a child for some trite wrongdoing, the fear of being left alone to fall asleep in a darkened room, the fear of losing a loved one, as well as the everyday fear of simply not knowing what tomorrow may bring. But, never in all her born days had Caitlan known the kind of paralyzing fear the likes of which presently set her whole being to trembling. She sat numbly on the straight-backed dining-room chair, gripping the seat so tightly that her flesh was stretched white across her knuckles . . . almost as white as the thin, drawn line of her mouth.

As she sat there, a jumbled mass of frightened nerves, a single thought kept pounding in her head. *Who were these men? What did they want of her and Rafe?*

Vaguely, she became aware of Rafe's hand, groping out at her in the darkness beside her. With a whimper, Caitlan released the viselike hold she had on the chair and grasped that welcoming appendage for all she was worth. Rafe did not say a word; he did not have to. The reassuring pressure of his powerful fingers as they gently squeezed her hand spoke volumes . . . everything would be all right, no harm would come to her, he would not let anything happen to her.

The sudden flicker of lamplight served to interrupt these comforting thoughts. Glancing up, Caitlan's terrified gaze became riveted upon the intruders. Indeed, she found that she could not take her eyes from the evil-looking men. There were two of them.

They resembled one another in build and size, and were about the same age—probably thirty-five or so—but that is where the similarity ended. One was blond, the other dark. One had pale green eyes so clear that Caitlan felt certain she could see straight through to his sinister soul, while the other had laughing brown eyes—eyes that sparkled with calculated mischief. One was clearly unkempt . . . unshaven, with dirty, wrinkled clothes, and a mouthful of broken, tobacco-stained teeth, not to mention the fact that he reeked to high heaven. Here again, it was like staring at some bizarre picture; the other was well dressed, with his hair neatly combed and his clothes—right down to the polish on his boots—impeccable. What Caitlan considered most bemusing was that the dark, brown-eyed man smelled of soap, as if he had momentarily stepped from a bath.

On the surface, the contrast between the two men was phenomenal . . . one looking oh so disgusting with his gaping, foolish smirk, the other appearing almost dashing. He looked so out of place, this dark, brooding man with the speaking brown eyes and, given different circumstances, Caitlan could have thought him to be curiously handsome. The cold reality was, however, this oddity of a man—for whatever reason—was presently aiming a gun at Rafe's chest. This fact alone gave Caitlan reason to think him to be the most wretched man alive.

Still, she could not help but think that the man—considering all his gentlemanly affectations—did not truly enjoy acting the part of a coldhearted ruffian. What Caitlan had no way of knowing was that—despite their looks—the men were equally treacherous. The sad fact was, a guileless young woman would presently come to understand the meaning of that age-old adage . . . "appearances often are deceiving."

The scraping of a chair across the pine floor made tiny slivers of prickly flesh race up and down Caitlan's erect spine. As a purely reflex action, she clung to Rafe even tighter. Looking up, her green eyes widened with fear when she saw the dark-haired man twirl the chair around and clump his foot atop the hard seat. Leaning forward over his bent knee, the stranger—the gun never wavering from its target—reached over to flick open Rafe's jacket. With a hollow laugh, he pulled the useless pistol from its holster and tossed it onto the table. Next, the man permitted his dark, devillike eyes a leisurely inspection of Caitlan's shapely figure, ogling her in a way that made her skin crawl. Then with a threatening chuckle, he settled his cold-blooded gaze on Rafe.

"So, we meet again, Bradrick."

"Yes . . . well, life is funny like that," Rafe drawled. "A man never knows how many sons of bitches may cross his path on a given day." Then icily, "What do you want, Rawlings?"

Caitlan could hardly believe her ears. Rafe knew these men!

"I think you know the answer to that. The very same thing we were after when we bushwhacked you up on the Yazoo Road a few weeks back. Jack and I thought we'd seen the last of you then, but I guess we were careless. It looks as if you're no worse for wear though." Rawlings's gaze returned to sweep over Caitlan, his expression cold and unfeeling. "Yeah, it appears as if the lady here has fixed you up good as new. It'd be a downright shame to undo all her fine work, wouldn't it, Jack?"

Caitlan's gaze flew to the other man and her heart very nearly leaped into her throat when she observed his demented mien. From the looks of him, he could happily murder the both of them without blinking an eye and not lose a wink of sleep.

Rawlings, hearing Caitlan's frightened gasp, laughed and said, "I suppose you're right, ma'am. Jack is the wrong man to confer with on that score. You see, old Jack there, he takes pride in his work. Why, it's almost like he truly enjoys what he does, but then, you'd know that already, ma'am. You've seen firsthand what old Jack can do to a man.

"Well, Bradrick," Rawlings barked. Dragging his foot from the chair, he went to stand in front of Rafe. "What's it to be?" he asked, bending close to intimidate Rafe with the deadly revolver.

"Go to hell," Rafe growled.

Rawlings scratched his chin with the barrel end of the gun and shook his head regrettably. "I do wish you'd reconsider.

You see, our employer is a patient man, but even he has his limitations. And he doesn't like to leave loose ends. Our instructions are to use whatever means necessary to get what we want.'' The man leaned even closer, his breath boring into Rafe's chin. "Please understand that we mean business. So, you can die easy, or you can die hard. Which will it be?"

Rawlings was given a prompt answer to his question, although one may safely wager that it was not the one he wished for. As he stood there smiling smugly at his captive, Rafe spit in the man's leering face.

"Son of a bitch!" Rawlings swore, wiping at the spittle that trickled down his cheek. Then with another angry oath, he brought the butt of the gun down across Rafe's cheek with a savage blow. "Okay," the man snarled, taking careful aim at Rafe's midsection. "Have it your way."

Caitlan heard the foreboding click of the revolver, and she nearly swooned from the maddening sound. This could not be happening. She must be dreaming. Caitlan squeezed her eyes closed and prayed, *Oh, dear God, please let this be a dream!*

Opening her eyes once more, she realized with a shuddering heart that her prayers had been futile; this was no dream. This nightmare was truly happening. The dark-haired man had a wild, ruthless look about him. There was no doubt in her mind that he was going to shoot Rafe.

No! her mind screamed. She could not allow this to happen. For seven of the longest, loneliest years of her life, she had made herself believe she never wanted to see Rafe's face again, hear his lazy chortle, or have him hold her in his strong embrace. Now, Caitlan knew just how big a fool she had been. Today, when Rafe had nestled her in his arms, all the old feelings had come rushing back. She had come so close to feeling truly alive again and Caitlan knew in her heart that, if anything happened to Rafe, she would die, too. She *must* do something! She could not sit idly by while this callous bastard took away her only chance for happiness with a blithe squeeze of a trigger.

"*NO!*" Caitlan's hysterical scream split the deathlike stillness. With no regard for her own safety, she sprang like a wild thing from her chair and flung herself across Rafe's body to shield him from the forthcoming deadly blast.

Instantly, a pair of strong arms came around her to gently calm her fears. And while Rafe did his level best to soothe his distraught protectress, he lifted a murderous gaze to Rawlings.

"Pull her off him, so I can get a clear shot," Rawlings snapped at his partner.

Jack Hayes took a step forward, fully intending to do as he had been ordered. But in midstride an idea occurred to him, causing his lip to curl up in a lecherous sneer. Splattering a stream of disgusting brown tobacco juice across Caitlan's spotless floor, the man wiped the excess dribble from his chin and said, "Hold on, Sam. Think on it. Mebbee we can get what we come for after all and have a little fun in the bargain." He nodded toward Caitlan. "You take my meanin'?"

Rawlings took a step back from Rafe, as if to give himself both the time and space to allow his anger to cool. Mulling his friend's words, his dark gaze lowered to rake over Caitlan with renewed interest. Running his shirtsleeve across his mouth, Rawlings muttered, "Yeah, I take your meaning." To Rafe, he said, "She mean anything to you?"

Rafe did not say a word, but Caitlan felt his entire body grow tense and his arms instinctively tightened about her.

"Yeah, she means sumthin' to him all right," Hayes answered his buddy's question, a stupid grin illuminating his face. "No man in his right mind would pay a hundrit dollars just to have vittles with a woman lessen she meant sumthin' to him."

Rawlings, who had been studying Rafe's face during his friend's summation, saw the question flare in the cerulean eyes and said, "That's right. We saw you at the carnival. You might have noticed if you hadn't been so preoccupied with your lady friend here." The dark-haired man stepped forward to casually fondle a brown-and-russet tendril that tumbled down Caitlan's back. She recoiled at his touch, but rather than dissuading him, the repellent man merely gave a bark of laughter—as if amused by her temerity—and one by one he began to remove the pins from her hair, continuing, "That's how we came to know for sure that you were still alive. Oh, we'd heard rumors, but you've been a hard man to track down . . . that is until today."

The last hairpin fell upon the floor with an ear-splitting "ping" and, Rafe, seeing the lustful gleam in Rawlings's eyes, rasped, "Leave her alone, Rawlings. This is between you and me."

"Not anymore it's not. The way I figure, you had your chance to do things our way. Now, me and the little lady here are going upstairs for a while. You've seen how I treat my women, Bradrick," Rawlings said, pulling a bowie knife from his boot and eyeing it with a perverse smile. "Maybe, once you've had a look at what's left of her, you'll feel more like cooperating with us."

Stuffing the ugly weapon back into his boot, he lifted a half-curious, half-taunting stare to Rafe and said, "Tell me, Bradrick. Is she really worth a hundred dollars?" A lewd grin twisted Rawlings's lips, and he added, "Never mind, I'll just find out for myself." With that, he plunged his fist into the tangled mass of russet-tinged curls and jerked Caitlan backward.

"No! Let me go!" Caitlan shrieked, truly terrified. "Rafe. *Rafe!*" she cried, her arms straining for the protective harbor from which she had been ruthlessly wrenched.

Sam Rawlings would rapidly discover that he had more trouble on his hands than he had bargained for. Though his threats had chilled her to the bone, Caitlan was not some meek lamb who would be led passively to the slaughter. Indeed, she fought him with the maniacal fury of a cornered animal, scratching at his arms and clawing at tables, chairs, the door facing, *anything* to frustrate his purpose. Caitlan waged a valiant struggle, but in the end, brute force won out over sheer will and Rawlings hauled her—kicking and screaming—from the room.

Rafe had never felt more helpless in his life. Ever since that bastard Rawlings and his lunatic henchman Hayes had caught him off guard on the back porch with Caitlan, he had been trying desperately to think of a way out of this seemingly impossible situation.

His heart had wrenched upon hearing Caitlan's frightened whimperings in the darkness beside him. Since Rawlings had not bothered to bind his hands—a stupid blunder for all the man's cunning—Rafe had clasped her fingers in his in an effort to reassure her. He had longed to do so much more than that.

To murmur words of comfort to her, tell her that everything would be all right, that he would protect her, keep her safe. But Rafe had been reluctant to voice a promise that he was not entirely certain he would be able to keep.

Rafe had come up against Rawlings and Hayes before. Indeed, he still bore the scars—mental and physical—as proof of that brutal confrontation. He knew them for what they were, a pair of ruthless, cutthroat bastards who would stop at nothing to get what they wanted. Therefore, Rafe had decided to bide his time and let them make the first move. True, he conceded, it was unfortunate he had lost his temper. But it had been bound to happen, what with that weasel-faced Hayes grinning at him like the village idiot and Rawlings gawking at Kettie, and goading him with that goddamn foxy smirk of his.

Rafe's head had still been reeling from the force of Rawlings's blow when Caitlan hurled herself between him and that madman's gun. For the life of him, Rafe could not imagine what had possessed her to react so impulsively. Whatever the reason, he was grateful to her; his own rash conduct had nearly cost him his life. Although, deep in his gut, Rafe did not believe Rawlings had truly meant to kill him . . . at least not yet.

No, Rafe had decided. There were still too many unanswered questions. The two thugs had no idea just how much he knew about their mysterious employer and who else, if anyone, he had told of his suspicions. Then, of course, Rafe still held the trump card . . . one vital piece of evidence that linked their nameless leader to a brutal crime. They had beaten themselves up—and Rafe—searching for it, and it had been right under their noses all the while.

If they only knew, Rafe had indulged in a self-satisfying round of silent gloating, tapping the floor with his right boot.

Rafe's smug countenance had been short-lived, however, as the men's vile, lewd suggestions about Caitlan began to filter through his complacent thoughts. With his hands figuratively, though not literally tied, he could do little more than glare at Rawlings and watch in helpless frustration as he wrested Caitlan from his arms and dragged her like an animal from the room. In that moment, Rafe had known what pure hatred was, making his whole being yearn for revenge. Even now the sound of Caitlan's near-delirious cries echoing down the stairway were almost too much for him to bear and, frantically, Rafe racked his panic-stricken brain for some means of escape.

Stay calm, man! You're no good to Kettie dead, was his self-admonition. Rafe realized that he must keep his head if he hoped to outfox his merciless foe.

Admittedly, with Rawlings preoccupied elsewhere, the situation was not as hopeless as it had been. Hayes was clearly not the type who would emerge the victor in a battle of wits. That kind of battle, however, was at present the least of Rafe's worries. As he mentally calculated his chances of overpowering his adversary, Rafe had to admit that Hayes did possess one slight advantage by way of the deadly pistol that he kept trained at his heart.

Another cry from upstairs sliced through Rafe like a razor-sharp knife. Shouting at himself that he must quickly think of a way to rescue Caitlan from that lunatic Rawlings, Rafe tore his gaze away from his captor and his eyes, wild with anguish, canvassed the room. The vivid blue spheres latched upon his revolver that lay on the table mere inches from his clenched fists—so close and yet so far—making Rafe's head whirl with the weighty decision before him. Should he make a grab for his gun and try to beat Hayes to the draw, or should he wait for Hayes to make a mistake . . . catch him unawares and jump him? Whatever he intended to do, Rafe knew he must decide without delay; every second he squandered that animal was upstairs with Kettie . . . doing God only knew what to her.

Rafe closed his eyes and cringed at the thought. He must not think of that or it would drive him mad. He must devote his sole concentration on escaping from the blackhearted rogue that stood gloating at him, openly defying him to try something. Once again, Rafe eyed his gun, thinking, *If I could distract the bastard for just one measly second*. . . . Rafe had no idea that his silent prayer was only moments away from being answered, and from a most unlikely ally.

The sudden toppling of the lamp on the table behind Hayes prompted the man to whirl in surprise. Wielding his gun toward the supposed intruder, Hayes's cocksure expression melted away to be supplanted by one of simpleminded wonder when he discovered that the meddler was only a cat. Too late, Hayes realized his blunder. Gulping down a sizable chunk of chewing tobacco, he wheeled back around just as Rafe lunged forward to grab his gun. As Rafe bolted from his chair, his hand caught hold of the corner of the table and lifted. Both men fired their weapons; a simultaneous explosion of gunpowder and lead reverberating throughout the chamber that achieved vastly differing results.

Whereas, Hayes's bullet became harmlessly imbedded in the table top that Rafe had improvised as a shield, Rafe's aim found its mark . . . a clean shot through the heart and Hayes lay dead upon the dining-room floor.

God bless that damn cat, came Rafe's bewildering thought and, without a backward glance, he sprinted from the room.

Thus abandoned, Beau voiced his considered opinion by mewing loudly. Then hopping down from the table, he trotted over to rub against one of Hayes's already stiffening legs. The striped tabby had no sooner begun this pleasurable exercise, however, than he was startled by another deafening gun blast from above stairs. Jerking away from the corpse, he scampered through the open portal.

Rafe was midway up the staircase when he heard the gun blast. Shocked and momentarily immobilized by the dreaded sound, he leaned against the wall to calm the frantic thundering of his heart. Taking the remainder of the stairs three at a time, he bounded down the corridor toward Caitlan's room. A more rational-thinking man would have approached the chamber with more caution, but Rafe did not have time for such luxuries. For all he knew, his Kettie lay wounded, possibly dying at the hands of that butcher Rawlings. Without regard for his own safety, Rafe lifted his gun into position and kicked the door open.

To be sure, Rafe had not known what horrors lay in wait for him behind the now splintered portal. But considering his thunderstruck expression, one may reasonably assume he did not expect to find Caitlan brandishing a derringer—still smoking from the recent discharge—and apparently in control of the erstwhile life-threatening situation. As Rafe stood gaping on the threshold, Rawlings clutched at his shoulder and stumbled sideways onto the bed.

Caitlan likewise weaved backward against the bedside table, groping at the edge for support. She had not been grievously wounded, but was merely reacting out of sheer emotional relief to the realization that the terrifying ordeal was mercifully over. Then a movement in the doorway caught her attention. Terrified that the dark-haired man's assistant had come to finish her off, Caitlan dropped the now useless derringer. Plucking Rawlings's gun from the bed, she pointed it at the opening. But upon seeing the tall, familiar figure lurking on the threshold, Caitlan's face broke into a tenuous smile.

"Rafe," she mumbled weakly. As the numbness began to wear off, she cried, "*Rafe!*" Her quivering limbs began to tingle with elation at seeing Rafe and, letting the gun fall from her trembling fingers, Caitlan staggered toward the beautiful sight.

"No, Kettie! Stay where you are!"

Too late, Caitlan heard Rafe's throaty warning, but all too soon she understood why he had voiced such a caution. In her joy at finding Rafe, rather than the despicable Jack Hayes in the aperture, she had completely forgotten about Sam Rawlings. As Caitlan stepped toward the door, Rawlings lunged upward from the bed and imprisoned her in a viselike grip. Holding her in front of him to shield himself against Rafe's revolver, Rawlings jerked the gruesome bowie knife from his boot and held it to Caitlan's throat.

Out of pure instinct, Rafe took a step forward.

"I'll cut her," Rawlings threatened, pressing the knife ever closer to Caitlan's slender neck. "Put the gun down, Bradrick. I'll cut her, I swear."

Rafe knew a moment of indecision, but as his blue gaze moved from Rawlings's deranged face to Caitlan's trusting— albeit frightened one—he knew he had but one choice. If he surrendered his weapon, Rawlings would kill them both. Therefore, Rafe knew what he had to do.

"You slimy son of a bitch," Rafe growled, inching forward. "I'd sooner kill her myself than let you have your filthy way with her." As if to give credence to his statement, Rafe aimed the gun barrel at Caitlan.

Now it was Rawlings's turn to doubt, and his hesitation would cost him his life. As he pondered Rafe's bold pronouncement, Caitlan suddenly grabbed hold of the hand that wielded the treacherous knife and jerked down with all her might. In the same motion, she lurched sideways toward the bed. A mere fraction of a second later, there was a flash of gunpowder and Sam Rawlings joined his partner in hell.

Caitlan landed crossways on the big four-poster. Before the gun blast's vibrations subsided in her ears, she pushed herself up on her elbows to stare blankly at Rawlings's lifeless body. Her hand flew to her mouth in a reflex action as she beheld the gaping hole in the man's forehead. Despite the gathering nausea that strangled her throat, Caitlan found that she could not turn her eyes away from the ghastly sight . . . a picture that would forever be branded upon her memory.

"Don't look."

Rafe's voice—strangely emotional—and sounding as if it were coming from a very great distance rather than the doorway, broke into Caitlan's stunned reverie. Still she could not make herself look away from where Rawlings lay sprawled across the floor.

"Don't, sweet pea," Rafe repeated, coming to stand between her and the gruesome scene. Taking hold of Caitlan's shoulders, Rafe shook her gently. When those horrified pools of green focused on him, he swallowed and asked, "Did . . . did that bastard hurt you?"

As of yet unable to find her tongue, Caitlan could only shake her head numbly in response, but that was enough. Rafe's heartfelt sigh of relief gently rippled her hair, and he snuggled his forehead against hers and mumbled a throaty, "Thank God!"

Vaguely, Caitlan became aware of his fingers digging into her upper arms. Then she was being pulled to her feet and dragged against Rafe's rock hard chest, his arms crushing her so tightly that she could hardly catch her breath. As he guided her toward the doorway, she heard his voice again, choking with emotion as it murmured against her hair, "Oh, thank God you're all right. I was nearly driven mad with worry."

Rafe, overwhelmed at finding Caitlan unharmed, discovered that his normally powerful legs would not support him. As he reached the threshold, he slumped against the door and slid slowly to the floor. Bracing Caitlan against his bent knee, Rafe pressed his quivering lips against the tangled wisps of hair along her cheek. Brushing the matted curls aside, he gazed at her as if to reassure himself of her well-being.

With a shudder for what he had very nearly lost, Rafe cradled Caitlan to him and groaned, "Aw, Kettie. I'm sorry to have put you through this. But it's over now, darlin'. They cannot hurt you now. It's over," he murmured, kissing her cheek once more and repeating, "It's over and you're safe. I'll never let anyone hurt you again."

Caitlan tugged her shawl more tightly about her shoulders and continued to pace along the back porch. She paused when she reached the edge and, with her fingers grasping the support pillar, gazed up at the full moon. Shuddering, she turned and walked the length of the porch to repeat the same gesture at the opposite end. It was not the crisp November night air that chilled Caitlan, however. Rather it was the frightening memories of the preceding evening; try though she might, Caitlan could not cleanse her head of those terrifying moments.

Every time she closed her eyes—as she did now—she could see Rawlings's leering face and hear his mocking voice, describing to her in minute detail every disgusting thing he intended to do to her. As she stood there, eyes shut, gripping the porch railing, Caitlan relived those final blood-chilling moments when Rawlings had backed her toward the bed.

She could almost feel his breath, nauseatingly hot upon her flesh, and see his leering grin as he crept ever nearer. She had been scared out of her wits, but when Rawlings had tossed his gun with a negligent gesture onto the pillows and begun to peel away his clothing, Caitlan had remembered the derringer. Knowing with a certainty that she would prefer death to letting this dog Rawlings defile her, she had inched backward toward the bedside table. Caitlan had very nearly shouted with glee when the sharp edge of the table dug into her backside but she had refrained, lest the madman that was stalking her somehow read her thoughts and thwart her plan. Her fingers had trembled as she groped behind her, fumbling with the drawer. Then, miraculously, the derringer was in her hands and she was pointing it at the vile man.

Caitlan had halfheartedly considered using the weapon on herself, but then the gun blast from downstairs had ripped through the house—and her heart—making her think the worst

. . . Rawlings's partner had murdered Rafe. That, coupled with the nagging fact that Rawlings stood before her, his snickering laughter taunting her, daring her to shoot him, had induced her to action. In that dreadful moment, Caitlan had known what she must do. Recalling Rafe's patient instructions all those years ago when he had taught her how to fire a gun in the meadow near Thistledown—adjuring her to gently squeeze, not jerk, the trigger—Caitlan shot Rawlings.

She had not mortally wounded the man, true. But she had succeeded in frustrating his purpose.

Then there had been that awful moment when the door had burst open and, Caitlan, thinking that Hayes had come to join his friend, had grabbed Rawlings's gun and pointed it at the intruder, prepared to fire again if necessary. The joy Caitlan had experienced upon finding Rafe in the aperture had been overwhelming, so much so in fact, that she had forced her quivering legs to carry her toward that wondrous haven. But in her eagerness to be enfolded in Rafe's secure embrace, she had forgotten about Rawlings.

Caitlan's pretty face tightened into a painful grimace as she recalled those harrowing moments when Rawlings had held the knife to her throat. But in an instant, it had been over. Rawlings lay dead upon her bedroom floor, an expression of mixed surprise and horror frozen upon his handsome face for eternity. Caitlan shivered with the gruesome memory and her eyes snapped open. Shaking off the mental image of Rawlings's dark eyes staring sightlessly into nothingness, she made her way over to the porch swing and sat down.

As her fingers nervously worked at the chains that suspended the swing from the porch overhang, Caitlan tried to remember what had happened afterward. It was useless, however. The fact was, the events that had transpired after Rawlings had been killed were pretty much a blur to her.

Caitlan remembered that a deafening pounding had been raised against the front door. The sound of gunshots in the middle of the night had quite naturally aroused the curiosity of the neighbors and several concerned nearby residents—including Mrs. Taylor from across the street, her broom at the ready—had come to investigate and render assistance. One man had run to fetch the sheriff while the others clustered

about, murmuring in hushed tones and speculating as to what
had transpired. Caitlan had been spared much of their idle
ramblings; Rafe had ushered her into the kitchen upon bringing
her downstairs.

When the sheriff had arrived, Rafe had turned Caitlan over
to Mrs. Taylor's capable hands. Caitlan knew that he had been
loath to leave her alone after all that had happened. She had
read it in the worried blue gaze he turned on her when he stood
up from the kitchen table in answer to the sheriff's summons.

"Don't you worry about her," Mrs. Taylor had said. "She'll
be as good as new once I brew her up a cup of my strong
coffee. I'll have one waitin' for you, too, young man. Now,
run ahead and explain these terrible doings to the sheriff. I'll
look after Miss Webber till you get back."

Rafe had disappeared with Sheriff Bodeker for hours it
seemed. In fact, the first shadows of dawn had already begun
to speckle the horizon before Rafe returned to the kitchen to
tell Caitlan that the bodies had been taken away and the rooms
restored to order. But she had been reluctant to venture back
inside the house proper. Even after Essie had washed away the
bloodstains and covered those stubborn blotches that refused
to yield to soap and water, Caitlan had persevered in her decision to avoid being reunited with those rooms in which so
much treachery had occurred. Instead, she had preferred to
remain in the kitchen, immersed in a hot bath from which she
had endeavored to scrub away every trace of Rawlings's disgusting touch.

Essie's soft-spoken suggestions and Rafe's outright surly
commands for her to go upstairs to her room and lie down had
been stubbornly ignored; Caitlan knew something they did not.
Every time she closed her eyes she was visited by a host of
ghostly apparitions; she simply could not wipe the gory images
from her head. This, in and of itself, made Caitlan feel fairly
certain she would never encounter another moment's sleep . . .
at least, not in that house. But by midafternoon, she had been
overcome by exhaustion and had dozed off in the back porch
swing. Rafe, who had been sitting beside her at the time, had
waited to make certain Caitlan was fast asleep. Then thinking
she would rest better inside, he had gathered Caitlan in his

arms, fully intending to carry her up to her room and tuck her into bed.

The sudden movement had jostled her awake, however, and Caitlan had grown almost hysterical when she realized what was happening. Clutching Rafe's sleeve, she had buried her face in his shirt and whimpered, "No! Don't make me go in there, not yet. I cannot bear it, Rafe. Please!"

Rafe, understandably shaken by Caitlan's distraught mien, had carried her to his room above the carriage house and settled her on his own bed instead. But when he prepared to move away, she had taken hold of his hand and coaxed him down onto the narrow berth beside her. Thusly nestled in Rafe's sturdy embrace—her head on his broad shoulder—she had fallen asleep. In fact, Caitlan had slept soundly the remainder of the afternoon and had awakened near dusk to find that Rafe had gone, the imprint of his head on the pillow they had shared the only indication that he had been there at all. But as her eyes had grown accustomed to the darkened room, Caitlan had been given cause to dread more than the mere fact that Rafe had gone off to tend to other matters while she slept.

His saddlebags lay draped across the back of the reupholstered wing chair, with his clothing folded in a neat pile on the seat, and his rifle leaned up against the arm. With a violent lurch of her heart, Caitlan had known intuitively what all this meant. Rafe was leaving . . . again. Her thoughts brought her outside.

"Meow," Beau droned at her feet, interrupting Caitlan's disheartening recollections.

Detecting the impatience in Beau's purr, Caitlan stopped the gentle swaying motion of the swing and allowed the cat to hop up onto the seat beside her. The sudden bouncing motion caused Caitlan to wince with pain and, with a grimace, she realized that all this serious reflection had caused her head to ache and the muscles in her shoulders to tighten into hard knots of searing pain. As she pressed a soothing hand to her temple, Beau—heedless of his mistress's discomfort—climbed onto her lap and, bracing his front paws on the front of her blouse, pressed his face closer to hers almost as if he, too, sensed something was wrong.

With a sigh, Caitlan settled the big cat on her lap. As she

methodically stroked his shiny coat, her head became filled with thoughts of tomorrow. Luckily today was Sunday and the tearoom had been closed all day, but Caitlan knew full well what the morning would bring, and she dreaded the thought. News of the bloody tragedy at Katie's Tearoom had spread throughout Vicksburg like wildfire. There was little doubt in her mind that, come the Monday dinner seating, the tearoom would be brimming with regular customers and bloodthirsty curiosity seekers alike. And they would all be looking for the same thing . . . juicy tidbits of gossip surrounding the mysterious killings.

"Why the long face, Kettie?" Rafe's deep voice plunged into the midst of her dismal thoughts. Without asking her leave, he nudged Caitlan's skirts aside and sat down beside her. "I was headed up to my room when I saw you sitting here. Hello, Beau," he said, burying his hand in the cat's soft fur, adding, "I hope your mistress gave you a fitting reward, seeing as how it was you that saved our necks last night." As the bored cat jumped down and scampered away, he turned to Caitlan and demanded, "Why aren't you in bed, young lady? And don't tell me you're still skittish about going back into this house. You'll have to get over your fears, honey. As much as I enjoyed taking a nap with you this afternoon, I'm afraid—"

"You're leaving, aren't you?" Caitlan brought Rafe's seemingly unending stream of chitchat to a halt with the baleful utterance of a single question. The query had been delivered with matter-of-fact clarity; there was no trace of accusation or bitterness in her voice . . . only sadness.

Realizing he had been found out, Rafe coughed and squirmed uncomfortably on the hard seat. "Uh, if you must know, I've just come from booking a cabin on the *Magnolia Princess*. She leaves tomorrow for New Orleans."

"The *Magnolia Princess*?" Caitlan repeated vaguely. "I'm surprised you could get a cabin. The riverboats are usually full of tourists and freight by the time they arrive in Vicksburg."

"Yes, well—" Rafe rubbed his chin and looked away. "I . . . happen to be on intimate terms with the owner." Standing, he took an awkward turn about the porch. Returning to stand in front of Caitlan, he planted his feet squarely before her and said, "How did you know?"

Caitlan laughed—a hard, brittle sound—and said, "I've come to recognize the signs."

Caitlan's scornful tone struck a nerve and, reaching down, Rafe forced her chin up until their eyes met in the moonlight. His voice was soft and low when he said, "It's not what you think, sweet pea. I was going to tell you, but there are . . . oh . . . so many things I wanted to explain to you first."

"You don't owe me any explanations," Caitlan snapped, slapping his hand aside in a petulant gesture. Swallowing her pride, she asked, "Since you're traveling by boat, what will become of your horse?" Caitlan held her breath, half hoping he would announce his intentions to return for the animal.

Instead, Rafe said, "I've made arrangements to take Wanderer with me on the *Princess*. But Kettie, please listen—"

"No." Caitlan shook her head. "I told you, you don't owe me any explanations." Her mood became pensive, as if she mulled some weighty decision.

A deep frown puckered Rafe's brow as he studied Caitlan's face, and he opened his mouth to offer an explanation despite her stubborn protestations. But when Caitlan focused her thought-filled green gaze on him, Rafe took a moment to reconsider. After all, he was not at all certain she would like him any better after he made a full and true confession of all the secrets he had kept from her since his arrival to Vicksburg.

"Rafe?" she murmured lowly, her cheeks dimpling in embarrassment at her bold thoughts.

"Yes."

"Will you do something for me before you go?"

"Of course I will, darlin'. Just name it." Rafe went down on his knee before her and, taking her hand in his, his mouth broke into a wide, adoring smile.

Caitlan swallowed hard, not sure that she would be able to put a voice to the scandalous proposition that had wormed its way into her brain the moment her eyes beheld those wretched saddlebags. But when her gaze mingled with his on the moon-drenched porch, she knew without a doubt that she could not let him leave again . . . never knowing when or if he would ever return. For in her heart, Caitlan knew she might never see Rafe again, and she was determined that he would not leave her this time, not with her still wondering. . . .

With a dark blush staining her cheeks—for in all honesty, she could hardly believe that she meant to seek fulfillment of her shameless thoughts—Caitlan fought off every logical instinct to the contrary and whispered, "Will you make love to me before you go?"

Chapter Twelve

Rafe jerked away from Caitlan as if he had been struck by a bolt of lightning and, clambering to his feet, leveled his startled gaze at her downturned head. Glancing about, as though he feared that some unseen eavesdropper might have overheard her shocking proposition, he lowered his voice to a raspy whisper and said, "Caitlan Webber! I'm surprised at you. Why, you must still be addled from last night's ordeal. Why else would you say such a damn fool thing to me?" Rafe trudged up and down the porch, waving his arms in exaggerated motions. Then coming to a standstill in front of her, he railed, "Have you completely lost your mind, woman?! Have you any notion as to what you just asked me to do? You cannot have meant it, Kettie."

"Yes, I did. I meant every word" came Caitlan's hushed reply, her gaze riveted on her hands that she clenched tightly in her lap. In an attempt to gauge Rafe's temper, she peeked up and caught a glimpse of his dogmatic stance—feet apart, one hand on his hip, the other wagging an outraged finger at her. Realizing his mood was tenuous at best, she lowered her eyes again and muttered, "I suppose this . . . means you don't . . . want me."

One look at Caitlan's forlorn countenance sufficed to melt

Rafe's stern resolve. Shoving a frustrated hand through his hair, he sank down onto the swing next to her. "Aw hell. Of course I want you, Kettie. I've wanted you ever since that day when I dragged you out of the brambles at Thistledown. Christ almighty, the thought of you and me together . . . making love . . . has gnawed at me for nearly fifteen years. And there hasn't been a single night since I moved into the carriage house when the idea of climbing those stairs and crawling into bed with you and loving you until the sun came up hasn't crossed my mind" was Rafe's throaty admission.

"Then . . . why haven't you?"

Rafe hunched his shoulders and said, "I have no clear-cut answer for you, Kettie. Mainly, I suppose I wasn't sure how you would take to the idea. And," he blew a long sigh, "because perhaps I think you deserve better. Someone who is willing to devote a lifetime to loving you, caring for you, not just one night or a few days."

Caitlan felt her heart shrivel into a lifeless lump in her chest and her voice was little more than a coarse whisper when she asked, "And you are not that someone?"

"I don't know," he said sadly, tears stinging his eyes. "I want to be, truly I do. It's just . . . well, darlin', you have to understand that a lot has happened to me in the past seven years. I haven't said much because you made it clear that day at the Washington Hotel that you didn't want to discuss the past. But the fact is, I've got some unfinished business to attend to; that is why I'm leaving tomorrow. Lord only knows when I will be able to return to Vicksburg, but I will . . . I promise I'll come back to you, honey. As soon as I take care of this unsettled business, I'll be back. Then I can start thinking about a wife and fam—"

"No, *you* have to understand, Rafe," Caitlan interrupted, her mien amazingly cool, considering the scandalous topic. "I am not asking for marriage. I just want you to make love to me. One night. One night after fifteen years. Is that too much to ask?"

Rafe, nonplussed for one of the few times in his life, leaned forward to rest his elbows on his knees. Lowering his face into his hands, he scratched his mustache, then turned his head sideways to look at her proud profile. After a moment, he said,

"Are you telling me that you have never . . . "

"*NO!*" came Caitlan's shrill whisper. Thoroughly embarrassed, she flung out of the swing and, turning her poker-straight back to him, stalked over to the porch railing.

Undaunted by the defensive shroud Caitlan had donned, Rafe went to stand behind her. Placing his hands on her shoulders, he turned her about and nudged her chin up, so he could gaze into her petulant face. His fingers lingered to gently stroke at her cheek as he murmured, "There's nothing for you to be ashamed of, sweet pea. I didn't mean to pry, nor am I poking fun at you. I'm just a little surprised, that's all. Hell!" he barked. "What's wrong with the men in this town? Are they all as blind and stupid as I am?"

"I don't want the men in this town."

Rafe cupped her face in his hands and his cerulean gaze grew serious as it stared into her eyes. In a voice husky with emotion, he asked, "What *do* you want, Kettie?"

"You," she replied softly and without a moment's hesitation.

Rafe, humbled by Caitlan's forthright admission, found that his tongue would not oblige him with a ready rebuttal. Consequently, he studied her upturned face by the moonlight for several thought-provoking moments and, when he spoke again, his tone was more serious than before. "Kettie? Are you absolutely certain this is what you want? I mean, surely you want to share that special moment with your husband. You've waited this long, sweet pea. Don't you think you should wait a little longer? Maybe the right man or at least a better man will come along."

"But that's just it," Caitlan mumbled wretchedly, reaching out to run one finger along his lapel. "The right man has come along . . . three times now. But before you run away again, I simply must know. Please, Rafe. Don't make me beg. Have I disgusted you? Is that why you don't want me?"

"No, never!" Rafe all but bellowed and, pulling away, jerked his hand through an already tousled mane. Taking hold of the railing to steady his flustered mien, he continued, "Good God, Kettie! You're not making this easy for me. Here I am, trying to spare your virtue, mind you, and you keep badgering me to take it. Then you keep looking at me like that—all sad-eyed and lonely—and try to make me feel guilty by saying I don't want you when you know damn good and well I do. I've told you as much. It's just that . . . well, dammit, woman . . . I don't want you to do anything you might regret later."

Though Caitlan could not bring herself to look at him, she placed her hand atop his and said, "I could never regret such a thing. When you kissed me yesterday, then later when I thought that awful man had killed you, I just . . . well, I have come to realize that making love with you is what I want more than anything. In fact, my only regret shall be if you leave tomorrow without loving me tonight."

"You flatter me, Kettie. But there's one thing I cannot quite figure out."

"Yes? What?"

Rafe leveled his unreadable gaze at Caitlan and said, "Why me? Why not Jeremy Cantrell or one of those other young bucks I've seen strutting around the tearoom lately?"

"What can I say to make you understand?" Caitlan splayed her hands in a helpless gesture. "I am not some giggly school-girl with an overactive curiosity. I am a woman in all ways except one. I don't want to merely experience having sex with a man." Her voice dropped to a breathy whisper as she said, "I want you. I want you to hold me, to feel you all around me, and I want to touch and hold you. I would rather have one night of making love with you than a lifetime with Jeremy or any other man in this wretched town. As for waiting . . . I have had enough of waiting, thank you. A lifetime of waiting. I don't want to wait . . . I *cannot* wait . . . another seven or eight years, or however long it takes this time before you decide to waltz back into my life . . . if you do at all."

Rafe made nary a sound, nor did he so much as twitch a muscle as he stood listening while Caitlan opened up her heart and revealed her most intimate thoughts to him. The worst was yet to come—or so she thought—for after Caitlan concluded this emotional appeal, several torture-filled moments dragged by while Rafe did little more than stand in subdued silence, his tall silhouette looming over her in the darkness.

Caitlan held her tongue and waited . . . hopeful. An eternity seemed to tick away in front of her and, with every passing moment, Caitlan's face fell a little lower. Eventually, she realized that Rafe must have been so thoroughly repulsed by her bold suggestion that he could not even bear to dignify her request with a reply. What other reason could there be for his prolonged reticence? With her shoulders drooping and her anxious smile now withered into a forlorn pout, Caitlan pushed away from the porch rail and turned toward the back door . . . feeling rejected and very much a fool. She had taken no more than two steps, however, when she felt a hand upon her wrist.

Before Caitlan fully understood what was happening, Rafe swooped her into his arms and strode toward the door, his gait matching the purpose that flashed in the crystal-blue eyes. Without saying a word, he shouldered the portal open and stepped into the darkened corridor. And his breath was warm and thrilling when he bent his head near hers to whisper, ''You won't have to wait, Kettie.''

The brilliant light of the November full moon cascaded through the upstairs window to wrap the couple in a circle of glowing light. They stood facing each other in the center of the room, hands touching, gazing at each other with nervous anticipation. Caitlan's anxiety stemmed from the fact that, not only was she about to make love for the first time in her not so young life, but it was with the very man she had conversely loved and hated . . . and wanted for nearly fifteen years. Whereas, her partner's apprehension sprang from an altogether different source.

Rafe was no stranger to a woman's boudoir, that much was certain. He knew what to do well enough. But this time would be different. This time he would be with Kettie. He had waited . . . they had waited . . . so long for this moment. Rafe wanted this night to be special . . . even memorable . . . for her. Realizing that if he stood there much longer, Caitlan might very well think he had changed his mind—or worse—forgotten what to do, Rafe stepped closer.

Caitlan stood as still as a mouse as Rafe lifted his hands to her hair and slowly stripped away the copper-colored hairpins. He then shook out the tangled curls and allowed the heavy tendrils to fall carelessly across her shoulders, a shimmery blanket of satin tumbling down her back. Next, those same powerful hands wandered down the front of her blouse to where she had knotted the lavender shawl at her bosom. As diligent fingers became embroiled in disengaging the irksome knot, they accidentally brushed each shapely breast, thereby sending little shivers of delight racing down Caitlan's spine.

Rafe, hearing her surprised intake of breath, finished untying the shawl. Tossing the frayed garment aside with a negligent gesture, he asked, "Did you like that?"

Caitlan, certain her voice would emerge as little more than a high-pitched squeak, bobbed her head up and down.

"Good. It gets better," he murmured against her cheek.

Lowering his sensual gaze, he locked his fingers around the topmost button of her blouse and slid the dainty fastener through the buttonhole. But as he began to systematically follow suit with the remaining buttons, Caitlan abruptly pulled away. His concentration thus interrupted, Rafe jerked his head up in time to see her step toward the highboy on the adjacent wall.

"What the—" He scratched his head, then demanded, "What's wrong? Where are you going?"

"My . . . my nightgown," she explained. Even as she struggled to pull the heavy drawer open, Rafe walked up behind her and pushed it closed again.

"You won't be needing it" came his perfunctory reply. "I want to feel you . . . *and* see you," Rafe added when he saw Caitlan look with longing at the open curtains.

"But—" Caitlan tried to protest, pinkening despite the chilly room.

"No buts," he told her. Pushing aside the heavy strands of brown-and-russet hair, Rafe pressed his lips against the side of her neck before moving upward to nibble at her ear where he murmured, "Trust me, sweet pea. I know what I'm doing. I'm almost certain you will like my way better."

Turning her around, his fingers became engaged once more in undoing those pesky buttons. Once this pleasant diversion was accomplished, Rafe tugged the garment free of the waistband and slipped it off her arms. Her skirt quickly followed, as did corset, shoes, and stockings, until she stood before him clad only in a threadbare chemise. Caitlan instinctively crossed her arms across her bosom to shield her near-naked state from Rafe's smoldering gaze.

That persistent gentleman merely responded by taking hold of her hands and, as he gently coaxed her arms away from the voluptuous mounds, he pulled her toward him. Rafe's warm gaze lifted from where the rosy tips of Caitlan's breasts strained against the thin cotton material of her undergarment to her expectant face. Drawing her near and in a voice rich with passion, he said, "I always knew you were pretty. In a moment, you will have to show me just how beautiful you are. But first—" His throaty discourse tapered off into a heady sigh as his lips descended upon Caitlan's.

This caress would prove to be quite different from the reunion kiss they had shared the day before. That kiss had been borne of a long-suppressed passion left simmering ever since that fateful July night when Caitlan had found Rafe lying nearly dead in the mud. Though this kiss was just as thrilling, it was conducted with considerably less urgency and a good deal more purpose. Rafe's mouth moved upon hers slowly, tenderly, as he reacquainted himself with those lips that he had been denied for so long. In fact, he whiled away several whimsical moments engaged in this most satisfying pastime.

With Caitlan snuggled closely against him, Rafe felt a tremor of excitement race through her body, and he pulled away to gaze down into her trusting face. Stroking her cheek with his thumb, Rafe smiled at her. Then he lowered his head to let his lips nibble along the slender column of her throat, his mouth wending its way ever lower while his hand slid down her back, along her trim waist, ultimately around in front to cup one heavy breast. Both instruments of pleasure arrived at the diverting object at the same moment and, while strong fingers tenderly massaged the fleshy mound, his teeth tugged at the nipple through the thin chemise.

Somewhere through the fog of his own tempestuous musings, Rafe became aware of Caitlan's breath, warm and moist against his ear—her tongue lightly flicking at the lobe—and he unthinkingly jerked away. Touching his fingers to the tingling region, Rafe grinned; he realized that his worries about stoking all those dormant embers of desire that Caitlan had buried deep inside for the past seven years had been for naught. With a quizzical shake of his head, he turned toward the bed.

"No," Caitlan whimpered, taking hold of his hand and

guiding it back to the breast that still quivered from his touch. "Don't stop now."

"Easy, Kettie," he cajoled, tweaking her chin. "We have all night. Besides, I would like to shed a few of my own clothes if you don't mind." With a mischievous wink, he added, "Suppose you come on over here and give me a hand."

Shrugging off his jacket, Rafe slid the suspenders from his shoulders and let them fall to dangle where they may. Then laying back crossways on the bed, he folded his arms behind his head and looked to where Caitlan stood frozen in the moonlight. "Well? What are you waiting for? You were the one who was so all-fired anxious to commence with this lovemaking, remember? Don't go turning skittish on me now." Realizing she had most probably suffered an attack of the jitters, he teased her by saying, "Come and help me get these boots off. And mind you have a care. You know how partial I am to my footwear."

At this reminder, Caitlan's momentary qualms vanished, and she marched over to the bed and grasped the proffered boot. Taking hold of his ankle with one hand and his toe with the other, she tugged and both the leather footgear and wool sock slipped off into her hand. There was a rebellious glint flashing in her eyes when she lifted the boot high above her head. And a syrupy-sweet smile spread her lips as she purposely let the boot slip from her fingers to fall against the hardwood floor with a resounding thud.

Rafe guffawed at her temerity and, envisioning the passion-filled night still to come, he extended his other leg.

Once again, Caitlan took hold of his leather-shod foot and yanked, but this boot did not budge. When after several attempts the footwear still refused to be dislodged, she turned about. And while Rafe braced his bare foot against her buttocks, Caitlan balanced his booted leg between her thighs and pulled. These efforts produced the expected results . . . well, almost.

As Caitlan tossed sock and boot atop the growing pile of discarded garments, she suddenly became aware of a curious tingling sensation along her thighs. With a start, she realized that Rafe was using his foot to rub up and down between her legs, but she had no sooner adapted to these thrilling bursts of pleasure than they stopped. A disappointed groan gathered in Caitlan's throat only to emerge a moment later as a startled gasp, and her right hand groped instinctively for the bedpost. Indeed, she clung to that post as if it were life itself and, closing her eyes, gave herself up to the thrilling wave of intoxicating feelings that washed over her.

There was a simple explanation for this latest upheaval in Caitlan's erstwhile latent emotions. Rafe, upon withdrawing his foot from where Caitlan snuggled it in that most provocative of places between her thighs, had become preoccupied with some sensual shenanigans of his own. As his foot slid backward, his big toe had brushed against the very essence of her womanhood and, feeling her jolt of surprise, he quite naturally lingered to massage the secret place with languid, meticulous strokes. Hearing Caitlan's confused moans of contentment, and longing to hold her against him so he could properly introduce her to that ultimate of ecstasies, Rafe abruptly halted the maddening motion. Caitlan did not stir until the last of those delicious sensations had ebbed, however, and she was prompted to do so only when Rafe's foot—still pressed intimately against her backside—nudged her back to reality.

At last, Caitlan found the strength to peel her fingers from the mahogany bedpost. She whirled about to face him—her cheeks flaming scarlet and her voice trembling ever so slightly—and demanded, "Wherever did you learn to do such a thing?"

Rafe very nearly choked when he heard Caitlan's forthright, albeit innocent, question. Propping himself up on his elbows, he regarded her with a tolerant eye. Clearing his throat, he said, "Kettie, darlin', I fear you have a great many things to learn about all this. The most important of which is . . . never question your lover as to the nature of his past liaisons when he is making love to you. It tends to pall one's ardor. Now climb on up here, woman, and help me get undressed."

"Well," Caitlan huffed and looked away, more than a little peeved by his evasive answer.

Her sullen disposition evaporated, however, when Rafe took hold of her hand and dragged her onto the bed with him. He positioned Caitlan so that she straddled his broad chest, then nodding for her to proceed, he settled back to savor this long-anticipated moment. Her fingers fluttered timorously as they unraveled the knotted neckerchief about his throat. Caitlan's trepidation became even more acute when she directed her attention to his shirt; as she undid each button, she had to inch her body a little lower in order to have access to the next fastener. By the time she freed the last button and pulled his shirt open to gaze upon Rafe's muscular hair-covered chest, Caitlan was trembling noticeably.

Her sudden attack of nerves could most likely be attributed to the fact that she presently sat astride Rafe's groin. The sensation of being pressed intimately against the hardened bulge that strained against his trousers, coupled with the knowledge that only a flimsy piece of cloth protected her from his tumescence, was almost too much for her to withstand. Caitlan felt herself go all giddy inside and, knowing that if she did not act immediately she might very well turn coward and flee, she lowered her quivering fingers to the front of his trousers.

Caitlan experienced some difficulty at first in wedging the buttons through the narrow openings, but when Rafe laid his hands upon hers to steady them, she swiftly accomplished her mission. Knowing she must act before she lost her nerve, Caitlan gripped the waistband and yanked downward. When her eyes caught a glimpse of his erect member, however, she became deathly still—her wide green gaze riveted to the awesome sight. Thus preoccupied with his nakedness, Caitlan could do little more than slide off him and watch as Rafe wriggled from his trousers and kicked them aside.

Finally free of his restrictive garments, Rafe turned back to Caitlan, the concupiscent gleam in those cerulean eyes having grown a shade darker with desire. As he reached for her, Rafe could not help but notice Caitlan's continued fascination with his swollen manhood. With a knowing chuckle, he said, ''And you thought I didn't want you. Just look at how much I want you, sweet pea . . . feel how much.''

Caitlan jerked away, truly horrified by his suggestion. Her hands flew to her crimson cheeks, and she whispered in a hushed tone, ''Oh, Rafe! I . . . I don't know if I can. Must I?''

Rafe was not untouched by the imploring look she turned on him. Heaving a conciliatory shrug, he said, ''Of course not, Kettie. Although I believe that one day you might like to very much. But I would never ask you to do anything that makes you feel uncomfortable or embarrassed.''

''But it would . . . please you?'' came Caitlan's timid inquiry.

''Right now, I would be pleased if you crawled back over here and kissed me.''

This request was one with which Caitlan was more than willing to comply. Scooting forward, she straddled his waist once more and bracing her hands along his shoulders, leaned forward to cover his mouth with hers.

This mutual commingling of lips began as an innocent gesture but rapidly grew into an all-consuming embrace. As Caitlan's lips trembled against his, Rafe buried his hands in her hair and pulled her tightly against him, returning her kiss with fervor while his hands explored the glorious curves that lay beneath the cotton material. Rafe moaned with pleasure as his hands roamed down her back to caress her hips and, drawing away, he nipped her lower lip with his teeth in a playful gesture. Finally, he directed his attention down the front of her chemise where the imprint of two rosy-tipped nipples could be plainly seen. The temptation to nuzzle those enticing peaks was too great to resist and, with a groan, he burrowed his face in the soft material.

When at last Rafe drew away, he pulled Caitlan to him again . . . kissing her mouth, her cheek, working his way around to her ear where he whispered in a voice thick with desire, ''Let me see you, Kettie.''

Caitlan, brown-and-russet hair tumbling all about her, brushed a kiss against his pleading mouth, then touching her lips to the bruise that marred his cheek—a gruesome reminder of the previous evening's horrors—she straightened. She hesitated only slightly before she lifted her arms and dragged the garment over her head. Growing suddenly self-conscious, Caitlan gathered the tattered cloth in her fists and hugged it to her breasts.

Rafe realized that Caitlan was not playing the coquette by design, rather it was her own insecurity that made her vacillate. Thinking to hasten her decision, he grabbed hold of the garment and gave it a tug, but still she resisted. In fact, it was not until Rafe flashed her a smile of encouragement that Caitlan grudgingly relaxed her hold. In that moment of indecision, Rafe snatched the undergarment from her fingers and flicked it over his head. While he drank in the exquisite beauty before him, the chemise fluttered unnoticed to the floor.

"Oh, my beautiful Kettie," Rafe breathed, pressing a kiss in the palm of her hand. "Just look how beautiful you are. I always knew you were, and not just here . . ." he touched her face, " . . . or here," he touched her breast, " . . . or even here," his fingers flitted across the brown-tufted triangle that safeguarded her femininity . . . but here, inside. Rafe tapped her breastbone where his fingers detected the frantic thrumming of her heart. "Nervous?" he interpolated.

"A little."

"Do you still want me to love you?"

"Yes! Oh, yes," Caitlan panted, breathless. "Please do, and right now."

"Soon" came Rafe's wicked chortle.

With Caitlan still straddling his stomach, her velvety-soft thighs hugging his hips, Rafe's powerful hands reached out to fondle the charming vision that hovered above him in the moonlight. Probing fingers set about a cursory exploration of the silken flesh, roaming down her sides to the rounded curves of her hips, back up across her flat stomach, and upward still to cup her breasts in his hands, skillful fingers squeezing each rosy peak until it stiffened with agonizing pleasure.

Caitlan could not help herself. She cried aloud from the sheer rapture of it all . . . this magical spell of sensual excitement that Rafe had woven about her.

Hearing her contented whimperings, Rafe tumbled Caitlan onto her back and his mouth descended on hers once more . . . this time hungrily, greedily. He felt her flinch slightly when he coaxed his tongue between her lips, but her trepidation proved transitory. Once she became accustomed to that intrepid organ's playful antics—as it plundered the secret mysteries of her mouth kept sacred for low these many years—she returned the caress in full. Indeed, Caitlan groaned with frustration when Rafe pulled his blistering hot lips from hers.

They did not remain unoccupied for long, however. Lowering his head to her breasts, Rafe kissed each tempting mound, alternately nibbling and flicking his tongue at each crimson peak until Caitlan writhed with desire beneath him, her breath coming in short, hot gasps. When his mouth returned to embrace Caitlan's, Rafe's hands picked up where his lips had left off. In fact, as their tongues mated and frolicked in delirious abandon, his hand slipped away from the alluring mounds of flesh to slither down across her stomach. He felt Caitlan shudder as he rubbed the inside of her thighs, then bristle as his fingers slipped between the moist crevice to stroke at the sensitive bud of her femininity.

"Relax, sweet pea." Rafe tore his mouth away from hers to murmur against her cheek. "We're almost there."

Rafe continued to whisper comforting words of encouragement to Caitlan as he brought his stiffened organ to the coveted opening of her womanhood. He did not immediately seek entrance, however. Wanting to assure himself that she knew what to expect, that she was indeed ready for him, Rafe massaged the volatile area with the pulsating shaft, and he obliged Caitlan to look at him by calling out her name. When those passion-filled pools of shimmering green met his, Rafe knew.

"This may hurt a little at first, Kettie," he warned, his voice hoarse with desire. "But not for long, honey. I promise, not for long." In the next instant, Rafe burrowed himself deep inside her.

Caitlan had never experienced such excitement . . . and pain. He had been right, there was pain, but only for a moment. Then as she grew accustomed to the glorious sensation of having his hardened shaft probing inside her, the pain was forgotten and there was only Rafe. Rafe, touching her hair, panting sweet nothings in her ear, kissing her, fondling her breasts, stroking that thundering pulse between her legs with his fingers while his demanding manhood plunged ever deeper between her thighs. Caitlan had never known such feelings existed and now that she did, she never wanted them to end.

Wrapping her arms about his neck, Caitlan clung to Rafe as she lurched upward to meet his powerful thrusts, each one thrilling her, sending a fresh wave of gooseflesh scurrying up and down her spine. She wanted so desperately to pleasure Rafe as well, but years of inexperience with the opposite sex had rendered her woefully timid. Consequently, Caitlan could do little more than fondle the rippling muscles along his back and arms, or stroke his beard, or press a kiss against his throbbing lips that moaned with pleasure. It was as she lifted her hand to brush a wayward lock of hair from his forehead that she became aware of a new sensation . . . something she had never felt before.

It began as little more than a scant tension somewhere in the depths of her being and seemed to intensify with each masterful surge between her legs. Conversely thrilled by the electric sparks that pulsed through her, and frightened by the mounting sense of urgency that seemed destined to drive her mad before she understood its meaning, Caitlan flung her arms about Rafe's neck and clung to him, crying his name over and over. In the next moment, she felt Rafe shudder in her arms and he, too, cried her name. As abruptly as it had appeared, the mysterious sensation fizzled, leaving her with a peacefully contented feeling, yet yearning for more . . . of what, she did not know.

As soon as his breathing returned to normal, Rafe rolled to his side and curled a protective arm about Caitlan's shoulder. Touching a finger to her chin, he coaxed her to look at him and his voice was low and consoling when he said, ''I'm sorry, sweet pea.''

''S-s-sorry,'' Caitlan stammered. ''Whatever for? It was . . . wonderful.''

''Was it?'' A dubious frown knit his brow as he considered her flushed face in the semidarkness. Stroking her cheek with the back of his hand, he murmured, ''I assure you, it *can* be better . . . for you at least. I don't think I could stand much more.'' Rafe chuckled and, pressing a fleeting kiss against her mouth, he climbed from the bed and walked over to the washstand. Caitlan watched, her curiosity raging, as Rafe poured water into the bowl. Next, he plunged the washcloth into the cold liquid, then wringing it dry, he approached the bed, saying, ''Let me show you just how wonderful it can be.''

Caitlan had no idea what he intended to do, but one may safely wager she did not anticipate Rafe's next maneuver. Walking around to where she lay, he sat down beside her and nudged her legs apart. His eyes never left her face as he lowered the washcloth to that secret place between her thighs. Ignoring her startled gasp, he tenderly and methodically washed away all evidence of her virtue and their lovemaking. Upon completing this diverting task, Rafe tossed the cloth aside and knelt down beside the bed. Grabbing her ankles, he pulled Caitlan around so that her hips touched the edge of the mattress and dangled her legs across his shoulders. Then before she fully comprehended his intentions, Rafe lowered his head.

At first, Caitlan was aghast. She didn't know whether to feel ashamed, disgusted or—

"Oh, God . . . *yes!*" she moaned, gripping the bedspread with convulsive fingers, her head writhing back and forth as she was consumed by the overwhelming sensations Rafe's zealous application sent coursing through her.

Every last vestige of Caitlan's moral outrage vanished as, within seconds, Rafe magically conjured that enigmatic feeling that had nearly driven her to distraction before. She lay there, every fiber of her being tingling with delicious anticipation as Rafe's hard tongue fondled her, touched her in ways Caitlan had never—in her wildest dreams—imagined possible. As the torturous pressure continued to build inside her, she ground her hips into the mattress, then thrust upward to strain against that most unlikely implement of pleasure. Each masterful flick of his tongue sent little bolts of lightning racing through her. It felt almost as if the bed were on fire—flames licking all about her—such was the intensity of her emotional upheaval.

And then it happened. All those wildly jumbled sensations came crashing together in a thunderous explosion of such excruciating ecstasy, such exquisite fulfillment that Caitlan could not help but cry aloud with the joy of finally knowing. But the pleasure did not end yet; Rafe continued to stroke her womanhood until the delicious tension-building sensation returned, coursing through her veins like liquid fire, riddling her body with convulsive tremors again . . . and again until—

"*Stop!*" she sobbed, slumping against the mattress. Turning her face into the bedspread, Caitlan cried . . . for the first time in a long while, she cried . . . great, huge tears and uncontrollable sobs of emotional release.

Understanding what had happened, Rafe gave Caitlan a moment to herself before he dragged her emotion-ravaged body to a sitting position and held her close. Brushing the matted russet-tinged curls from her cheek, he pressed a kiss against her mouth. Upon tasting the salty tears that drenched her face, Rafe cursed himself, thinking he must have pushed her too far. It was obvious she was not ready. He should have waited. Recriminations aside, he lifted Caitlan into his arms and, sweeping the bedclothes back, laid her upon the sheets. Climbing in beside her, Rafe gathered her in his arms and rocked her back and forth until her sobs subsided.

"There, there, honey. Shh," he cooed, stroking her hair. "I didn't mean to make you cry. Did I hurt you, sweet pea?"

Choking back a sob, Caitlan reached up to clutch his shoulder. Her voice, though unsteady, was nonetheless passion-filled when she said, "No! Not at all. It was . . . was . . . oh . . . exquisite. I've never felt anything quite like it. Indeed, I . . . I—" she choked again, " . . . I didn't know."

"I know, darlin'." He squeezed her to him. "It can be a bit overwhelming the first time."

"And the second," she informed him.

"Yes." Rafe laughed, dropping a kiss to the top of her head. "And the second. But now that you know all the delicious secrets of this lovemaking business, do you think you will be ready for me the next time we make love?"

"Uh huh," she murmured, trailing her fingers through the thick carpet of hair that adorned his wide chest. Caitlan entertained herself in this fashion for a short while, then a coy grin curled her lips when she whispered, "Rafe?"

"Yes?"

"Just when do you think that might be . . . the next time, that is?"

* * *

Caitlan felt rather than heard the chuckle rumbling in Rafe's chest, and she pulled away to look at him. Within seconds, her quizzical frown changed to a knowing smile; Rafe guided her hand from his chest down to that intimidating length of masculine flesh that had already grown hard again from wanting her. As he pressed her down into the pillows, Caitlan was vaguely aware of his throaty murmurings.

"Soon, Kettie. *Very* soon."

And Caitlan was ready for him. The next time . . . and the next . . . and the next. . . .

* * *

Caitlan stood at the kitchen sink, clad in her nightgown and robe, her brown-and-russet curls tied back with a length of lavender ribbon. From the looks of her radiant complexion and the smile that twittered in her eyes, one would be hard-pressed to believe that she had not had a single wink of sleep the night before. It was barely six o'clock, but Caitlan—full of nervous energy—had come downstairs just before five, thinking to get an early start on the day's cooking. As she stood there, her hands immersed in soapy dish water and her thoughts wandering back to the delicious memories of the night just spent, she felt a hand creep around her waist and boldly slip between the opening of her robe to fondle her breast.

"Morning," Rafe breathed against her neck.

"Good morning," she returned, turning her face toward his to accept his kiss.

"Why didn't you wake me?" he asked, yawning. Tossing his jacket across a chair, he stepped over to the counter and poured himself a cup of coffee.

"Because I never would have made it down those stairs this livelong day if I had," she informed him, giggling at her own shameless admission. "Besides, you looked as if you could use the sleep. Sit down, Rafe. I made breakfast for you."

Caitlan filled a plate for Rafe, then pouring herself a cup of coffee, sat down across from him at the kitchen table.

"Aren't you going to have anything?" Rafe asked, taking a forkful of scrambled eggs and chewing with relish.

Caitlan shook her head, explaining that she had already eaten and watched with amusement, then amazement as Rafe devoured the plate of food in very short order. Standing, he walked over to the stove and refilled his plate from the pans that sat warming in the oven. Caitlan could hardly believe her eyes when she saw the tremendous serving of eggs, sausages, bacon, grits, and biscuits he carried back to the table. Setting the plate down, Rafe crossed to the ice box and, yanking the door open, bent forward to peer inside. He stood there for a long moment, one arm draped negligently across the door, scratching his left side with his right hand, his pensive gaze surveying the interior.

Suddenly he lifted his head and turned toward Caitlan. "Is there anymore of that blackberry cobbler left from the other day?'' he asked, grabbing the milk jug and helping himself to a glassful before returning to the table.

"Goodness gracious, Rafe!" Caitlan exclaimed, going to fetch the requested pastry. "A body would think you had not eaten for a week."

"Listen, Kettie," Rafe countered amid bites of food. "I just spent the night making love to a woman just about every which way a man can except for standing up. I'm starving! So, quit nagging at me, woman, and bring me that dish of cobbler." Though his tone was gruff, there was a smile dancing about the blue eyes which lit up even brighter when he added, "Oh, and how about some peach preserves for my biscuits?"

Caitlan, a pensive frown quirking her brow from something he had said, placed the requested delicacies in front of him and sat down. Picking up her coffee cup, she took a contemplative sip and rested her elbows on the table. As she peered at him across the top of the steaming cup, Caitlan was persuaded to ask, "Standing up?"

Rafe was in mid-chew when the provocative question reached his still drowsy ears and, glancing up, he nearly choked when he saw her demure expression. "Oh, God, Kettie. Now?" he groaned. "Can I at least finish my breakfast first? Just sit there and talk to me for a spell while I rebuild my strength. Tell me, have you given any thought to what I asked you last night?"

"Rafe." Caitlan sighed, sitting back and crossing her arms in front of her. "I simply cannot go to New Orleans with you. Not now anyway."

"Why not?"

"Why not?" she repeated, incredulous that he should ask. "Well, for one thing, there is the tearoom. I cannot run off willy-nilly only after just getting it up and running. It would not be fair to Essie."

"What wouldn't be fair to Essie?" asked the very same young lady upon entering the kitchen.

Knowing full well that it was useless to try and keep a secret from Essie, Caitlan shrugged and said, "Oh, Rafe has invited me to accompany him to New Orleans, and he will not accept the fact that I cannot leave you alone to manage the tearoom."

"Has he now?" Essie looked from one to the other and,

after considering Rafe's glib expression, the mountain of food before him, and Caitlan's glowing face, she put two and two together and grinned. "So, that's how it is, is it?"

"That's how what is?" Caitlan demanded.

"Never mind," Essie trilled, joining them at the table. "I just knew all them 'sweet peas' and 'darlin's' he's been throwin' around all casual-like would eventually get to you, that's all. Now stop worryin' about me and this place and go with him," she urged. "I'm not sayin' I can cook as good as you . . . but almost. Anyway, the customers won't be able to tell the difference cause I'll use your receipts. And I can get my sisters Eliza and Eugenia to help out while you're gone. Just how long are you fixin' to be gone anyway?"

"I'm not fixin' to be gone at all" came Caitlan's agitated rebuttal. "So, stop pestering me about it."

"Well, you just change your mind, Katie. You've earned some time away from this place, what with Hezekiah runnin' off the way he did, and those men shootin' up the place the other night. Did you ever figure out what they were after? Well, no matter." She dismissed the question as quickly as she had voiced it and helped herself to a piece of bacon from Rafe's plate despite the glaring look he threw at her. Essie polished off the bacon, then dusting her hands together, stood up. As she strolled over to collect the broom and dustpan from behind the door, she said, "I'm going to sweep out the dining-rooms before time to open up. But you think about what I said, Katie. The place will be here waiting for you when you get back."

Caitlan waited until the door closed behind this whirlwind, otherwise known as Essie, before addressing Rafe. "There are other reasons besides the tearoom, you know."

"Name one."

"I haven't the proper clothing."

"I am fairly certain there are dress shops in New Orleans," Rafe countered, pushing the near-empty plate of food aside and rocking back in his chair.

"And money. I haven't . . . *you* haven't for that matter . . . the money for such an excursion."

"Excuses, lame excuses." Rafe thumped his fist against the table. "Dammit, Kettie. You're so all-fired worried I won't come back . . . I know you are . . . even though I told you last night I would. Well, I'm offering you a way to make sure I do.'' His voice deepened, and he looked at her with those soulful blue eyes and whispered, ''Come with me.''

Before Caitlan could answer, the door flew open again and Essie hurried across the threshold, bursting with news. ''Katie, there's a reporter from the *Daily Sun* outside. He wants to know if you'll talk to him about what happened here Saturday night. What do you want me to tell him?''

Caitlan mulled her reply for a long moment. Swallowing hard, her eyes found Rafe's across the table and she murmured, ''Tell him I don't have time right now. Tell him . . . tell him I have to get ready to leave for New Orleans.''

Essie clapped her hands together with glee upon hearing Caitlan's reply. Muttering something about going to fetch her sisters and tell them the news, she whirled and ran from the room.

To be honest, Rafe felt like clapping his hands and jumping up and down for joy himself. But considering his advanced years, he decided that a more dignified reaction was expected of him. Standing, he walked around the table to Caitlan and tilted her head back. Touching his lips to hers, he murmured, ''A wise decision, ma'am.''

Feeling suddenly amorous and, remembering their naughty conversation from before Essie came in, Rafe pulled Caitlan from her chair. Hoping to avoid any similar interruptions, he stepped to the door and shot the bolt. Then proffering his hand, he said simply, ''Come here.''

Chapter Thirteen

The shrill cries of the steamboat whistle shattered the afternoon stillness as it sounded the *Magnolia Princess*'s impending departure. Caitlan and Rafe had already boarded the majestic stern-wheeler and, while he went off to find their cabins and make certain that everything was in order, she remained on deck. Taking up a stance beside the railing, Caitlan directed her gaze toward the pier and the hubbub of activity that was taking place thereon. While she appeared to be enthralled with watching as cargo was hoisted into place and the last of the passengers were herded up the gangplank, in truth, her thoughts were elsewhere.

Caitlan was having second thoughts about her impetuous decision to accompany Rafe to New Orleans. What had she been thinking when she accepted his invitation? And what Rafe must think of her for having said yes to him, she could just imagine. Only lewd, immoral women acted in such a brazen fashion and Caitlan was neither of those things . . . at least, she had never been before. Her musings drifted back to the night of uninhibited passion she and Rafe had shared, and a whimsical smile lit up her face. Then with a stern, self-admonishing shake of her head, Caitlan brought her wandering thoughts back to the matter that presently troubled her.

She should have waited for him to come back, Caitlan decided. Rafe had promised he would return to her just as soon as he took care of some plaguey business matter. Her brow crinkled with a frown as this rumination brought her to an altogether different dilemma . . . Rafe. There was so much she did not know about him. Seven years was a long time. People changed. She certainly had. And then there was this dreadful business with Rawlings and Hayes. Caitlan had wanted to question Rafe about it, but between making love until the wee hours of the morning and scurrying to get ready for this trip, the opportunity had not presented itself. Everything had happened so fast—like a whirlwind—but now that she had time for cool-headed reflection, Caitlan realized she had most probably made a mistake.

Rafe would understand, Caitlan told herself. She would find him and simply explain that she had changed her mind.

But as she took a halfhearted step away from the rail to do just that, Caitlan discovered that she was too late. The gangplank had been raised into position for traveling and, as the calliope launched into a deafening melody, the riverboat lurched and backed away from its mooring. For better or worse, she was committed. But to what?

Even as the word formed an image in her brain, Caitlan refused to allow her hopeful heart to embrace it . . . marriage. Thus far, Rafe had made only a fleeting reference to the hallowed state of matrimony. But Caitlan remembered a time— a lifetime ago—when talk of marriage had driven him away for five years. Caitlan could not chance that happening again. Regardless of what the town tabbies may say about her—and there would be gossip, of that she was certain—she resolved to accept Rafe's terms for the time being. And when he asked her . . . if he asked her . . . only then would she open up her heart to him. Until then, Caitlan would be patient and wait for him . . . as she always did.

"Penny for your thoughts," Rafe said, sidling up beside her at the deck railing.

"Ha! There you go, squandering your money again." Caitlan gave a nervous laugh, grateful that, since Rafe was willing to buy her thoughts, he had not been able to read them. "They are hardly worth it, I assure you. Besides, I should very well

think that you would need to keep every last one of your pennies
just to pay for this excursion. For how you can afford such an
extravagance on the piddling salary I pay you is a mystery to
me.''

''Yes . . . well,'' Rafe coughed awkwardly, taking hold of
her hand and tugging her away from the railing, ''perhaps we
will discuss that later. For now, suppose I escort you to your
cabin,'' he offered, tucking her hand under his arm.

Thus they strolled along the wide deck arm in arm in companionable silence, watching as the Vicksburg skyline shrank
and vanished altogether when the *Magnolia Princess* rounded
a bend in the river.

''Isn't she beautiful?'' Rafe asked conversationally.

This question, which came from out of the blue, understandably caused a jealous spark to flare in a certain young lady's
breast. Caitlan instinctively glanced about the deck, expecting
to see some ravishing damsel who had caught Rafe's eye. She
saw no one out of the ordinary in their immediate vicinity,
however.

Frowning, she asked, ''Who? Where?''

Rafe, cognizant of Caitlan's green-eyed reaction to his statement, squeezed her arm and chuckled. ''No, silly. I'm talking
about the *Princess*. She's impressive, don't you think?'' Without waiting for an answer, Rafe launched into a stream of
nautical chitchat about the vessel.

''The *Magnolia Princess* is the biggest and fastest steamboat
on the Mississippi,'' he explained. ''She's over three hundred
feet long and can clip through the water at up to twelve knots;
that is upstream and in the roughest current. There are at least
twenty-five staterooms on this deck and another fifty on the
one above us. Why, the boat even has a nursery for children.
And the cargo space? Have you ever seen anything like it?
They loaded every bit of three thousand bales of cotton on
board and another eight thousand sacks of cotton seed . . . unless I miss my guess. And the salon, you really must see it,
Kettie. There's not a finer dining establishment on the Mississippi . . . well, with the exception of a certain tearoom in
Vicksburg which I happen to be mighty partial to.'' Blue eyes
twinkled down at her. ''What do you think, Kettie?''

Caitlan, who had listened patiently while Rafe extolled the

riverboat's virtues with all the enthusiasm of a little boy telling his nanny about his first pony ride, shrugged and said, "Well, from the way you talk about this floating palace, one would almost think it belonged to you."

Rafe paused before a cabin door and inclined his head to indicate they had arrived at her quarters. Pushing the portal ajar, he nudged Caitlan across the threshold. Then he scratched his chin, grimaced and said, "But that's just the thing, Kettie. The *Magnolia Princess* does belong to me. I own her . . . lock, stock, and stern-wheel."

"Are you sure you won't try just a bite of this lobster?" Rafe cajoled, holding a forkful of the savory meat before Caitlan's lips as if trying to coax a small child to eat. "It's delicious," he told her for at least the fourth time. But when it became apparent that no amount of wheedling would tempt Caitlan from her foul mood, Rafe let the utensil clatter against his plate, swearing, "Dammit, Kettie! What's gotten into you?

"You acted like a goddamn madwoman this afternoon, screeching at me to stop the *Magnolia Princess* and let you off. The mere idea. What did you intend to do . . . swim back to Vicksburg? Then when I explained that we would be stopping in Natchez for the night, you behaved in an oh so mature fashion by slamming the door in my face—refusing to talk or listen to me—saying only that I should let you know when we arrived, so that you could get off.

"And now this." He splayed his hands in an all-encompassing gesture. "You declined my invitation to dine in the grand salon. What was it you said? Oh, yes . . . 'I'd rather walk naked down Washington Street,' " he quoted her exact words. "A charming image, I grant you, but hardly something I would expect a *lady* to say," he scolded in his most haughty voice.

Knowing his next action would only irritate her all the more, Rafe reached inside his jacket and retrieved a cigar which he proceeded to puff alight from the candle on the table. Leaning back in his chair, he continued to air his somewhat lengthy list of complaints.

"I do admit I probably exhibited poor judgment when I suggested you might like to wear one of the frocks hanging in the armoire. Although I daresay it hardly warranted you hurling that music box at my head. I didn't mean to offend you by making the gesture, Kettie. I merely thought you might like to put aside your homespun for one evening and wear something a little more fashionable for a change. You used to love to wear pretty clothes,'' Rafe reminded the stony visage that sat opposite him. ''But once again, I apologize if I offended you.''

Rafe grew silent for a moment as he considered Caitlan's unyielding countenance. Blowing a cloud of smoke in her direction, he raised one dark eyebrow and drawled, ''Kettie, dear, you cannot truly believe I've been a monk for the past seven years.''

In answer to this bold statement, Caitlan merely pulled herself poker-straight in her chair and continued glaring at him, saying not a word, yet speaking volumes.

Rafe held a tight rein on his emotions; he had never wanted to throttle anyone more dearly than he did Caitlan at that moment. Though his jaw had begun to twitch, Rafe held in his anger and thumbed at the mangled pile of tissue paper that lay in the middle of the floor. Caitlan had promptly consigned the peace offering to this humbling station when he had presented it to her upon entering the cabin.

''As for the shawl, it was a gift chosen especially for you'' came his softly spoken admission. ''I stopped by Madame Cognaisse's shop earlier today, and she helped me select the shawl for you, explaining she had seen you admire it on several occasions.

''So, here we sit. We could be . . . should be . . . in the salon, making small talk over a leisurely supper, enjoying the entertainment, and mingling with the other passengers,'' he told her, resentment creeping into his voice. ''But no, you insist on locking yourself in this cabin and behaving like a stubborn, willful brat . . . refusing to eat or talk. You won't even let me explain why I thought it was necessary to keep my little secret all these weeks. Damn, even a criminal is given a trial before he's convicted,'' Rafe informed her. Then having tolerated enough of her standoffish mien for one evening, he jumped from his chair and shouted, ''Christ almighty, Kettie! The way you're carrying on, I almost believe you would prefer it if I were a pauper.''

When this accusation failed to evoke any reaction from Caitlan, Rafe turned and stalked to the door that connected her cabin with his. "*Women!*" he spat, shoving a frustrated hand through his hair. "A man could go stark raving mad trying to please them, for it cannot be done." And upon muttering this passionate declaration, Rafe exited the room.

Caitlan, in turn, relaxed her inflexible mien the moment the door closed behind Rafe. With a sigh, she admitted—begrudgingly and only to herself—that he had been within his rights to scold her on all counts . . . well, *almost*. He should have known that she could not have liked having the knowledge that other women had shared his living quarters, had in fact, been intimate with him in this very room, flung in her face. Closing her eyes, Caitlan took a deep breath, determined to burn these hurtful images from her mind. After all, Rafe was with her now, and that was all that mattered.

Thus mollified, and with the threat of a long, lonely night— possibly a lifetime—hanging over her head should she not attempt to make amends with a certain headstrong gentleman in the adjoining cabin, Caitlan swallowed her pride and pushed away from the table. She was about to stand when she caught a glimpse of the crumpled mound of tissue paper that she had discarded earlier. Within moments, a positively wicked grin appeared on her face; a shameless idea had popped into her head. Knowing she must act before her courage waned, Caitlan plucked the cashmere shawl from the floor.

Rafe was still sitting in the wing chair where he had hurled himself upon taking his leave of Caitlan, a brooding thundercloud of emotion, when he heard a tentative rapping at the connecting door. Disregarding the summons, disgruntled fingers unraveled the neatly tied cravat at his throat and jerked open the top two buttons of his silk shirt so that he could breathe. When the tapping continued, Rafe told himself that he had endured more than enough of that young lady's churlish disposition for one day, and that if he were subjected to another of Caitlan's stone-cold gazes, he would very likely wring her neck. Thinking that if he ignored her long enough, Caitlan would tire of her little game and go to bed, Rafe reached for the whiskey bottle on the table to his right and tilted it toward the glass he had drained only moments earlier.

But Rafe's nonresponsive tactics failed to bring about the desired results and, when it became apparent that Caitlan was not going to give up, he leveled a darkling look at the door and barked, "Go away, Caitlan!"

On the other side of that wooden barrier, the object of this hostility understandably blanched. Rafe had used her Christian name . . . a sure indication of his pique. Summoning her nerve, Caitlan squared her shoulders and pushed the door open despite Rafe's command to the contrary.

"Dammit, Ket—"

Whatever admonition Rafe had been about to voice fizzled summarily upon his tongue. In fact, he very nearly choked on his words when he saw the stunning vision standing in the doorway. Caitlan projected a charming pose indeed, framed as she was by the candlelight from the adjoining room, her hair tumbling freely all about her. And she was wearing the cashmere shawl that Rafe had given her . . . that and nothing else.

"Kettie" came Rafe's hoarse whisper.

Rafe's disbelieving eyes never wavered from the doorway as his trembling fingers brought the whiskey glass to his lips. He quaffed the potent libation in a single drink.

Before Rafe could speak another word, Caitlan padded across the floor and curled up on his lap like a kitten. Coiling her arms about his neck, she rested her head on his shoulder and purred, "Shh. Let me talk."

Rafe thought that an exceedingly good idea since the enticing bundle that had brazenly sprawled herself across his lap had quite rendered his tongue useless.

"You were right . . . I was being stubborn," she admitted, pouting at him with those wondrous green eyes. "But you were also very much wrong," Caitlan accused, walking her fingers up his chest to toy with the tuft of dark, curly hair that peeked out the opening of his shirt. "I'm not displeased to discover that you have become successful. Quite the contrary; it appears you have amassed a great fortune and for that you are to be congratulated. Knowing you as I do, I realize you have worked hard to get where you are. No, I would not *prefer* having you as the pauper you pretended to be, even though I was perfectly happy being with you when I thought you were penniless. What I don't understand is . . . why did you keep your wealth such a secret from everyone, especially me? Don't you trust me?''

"Aw hell, Kettie. Of course I do." He snuggled her against him. "It's just that, when I woke up and found you taking care of my busted, broken body . . . hell, I didn't know what to think. I was in so much pain, all I could think about was Rawlings and Hayes and what they did to me. I didn't want to risk them hurting anyone else, especially you. I knew that, if word got around town that you were looking after some rich fellow, they would figure things out and come looking for me. But nobody would give a damn about some poor, penniless fool who was so stupid as to go and get himself ambushed by a couple of thugs.''

"You could have told me later," Caitlan grumbled. "You had plenty of opportunities.''

"Well," Rafe scratched the back of his head and hunched his shoulders, "that's just it, Kettie. By the time I stopped worrying about those two bastards—a might too soon as it turned out—there *you* were. I could hardly justify staying on at Tuttle's or . . . later . . . with you at the carriage house when I had the means to buy the whole damn town if I took the notion. I—'' He faltered and tilted Caitlan's head back, so that he could gaze down at her face. Reading the encouragement in her eyes, he said, "I just wanted the opportunity to get to know you again . . . get close to you. I thought I stood a better chance of doing so if you believed me to be down on my luck. Believe me, sweet pea,'' Rafe murmured, caressing her cheek with his knuckles, "I never meant to hurt or deceive you.''

"I know," Caitlan murmured. Sighing, she offered Rafe her lips. They kissed and, when after several wistful moments they pulled apart, she glanced about the richly decorated cabin and asked, "Just how rich are you anyway?''

"Ha!" Rafe blurted, taken aback by her candor. Chuckling, he pursed his lips and said simply, "*Very.*''

"I see," she mumbled, her fingers fondling the elegant material of his jacket.

Noticing the contemplative crook of her brow, Rafe was

prompted to inquire, "What's wrong? Are you still angry with me?"

"No."

"Do you still want me to make arrangements in Natchez for you to go back to Vicksburg? I don't want to, mind you," he told her flatly. "But, if that is what you want, I'll do it for you."

Caitlan shook her head. "No, I want very much to continue on with you to New Orleans, however—"

"Yes?"

"If time allows, I would like to leave the *Princess* long enough to shop for a new dress or two. I do thank you for extending the use of the garments in my cabin, but I cannot bring myself to wear them. Please understand, I don't harbor any resentment about your past and the women you have known. Indeed, I have no right. But neither should you expect me to prance about in the clothing you purchased for them.

"Now, I brought a little money with me," Caitlan explained. "And, well . . ." she absently fingered Rafe's dark blue satin coat and heaved a weary sigh, "I would not like to embarrass you with the shabby state of my wardrobe. Although I might as well tell you right now that I do not intend to go putting on airs. I know my place, and there will be no hoops nor yards and yards of silks and taffetas. Just a serviceable—albeit fashionable—ensemble will do quite nicely."

"Why don't you wait until we get to New Orleans?" Rafe suggested, twirling a heavy curl that dangled about her breast. "There are several shops within walking distance of the hotel where we will be staying. You may buy whatever you wish."

Caitlan considered this, then said, "I don't know. I cannot afford to be too extravagant."

"Kettie, I have money—"

"No, Rafe." Caitlan shook her head, her green eyes flashing with determination. "I won't have you buying my clothes. Everyone will think I'm your . . . Well, people are thinking quite enough already, I am certain. I'll not wittingly give them fuel to add to their wicked thoughts."

"Call it a loan."

"What?"

"Let me lend you the money you need. Better yet, let me

invest in the tearoom. You can pay me back out of each quarter's profits.''

Caitlan mulled Rafe's offer. He made it sound so logical, so easy . . . too easy. Looking doubtful, she said, ''I don't know, Rafe. What if the tearoom doesn't turn a profit?''

''Hell *and* damnation, if you haven't turned out to be a troublesome thing,'' Rafe swore in frustration, shaking his head. ''You used to be sweet and docile. What happened to you, Kettie?''

''I grew up.''

''Yes,'' he noted, running his finger around one voluptuous breast. ''Yes, you did. And quite nicely, I might add.'' He smiled with pleasure as the nipple grew taut and thrust out proudly against the palm of his hand.

Caitlan, realizing that the conversation had taken an amorous turn, taunted him by saying, ''I thought you wanted to spend the evening in the grand salon.''

''What? Go there now? With you, dressed like this?'' Rafe sputtered. Seeing the impish gleam in Caitlan's eyes, he pushed her from his lap, crying, ''Hoyden!''

As Caitlan sat upon the hard floor, rubbing her smarting buttocks and glaring up at him, Rafe leaned close to murmur, ''Although I will allow that you're a bit overdressed for what I have in mind. Shall we?'' Rafe cocked his head toward the four-poster that headed the far wall.

He did not have to ask a second time. Seeing Caitlan nod her head eagerly, Rafe laughed and scooped her from the floor and into his arms. Striding over to the bed, he nestled her against the turndown sheets, then set about removing his own clothing.

As Caitlan rolled to her side to watch him go about his evening ablutions, she felt obliged to tell him, ''You were also wrong about not being able to please a woman.''

''Really?''

''Yes. You have brought me a great deal of pleasure,'' she told him, her cheeks pinkening with embarrassment when she observed his shameless expression. ''And not just *that* way, but when you helped me deal with Harriet, and all the things you did around the tearoom when I know you must have wished yourself elsewhere a thousand times, and . . . and this shawl.''

She smoothed the delicate fabric with a loving hand. "Thank you for my shawl. I shall treasure it always."

"It suits you," Rafe said, walking over to the bed and climbing in beside her. "I fear, however, that it is very much a nuisance at the moment. May I?" He extended his hand and helped peel the shawl away from her shoulders. Tossing the costly garment onto a nearby chair, Rafe devoted his undivided attention to more pleasurable pursuits.

Coaxing Caitlan back against the pillows, Rafe made as if to press a kiss against her sensuously full lips when he noticed her puzzled frown. "What's troubling you now, sweet pea?" he murmured against her throat.

Looking up, Caitlan brushed her hand across his forehead and asked, "Just what other great lurking secrets are you keeping from me, I wonder?"

Rafe, thinking back to the furious reaction his earlier confession had wrought, thought for a moment. With a nervous laugh, he rolled on top of Caitlan. Pinning her legs beneath his, Rafe lowered his head to nibble at the tip of one breast. While he appeared to be completely enamored of this diverting pastime, he allowed his hands to creep up Caitlan's shapely arms to her wrists where he imprisoned both her hands in his. Next, Rafe removed his lips from that alluring mound of flesh to burn a trail of intoxicating kisses along her collarbone, to her mouth, and around to her ear.

Deciding that now was as good a time as any to tell her, he shrugged and whispered, "Kettie, darlin', about Hezekiah . . ."

The riverboat journey from Vicksburg to New Orleans took five days. Fortunately for Rafe, Caitlan did not spend the entire voyage pouting at him after he divulged the part he had played in helping Hezekiah rescue his Abigail from the Cantrell plantation. Although Caitlan was sad that Hezekiah was gone, at least she knew he was happy and—more importantly—safe with Abigail far away from Mississippi and the men Jeremy had sent looking for them.

It would seem that Rafe had taken care of everything. He had secreted the couple on another of his riverboats—the *Louisiana Belle*—that was traveling north to Cincinnati. From there, he had made arrangements for Hezekiah and Abigail to journey on into Canada . . . Toronto to be exact. Rafe had explained that he had friends in the Canadian city who would look after Hezekiah and Abigail and help them get settled. Rafe had also promised her that, as soon as it was safe to do so, he would give her an address where she might get in touch with her longtime friend and champion.

Thus pacified, Caitlan had swallowed her initial vexation at Rafe for his duplicity in the affair. After all, she had sent Rafe to prevent Hezekiah from making a terrible mistake, not render him assistance. Realizing that she could either put on a long face and mope about the cabin for days on end, or put the unhappy incident behind her and enjoy her time alone with Rafe, Caitlan promptly opted for the latter.

In the days immediately following, Caitlan spent hour upon glorious hour exploring the *Magnolia Princess* with Rafe. The grand salon proved to be everything he had said it was, from the crystal chandeliers with ornate candelabra to the filigree paneling of natural cherry wood with inlaid arches. The riverboat's china was decorated with hand-painted pictures of the stern-wheeler and the silver was engraved with the riverboat's likeness and initials. All the furniture, from the grand salon to the bridal suites—of which there were three—to the staterooms, had been made in France of heavy walnut with an inlay of rosewood and displayed the initials "MP" in carved wreaths of holly.

Entertainment was provided for young and old alike. Although gambling was not a popular activity with all the passengers, it was permitted in restricted areas of the boat and was carefully monitored at all times.

The five-day excursion passed quickly; when Rafe was not escorting her about the deck, introducing her to the captain and the crew and mingling with the passengers, they could be found dining in the salon where they oftentimes lingered until the wee hours of the morning, dancing and listening to the orchestra. Once, Rafe even went so far as to engage Caitlan in a friendly game of cribbage, at which she soundly trounced him. And, of course, when they were alone together in his cabin, they could very often be found composing their own passionate melodies upon the chamber berth.

Opulence and elegance. Those were the words that sprang to Caitlan's mind whenever she glanced about her plush surroundings. She did so now as she lounged in a tub of scented water in her cabin, and she felt a pang of regret when she thought of how she would presently be leaving all this grandeur behind. Lathering the washcloth with a bar of rose-scented soap, Caitlan lifted her leg from the water and began to scrub the shapely limb with the fragrant cloth.

Sighing, she asked, "What did you say the name of the hotel was where we will be staying?"

Rafe's newspaper made a rustling sound as he lowered it and leveled a tolerant eye at the watery vision who sat not more than five feet from him. His gaze narrowed as he leaned forward to pluck a piece of buttered toast from his breakfast plate. He took a contemplative bite, chewed, and, with all the petulance of a gentleman who has been pestered with a particular question several times over, said, "The St. Charles. Hell, Kettie. It's only the finest hotel that New Orleans has to offer. It cannot be that troublesome a name to remember."

"I know. I'm just feeling a little blue about leaving the *Princess*. I had a delightful time on our trip down from Vicksburg. Indeed, I cannot recall when I enjoyed myself more," she said with a dreamy lilt in her voice and leaned back against the cool copper tub.

"Yes . . . well, all I can say is you've gone all soft in the head if you prefer this riverboat to all that New Orleans has to offer." He rubbed a thoughtful hand across his bearded cheek and a waspish smile lit up his face. "Hell, if I didn't know better, I might think you were dawdling in that bath in the hopes I might join you. But Christ almighty, after last night and this morning, I thought you would have had enough to keep you until noon at least."

"Ooh, *you*!" Caitlan seethed—though not angrily—at the smug look he turned on her. Without truly thinking of her actions, she hurled the soapy washcloth at his arrogant head.

Rafe easily dodged the dripping airborne missile and stood up. Snatching a monogrammed towel from the chest of drawers behind Caitlan, he advanced toward the tub. "Come on, sweet pea," he wheedled. "All of New Orleans awaits to be explored. You cannot mean to set up housekeeping on the *Princess*.''

"You have," she reminded him.

"That's different," Rafe countered. "The *Princess* has become my main residence, that's true. But I also maintain rooms in New Orleans and St. Louis. For you see, darlin','' he squatted down beside the tub and allowed his index finger to have its way with her collarbone, ''as much as I love this riverboat, every now and again I do enjoy going ashore. Now, climb on out of there and get dressed. Time's a wastin'.''

"But why is that, I wonder?"

"What?''

"Why did you never buy your own place . . . a home or a plantation? I can just see you riding out to oversee the planting and harvesting of acres and acres of rich farmland.'' A winsome smile lit Caitlan's eyes as she visualized this image to be supplanted a moment later by a question, which she asked, ''Whatever happened to your father's plantation near Nashville?''

"Sold upon his death'' came his blunt retort. "I had no need of it, and I had no desire to return to Tennessee. My future—my destiny—did not lie there. As for owning a rambling home of my own,'' he said, shrugging those magnificent shoulders of his, ''I've never had need of one.

"Now," Rafe said, tweaking her nose and, adopting a haughty air, ''if you can be persuaded to dispense with the asking of trite questions, we shall be on our way. Come on, honey,'' he cajoled, waving the towel in front of her in a beckoning gesture. ''There is someone I'm anxious for you to meet. She's a sweet little bundle. Indeed, I can hardly wait to hold her in my arms again.''

Knowing full well that this ambiguous announcement would succeed where all else had failed, Rafe smiled to himself as Caitlan all but jerked the towel from his fingers. Standing, he turned toward his cabin, thinking he would let his surly miss mull this unexpected development for a while. It was a rakish grin that adorned his mouth and a jaunty step lightened his gait as he stepped across the adjoining threshold, the refrains of Caitlan's splashy exodus from the tub resounding in his ears.

* * *

Caitlan sat opposite Rafe in the carriage as it trundled through the streets of New Orleans and wiggled restlessly against the leather squabs. One may very well believe her anxiety to be the result of Rafe's startling pronouncement. While he most certainly was to blame for unsettling her nerves, Caitlan's present distress was the consequence of an altogether different dilemma.

The door had not even swung closed behind Rafe's haughty countenance before Caitlan had scrambled from the bathtub. She had dressed in haste and now—the outcome of her hit-or-miss efforts in toweling dry—her chemise clung to her damp skin. Fully cognizant of the quizzical stare that Rafe directed at her, she ignored him and tugged at the offensive garment in an attempt to feel less constricted. Caitlan could not even take pleasure in the knowledge that she was wearing the new rose-colored silk blouse with the lace trim she had purchased in Natchez, nor the deep blue skirt with the rose ruching about the hem. She looked pretty, better than she had in years, and Rafe had to go and spoil everything by telling her how excited he was about getting to see some other woman again. Sometimes the man went too far.

"How much farther?" she grumbled, crossing her arms across her heaving bosom.

"Several more blocks, I fear," he told her, biting back the chuckle that tickled his throat. To himself, he thought, *Temper, temper, my fine miss. It's precisely that petulant disposition of yours that kept us apart the past seven years. For had I not been made to believe you were dead, I would have come knocking on your door long ago ... unfortunate letter or not.* His musings having turned to this touchy subject, Rafe lifted a pensive mien to Caitlan. Reaching across the narrow aisle that separated them, he coaxed her hand into his and said, "Do you know what I was just remembering?"

"No. What?"

"The second time I came riding back into your life." Rafe felt Caitlan go rigid, beginning with the tips of her fingers and, hoping to avoid an ugly scene, he hastened on, "Now, don't poker up at me like that. I don't understand why you behave this way every time I mention the past."

"And I don't understand this perverse fascination you have

with days gone by,'' Caitlan returned. ''They are over and done, Rafe. Leave them be.''

''No. They are important to me—these memories I have of you—as important to me as you are now. And I hold them dear. Hell, that's what kept me going all these years, Kettie. Didn't you know that?'' He nudged her knee with his and obliged her to look at him. ''Tell me, do you recall what you were doing when I rode up the drive at Thistledown that spring morning?''

Caitlan nodded, then finding her voice, said, ''I was cutting a basket of flowers—daffodils, I think—along the driveway.''

''That you were. And when I climbed down from my horse, you smiled up at me and said, 'Hello, Rafe,' just as pretty as you please, as if you had been expecting me . . . as if you had known all along in your heart that I would come back to you.'' Rafe moved across the aisle to settle himself beside Caitlan. Draping his arm about her shoulder, he nuzzled his chin against her hair and said, ''You were right about why I left the first time, Kettie. The notion of getting married, settling down with one woman and starting a family, scared me half out of my wits.

''Josie was right. We were both too young, and I didn't have much to offer a bride. That's why I left, Kettie—to make my fortune, so you would be proud of me, so we would have a secure future together. I do admit that it was wrong of me not to come and tell you all this myself, but I could not bear to see your pretty face when I told you of my plans. That's why I left the way I did . . . why I asked my sister to bring you the news. The two of you were friends at the time. I thought Josie could perhaps soften the blow.''

''You were wrong'' came Caitlan's hollow murmur.

''I know, honey,'' Rafe replied, holding her tight. ''And I'm sorry I put you through all that. But I did come back, darlin','' he reminded her. ''It took me all of five years, but I did come back.''

Since Rafe seemed determined to rehash the past, Caitlan decided that she would have her say. ''But why did you leave again so soon? You came to Thistledown off and on for a year and then you were gone again, leaving only that letter . . . oh, that mean, hateful letter, Rafe. How could you do that to me

. . . after you told me you loved me? How could you? Why?''
she sobbed, near tears.

"I know. I know, darlin'." Rafe patted her arm in a consoling gesture. "You had good reason to hate me, despise me
for what I did, but believe it or not, I can explain that, too.
And perhaps I shall . . . later. But first, I have a bone to pick
with you. Oh, you got back at me, didn't you, sweet pea?''
he accused, unaware of the bemused frown that furrowed Caitlan's brow.

"What do you mean?'' she asked, genuinely confused.

"Oh, that's rich, pretending you don't remember after all
these years," Rafe chided, tapping her nose with his finger.
"I should box your ears for you now that I have my hands on
you. God, I nearly went mad when Josie sent word that you
were dead."

"What?!" Caitlan exclaimed, pulling away from him.
"Whatever are you talking about, Rafe?"

"Don't play coy, Kettie. You know damn good and well
what I'm referring to . . . how you evidently convinced Josie
that it would be in everyone's best interest if I were led to
believe you had died in a riverboat explosion. There was one
about that time, as I recall. The *Natchez Queen* was on her
way upriver to St. Louis when she caught fire one night and
sank. Over half her passengers were lost . . . either drowned or
blown to bits. Josie told me you were on board, that you—
like your mother before you—had run off with the first fella
that came along after I left. When the truth of the matter was
little Kettie Webber just wanted to discourage the only man
that ever truly loved her from darkening her door again. Well,
it worked all right. It cost us seven years of being together,
but it worked. I haven't been back to Foxborough Hall or
Thistledown since the day I received Josie's letter.

"Christ, how I hated you when I first learned of what you
did," he told her, his voice filled with angry emotion. "But
I soon got over it, because I remembered what we had. And
for seven years, the image I carried in my heart was of you—
my Kettie—all broken and lifeless, floating facedown amid the
debris of an exploded riverboat. I'd say I have been repaid in
full, wouldn't you, Kettie?''

Caitlan did not make an immediate attempt to reply to his

horrifying accusations. Indeed, she sat in stunned silence, unable to speak. All she could do was clutch at his sleeve while her mind screamed, *Lies, all lies*! She longed to tell Rafe this very thing, tell him that Josie—for whatever reason—had made up this incredible lie. He must believe her . . . she would *make* him believe her, if only she could make herself talk.

As fate would have it, the conveyance came to a stop before Caitlan regained the use of her tongue. Without waiting for the driver to hop down from his perch, Rafe pushed open the door and stepped out. Proffering his hand, he helped Caitlan alight.

Caitlan barely took note of her surroundings as Rafe led her through a creaky iron gate and into a courtyard that was encased by a high stone wall. She followed along blindly as he escorted her across the stone-flaggings to a door. As Rafe knocked upon the huge portal, Caitlan's flustered mien began to show signs of improvement, and she had just opened her mouth to address Rafe, when something occurred to freeze her comment on her lips. The door in front of them was opened by a woman wearing a nun's garb.

A convent! Rafe had brought her to a convent. But what on earth for? Completely mystified by this unexpected turn of events, Caitlan could do little more than stare in gape-faced wonder at the sister.

Through the fog that had inveigled her brain—turning it to mush—she heard Rafe say, "Good morning, Sister Angelica. Is she ready?"

"Yes, Mr. Bradrick. We received your dispatch yesterday afternoon." The oval-shaped face peeped out at him from the folds of the black and white wimple. Smiling at Rafe and, turning a curious—albeit polite—expression on Caitlan, she said, "Rebecca has been waiting patiently all morning."

"Shame on you, Sister," Rafe scolded the young woman. "I thought you gave up telling lies—even white ones—when you took your vows. If I know my little spitfire, she has been bouncing up and down, squealing with glee ever since you told her I was coming to see her." One glance at the nun's face verified his supposition and, smiling widely, Rafe said, "Where is she?"

He tried to look down the long hallway beyond Sister Angelica, but to no avail.

"She's right here." The sister indicated a tiny hand that clung to her habit. "She seems a bit frightened today. Perhaps it is the beard?" Sister Angelica suggested. "You did not have one the last time you visited, as I recall."

"Of course. It's been several months," he said with a regrettable sigh. Kneeling down before the open portal, Rafe stretched his arms out in a welcoming gesture to the small child who peeked out at him from behind Sister Angelica's wide skirt. And a broad grin spread his lips when he said, "Come on, Becky. Come to Daddy Rafe."

Chapter Fourteen

❧❦❧

Caitlan stood in the hotel room doorway and watched in subdued silence as Rafe tucked the small child in for her afternoon
nap. As might be expected, the nearly two-and-a-half-year-old
Rebecca protested—and loudly so—at being forced to lay quietly upon the bedsheets when all she truly wanted to do was
play with her ''Daddy Rafe'' and the new toys he had bought
her. Despite her throaty cries to the contrary, the counterpane
had no sooner been snuggled under her chin than Rebecca—
worn out from the day's excitement—quieted down.

While Rafe tended to the little girl, Caitlan crept closer to
observe as he murmured soft reassurances to the child and
stroked with loving tenderness the mass of dark brown ringlets
that covered Rebecca's head. Caitlan came to stand at the foot
of the bed, her hand gripping the bedpost, and a lump tightened
in the back of her throat as her gaze took in the poignant scene.
Huge brown eyes, wide with suspicion, remained riveted upon
Rafe's face, and Rebecca wrapped her tiny hand around his
thumb and held on for all she was worth. Eventually, the little
girl was comforted by the soothing sound of his voice, and,
as her eyelids began to droop, she shifted to her side, plopped
her thumb in her mouth and drifted off to sleep.

Caitlan observed the peacefully slumbering child—the

mouth that, although she slept, sucked relentlessly upon the tiny thumb and the fingers that clutched Rafe's bigger hand for security—and wished that she might be as easily pacified. In reality, she knew it would take a good deal more than a few moments of sleep to assuage her rampaging thoughts. The truth of the matter was, Caitlan still had not recovered from this latest surprise—of a rapidly growing list—that Rafe had sprung on her. Throughout the day, as they shopped for toys and ate lunch in the hotel dining-room, Caitlan had been plagued by a single nagging thought . . . Rafe had fathered this beautiful little girl.

With the recurrence of this heartrending reminder came a rush of irrational feelings, not the least of which was jealousy. As unbidden tears of anguish gathered in her eyes, Caitlan turned away from the bed; she feared that, if she remained, she would burst out howling at any moment. Knowing full well that such maudlin behavior would give rise to a host of questions that she was not prepared to answer, Caitlan took a step toward the door.

"Wait" came Rafe's hushed whisper.

Caitlan did as he requested; indeed, she was shocked into immobility by the mere fact that he was aware of her presence. She had not thought he noticed her, preoccupied as he was with getting Rebecca settled down for her nap. Her exodus thus forestalled, Caitlan turned back to watch as he executed his own escape. As she looked on, Rafe very carefully peeled the child's fingers away from his thumb. Before this desertion could be translated to her sleeping brain, he replaced his hand with the toy he had purchased for her that day.

Caitlan gazed on, dubious that this age-old ploy would be successful, and wondered again at the child's unlikely toy selection. As Rebecca's fingers curled about the wooden soldier, Caitlan shook her head, remembering the scene in the toy store earlier that day.

"Pitty," Rebecca had said, her eyes lighting up with excitement when she saw the shelf lined with an entire battalion of the brightly painted replicas. No amount of cajoling had convinced the little girl that the toy soldier was an inappropriate plaything for her. Nor had Rebecca been swayed from her decision when Caitlan tempted her with a new dolly. Rebecca had merely clasped the wooden figure more tightly in her fists, saying with determination, "Mine!"

Rafe had purchased the toy soldier and the doll, as well, but it was the colorful military figure that had commanded Rebecca's attention throughout the morning and lunch, right up until naptime. As Caitlan watched Rafe ease himself up from the bed, she hunched her shoulders and sighed. One thing was certain . . . she had a lot to learn about children.

Caitlan felt Rafe's hand on her elbow, nudging her forward. With a parting wishful look at Rebecca, she turned away from the bed and the couple tiptoed soundlessly from the room. Upon reaching the sitting-room, Rafe left the door open just a crack, so they might hear her when she wakened, then turning away, he wiped his hand across his brow.

"Whew! I had forgotten how difficult it can be putting her down for a nap. Becky hates them, but she grows downright cranky by suppertime if she hasn't had her sleep," he explained, striding over to the mantelshelf and the wine decanter that sat thereon.

Rafe poured himself a generous serving of the libation, but as he lifted the glass to his lips, he caught Caitlan's reflection in the gilt-framed mirror that hung over the fireplace. Noting her dejected mien, he put the glass aside and swiftly returned to her side. He was understandably surprised to see that the usually calm green eyes glistened with unshed tears.

Drawing her close, he wrapped her in his sinewy embrace and asked, "What is it, Kettie? This isn't like you. Why the tears?"

Caitlan hunched her shoulders and looked away, unable to meet his probing gaze. "I just feel so . . . inadequate," she mumbled against his broad chest. "And I . . . I don't think Becky likes me very much. Not that I can blame her, I suppose. I fear I know precious little about taking care of children," came her wretched admission.

Rafe chuckled and held her more tightly in his embrace. Dropping a kiss against the top of her russet-tinged head, he whispered, "You'll do just fine, honey. As for Becky, you need to give her a little time to get to know you is all. She'll come around, mark my words." He nudged Caitlan's chin to enable him a better view of her pretty face. "Better?" Rafe felt obliged to ask when he could see no visible sign that his speech had helped ease her troubled disposition.

Caitlan nodded, albeit it was a halfhearted gesture. Swallowing the knot that had been lodged in her throat for much of the day, she summoned the courage to ask, "What about Rebecca's mother, Rafe? What has become of her?"

Caitlan gladly accepted the glass of sherry that Rafe extended and, settling back against the sofa, she watched as he collected his wineglass from the mantel. She noted with some chagrin that his countenance had grown grim, a fact that could be evidenced by his actions; he quaffed the contents of the glass in a single motion and refilled the goblet before turning back to her.

Feeling suddenly ill at ease, Caitlan took a nervous sip of her own libation and said, "Rafe, I . . . I did not mean to pry. You don't have to—"

"No, it's all right, Kettie," Rafe assured her. "Actually, I should have confided much of this to you weeks ago. It's just that . . . well, honey, it's a difficult story for me to tell." He came to stand in front of her, the intensity of his brooding gaze making Caitlan think she ought not to have pestered him about Rebecca's mother. "You see, darlin'. Becky's mother is dead . . . murdered . . . butchered horribly—it's my guess—by the same two bastards that held us prisoner in the tearoom."

"Oh, no!" was Caitlan's shocked response, one hand flying to her mouth in dismay. "How dreadful! And how awful for you. You must have . . . loved her quite dearly."

"What? Loved her—" A perplexing frown creased Rafe's rugged brow as he stared down into Caitlan's upturned face. Reading the hurt she could not hide in those bewitching green eyes, Rafe sat down beside her. Taking her hand in his, he hastened his explanation, "No, sweet pea, you misunderstand. Becky is not mine. I mean, I *am* her legal guardian, but I'm not her real father. Let me explain.

"Do you remember asking me in the carriage this morning as to why I left so abruptly seven years ago? Well, the answer is a relatively simple one. I was called home to Nashville because Father had taken suddenly ill. He lingered near death for a month or so until . . . finally, one night he quietly slipped away. I believe I told you already that I had no need of a plantation, nor did I wish to remain in Tennessee. You see,'' he lifted his hand to cuddle her chin, ''by that time, I had received Josie's letter about you and all I could think about was getting away . . . striking out on my own.''

Once again, Caitlan was reminded of the terrible lie his sister had concocted. A bitter denial formed on her tongue but before she had the chance to launch her defense, Rafe continued.

''I buried Father alongside Mama in the family cemetery, then put the place up for sale. Wesley and Josie already had their hands full running Foxborough and, quite frankly, I would have sooner sold the place to strangers than let my brother-in-law get his greedy hands on it. But,'' Rafe plopped his feet on the footstool in front of him, ''as it turned out, I didn't have to. Ethan Meadows, a longtime friend and neighbor, came forward and offered to buy Shadow Vale. Ethan was making plans to marry his childhood sweetheart and wanted to make the plantation a home for himself and his soon-to-be bride.

''And so it was done. Ethan bought Shadow Vale and, with my share of the proceeds, I invested in the *Magnolia Princess*. I hadn't heard from Ethan in years. Oh, we exchanged an occasional letter, and I heard through mutual acquaintances that Shadow Vale was thriving under his care. But it wasn't until last year about this time that I had the opportunity to see Ethan again.''

At this point, Rafe grew silent, almost pensive. Caitlan, wishing to be supportive, placed a comforting hand upon his shoulder and murmured, ''Yes. What happened?''

''Ethan sent word that he was shipping his crops downriver to market in mid-December and wanted to know if I could meet him in New Orleans. He brought his family with him— his wife Jenny and little Becky—on a holiday, so that Jenny might explore the shops and the two of them could enjoy the city's entertainments. Luckily, as it later turned out, five-year-old Ethan, Jr., had come down with measles prior to the outset of their journey and had to be left behind with his nurse.''

Rafe, more disturbed by the recounting of his tale than he would have willingly admitted, loosened his neckcloth and dragged his feet from the footstool. He took a long draft of wine to relieve his parched throat and set the half-empty glass on a side table. Then Rafe leaned forward and, resting his elbows on his knees, he buried his face in his hands in a helpless gesture.

Caitlan thought he had never looked more vulnerable. Wanting to help—yet not knowing what to do—she smoothed her hand along the muscular contour of his back and whispered, "Go on."

After a moment of silence, Rafe drew a long breath and said, "I spent the better part of a week here in New Orleans with Ethan and his family—Becky included, she was barely eighteen months old at the time—talking over old times and seeing the sights. Ethan told me of the changes he had undertaken at Shadow Vale and invited me to accompany them back to Nashville for a visit, so I might see for myself that the plantation was indeed prospering, that—in his own words—he had not let the place go to wrack and ruin. Thus, we set about making plans for the return journey to Shadow Vale."

Rafe stood up and began to pace the length of the room as he continued his narrative. "We took the *Magnolia Princess* as far as Natchez. Our plans were to travel the rest of the way overland, but I was delayed for a day with a mechanical problem on the *Princess*. Jenny couldn't wait, however. She was anxious to get home to see how young Ethan, Jr., had fared in her absence, so they set out without me with the understanding that I would come as soon as I could." Rafe strode over to the table to claim his abandoned wineglass. Drinking down the contents, his voice was gritty and strained when he said, "I found them—rather what was left of them—by nightfall the next day."

"Oh, Rafe. No!" Caitlan gasped, her heart going out to the tortured man.

Knowing him as she did, Caitlan imagined he blamed himself for what had happened. Rafe undoubtedly believed that, if he had accompanied his friends from Natchez, he could have somehow prevented this horrible tragedy. Noting that Rafe had drained the goblet and was presently eyeing the decanter with a purposeful eye, Caitlan stood up. Putting her own drink aside, she stepped to him.

"That won't help, you know."

"Yes, it will," he vowed. "It helps me forget."

"Very well then." Caitlan eased the fragile stemmed glass from his agitated fingers and walked to the mantelshelf. Upon pouring another serving of burgundy, she turned and proffered the goblet to Rafe, saying, "Here it is, if you need it. I think, however, you would be better served if you stopped blaming yourself. It was not your fault. You couldn't have known—"

"That's not the point, Kettie!" Rafe shouted, shoving his hand through his hair in a desperate motion. "Don't you understand?" He knocked the glass aside and grabbed Caitlan's shoulders in a ruthless grip. "I should have been with them. I could have made a difference."

Caitlan, wincing from the painful fingers that dug into her flesh, glanced sideways at the shards of broken glass on the hearth and the bloodred drops of wine that trickled down the front of the mantelpiece. Biting back the fearful cry that trembled on her lips, she wrenched herself free of his hurtful grasp and flung herself against his chest. Wrapping her arms about him, she sobbed into his shirt, "But don't you see? If you had been there, you might have been killed, too."

This sudden outburst brought Rafe's enraged emotions back to the matter at hand and, summoning his wits about him, he held Caitlan close and said, "I suppose we'll never know, honey. But I cannot help but think I could have done something."

"What . . . what did you find?"

"Oh, sweet pea." Rafe sighed, lifting her chin and caressing her cheek with his thumb. "You're better off not knowing. I still have sleepless nights over it. Suffice to say they had been murdered and robbed. The huge sum of money Ethan had received from the sale of his crops was missing, along with the rest of his valuables. The bastards even took Jenny's wedding band."

"And Becky?"

"Thankfully, they had not harmed her," Rafe explained. "She was sitting beside Jenny's body when I found her, her little face all red and puffy from crying. She was tugging on her mama's dress, trying—I don't know—to get her to wake up, I suppose." He dashed an impatient hand across his face to wipe at the tears that stung his eyes. Pulling away from Caitlan, Rafe walked over to the window and, drawing the heavy draperies aside, looked out at the bustling city below. "Jenny and Ethan had been dead for hours. Lord only knows what might have happened to Becky if I hadn't come along when I did.

"At first, I thought it was a blessing, you know, that those butchers had spared her. Then I realized it was just more of Rawlings's demented doings, leaving an infant alone in the wilderness to fend for itself. If Becky had wandered into the woods—" Rafe's voice tapered off, and he gave an involuntary shudder.

"But you did find Becky before anything ghastly happened to her, and she is safe with you. Indeed, I think she is a very lucky little girl to have someone who loves her as much as you obviously do. And she adores you, too. You must know that, Rafe."

In response, Rafe merely nodded and continued to stare out the window.

At a loss as to what she might say to comfort Rafe's grieved heart, Caitlan knelt down at the hearth. She busied herself with raking in the broken pieces of glass, but she could not take her eyes from that stormy countenance for very long. Eventually, she offered, "How is it that you came to be Becky's legal guardian? Did she have no other family? Whatever happened to Ethan, Jr.?"

"Both Ethan's and Jenny's parents were deceased," Rafe replied. "Ethan was an only child and there were no other relatives on his side of the family who were willing to take on the responsibility of rearing two small children. Jenny had a sister, but she made it plain that she didn't have time to be bothered with children. She was living in New York at the time, trying to make a name for herself in the theater. I don't know where she is now, nor do I care . . . as long as she stays away from Becky. She had her chance to do right by her.

"My attorney did locate a cousin in Memphis who was willing to adopt Ethan, Jr. But, seeing as how he and his wife already had five daughters of their own, they couldn't see their way clear to taking Becky. So, I decided that, since no one else seemed to want the little ragamuffin, I'd take her," Rafe said, as if assuming the guardianship of a small child was the most natural thing in the world a single gentleman could do.

A hint of fatherlike pride crept into his voice as he added, "My lawyer drew up the appropriate documents and I brought her here. I'm not around as much as I'd like to be, but I do spend a considerable amount of my time in New Orleans. When Becky gets old enough, I'll take her with me on the *Princess*. As for now, when my business takes me out of the city, the good sisters at the convent look after her for me. But when I'm in town, Becky stays with me," Rafe said as if he dared anyone to question his child-rearing philosophy.

"Do you think you will ever tell her about what happened to her mama and daddy?"

Rafe straightened as the force of this question hit him head-long. "I don't know" came his truthful answer. "To be honest, I've never given it much thought." Shrugging his broad shoulders, Rafe said, "Perhaps someday when she is old enough to understand. Becky is too little to remember what happened to Ethan and Jenny, although there are times when she awakens in the night—terrified—and I have to cuddle her until she falls asleep again. Becky thinks I'm her daddy, and I have to admit that I kind of like that," he said, turning from the embrasure.

Upon finding Caitlan on her knees, cleaning up the mess he himself had created, Rafe swore and rushed forward. "Leave that be! You're no longer that Tuttle woman's minion," he snapped.

Caitlan bristled at the insulting reminder and instinctively clenched her fist. She was given reason to regret her impulsive reaction; a jagged piece of glass pierced the palm of her hand, causing her to gasp aloud with pain. As she stared blankly at the injured region, an ugly red stain began to spread across the palm of her hand.

Rafe, realizing what he had unwittingly caused, dragged her to her feet. "Oh, God! I'm sorry, darlin'. I didn't mean to bark at you. Does it hurt?" he asked, staring down at the afflicted area. With meticulous precision, Rafe plucked the shard of glass from her hand and, pulling a handkerchief from his pocket, carefully wrapped it about the wound to stanch the flow of blood.

Then Rafe obliged her to look at him by bumping her chin up with his index finger. Kissing her, he pulled away and gazed down into Caitlan's petulant face. "I'm sorry, sweet pea," he repeated. "I wouldn't hurt you for the world. You know that, don't you? Will you need a doctor, do you think?"

Despite all that had occurred, Caitlan found herself smiling. "Of course not, silly. It is but the tiniest scratch, after all. It will stop bleeding in a moment."

"Well, if you're certain." Rafe studied her face, then taking hold of her uninjured hand, he led her to the sofa. He pulled Caitlan down beside him, settling her in the crook of his arm. "I ought not to have snapped at you, I know," he said. "It's just that I've been on edge lately, trying to discover the identity of the mastermind behind my friends' murders."

"What?!" Caitlan blurted, looking up into that troubled face. Her brow knitted into a confused grimace when she said, "I thought you said the two despicable creatures who accosted us were the ones who murdered Becky's parents."

"Oh, Rawlings and Hayes had a hand in it, that's for damn sure. But neither one of those buffoons was smart enough to plan the cold-blooded crime. You see, Kettie," Rafe explained, coaxing her head down onto his shoulder, "this was not the first villainy of this sort to occur along that stretch of woodland highway. Thefts and murders have been happening off and on for ten years or more. Whoever is behind all this treachery has been ingenious. There's no rhyme or reason to his madness. He strikes at whim and has never left behind one shred of evidence that could lead to his identity. That is," Rafe drawled, a satisfied smile parting his lips, "until now."

Upon saying this, Rafe withdrew his arm from about Caitlan and leaned forward. A curious frown adorned her otherwise pretty face as she watched him cross one muscular leg over the other. Then pulling a penknife from his pocket, he began to fiddle with the heel of his boot. As Caitlan looked on—her expression incredulous—Rafe pried the heel free of the boot proper and turned to her.

"Do you remember how concerned I was about my boots when I first awakened at the boardinghouse?"

A sheepish blush burned Caitlan's cheeks as she recalled her impetuous outburst that night. With a guilty smile, she mumbled, "Yes, I remember."

"This is why." Rafe tipped the hollow boot heel over and dumped its contents onto Caitlan's lap. "This is the only piece of evidence available that will eventually lead me to the ring-leader of this deadly band of marauders. Ethan evidently put up quite a struggle before his death; he was clutching this in his fist when I found him. This and a small swatch of silk cloth—a neckcloth, I am certain—to which it was attached. Rawlings and Hayes couldn't have come up with a sawbuck between them if their lives depended on it. Oh, Rawlings played the dandy well enough, but he couldn't afford anything this fancy. It had to belong to their leader.''

Caitlan gazed down at the decorative tiepin that lay twinkling in her lap and, picking it up, she examined it closely. It was a costly bauble, there was no denying that. Considering its unusual design—that of two elaborately crafted initials, a ''J'' and a ''C'', with the latter slightly overlapping its predecessor, and what with each letter made up of three alternating rows of rubies and diamonds—Caitlan surmised the tiepin was more than likely one of a kind.

Noting that the gold sheath had been broken, probably when Ethan ripped it from his assailant's throat, Caitlan handed the pin back to Rafe and asked, ''Is this what those two men were looking for when they attacked you near Vicksburg?''

''Uh huh.''

''And again when they came to the tearoom?''

Rafe nodded.

Caitlan mulled this information over and said, ''Obviously, you have made it public knowledge that you carry this piece of incriminating evidence on your person. Tell me, just how did you intend to find this supposed ringleader? Did you believe he might approach you and kindly ask you for the return of his trinket when he learned you had it?''

''No,'' Rafe drawled, amused by her sarcastic reaction to the efforts he had put forth thus far in tracking his unknown nemesis. ''He did pretty much as I expected . . . he sent his two henchmen after me. That's how I learned Rawlings and Hayes were involved. And one day soon, mind you—my doubting miss—I shall know their leader's identity as well. I'll flush him out in the open and heaven help him when I do,'' Rafe vowed. Dropping the tiepin back inside the hollowed-out heel, he added, ''Besides, my adversary doesn't know precisely what it is I have in my possession, or how I came by it. I only let it be known that I have a piece of evidence . . . it could be anything as far as he's concerned. Meanwhile, I'll keep going from town to town, talking with all the local jewelers in the hopes that they have either heard of or had a hand in the craftsmanship of this gaudy little pin.''

"And in the meantime, anyone you meet with the initials 'J.C.' is suspect," Caitlan interpolated.

"Yes." Rafe pounded the heel back into place and, stretching his long legs out in front of him, settled back and draped his arm about Caitlan once more. "All except for that Jeremy Cantrell fella you're so partial to," he teased. "You see, Kettie. It wasn't pleasure of the flesh I was seeking when I spent all those hours at Sadie's place back in Vicksburg. I made arrangements for a couple of my men to meet me there whenever the *Princess* was in port. They would bring me money and keep me posted on business matters and what have you. So, I had one of them check out your would-be beau and, as it turns out—except for the fact that his wives seem to expire with unnatural regularity—he's as clean as a hound's tooth.''

"That's good to know," Caitlan huffed, crossing her arms over her indignant bosom and turning away from him. "Perhaps I'll just go back to Jeremy. He's gentle and kind, and he rarely ever provokes me the way you do. I daresay life with Jeremy would be most . . . pleasant.''

"Life with that pompous ass would be a dead bore and you know it" came Rafe's matter-of-fact taunt. "Now, don't you go turning that cold shoulder on me, or I just might be tempted to come over there and warm it up for you. Trust me, darlin', that's one thing old Rafe is good at, but you know that already, don't you?" he teased, grabbing hold of her arm and dragging her onto his lap.

As if to prove his point, Rafe deftly unbuttoned her blouse. Sliding the silk material from her shoulder, he lowered his mouth to the enticing flesh and allowed his lips to have their way with her milky-white collarbone.

Caitlan permitted him several moments of uninterrupted play before asking, "Am I to assume this impromptu excursion to New Orleans has something to do with your quest to find your friends' murderer?''

"Uh huh," Rafe murmured against her throat.

Dragging his blistering-hot lips from the shapely column, Rafe directed his passion-filled gaze toward the bedchamber door behind which little Becky slept. From the expression on his face, Caitlan supposed him to be mentally calculating how much time they had to themselves before the child awakened. Evidently, he decided it was not long enough to conduct whatever sensual torture he had in mind. Deciding their frolicking would have to wait until later, Rafe gave a frustrated sigh and rebuttoned her blouse.

Pushing her from his lap, he commented on her earlier question in greater detail by explaining, ''Sheriff Bodeker and I had a long chat the night he came to the tearoom. I told him pretty much what we discussed today and, although he advised me to let the law handle the investigation, he did give me the name of a man here in New Orleans . . . a man that Sam Rawlings used to work for. His name is J.D. Calhoun, and I believe he may lead me to the ringleader. Indeed, he just might be the 'J.C.' I'm looking for. That's why I'm here, Kettie . . . to find Mr. Calhoun.''

Caitlan lay on her side, her face turned away from the twinkling shadows of morning that glistened through the curtains. Her arms were curled possessively about the down-filled pillow, and the long lashes that splayed across her cheek like black satin feathers were a sure indication that she slept soundly. That is until she became vaguely aware of a finger poking her in the back, tentative at first. But, as Caitlan ignored it—in the hopes that its owner would grow weary and leave her to awaken in her own good time—the probing appendage prodded more persistently.

''Go away, Rafe.'' Caitlan gave a drowsy grumble, tucking the bedsheet more firmly under her chin and burrowing her face in the soft bolster.

To which a demanding little voice squealed, ''Hey!''

Caitlan, surprised to discover it was Rebecca and not Rafe who was pestering her, rolled onto her back. Propping herself up on her elbows, she yawned and focused her sleepy gaze on the tousle-haired child.

''Hey yourself'' was Caitlan's hoarse rejoinder. Glancing about the chamber for a certain tall gentleman, and not finding him, she was obliged to ask, "Just where has Rafe . . . uh . . . Daddy," Caitlan corrected herself, "gone off to this morning?"

In reply, Becky merely hunched her tiny shoulders and gurgled, "Daddy go."

"I see." Caitlan mulled this nonspecific piece of information. Noticing the sadly crumpled note that the child twisted in her chubby fists, she ventured, "Is this for me?" Caitlan acknowledged Becky's bobbing head by plucking the wrinkled missive from the little girl's clenched hands.

While Caitlan read the short letter, Becky scrunched her hands together and pressed them down onto the mattress between her crossed legs, jabbering, "Me go, too. Me go pootie."

"What's that you said, sweetie?" Caitlan glanced up from the page of boldly scrawled script. "Pootie?" she repeated, clearly baffled by Becky's childish rhetoric. Then noting the imploring expression that contorted the little face that stared up at her, Caitlan understood the child's meaning. "*Oh!*" she exclaimed, flinging the sheet aside and jumping from the bed. "Come on then." She whisked Becky into her arms and marched straightaway to the water closet.

"I don't know what your daddy was thinking, leaving the two of us alone like this," Caitlan mumbled, fussing with Becky's nightclothes. Once the child was settled, she continued, "He knows perfectly well that my child-rearing skills are lamentable at best."

While Becky answered the call of nature, Caitlan reread Rafe's brief note. "Humph!" she grunted, unaware that Becky's brown gaze was trained on her face in rapt fascination. "It appears as if your daddy has forsaken us for the better part of the day. He says he has gone off to make inquiries about that Calhoun fellow and to see about employing a nursemaid to help look after you. He very likely will not return to the hotel until late afternoon and says we should make the best of our day without him." With a small sigh, Caitlan folded the rumpled paper and smiled down at Becky. "Well, little one. What do you suggest we do first?"

"Hungee," Becky chirped without hesitation.

Caitlan laughed, gently riffling her fingers through Becky's dark brown mane. ''Yes, I quite agree. Breakfast sounds like just the thing.''

They enjoyed a scrumptious breakfast in the St. Charles dining-room before Caitlan and her young charge set off for Jackson Park. The waiter, who had served them at breakfast, had suggested the outing while they dined and even provided Becky with a napkin full of bread crumbs to feed the ducks. Upon arriving at the park, Caitlan settled herself on a stone bench to observe Becky as she chased—and was chased by— the ducks that inhabited the park. She and Becky contented themselves by whiling away the morning amid the park's idyllic setting.

In fact, Caitlan could have been persuaded to remain until the early afternoon had an unfortunate incident not occurred. One of Becky's feathered friends accidentally nipped her finger as it lunged for one of the coveted bread crumbs. Huge tears were tumbling down Becky's cheeks by the time Caitlan gathered the child in her arms. After determining that little Becky had been more frightened than hurt by the animal, Caitlan decided they had enjoyed enough of the park's amenities for one day. Pressing a kiss against the tip of the assaulted appendage that Becky thrust under her nose, Caitlan gathered up their belongings and they exited the park.

They lunched at a local café, then realizing it was growing near Becky's naptime, as well as approaching the hour when Rafe had said he would return, Caitlan decided it was time to go back to the hotel. She found her progress somewhat impeded by the shops that cluttered the street, however. She paused now and again along the sidewalk to peer in a store window if a particular item chanced to catch her eye.

''Pitty'' came Becky's unsolicited comment, as Caitlan contemplated a royal blue velvet cloak that hung in a shop window.

''Yes, it is,'' Caitlan concurred. ''Very 'pitty' indeed.''

Taking one last wistful look at the luxurious cloak with matching blue satin frogs and a lighter blue piping around the edges, Caitlan started to turn away when a voice behind her said, ''Just say the word and it's yours, Kettie.''

''Kitty?!'' Becky squealed, straining to look down at the ground.

''No, sweetheart,'' Caitlan explained with a tolerant smile.

"Not *kitty,* Kettie. That's me. That's my name. Can you say Kettie?"

The little girl bobbed her head up and down with an excited motion, saying happily, "Kitty."

"That's close enough, I suppose," Caitlan murmured on a sigh. Glancing up into Rafe's handsome face, she said, "Thank you for offering to buy the cloak for me, but my shawl shall do nicely."

"Mississippi winters can grow downright chilly," Rafe reminded her, but seeing the stern set of Caitlan's jaw, he gave up trying to convince her and said, "I was just on my way back to the hotel when I saw you and had my driver let me out. What have my girls been up to all day?"

Before Caitlan could muster a response, Becky offered this gleeful reply: "Ducks!"

"Oh my. That sounds like great fun," Rafe said, reaching out to take the child from Caitlan's aching arms.

Normally, this was a gesture that brought great joy to the little girl's heart. Both adults were therefore mystified when Becky shied away from his proffered hands. Instead, she wriggled and pushed against Caitlan's breast, demanding, "Down!"

Caitlan complied with the child's wishes, but Becky's feet had no sooner struck the sidewalk than she reached up to latch onto one of Rafe's fingers. She pulled and yanked on Rafe's hand to no avail until, thoroughly frustrated, Becky appealed to Caitlan by saying, "Kitty. Ducks!"

"I believe she wants to introduce you to her newfound friends," Caitlan explained.

"Do you mind?"

"Of course not," she replied, stepping down from the sidewalk and onto the thoroughfare. "Come along, Becky. Bring your daddy with you." To Rafe, she said, "The park is just across the way."

Rafe gave a bark of laughter as he observed the gathering of ducks scatter in all directions—the smarter ones heading for the pond—as Becky toddled into their midst once more. Calling out for her not to go near the water, Rafe settled back against the bench and watched her gamboling with a spiraling sense of fatherly pride. Reaching out beside him, he covered Caitlan's hand with his own and gave it an affectionate squeeze.

"I knew you two would get along just fine."

"It's easy to get along with Becky. She won't allow it otherwise," Caitlan said with a chuckle. Her mien grew more serious as she said, "I understand now why you took her to raise as your own, why you couldn't turn your back on her like everyone else did. She is a darling little girl."

"You didn't mind playing nursemaid for the day then?" Rafe asked, watching her face for her reaction.

"No, I didn't mind," Caitlan assured him, tucking her arm in his and scooting closer to cuddle against him. "In fact, I rather enjoyed myself. How about you? Did you have any luck locating your Mr. Calhoun?"

"I asked around . . . made a few inquiries" came his ambiguous reply. "I let it be known that I was anxious to speak with him."

Caitlan averted her eyes from where Becky played with a little boy who had wandered over from another group of children and twisted around to look up at him. "I don't understand, Rafe. Why is it so difficult to arrange a meeting with this man? Is he as important as that?"

Rafe observed as Becky ambled back over to them and raised her tired arms to Caitlan. A feeling of contentment washed over him as he watched Caitlan pull the sleepy-eyed little girl onto her lap and cradle her to her breast.

Reaching over to stroke the child's hand, Rafe answered, "Perhaps not nearly so important as disreputable. You see, honey, J. D. Calhoun is what is known as a moneylender. He is a powerful and influential man. Indeed, he is the most feared and revered man of his ilk from here to St. Louis . . . his reputation extends that far.

"From what I can find out about him, he's honest . . . well, as honest as a man can be in his line of work," Rafe said with a wry twist of his sensuous mouth. "So, I'll humor the man and play his game for a time. But mark my word, some day very soon—one way or another—the notorious Mr. J. D. Calhoun and I will come face to face."

Chapter Fifteen

❦❦❦

The infamous J. D. Calhoun was determined to maintain his anonymity, it would seem. Despite Rafe's diligent efforts to track down the enigmatic man, November had long since given way to December's chilly breezes and still the reclusive man had not acknowledged Rafe's request for an interview. The Christmas season was nearly upon them, a time when most hearts were lightened with a festive holiday spirit. The mood that had settled upon the two adult occupants of the fashionable suite of rooms on the third floor of the St. Charles Hotel was far from merry, however. Both Rafe and Caitlan had grown moody and anxious, albeit for different reasons.

Rafe's chagrin stemmed from his own inability to locate Mr. Calhoun, as well as the fact that the trail that led to the identity of his friends' murderer was growing colder with every passing day. Whereas Caitlan's distress was of a more self-directed nature . . . guilt.

It is true that old habits die hard, for Caitlan, having spent so many years under Harriet Tuttle's daunting tutelage, was feeling remiss about leaving Essie alone to manage the tearoom while she romped with Rafe for weeks on end in the most elegant city the deep south had to offer. Even though Essie had written time and again to tell of the business's continued success and to assure Caitlan there was no need for her to hurry back to Vicksburg, the tearoom's namesake remained skeptical. After all, she was accountable for the restaurant. It was irresponsible of her to expect Essie to go on managing the tearoom indefinitely.

The only one who remained unaffected by all these grown-up woes was little Becky. Although she was much too young to understand the significance of the approaching holiday, she realized that something special was in the offing. There was much hustle and bustle, what with decorating the sitting-room with sweet-smelling pine branches, bright red ribbons, holly wreaths, and candles. Not to mention all the hushed murmurings about the impending visit from Saint Nicholas. It is little wonder that the excited child could barely be persuaded to go to sleep at night and refused to take her afternoon nap altogether.

With Christmas morning less than a week away, Caitlan was having second thoughts about leaving the fidgety little girl with the nanny—Mrs. Fitzhugh—while she accompanied Rafe to the theater on Saturday evening. Not that she found the kindly gray-haired woman lacking. Indeed, Mrs. Fitzhugh acted more like a cuddly old grandmother than the curmudgeon nursemaid Caitlan remembered having as a child. Caitlan realized that Becky would be well looked after, but deep in her heart, she knew something else.

Rafe could not continue in the same vein much longer; he could not remain in New Orleans forever. Sooner than Caitlan might like, Rafe would resume his quest for the murderer of Becky's parents, she would return—alone—to Vicksburg, and little Becky would go back to the convent until Rafe's next sojourn to the city. She did not look forward to that dreaded moment of separation. Knowing that her time remaining with Becky was limited to but a few precious days, she suggested they forgo the theater that night. Rafe, however, remained adamant that they go.

As she sat next to him in the plush theater box, her hand clasped in his, Caitlan had to admit she was glad Rafe had coerced her into attending the performance. It was not a droll tragedy that was presented that evening, rather a witty comedy . . . precisely what Caitlan needed to boost her melancholy spirits. But when they exited the theater, intending to walk the few blocks back to the St. Charles where a midnight supper awaited them, Caitlan suffered an abrupt reversal of feelings. Indeed, she was given every reason to regret she had allowed Rafe to overturn her earlier decision to cancel the outing.

As they turned up the street, two men stepped from a nearby alleyway and approached them. Without saying a word and, before either of them had guessed what was about to happen, one of the men wrested Caitlan's hand from Rafe's arm and jerked her back into the shadows. The other man shoved a revolver into Rafe's ribs and commanded him to accompany him. While Caitlan watched—helpless and frightened—Rafe was forced to walk a few feet up the street where a carriage sat waiting beside the curb. In the next instant, Rafe was pushed inside, the conveyance trundled away, and the sinister-looking man—a wicked sneer curling his upper lip—turned back toward Caitlan.

Rafe had a fleeting glimpse of Caitlan's terrified face before the carriage window was slammed shut. Knowing he must keep his head about him if he hoped to discover his kidnapper's purpose, he leaned back against the leather squabs and tried to make out his companion's likeness across the darkened coach. When his efforts proved futile, Rafe glanced down at the tip of the cane that had been thrust into his chest to prevent him from climbing back out of the vehicle and running to Caitlan's assistance.

Fighting back the urge to wrench the stick from his adversary's hands and break it over his head, Rafe growled, ''If those two thugs so much as—''

''Miss Webber won't be harmed, Mr. Bradrick,'' interpolated the feminine voice from across the narrow aisle. ''Assuming, of course, you do as you're told. I do apologize for the theatrics, but it was a necessary precaution, I fear. It was you who insisted on meeting with J. D. Calhoun in person, after all.''

''Wait just a goddamn minute,'' Rafe blurted, bewildered by the lady's insinuation. ''Are you telling me that *you're* J. D. Calhoun?''

''That surprises you? I had hoped you might be a man of

some intelligence,'' she scoffed. ''But it appears you are just like the others of your sex who believe that only a man is capable of scheming, conniving, unscrupulous doings. When the truth of the matter is, my gender has been at it much longer than yours.'' She gave a short laugh before assuming a businesslike demeanor.

''To answer your question; yes, I'm J. D. Calhoun. And that, sir, you must realize, is privileged information. I pride myself on my privacy and trust that, once this interview has concluded, my secret will be safe with you.''

This final statement was said in deliberate tones that gave Rafe little reason to doubt that the consequences would be dire should he decide not to honor the mysterious woman's express wishes.

''I'll do whatever you say, ma'am,'' Rafe said, pushing the fancy walking stick aside. His voice lowered to a gravelly whisper and the foreboding expression in his eyes—had they been visible in the blackened coach—would have given the woman pause when he vowed, ''But I promise you this; if you've misjudged your men and something happens to my Kettie, their lives—and yours for that matter—won't be worth spit.''

Rafe had no way of knowing that his daring speech brought a smile to the woman's lips. Her tone was devoid of humor, however, when she reminded him, ''You are in no position to make threats, Mr. Bradrick. I give you my word that Miss Webber will not be harmed. Like it or not, you'll just have to trust me. My men will escort her back to the St. Charles and await our arrival. As I explained, precautions have been taken to ensure my safety. Therefore, if you should be so foolhardy as to prevent me from meeting my men at the hotel, then . . . '' the woman spread her hands in a helpless gesture, '' . . . well, let's just say they have their orders.

''But let's not dwell on unpleasantries. Let's get down to business, shall we?'' Miss Calhoun suggested, withdrawing a cigarette from her reticule. ''After all, the sooner we conclude our little chat, the sooner you may return to Miss Webber and the midnight supper that awaits you.''

''It would appear you have me at a disadvantage, ma'am. You seem to know a great deal about me, while I know precious little about you," Rafe said, stretching his long legs out in front of him and folding his arms across his chest. Though he gave the appearance of having relaxed his guard, his every sense was attuned to the woman's slightest movement.

"That's the way I conduct business, Mr. Bradrick. You see, being an astute businesswoman, I make it a point to have the upper hand in every situation," she said with a coy toss of her head that led Rafe to believe the lady's "take-charge" philosophy carried over into her intimate life as well.

Rafe cleared his throat but made no further comment, lest the lady take it into her head that he could be persuaded to stray down that sensual path. Make no mistake about the matter; Rafe was no saint. Had this meeting taken place a few months earlier, he might have allowed himself to be seduced by the mysterious woman and the dangerous aura she exuded. But now there was Kettie, and the only thing the Calhoun woman had that was of any interest to Rafe was information about Sam Rawlings.

A brief splash of light suffused the compartment for a fraction of a second as Miss Calhoun flicked a match down the carriage wall. As the stench of sulfur pervaded the enclosure, Rafe studied the woman as she brought the flame toward her face and puffed the cigarette alight. In the next moment, the fire was extinguished and Rafe was in the dark once more. He still had no inkling as to what the enigmatic woman looked like, however. Although the fleeting burst of match light had given him reason to believe he was dealing with a handsome woman not so very many years his senior, the brim of her large hat had concealed much of the woman's face from his watchful gaze.

Upon exhaling a puff of smoke, Miss Calhoun tapped the slender rod to dislodge the burned ash. Realizing that her companion was not interested in pursuing the pleasures of the flesh, she adopted a no-nonsense tone, saying, "My friends call me J.D. You may call me Miss Calhoun. Now, what do you want, Mr. Bradrick?"

Rafe assumed much the same mien, saying simply, "Sam Rawlings."

"Yes? What about him?"

"I understand he used to work for you."

"Yes . . . lamentably," she drawled, making some offhand gesture. Though Rafe was oblivious to her change of expression, J.D.'s eyes glistened with admiration as she added, "And I understand you did the citizens of Vicksburg a service by killing the good-for-nothing bastard."

"I had little choice in the matter, considering he was about to take his bowie knife to the finest woman God ever put on this earth" came Rafe's dry reply.

"Ah, that would be Miss Webber," J.D. surmised. Taking a contemplative draft of her cigarette, she exhaled and said, "It appears the lady holds a special place in your heart."

"She does."

"You would be wise not to make your enemies privy to such intimate details of your personal life. It puts one at a disadvantage during critical negotiations," she advised him.

"Thank you. I'll keep that in mind. Now, about Rawlings?" Rafe prompted, growing impatient.

"As I said, the man used to work for me, but I gave him his walking-orders several months back . . . more than a year ago, I believe." J.D. inhaled one last time on the cigarette before dropping it to the floor with a negligent motion and crushing the flame with her shoe. Then she explained, "You must understand, Mr. Bradrick, that—regardless of the nature of my profession—I do have a reputation to uphold. My clients are a special breed who often need to be persuaded that it is in their best interest to settle their debts.

"Rawlings was one of my money collectors. He possessed a raw, untamed talent, but no finesse when it came to dealing with people in a civilized manner. Rawlings proved to be little more than a ruthless, bloodthirsty ruffian. Word got about." The Calhoun woman made a careless gesture with her hand. "Rawlings was scaring both my regular and potential customers away. He was, in short, bad for business. I had no recourse but to let him go."

Rafe noticed with a pang of trepidation that the conveyance was drawing to a stop. He felt the carriage lurch to one side as the driver heaved himself down from his lofty perch and, fearing he was but moments away from being tossed out on his ear by the domineering woman, he asked, "Do you have any idea as to what became of Rawlings after he left your employ?''

''Not so fast, Mr. Bradrick,'' J.D. said, a devilish grin twinkling in her eyes. ''Again, you surprise me. Being a successful entrepreneur in your own right, surely you must realize that a shrewd businesswoman—or man for that matter—does not simply hand over valuable information. I do expect something in return for my trouble,'' she murmured.

To emphasize her point, J. D. Calhoun tilted her head to one side so that Rafe could see the sensuous slant of her mouth. Then catching a thoroughly surprised gentleman off guard, she leaned forward to rub her hand suggestively along the inside of his thigh.

It was the middle of the night and Rafe stood staring out the bedchamber window, his unseeing gaze focused on the moon-drenched street below. Sleep had proved to be an elusive thing this night, and not wishing to disturb his bedmate with his tossing and turning, Rafe had forsaken the comfort of his bed for the lonely vigil at the embrasure. As he stood there, lost in thought, his ears detected the sound of the shifting mattress, followed immediately by the padding of bare feet across the floor. In the next instant, a pair of shapely arms slithered about his waist and a cheek nuzzled his back.

''Come back to bed,'' urged a drowsy voice.

''In a moment, darlin','' Rafe promised, taking hold of Caitlan's hand and dragging her around in front of him. ''I'm thinking.''

''About what?''

''Oh, a number of things.'' He sighed, drawing her back against his chest. Clasping his hands beneath her breasts, Rafe pressed a kiss against the top of her head and said, ''About tomorrow, about leaving Becky again, about what I'll find in Baton Rouge . . . if anything. But mostly, I've been thinking about what you told me this morning just before Becky came tearing into the room to tell us that old St. Nick had visited her during the night.'' Rafe smiled at the memory of the child's beaming face.

Shaking his head, he said, ''Honey, I swear I don't know what provoked Josie to make up that dreadful lie about you being dead all these years, but I'm determined to find out. Now, I know you're anxious to get back to Vicksburg because you feel you've been neglecting Essie and the tearoom, but I was wondering . . . ''

"Yes? What have you been wondering?" Caitlan gave his hand an encouraging squeeze when it appeared he was reluctant to continue.

"Aw hell, Kettie," he blurted, turning her around to face him. "You've been away this long, a few more days shouldn't matter one way or another. Come with me to Foxborough Hall. We'll confront Josie together and, together, we'll get to the bottom of all her lies.

"Besides, Miss Calhoun said Rawlings took up with some rich planter up near Baton Rouge after she let him go. Who knows? If I'm lucky, I'll be able to kill two birds with one stone. Please say yes, honey," Rafe implored her. "Please."

Caitlan required all of two seconds to ponder her answer before she smiled up at him and said, "Of course I'll come with you. You need only ask." Her mood grew pensive and, turning away, Caitlan pulled the lace curtain aside to stare out into the night.

"What is it, darlin'? Did I say something to upset you?"

"No." Caitlan shook her head. "I guess it's my turn to think, is all."

"About what?"

"Becky," Caitlan said, her voice infinitely sad. "She knows we're leaving; I'm sure of it. You see, she spent the evening helping me pack. At least, Becky thought she was being helpful. Actually, every time I turned around, the little angel was underfoot. She would come scurrying into our room dragging a toy or piece of clothing after her. Then she would shove the item into my hands—expecting me to pack it in one of our bags, I'm sure—and toddle off to find another.

"Oh, Rafe," she whimpered, turning about to bury her face in his chest. "I'm certain Becky believes we are taking her with us. We're going to break her little heart tomorrow when we take her back to the convent. You know that, don't you?"

"Yes, Kettie. I know it all too well," Rafe informed her, his tone sounding as empty as she felt. Tipping her head back so that he could study her face by the moonlight, he was surprised to find that her eyes sparkled with unshed tears. Brushing a kiss alongside her cheek, he murmured, "Don't cry, sweet pea. It cannot be helped, I fear. As much as I would love to have Becky with me all the time, it simply isn't practical at the moment. Besides, I don't know what treachery awaits me in Baton Rouge. I'll have enough on my mind, worrying about what might happen to you. The little one is much safer here in New Orleans, I promise you."

"I know," Caitlan murmured, heaving a wretched sigh. "It's just that I've come to . . . love her so very much. I cannot bear the thought of hurting her."

"I know, Kettie. And she loves you, too." He cuddled her chin between his thumb and forefinger, his eyes searching her unhappy face. "But let's not dwell upon sad thoughts for now. Let's just go to bed, shall we? We've got a busy day tomorrow, and—"

"I'm not sleepy anymore," she interrupted.

"Well, now that I've thought on it," Rafe drawled, rubbing her chin, "neither am I" was his throaty murmur. He lowered his head and allowed his lips to blaze a trail of hot kisses from her mouth, down her throat, to the opening of her nightdress.

Caitlan, understanding his meaning, did not cavil when Rafe tumbled her to the floor. Indeed, she welcomed his caresses with open arms. Caitlan lay back on the thick-piled rug as Rafe hovered above her in the semidarkness and watched in breathless anticipation as he removed his robe. The sight of his nakedness, bulging muscles rippling in the moonlight, was an image that always sent a tremor of excitement pulsing throughout her being. Likewise, it was a view that Caitlan never grew tired of seeing and, anxious to be in his arms—to taste his lips on hers, to have his powerful body writhing in rhapsodic splendor against her own—she wriggled out of her nightgown and pulled Rafe down on top of her.

In the afterglow of their passion, as they lay side by side on the floor, their glistening bodies drenched in moonlight, Caitlan rolled onto Rafe's chest. Propping her chin on her hands, she gave a contented sigh and stared down with loving eyes into his handsome face.

Eventually, after giving a sudden nagging thought due consideration, she asked, "Was she pretty?"

''*What?!*'' Rafe exclaimed, thoroughly stunned by the un-expected question. ''What the devil are you talking about, Kettie? Was who pretty?''

''That Calhoun woman. Was she?''

Rafe pondered his response carefully; although Caitlan tried to effect a nonchalant mien—as if the essence of his reply did not truly matter one way or the other—he knew better. Finally, he gave a great bark of laughter and said, ''Christ almighty, woman! How the hell should I know if she was pretty or not? She kept her face more than half covered the whole time with some hideous hat. Besides,'' he growled, pulling Caitlan against him, ''I wasn't interested in her looks . . . I've got me a pretty woman already. I was after information.''

''And you're absolutely certain she's not the 'J.C.' you're looking for?''

''Positive,'' Rafe replied, running his hands along Caitlan's back, down over the contour of her hips where he gave her buttocks a satisfying squeeze.

''How can you be so sure?''

Rafe hunched his shoulders and shivered with delight at the gentle vibrating motion of her breasts against his chest. Ex-haling a heady breath, he said, ''I just am is all.''

A pout found its way to Caitlan's lips, and, as one wayward finger began to trace abstract figures in his neatly trimmed beard, she complained, ''I suppose you should know better than I. After all, you were gone for hours that night—alone with her—after she whisked you away from the theater.''

''Kettie,'' Rafe droned, his tone indicative of one who has been forced to recount a particular thing several times over. ''I've explained at least a dozen times what happened that night. Miss Calhoun—and mind, she doesn't want the fact that she's a woman bandied about—took me to a secluded place where I could meet her daughter. In exchange for information about Sam Rawlings, I agreed to personally escort young Ame-lia to some fancy boarding school up St. Louis way when she begins classes next fall. That, my dear, is all there was to it,'' he informed her, tweaking her nose and planting a playful kiss against her petulant mouth.

''You swear that's all that woman wanted with you?'' Cait-lan murmured, her expression doubtful.

"I'm not saying that's all she *wanted,*" Rafe declared with an arrogant quirk of his brow. "What I'm saying is; that's all she got . . . my word that I'd take her daughter to St. Louis next fall." Then muttering some unintelligible oath under his breath, he shook her and said, "Good God, Kettie, haven't you figured it out yet?"

"What?"

Taking Caitlan's face between his large hands, Rafe stroked her cheeks with his thumbs and his expression softened when he looked deeply into her eyes and whispered, "I love you, darlin'. I always have. I don't want anyone else."

Becky sat patiently on Caitlan's lap—well, as patiently as any two-and-a-half-year-old can sit for any length of time— while Caitlan rearranged the ribbon in her dark brown curls for at least the fifth time. As the small child pounded the edge of the dressing table with the brightly painted toy soldier Rafe had bought her the day they arrived in New Orleans, Caitlan viewed her lopsided efforts in the mirror and sighed.

"I'm sorry, love, but that's the best I can do. I'll learn to do better, I promise," Caitlan whispered into Becky's hair and, wrapping her arms around the little girl, hugged her tightly.

"Okay, Kitty," Becky gurgled happily. Lifting her hand to the cockeyed satin frippery, she patted the ribbon and gave it her approval by saying her standard byword, "Pitty."

"Yes, you are. Very pretty, indeed," announced a masculine voice behind them. Blue and green gazes met in the mirror for a fleeting moment before Rafe clapped his hands together. Forcing a cheerful smile to his face, he said, "Well, now. All the baggage has been loaded onto the carriage. Are my girls ready to leave?"

"Ready!" Becky squealed, lifting her arms to Rafe. "Me go Daddy."

Caitlan remained seated for a long moment after Rafe carried the animated child from the chamber. Choking back the sob that trembled on her lips, she braced her hands on the dressing table and pushed herself up. Then with a disconsolate sigh, she gathered the royal blue cloak—a Christmas present from Rafe—about her shoulders, collected Becky's coat and bonnet from the bedside chair, and followed them from the room.

The carriage ride to the convent was pretty much as one might expect. Becky alternated between Caitlan and Rafe, climbing from one lap to the other. The couple remained unusually reticent during the short excursion. In fact, the vehicle was deathly still except for Becky, whose nonsensical gibberish and singsong nursery rhymes reverberated throughout the tiny compartment. While Becky chattered on in idyllic ignorance of the impending separation from her loved ones, Caitlan clutched at Rafe's sleeve, unable to withstand the unbearable pressure that was building in her chest.

It was as the conveyance made the wide turn onto the thoroughfare on which the convent was located that Becky sensed something was amiss. She was bouncing up and down on Caitlan's lap at the time, playing with the satin frogs that adorned the new cloak, when she suddenly took note of Caitlan's forlorn expression. Frowning, Becky clasped Caitlan's face in her chubby hands and tilted her head this way and that, as her big brown eyes scrutinized Caitlan's downcast countenance.

Finally, she said, "Kitty sad." And before Caitlan realized what the child was thinking, she bounded forward and pecked Caitlan on the cheek. Sitting back, Becky looked at Caitlan once more—her little face full of concern—and asked, "Better?"

"Oh my, yes. Much better" came Caitlan's hoarse whisper as she clasped Becky's hand in hers and brought it to her lips. Kissing the tip of each tiny finger, she fought back the desolate tears that prickled her eyes and murmured, "Thank you, sweetie. I . . . I love you."

"Love you," Becky assured the visibly distraught woman, patting her cheek.

Caitlan was beside herself with misery. Here she was, a fully grown woman, being consoled by a little child . . . a child that adored her, trusted her . . . a child she would presently abandon to another's care. If anyone would have told Caitlan six weeks earlier that this precious little life would come to mean so much to her, she would have scoffed at them. The unhappy truth was, Caitlan's heart was breaking and there was nothing she could do to make the incredible ache go away.

It was on the tip of her tongue to ask Rafe to please reconsider what he was doing when the carriage rolled to a stop and the driver jumped down from his seat to throw the door open. The sudden disturbance caught Becky's attention, and she glanced out the opening. Upon seeing the familiar stone wall that surrounded the convent, Becky's visage underwent a dramatic change. Scrambling from Caitlan's arms, she clambered atop Rafe's lap and flung her tiny arms about his neck, clinging to him in sheer desperation.

"*NO!*" Becky shrieked, burying her face in Rafe's neck. "Me go Daddy! Me go, too!" she wailed, dissolving into tears.

"Not this time, princess," Rafe whispered, holding the child close for a moment. "Soon. Daddy Rafe promises we'll be together soon." His voice was husky with emotion as he made this vow.

Though Rafe's soft murmurings sufficed to calm Becky's hysterical screams, her little body trembled with uncontrollable sobs as she held fast to his overcoat. Laying her head upon Rafe's shoulder, Becky made it understood that no amount of cajoling would persuade her to change her mind. She knew what was best for her, and she wanted to be with her daddy.

"Me go, too," she insisted, whimpering softly against his neck. "I be good."

"I'm sorry, Becky," Rafe choked out, obviously near tears himself. Obliging the little girl to look at him, he scolded, "Listen to me. You know Daddy Rafe loves you. I'm not about to leave you here forever. I'll come back as soon as I can. Now, be Daddy's brave, little princess," he cooed, brushing the tears from Becky's cheeks and pressing a kiss to her forehead. Knowing he must act before his own composure shattered, Rafe squared his shoulders and stood up.

This movement prompted another wildly emotional outburst from the little girl, whose hysterical protests suffused the conveyance once more. As Rafe prepared to exit the compartment, Becky's eyes fell upon Caitlan and, certain here was a sympathetic friend who would champion her cause, she reached out to grab hold of Caitlan's cloak.

"Kitty, *nooo*!" Becky sobbed, clutching the garment in her tiny fist, her imploring eyes awash with a fresh flood of heart-rending tears.

It was more than Caitlan could bear. Her arms flew upward in a reflex action as if she would wrest the child from Rafe and cuddle her to her breast. Instead, Caitlan caught hold of Rafe's sleeve in a beseeching gesture and gasped, "Oh Rafe! Perhaps—"

"No!" he snapped, tugging Becky's hand free of the expensive garment. Realizing that Caitlan wanted only what was best for the child, his tone grew more reasonable when he added, "I know it's hard, Kettie. But you must know in your heart that Becky is better off here for now. She'll be fine," Rafe said, flashing her a reassuring smile.

With that, he exited the conveyance, leaving Caitlan to await his return. For that, she was grateful; there was little doubt in her mind that her wobbly legs would not have carried her as far as the gatepost, let alone through the wide courtyard. As for Becky, Rafe was right. Deep in her heart of hearts, Caitlan knew the little girl would be all right once they were gone. She was not so sure the same could be said of her own peace of mind, however.

Breathing a beleaguered sigh, Caitlan leaned forward to peer out the open coach door. In the ensuing moments—as she observed the poignant scene unfold in the courtyard—she was compelled to press a hand to her lips to smother the sob that gathered there. Caitlan had no idea what Rafe said to Becky to soothe her frazzled mien, but as she watched, the little girl's hysterical screams gradually gave way to less heartbreaking whimpers of disappointment. Then screwing up her face in a pout, Becky bussed her self-appointed daddy's cheek with her wet mouth and went—albeit begrudgingly—into Sister Angelica's waiting arms.

As Rafe turned to make his way back to the carriage, a little hand lifted and gave a tremulous wave of farewell at his departing back. He was about to pass through the gatepost when Becky's lonely sounding, "Bye-bye, Daddy. Me love you," fell upon his ears.

Rafe stopped dead in his tracks and wheeled about, and it took every ounce of strength the big man possessed to keep from running back up the sidewalk and whisking the precious bundle from the nun's arms. Instead, he forced a smile to his lips, returned her wave, and said, "Bye-bye, princess. Daddy loves you, too. I'll come back for you, sweetie, just as soon as I can.'' Upon making this promise, Rafe flung himself inside the carriage and signaled the coachman to drive on.

Neither Caitlan nor Rafe said a word as the vehicle pulled away from the convent. Indeed, they each required several moments to restore their respective composures following the emotional leave-taking. But, as luck would have it, little Becky herself—although inadvertently—proved instrumental in uniting two separately grieving souls as one.

As the coach trundled free of the city and rounded a curve, Caitlan felt something roll against her shoe and, bending down, she discovered Becky's coveted wooden soldier. Realizing the child must have dropped it during her hysterical outburst, Caitlan plucked the precious plaything from the floor. Leaning back against the leather cushions, she fingered the colorful toy, her expression glum. And this time when the tears came, she made no attempt to dissuade them as they trickled down her cheek.

Somewhere in the depths of her misery, Caitlan became aware of a strong, comforting arm that Rafe slipped around her shoulders. And through her tears, she saw him slide his free hand over hers . . . the two of them—together—nestling a cherished memory of Becky in their clasped hands. Leaning into the circle of his arms, Caitlan took comfort in Rafe's nearness, although she gleaned little satisfaction in her memory of Becky's crestfallen face as she watched her daddy stride out of her life.

Poor little one, was Caitlan's unspoken thought. *It doesn't get any easier when you grow older, I fear*.

After all, no one knew any better than she how heartbreaking it was to be forsaken by Rafe . . . to be left alone for years on end with only lonely memories to brighten an otherwise desolate existence. This vein of thought prompted an eerie sensation to prickle her spine and, recalling what occurred the last time she had been encumbered with a sense that some portentous happening loomed in her future, Caitlan wisely shooed the bothersome feeling away. With a sidelong glance at Rafe, she gave her head a stern shake, snuggled closer to him and resolved not to think on that now . . . the time when Rafe would leave her again.

*   *   *

Since the *Magnolia Princess* had not returned from its latest
run upriver, Rafe was forced to make alternate travel arrangements for them. They had no choice but to make the journey
overland, but rather than travel by way of public stagecoach,
Rafe hired a private coach and team, as well as a driver and
outrider—Zeke and Thom, albeit Caitlan could never seem to
remember which was which—for the duration of the trip.
Though the expedition got off to a prodigiously rocky start—
what with that distressing scene at the convent—by the time
they stopped for lunch at a quaint country tavern, both Caitlan
and Rafe were feeling more the thing.

The small entourage arrived in Baton Rouge by the afternoon
of the following day. They did not stay the night, however.
Rather they paused only long enough to partake of a light meal
and rest the horses before embarking on the next stage of their
journey. Rafe explained that he preferred to get them settled
at Foxborough Hall with his sister and brother-in-law before
beginning his search for the elusive owner of the diamond and
ruby JC-shaped pin. With this decision made, the couple traveled on until just before nightfall, stopping to pass their last
night on the road at a cozy roadside inn.

As Rafe was helping Caitlan into the carriage the following
morning, he noticed her disheartened air and, thinking back,
he recalled that Caitlan had been unusually taciturn during
breakfast. Dismissing her lackluster mien as weariness from
their whirlwind trip, Rafe settled her inside the conveyance,
then went to slip Wanderer a carrot before tethering him to the
back of the coach and answer any last-minute questions the
driver might have concerning directions and whatnot. When,
however, they had been on the road for more than an hour and
his attempts to engage Caitlan in casual conversation had been
rewarded with little more than an indifferent shrug or morose
sigh, Rafe knew that fatigue was not the problem.

Determined to coax Caitlan into a more jovial mood, Rafe
swung himself around onto the opposite seat facing her. Nudging her knee with his, he said, "All right, Kettie Webber. Out
with it."

"Hmm?" Caitlan murmured, dragging her listless gaze from
the window where she had been watching the passing land-
scape. "Whatever are you talking about, Rafe?"

"I want you to stop looking so gloomy and tell me what's bothering you."

In response to this, Caitlan merely averted her gaze back out the window and said, "You're mistaken. I'm fine. What makes you think something is bothering me?"

"Lord, Kettie, you've been throwing out signals ever since we pulled out of Baton Rouge yesterday" was his blunt pronouncement. "In fact, I've been thinking you weren't quite yourself when you joined me at the breakfast table this morning. But the clincher came about thirty seconds ago when I asked if you'd like to strip naked and take a dip in that pond we drove by a ways back and you said," and here Rafe quoted, mimicking Caitlan's woebegone sigh to perfection, " 'That would be nice, I suppose.' "

"You're right, of course," Caitlan conceded, a mischievous half smile spreading her lips despite her heavyhearted mien. "I don't know what I could have been thinking to have said such a thing. It's much too cold to go swimming."

"Oh no you don't. That's not what I meant and you damn well know it. So, don't go thinking you can pull the wool over old Rafe's eyes that easily. It will take a damn sight more than a saucy reply and a flirtatious smile to convince me otherwise," he informed her. "Tell me, darlin'. Because, if you don't confide in me willingly, I may be forced to take extreme measures—perhaps tickle you—until you fess up. And you know . . . that I know . . . exactly which spot to aim for first," Rafe threatened, throwing Caitlan a meaningful look. Then cracking his knuckles, Rafe gave all ten fingers a purposeful wiggle and made as if to lunge across the aisle toward her.

Caitlan regarded those potentially pesky digits with a wary eye and, before Rafe had a chance to suit his actions to his words, said, "Don't, Rafe. Please. Give me a moment and I'll tell you what has been on my mind all morning."

It was the imploring look in her eyes more so than the serious-sounding tone of her voice that persuaded Rafe to do as she asked. Leaning back, he folded his arms across his chest and waited for Caitlan to begin.

Staring down at the hands she had folded primly in her lap, she eventually said, "This was all a huge mistake. I should not have come with you."

"The hell you—"

"No, let me finish" was Caitlan's firm admonition when Rafe would have interrupted her. "Do you remember all those weeks ago when we were sitting in Harriet's kitchen and you asked me how I came to be living in Vicksburg?" Observing Rafe's silent nod, she continued, "Well, it's not a happy story. You see, it all began when my brother Brendan was killed in a duel six years ago by Page Wilkerson."

"Aw, honey, no. I didn't know. How awful for you. But Wilkerson, you say?" Rafe questioned, obviously surprised by this revelation. "As I recall, he was the best marksman in the parish. What could your brother have been thinking to pick a fight with the likes of Page Wilkerson?"

"Actually, it was the other way around. Page provoked Brendan by saying unkind things about Mother. I know," Caitlan threw up a hand to forestall Rafe's ensuing comment, "Page Wilkerson was not the first to make lewd references about our mother, nor will he be the last, so long as your sister's husband is alive, I fear," she added with a begrudging snicker. "Anyway, the two of them met early one morning and, when it was all over, Brendan lay dead in the wet grass. All from some idiotic sense of family honor for a woman who had—I'm sure—long since stopped thinking of him as her son."

Rafe thought it singularly peculiar that, during the recounting of this devastating tale that Caitlan retained remarkable composure. Not so much as a single tear glistened in the vibrant green eyes, nor did her voice falter. Had he asked, she could have explained the reason for her apparent detached mien. In truth, Caitlan had relived that terrible morning when she learned about the duel in her mind and dreams so often that she had become numb with the thoughts of it.

"Papa was never the same after that," she continued, blowing a sorrowful sigh. "He began to drink and to gamble away huge sums of money. Soon there was nothing left . . . except Thistledown. And eventually, Papa's debts grew so immense that he was forced to sell our home as well. I know it's ironic, but in the end—with the exception of a few personal belongings—Papa sold the plantation to Page Wilkerson and the three of us set out for Vicksburg."

"Three?"

"Hezekiah came with us, too," she explained. "What with his bad leg and all, not to mention the fact that he was totally devoted to Papa and me . . . well, I suppose Page realized Hezekiah would be more trouble to him than he was worth in the long run. When we arrived in the city, we took up residence at Harriet's boardinghouse until Papa succeeded in squandering what little proceeds he had made from the sale of Thistledown . . . and was in debt for a good deal more." Caitlan paused to stare out the window, holding onto the leather hand strap so tightly that her knuckles made a distinct impression in her glove where the material stretched taut across her hand.

She indulged herself in a moment of quiet reflection before saying, "Within six months, Papa was also dead. It was a . . . a suicide," Caitlan mumbled the dreaded word. Taking a deep breath, she looked at Rafe and said, "Sheriff Bodeker brought word to me in the middle of the night. I have often wondered how Papa could do such a thing, but I suppose the pressure finally got to him. You know, I was only ten years old when Mother ran off with Mr. Carter, so I didn't truly understand what a blow that was to Papa's pride until I was older. He loved her so very much and the memory of her desertion must have eaten away at him all those years. The final blow came when Brendan was killed. I can only speculate as to why Papa did such a ghastly thing, but I think it was because he had come to believe that dying was easier than living.

"You know, Rafe, there are times when I'm inclined to agree with Papa's way of thinking," Caitlan told him, her straightforward comment catching him unawares. Smiling at the disapproving frown that shadowed his otherwise handsome face, she said, "Don't misunderstand me, I do not condone what Papa did. I'm just saying I have recently come to terms with his reasons for doing so.

"And I'll tell you something else . . . living with Harriet the past five years to work off the debts Papa left behind has been no easy task, to be sure. But I had no idea that coming home would be this hard. It has stirred up a lot of unhappy memories for me. Are you certain I will be welcome at Foxborough Hall?" Caitlan asked, turning her doubtful gaze on Rafe. "Josie and I used to get along well enough, I suppose, but Wesley has never forgiven me for what Mother did.''

Rafe had listened patiently throughout Caitlan's lengthy discourse, thinking it wise to let her purge herself of these sorrowful memories while she was of a mind to do so. But now that she was finished, he was determined to have his say.

Leaning forward, Rafe gathered her hands in his and said, "Now, you listen to me, Kettie. What John Carter and your mother did was scandalous, shameless—even by my standards—there's no denying that. But you are not to blame for what they did." Noting that his words did little to assuage the brooding frown that turned down the corners of her mouth, he tugged on her hands and his voice was soft when he said, "Come here."

When Caitlan demonstrated an irritating reluctance to comply with his wishes, Rafe merely pulled her from her seat and settled her on his lap. Untying the satin ribbons at her throat, he removed her bonnet and tossed it onto the opposite bench. Then he cuddled her face in his large hands and his eyes deepened with passion as he lowered his lips to hers and kissed her . . . tenderly, lovingly.

When—after several delicious moments—he pulled away, Caitlan felt safe, protected. As she curled up against him, she heard Rafe say, "Put aside your fears, sweet pea. If my brother-in-law knows what's good for him, he'll conduct himself in a manner befitting a well-bred southern gentleman. Hell, I've lent Wesley so much money over the years—and mind, he's not so much as offered to repay a single penny—that I feel as if I own part of Foxborough Hall. The very least he can do is provide his benefactor . . . and his benefactor's very lovely traveling companion," he bussed Caitlan's cheek and grinned at her, "with accommodations for a few days."

Then his mood grew pensive as he entwined his hand with hers and said, "Josie, on the other hand, is a different matter altogether. I'm afraid my dear, baby sister may not be too pleased to see her long-departed brother when she learns what I've come for . . . the answers to some long overdue questions."

Chapter Sixteen

Wesley Carter was a bitter, little man. From the top of his sorely balding head to the bottom of his stocking feet, he stood no more than five feet, seven inches tall . . . if that. But what he lacked in physical stature, he overcompensated for in his emotional—and extremely explosive—demeanor. Indeed, Wesley Carter's business associates and neighbors were the first to agree that he was nothing if not an aggressive, calculating, and oftentimes ruthless, businessman. Wesley was also a shrewd man, however. For although he inwardly seethed at the fact that the daughter of the harlot who had lured his father into a life of sin and degradation presently sat at his dining-room table, outwardly he effected the mien of a most gracious host.

Smoothing the dark brown hair at his temple—of which there was precious little—with a negligent hand, Wesley reached for his wine glass. Taking a sip, he savored the dry Chablis for a moment before commenting, "I'm sorry I wasn't here to welcome you when you arrived yesterday, Rafe. Business matters detained me in Lafayette longer than I anticipated. I had to ride like the wind to make it back to Foxborough before night-fall. And then to have such an . . . unexpected surprise waiting for me. I cannot tell you how good it is to see you again."

Wesley smiled, although an astute observer would have noticed that his seemingly delighted expression did not quite reach his eyes. "How long has it been since Josie and I had the pleasure of your company at Foxborough, Rafe . . . five, six years?"

"Seven."

"It's been that long, has it? My, my." Wesley shook his head, signaling for the servant to remove his plate and bring on the next course. Settling his stony black gaze on Caitlan, he said, "And you've brought Katie Webber with you. It's been an age since we've seen you, as well. What have you been doing with yourself all these years, Katie?"

Caitlan, who was finding it difficult to relax under Wesley's daunting stare, dabbed at her lips with her linen napkin and said, "I've been keeping busy, Wesley."

"Don't be so modest, honey," Rafe scolded, reaching out beside him to capture Caitlan's tremulous hand in his. "Actually, Kettie's done quite well for herself considering all the adversity she's had to overcome. Why, she even runs her own business—a successful one, mind you—up in Vicksburg," Rafe said proudly. Pressing a kiss against the slender appendage, he gave Caitlan a reassuring wink and offered his full attention to his meal and the conversation taking place at the table.

"Really?" Wesley drawled, taking in Rafe's blatant show of affection with a cool eye. Helping himself to a heaping spoonful of potatoes that a servant tendered at his left side, Wesley droned, "That certainly is interesting. But what about you, Rafe? What brings you back to Pointe Coupee Parish after all these years? Josie tells me you gave her quite a surprise when you drove up to the house yesterday."

"That's an understatement! You should have seen the look on Josie's face when we stepped out of the carriage, Wesley, especially Kettie." Rafe laughed, his all-observing gaze settling on his sister's face directly opposite him. "Yes, it was fairly obvious that Kettie and I were the last people Josie thought to find trundling up her driveway yesterday morning."

In response to this sally, the blond-haired, green-eyed, one-time beauty pulled a face at her sibling and said, "Well now, just what did you expect, Rafe? I haven't had as much as a single letter from you in over a year. Mercy sakes, I didn't know if you were dead or alive. Is it little wonder my eyes nearly popped out of my head when I saw you?''

"No, Josie. I suppose not.'' Rafe gave a good-natured chuckle, tearing off a piece of the piping hot bread one of the maids had set down in front of him. Reverting his gaze to Wesley, he said, ''As for my reasons for dropping in on you like this, it's partly social, partly business . . . mostly business, I guess.''

"We'll have none of that talk at my dinner table, thank you,'' Josie announced in no uncertain terms. ''You and Wesley can very well put aside your boring business discussion until after Katie and I have taken ourselves off to the drawing-room. I want to hear all about New Orleans. Why, I've been so busy with the children and running this house that I can't even recall the last time Wesley took me to Baton Rouge, let alone all the way to New Orleans. What was it like, Katie dear? Did you do much shopping?''

Caitlan could tell from the disdainful look that Josie cast in her direction that the woman thought it was obvious from the modest cut of her plain gown that she had not used her time in New Orleans to good advantage. Still, Caitlan thought it only polite to answer, ''No, actually, we—''

"Mrs. Carter!'' interrupted a high-pitched feminine voice from the dining-room threshold. ''May I have a word with you, please?''

The abrupt arrival of the children's governess served to cut Caitlan off in midsentence. Although Wesley and Josie accepted the invasion as if it were an everyday occurrence, their dinner guests viewed the proceedings with a decided bemused air. Though she was not given leave to do so, the agitated governess scurried into the room and walked straightaway over to Josie where she bent to whisper some secret intelligence in the woman's ear.

Though Josie did her best to mask her displeasure with the intrusion, she could not hide the irritation that crept into her voice when she said, ''I've told you time and again, Miss Pendleton, that you simply must learn to manage the children if you hope to remain in our employ.''

When, however, Miss Pendleton made it plain that she was not about to brave the horrors of the third-floor nursery unassisted, Josie blew a disgusted sigh and said, "Oh, very well then. Run along." She shooed the governess away with a dismissive wave of her hand. "I'll be along in a moment."

Josie waited until the young woman had exited the dining-room before she railed on her husband. "Really, Wesley! I declare I don't know what I'm going to do with that woman. One would think that, in this day and age, a body could find decent help for the nursery. Granted, the children—especially the boys—are rambunctious little darlings, but they are hardly the monsters that Miss Pendleton would have everyone believe." Standing, Josie tossed her crumpled napkin onto the table, grumbling all the while, "I suppose I'd better go see what I can do to settle them down, else there'll be no living with that woman."

Caitlan felt Rafe give her knee a gentle squeeze and, correctly surmising that he wanted to have a word alone with Wesley, she asked, "Might I go along with you, Josie? I mean, if it wouldn't be an imposition. I doubt if I'll be much help to you, but I would love to meet the children. I've heard them laughing in the hallway and seen them playing on the lawn, but I haven't had the opportunity to talk to them yet. May I?"

Wesley gave his wife a meaningful look and, interpreting his expression in much the same way Caitlan had deciphered Rafe's groping gesture, Josie shrugged her shoulders and said, "Feel free to do as you like, Katie. The children always enjoy meeting a new face." Then offering up her next comment as if it were an offhand statement when, in truth, the barb had been well thought out, Josie chatted, "You have no idea how lucky you are, Katie . . . you know . . . that you'll never have children of your own to contend with. They can be such precious angels, but they're also a tremendous responsibility."

After the dining-room door closed behind the departing women, Wesley motioned for the servants to clear away the place settings. When the decanter of port had been placed in front of him, he poured each of them a glass of the flavorful drink and selected a cigar from the box a servant held open before him. He lit the cigar from a match the same diligent domestic proffered and, leaning back in the straight-backed chair, Wesley took a contemplative puff and leveled his ponderous gaze at Rafe.

Exhaling, he said, "It would seem that old habits die hard with you, Rafe." Wesley nodded toward the chair that Caitlan had recently vacated. "No offense intended" came his hasty postscript when he saw the darkling look gathering in the blue eyes that returned his stare.

"None taken," Rafe grunted, following Wesley's example of puffing his cigar alight and making himself comfortable on his chair. "But I would hardly call Kettie a habit. I hadn't laid eyes on her in seven years until back in July, and then it was Kettie who found—rather stumbled across—me one night on a rain-drenched bluff up in Vicksburg. I had been bushwhacked by a couple of good-for-nothing lowlifes and left for the buzzards. Hell, the fact is, I was more than half dead when Kettie found me and took me back to her place. She saved my life, Wesley . . . literally forced me to live when I had pretty much given up on the idea.

"I don't know if it's fate or just plain coincidence that keeps throwing me and Kettie together, but I do know this much . . ." Rafe paused and bent sideways to tap the cigar against the brass spittoon the servant had placed on the floor beside him before exiting the room and leaving the men alone to conduct their business in private. Pulling himself erect once more, he continued, " . . . I almost lost Kettie twice before, I don't intend to let her slip away this time. After all, how many chances at happiness is a man entitled to in one lifetime? I've already had two . . . three if you count this time. Hell, I may not get another. No, Kettie's not a habit, Wesley . . . she's my life."

Wesley fiddled with the stem of his drinking glass for a moment as he considered, not only the essence of Rafe's discourse, but his reasoning behind making him aware of his personal feelings insofar as the Webber woman was concerned. Taking a satisfying draft of the liquid, Wesley said, "I know what you mean, Rafe; I feel the same way about your sister. I hope you don't mind me asking this, but are you sure Katie shares your sentiments? After all, you know how she reacted the time you were called home to tend to your ailing father."

"If it's all the same to you, Wesley, I think I'll wait and pick that particular bone with my sweet, little sister" was Rafe's ambiguous comment. Rolling the end of his cigar around on the tip of his tongue, he said, "I do have a favor to ask of you and Josie, however.''

"Yes?"

"I have some business—a private matter—to settle back in Baton Rouge,'' he explained. "It shouldn't take more than a day or two, and I was hoping I could leave Kettie here at Foxborough while I took care of it. I could take her along with me but you know how bored women get when we men are conducting business in town.''

"Don't I though.'' Wesley laughed. "You should hear Josie, although I have to admit, if I point her in the direction of the nearest dress shop, that usually pacifies her. I'm sure Josie won't mind if Katie stays. In fact, she'll most likely enjoy the company.''

"What about you, Wesley? How do you feel about Kettie staying here?'' Rafe posed the delicate question and watched closely for his brother-in-law's reaction.

Knowing full well that Rafe would see through any attempt to hide his true feelings, Wesley smoothed his hand across his bald spot—a habit that always seemed to materialize whenever he was the least bit nervous—and said, "I cannot honestly tell you that I'm overly fond of the idea of having that Webber woman's daughter in my home for any great length of time, but we'll get along well enough for a day or two, I should imagine. Besides, Rafe, you're Josie's brother. If Katie means as much to you as you say she does, I have a sneaking suspicion you'll be adding her to our little family circle one day soon.''

"Kettie is not to blame, you know.''

"Please, Rafe.'' Wesley threw up a silencing hand and reached toward the table to help himself to a second serving of port. "We have been down this road before. I've said Katie can stay. Let's leave it at that, shall we? Now, tell me what you've been doing since you arrived. Have you had a chance to visit any of your old haunts?''

"Kettie and I took a drive over to Thistledown this morning. That was an eye-opening experience, as you can well imagine,'' Rafe commented, a grim expression furrowing his brow. "It damn near broke Kettie's heart to see how the present owner has let the plantation go to ruin. It's a disgrace. Why, the house is practically falling down and the fields have all grown wild. An idea has been nagging at me ever since we came back from Thistledown. I've been thinking about it all day and I'm about to come to a decision.''

''Oh? And what might that be?''

''I'm thinking about buying that plantation and putting it back in working order. It would please Kettie, I'm sure of that,'' Rafe said, taking a sip of wine and smiling to himself as he envisioned Caitlan's reaction when he told her what he was planning.

His wistful ruminations were ruthlessly invaded a moment later by Wesley's incredulous voice, saying, ''Rafe, have you taken leave of your senses? Haven't you been reading the papers? There's a war brewing, man! South Carolina has already seceded from the Union and other states are sure to follow. Hell, talk of secession has been the rage in Mississippi and Louisiana for months now. This is not the time to be worrying about pleasing your woman. It's time to worry about holding on to what you've got—I expect the Yankees would like to get hold of those riverboats of yours—not plunge yourself deeper in debt.''

''I expect you're right, Wesley,'' Rafe conceded. ''But, be that as it may, I rode over to see Page Wilkerson this afternoon. Kettie told me that her father sold Thistledown to him before they moved to Vicksburg, so I thought I'd test the waters . . . you know . . . hint around that I was interested in buying if he was interested in selling. Come to find out, Wilkerson doesn't own the plantation either. As it turns out, he was merely acting as an agent for some attorney up in Natchez when he bought the property from Lawrence Webber. The lawyer, in turn, was representing his client, so the long and the short of it is, Page claims that he doesn't have the slightest clue as to who owns Thistledown.''

''My, that is a puzzle, isn't it?'' Wesley said, downing his second glass of port in a single gulp. Before he could pour himself a third, Rafe continued.

''Yes, it is. But I fancy I could solve it quick enough if I had the time to run up to Natchez and search through the courthouse records. It would take some digging, but I would eventually find what I was looking for, I expect.''

''I expect you would'' was Wesley's wry retort.

''As I said, I don't have time to enact such a plan at the

moment, especially since I intend to set out for Baton Rouge the day after New Year's.'' Rafe leaned forward to refill Wesley's glass and, pouring himself another half portion, said, ''I was hoping I might prevail upon you to help me.''

''What would you have me do?''

''I don't expect you to go all the way to Natchez. If it comes to that, Kettie and I can always stop over there on our way back to Vicksburg.'' Rafe quickly put—or so he thought—Wesley's fears to rest. ''But you could ask around while I'm gone,'' Rafe suggested. ''Talk to your neighbors, see if they recall anyone in particular who showed an interest in Thistledown. I know it's been a few years, but you never know what kind of things people store away in their memories. Would you be willing to do that for me, Wesley?''

''Why, yes. Yes, of course,'' Wesley said, his hand automatically lifting to stroke at his bald spot. ''I'd be happy to.''

The full January moon hovered among the twinkling stars in the Louisiana sky and shined its shimmering brilliance down upon the Foxborough Hall plantation. As the stately, white-columned mansion basked in the glow of the celestial body, a beam of light wended its way through a second-story window to gently waft across the face of the slumbering miss who rested peacefully upon the chamber bed. In fact, it was the first truly restful sleep Caitlan had enjoyed since she and Rafe had taken their leave of little Becky in New Orleans a week earlier.

Caitlan slept soundly, oblivious to the fact that a shadowy figure crept in cautious silence along the corridor toward her room. She stirred slightly as the sound of the creaking door being pushed open penetrated her dreams, but after a moment, Caitlan moaned a drowsy sigh and snuggled farther down in the big cherry four-poster. Thus mindful that there was no danger of immediate discovery, the intruder took up a stance at the foot of the bed to observe for a moment.

The moonlight streamed through the window, bathing Caitlan's face with its luminescence and causing her face to glimmer with a radiant luster. As the invader watched, Caitlan twisted from her side to her back, kicking off several layers of bedclothes in the process. Knowing that the chill of the room would eventually prompt her to waken and initiate a search for the errant blankets, the shadowy figure stepped around the foot of the bed. Purposeful fingers had just taken hold of the bed coverings, however, when Caitlan's eyes fluttered open, and she sensed rather than saw that someone hovered above her in the darkness.

Acting from instinct, she started to scream but was prevented from doing so when a hand was clamped firmly across her mouth. Caitlan felt the mortal terror gather in the pit of her stomach and her limbs went limp, leaving her momentarily helpless against her stronger adversary. The panic that spurted throughout Caitlan's being was mirrored in her eyes and just when she thought she might actually swoon from the fear of not knowing what was about to happen, the dark figure spoke, filling her with an altogether different emotion.

"Don't scream, Kettie! It's me, darlin'," cooed a familiar voice. "Did I frighten you, sweet pea?"

With an angry glare, Caitlan shoved the oppressive hand aside and hissed, "What do you think? You come skulking into my room in the middle of the night and wake me from a sound sleep. Of course you frightened me, Rafe!" Caitlan slapped his arm with a peevish gesture and flounced onto her side.

"Aw hell, Kettie," Rafe grumbled, climbing onto the bed and snuggling up against her rigid back. "Don't poker up at me. I'm sorry if I startled you, honey." Rafe tossed the long brown-and-russet braid across Caitlan's shoulder so he could nuzzle her neck. Nibbling a sensuous path around to her ear, he murmured, "I couldn't help myself. I was lonesome for you, sweetheart. We haven't slept together since we left New Orleans, what with you hell-bent on observing the "proprieties" at the inns where we stayed overnight. And I'm sure I don't know what my sister was thinking by giving us rooms on opposite ends of this rambling mansion."

Caitlan, greatly mollified by Rafe's pouting admission and the hand that tenderly stroked her arm, wiggled onto her back to look at him. Noting that, in the shadowed moonlight, he looked rather more like a disgruntled schoolboy than a strapping man of thirty-six, she smiled knowingly to herself and said, "I know precisely what Josie was thinking when she made the room arrangements as she did. She was hoping to prevent us from doing what she undoubtedly suspects we have been doing—and that which you are presently contemplating—for sometime now.''

"Well, if that's the case, my uppity sister can very well keep her nose out of my business. What I . . . we . . . do in the privacy of our own bedchamber is none of her concern" came his surly retort.

"It is when we are guests in her home," Caitlan reminded him, lifting her hand to bury her fingers in his beard and caress his cheek. "I'm certain Josie just wants to avoid any unnecessary gossip. You know how servants talk. And then there are the children to consider. We would not want them to ask any embarrassing questions."

"Oh, bother Josie's pack of young hellions. As if they notice anything besides themselves," Rafe grunted.

"Shame on you, Rafe. You're their uncle, after all," Caitlan scolded. Recalling how the children had run amok since their arrival, she laughed despite her attempt to remain stern. "Although I must admit they are quite a handful; they're always creating mischief and causing Miss Pendleton a world of grief. All except for young Percival—mind you, he insists on being called P.J.—"

"And who can blame the lad?" Rafe blurted. "I cannot imagine what my sister could have been thinking when she saddled that boy with a pansified name like Percival. He'll no doubt have to prove his mettle with every snot-nosed bully that comes along, stewing for a fight."

"No doubt," Caitlan agreed, twisting onto her side to face him, their noses mere inches apart on the pillow. "I'm ashamed to admit it, especially after what I just said to you, but of the three children I've met, P.J. is by far the most personable. Daniel is downright wicked—he puts me in mind of Petey Wilson back in Vicksburg—and little Emma . . . well, for a four-year-old, she certainly is a bossy little miss. She's not at all like our . . . your Becky," Caitlan corrected, lest Rafe think her presumptuous. "And as for Wesley, Jr. . . . well, I've not met him, of course, since he is away in Virginia at a military academy, but I have seen his picture and it gave me the shivers. The resemblance to his father is uncanny.''

"What do you mean?" Rafe asked, a mischievous glint twinkling in his blue eyes. "Is he short, bald, and potbellied?"

"No, silly!" Caitlan chided, striking out with the palm of her hand and catching him squarely in the chest.

The unexpected blow took Rafe by surprise; indeed, it very nearly toppled him from the bed. He regained his balance quickly, however, and retaliated by dragging an unprotesting Caitlan onto his chest.

"I simply meant," Caitlan continued, heedless of the interruption, "that Wesley, Jr., looks remarkably like his father, right down to his thin-lipped snarl and the forbidding glint in his black eyes. P.J. says he's an ill-tempered young man, as well."

"Just like his father," Rafe interpolated. Screwing up his face in a thoughtful frown, he regarded her for a moment and said, "It appears that my woefully named nephew has wormed his way into your heart."

"I feel sorry for him." Caitlan shrugged, pressing her ear to his chest and deriving much comfort in the strong rhythm of his heartbeat. "P.J. behaves like a perfect, little gentleman—well, most of the time; he is, after all, only seven—and yet Josie and Wesley ignore him. I believe I've figured it out, though."

"Figured what out, honey?"

"Why Josie and Wesley treat poor P.J. the way they do," she explained. "P.J. favors his grandfather—Mr. Carter—in both looks and temperament. Since Wesley has never forgiven his father for running off with my mother, it stands to reason that he could not tolerate a child who bore such a striking resemblance to him."

The room grew silent then, the only thing of which either of them was conscious being each other's nearness and the faint ticking of a clock in the darkness. Caitlan gave an involuntary jerk when that same timepiece on the corner table chimed three o'clock.

Stirring, she brushed a wayward curl from her face and asked, "What time will you be setting out for Baton Rouge?"

"Mandy sent word by one of the servants that she would have a hearty breakfast waiting for me in the kitchen at half past five. I suppose I'll get on the road shortly after that. I'll be taking Wanderer instead of the carriage, so"—Rafe brought Caitlan's face up to his and placed a kiss against her down-turned mouth—"I'll be able to make the trip to and from the city in half the time."

"And you'll be back tomorrow night?"

"Friday afternoon at the latest," he promised. "But don't you worry your pretty head; Zeke and Thom have assured me they will look after you while I'm gone. If you need anything, just let them know. You may want to take P.J. out for a romp, or go visit some childhood friends. But whatever you do, don't mope around this house thinking my sister will entertain you. Near as I can tell, all she does is sit around on her backside, eating boxes of chocolates while the servants wait on her hand and foot. Then she takes to her bed, pleading a sick headache at the slightest sign of trouble in the nursery."

"Yes, for all her talk, Josie doesn't seem to care much for her motherly duties," Caitlan offered. Thinking to steer the conversation down a more personally gratifying path, she said, "Don't give me a second thought, Rafe. I'm certain I can manage for a day or two without you even though I will . . . miss you," she murmured against his lips, her green gaze deepening with desire.

"Will you now?" Rafe whispered, his warm breath coating her cheek. "Perhaps I should leave you some . . . er . . . token to remember me by?"

Caitlan's affirmative response emerged as little more than a contented whimper when his lips converged upon hers. As Rafe kissed her, she ran her hand down the front of his shirt to his waistband where she hesitated but a fraction of a second before allowing it to continue its playful trek downward. Caitlan's dubious efforts were rewarded moments later when she heard Rafe's heady intake of breath as her tentative touch flitted across the hardened bulge in his trousers. His passion-filled groan of delight was immediately followed by a wicked chortle which caused Caitlan to frown and direct a quizzical gaze at him.

"What?"

"Nothing, sweet pea," Rafe answered, tweaking her chin before his fingers became engaged in the diverting task of undoing the buttons of her nightgown. "I was just wondering what your opinion of Josie and propriety was at this particular moment.''

By way of an answer, Caitlan pushed away from him to sit on her knees. As he watched—ever gratified—she pulled her nightgown over her head and tossed it to the cold floor. Then she straddled Rafe's waist and, with her pale body shimmering above him in the moonlight, Caitlan made short work of his shirt buttons. Shoving the soft material aside with an impatient gesture, she allowed her fingers to fondle the muscular flesh and marveled at the sinewy strength of him. Finally, she slowly leaned forward to embrace him, the stiff peaks of her breasts digging into his skin, wreaking havoc with his already spiraling passions.

Just before Caitlan's lips enclosed on his, she gave a throaty sigh and moaned, ''Bother them both.''

Caitlan shivered as the night breeze brushed across her face and pulled her heavy cloak more snugly about her. Strolling along the garden path, she came upon a stone bench and sat down. As her wandering gaze lifted to the stars that twinkled out from behind a hazy covering of clouds, her thoughts quite naturally turned to Rafe. Vaguely, she wondered if he might be staring out a Baton Rouge hotel room window at the sky, thinking of her . . . missing her as much as she missed him. On this melancholy thought, Caitlan gave a little sigh and took solace in the fact that he had been gone from Foxborough Hall one entire day already. If all went well in the city, he would return the following evening.

With this comforting thought foremost in her mind, Caitlan's reflections turned to the day just ended. Rafe had been right about Josie. She had proved to be an indifferent hostess at best. Thus, after breakfast, Caitlan had prevailed upon Zeke to escort her on a morning visit to an old friend's house. Then in the afternoon, following an adventuresome luncheon with the children in the nursery, she and P.J. had set out for a long walk. Not that Caitlan had meant to openly exhibit a preference for P.J.'s company over the others, but since Daniel was being punished for an earlier misdeed and Emma was destined for a nap, circumstances had merely worked out to Caitlan's advantage.

Thinking back on her outing with the little boy brought a smile of fond remembrance to Caitlan's eyes. Even though the invigorating excursion had left her with blistered feet and an aching lower back, upon reflection, Caitlan knew that she would not have forgone a single moment with the child. They had tramped all over the hills and meadows of Foxborough and neighboring Thistledown, but the highlight of their adventure had come on their return to the mansion by way of a country lane when they happened upon a traveling tinker and his wife.

Caitlan's smile deepened as she recalled how P.J.'s little face had come alive when he saw the brightly painted wagon with the huge signboard. Sprawled across the top of the sign in bold, black letters had been the expected . . . TINKER . . . followed by a general listing of the types of repairs available. It was, however, the lower half of the sign that had caught P.J.'s impressionable eye. For it contained the fleshy drawing of the palm of a hand and was accompanied by bloodred letters proclaiming . . . "Madame Griselda, Teller of Fate and Fortune."

Needless to say, Caitlan had been hard-pressed to keep the child from gaping at such an extraordinary sight. When the colorfully clad owners of the stalled wagon espied the passersby, they had prevailed upon them to stop and visit with them for a while and tell them about the countryside. Caitlan had been suspicious of their motives at first, but her fears had vanished once she realized the middle-aged, travel-weary couple was merely lonesome for company. As the woman went about preparing a meager meal for herself and her husband, the tinker had regaled an ever attentive P.J. with tales of his homeland.

Even though the man had spoken with a heavy accent— making it difficult for Caitlan to understand his every word— P.J. never took his fascinated gaze from the storyteller. All too soon, the time had come for them to leave, and P.J., disappointment registering plainly on his face, had stood up from the tree stump and prepared to follow Caitlan. As a parting gesture, the man had thrust a musical pipe that he himself had carved from wood into the boy's hands and turned his hopeful gaze on Caitlan.

Understanding his implied meaning, Caitlan had delved deeply into her skirt pocket and found a solitary coin. She had apologized for the paltry amount, explaining that they had gone walking and not anticipated the need for money. The man had accepted the small gratuity with an acquiescent smile and bid them farewell. But as Caitlan and her happy companion stepped back onto the roadway, the man's wife had abruptly ceased stirring the contents of the steaming cauldron and run after them.

"Wait! I tell fortune before you go," Madame Griselda had called out to Caitlan in her thick dialect.

Thus summoned, Caitlan had paused to await the woman. Her expression had been apologetic when she said, "I'm sorry, Madame Griselda. Perhaps another time. You see, I haven't any more money with me. I cannot pay you for your trouble."

"No trouble," the woman had assured Caitlan with an elaborate gesture. "And no charge. You and the boy have given us pleasure, now I help you. I see you are in love."

Caitlan, taken aback by the woman's forthright pronouncement, had given a nervous giggle and said, "You can see that in the palm of my hand?"

"No, that I see in your eyes. The palm tells another story." Madame Griselda had grasped Caitlan's hand and peered closely at the open palm for several moments. She had clucked her tongue and her tone had been full of portent when she said, "You must beware. There is one who wishes you much harm. I sense blackness all about you . . . and coldness." The woman shivered for good measure and folded Caitlan's hand closed, saying sadly, "The signs foretell of many dark, terrifying hours in your future. But you must have trust in the one you love. Think of him . . . only of him . . . for he loves you truly and only he can save you from this misfortune."

Caitlan had contrived to put the woman's soothsaying nonsense from her head for the remainder of the outing with P.J., and she had suffered through the evening repast with her nonconversant hosts without the nagging premonition returning to plague her. But alone as she was, seated in the spacious garden, the chilly evening breeze lapping at her billowing cloak, Caitlan was unable to prevent the tingling of prickly flesh that arose along her spine. Feeling suddenly cold and ill at ease,

Caitlan returned to the mansion.

She let herself into the house through the French window that led into the dining room. Upon stepping into the corridor, Caitlan became aware of loud voices coming from the drawing-room and, assuming that Josie and Wesley were embroiled in a heated argument—and not wanting to intrude—Caitlan entered the first room she happened by . . . the library. Even though a cozy fire crackled in the fireplace, Caitlan did not immediately take off her cloak; she was still chilled from her walk in the garden. Instead, she strolled about the room, glancing at the expensive leather-bound volumes that lined the bookshelves.

Vaguely, Caitlan wondered at how Wesley had come to be in possession of so many impressive titles. Frankly, he did not strike her as the scholarly type. And, she noted with a cynical chuckle that, considering the number of expert volumes Wesley held in his library on agriculture, it was a shame he did not use them to better advantage. His cropland was in a sorry state. Both Rafe and Caitlan had thought it singularly peculiar that, while the mansion boasted a serving staff that was second to none, there were no field hands to speak of.

This had raised another perplexing question in Rafe's mind, which he had confided in Caitlan. Since it was obvious that the Foxborough fields had lain dormant for several planting seasons, he could not help but wonder at his brother-in-law's source of income. It had to be substantial, considering that Wesley and Josie spared no expense on personal luxuries. This nagging quandary was swept from Caitlan's head a moment later, however, as she made a puzzling discovery of her own.

Caitlan's happenstance browsing had led her to a section containing novels of romantic fiction and books of poetry. One in particular caught her eye and, out of curiosity, she pulled it from the shelf, opened the cover and read the handwritten inscription. Then she understood the basis for the eerie sense of familiarity that had haunted her since she had stepped into the room . . . this was her father's library. From the huge oak desk, to the leather chair behind it and the oriental rug spread before it, right down to the rare book of poetry she held in her trembling fingers—a book her father had gone to great lengths to purchase for her mother when he was courting her—this was the Thistledown library.

But how could that be? Her father's library had been sold intact, along with everything else connected with the plantation, to Page Wilkerson. That being the case, how had Wesley come to own Lawrence Webber's valued collection?

Caitlan's head swam with the weighty conundrum, and she stumbled over to a chair and sat down. Looking about her—and truly seeing—for the first time, she was amazed by what she saw. It was as if someone had somehow contrived to pick up her father's library at Thistledown, then set it down at Foxborough Hall. The two rooms were identical . . . well, almost. Were it not for that nauseating life-size portrait of Wesley hanging over the mantelpiece they would be exactly the same.

Caitlan eyed with longing the brandy decanter across the way, and for the first time in her life, she felt as if she truly needed a drink to help steady her nerves. Laying the book of poetry aside, she pushed herself to her feet and prepared to suit her actions to her thoughts. A sidelong glance at Wesley's portrait drew her to the mantel instead. Caitlan felt strange, as if she were on the brink of some important discovery, only she had no idea what it might be. Remembering where her premonitions had led her before, she examined the portrait closely.

Granted, there was nothing remarkable about the picture at first glance. Wesley stood at a slight angle from the viewer, rigged out in full evening dress. He wore his top hat—to hide his baldness, she suspected—at a jaunty angle, and his shiny black boots showed nary a smudge. In one hand, he gripped an ornate walking stick while the other rested on his hip, pinning back the edge of his dress jacket to show his waistcoat to advantage. His face held its customary bored expression and there was not so much as a hint of a smile lurking around those cold, black eyes. In short, Wesley looked pretty much as he always did.

Feeling a little disappointed, Caitlan blew a disheartened sigh and made as if to turn away from the mantel. But as she moved her head to one side, something she had not noticed before caught her eye, giving her pause. Facing the portrait once more, Caitlan settled her steady green gaze on Wesley's cunning face, then slowly lowered it until she found what she was unwittingly looking for. There nestled amid the folds of his elaborately tied silk neckcloth was a diamond and ruby tiepin fashioned in the initials "J.C."

Staggered by this totally unexpected revelation, Caitlan took a faltering step backward and one hand flew to her mouth to smother the startled cry that sprang to her tongue. Groping for the chair behind her to help support her withering countenance, a terrifyingly inconceivable thought flashed through Caitlan's brain like a recurring bolt of lightning. Wesley was the murderer that Rafe had been searching for all these months. Wesley was the infamous "J.C." . . . a man who—from Rafe's accounts—was capable of carrying out the most savage and brutal of crimes.

But how was that possible? Wesley's initials were different from that of the pin. Giving herself an admonishing shake, Caitlan told herself that she mustn't dwell on the matter, lest she confuse the issue. After all, she had all the proof she needed; indeed, it twinkled down at her—taunting her—from Wesley's self-indulgent portrait. The perplexing riddle could be sorted out later, but first she had to get in touch with Rafe. He must be found without delay and made aware of her discovery.

Having reached this decision, Caitlan's foremost thought was to find Zeke and have him ready the carriage for traveling. She could not bear to wait until morning; she wanted to put as much distance as possible between herself, Foxborough Hall and its ruthless owner before the first light of day. With this objective in mind, Caitlan whirled to run from the room and ran straightaway into the very villain she was trying to avoid.

"Wesley!" His name emerged as little more than a high-pitched squeak, but considering the circumstances, Caitlan was to be forgiven her squeamish reaction. Lowering trembling fingers to her breast as if to quell the frantic pounding of her heart, she forced a smile to her lips and said, "You gave me quite a fright."

"Did I?" Wesley drawled, his tone far from apologetic. Stepping around her, he lifted his contemplative gaze to the painted canvas above the mantel and said, "From the looks of you, something upset you long before I happened by."

Though he kept his studious black gaze focused on the picture, he continued to direct his comments to her. Drumming the mantelshelf with his fingertips, he mulled aloud, "Now, I wonder what you saw in my portrait that has caused you such distress."

"Nothing," Caitlan replied, hoping desperately that the fear in her heart had not been echoed in her voice. And though she very nearly choked on the compliment, she forced herself to add, "Indeed, I think you look . . . handsome."

"Spare me your flattery," Wesley spat, unimpressed.

Wheeling from the portrait, he stalked over to Caitlan and, without warning, slapped her across the cheek. Her head was still reeling from the stunning blow when she felt her shoulders grasped in a savage grip. Wesley shook her viciously, his hateful voice shouting through the haze that enveloped her, "Tell me, bitch! Tell me what you know. I'll hit you again, I swear!"

Oddly enough, Caitlan was no longer afraid . . . now, she was furious and aware of only two things. One, Wesley's bald spot had grown bloodred, like mercury rising to the top of a thermometer on a hot day, and two, she would die before she would tell this bastard anything. Summoning all her mettle, Caitlan spat in the man's eye.

"Wesley! Have you gone stark-raving mad?!" Josie screamed from the doorway.

Wesley, who had drawn back his fist to deliver another punishing blow to Caitlan's unprotected face, halted in mid-swing. Wiping the spittle from his face with his handkerchief, he glared at his wife and rasped, "She knows."

"What do you mean, she knows? That's not possible," Josie said, giving Caitlan a nervous look. "Now, let her go, Wesley. You don't want to have to explain this to my brother when he returns. As you know, Rafe can be most . . . disagreeable."

"To hell with your brother!" Wesley cried, his scowl deepening. "Look at her, Josie. I tell you, *she knows*."

Josie allowed her fretful gaze to drift back to Caitlan. After considering her for a long moment, she gave her shoulders a resigned shrug and said, "What are you going to do with her?"

"I'll tell you what I'm going to do," he snarled, wrenching Caitlan around in front of him and twisting her arms painfully behind her back. "What I should have done years ago. Give me your sash." Wesley nodded at the knotted belt that secured his wife's dressing gown.

Once he had bound Caitlan's hands securely behind her, Wesley stuffed his handkerchief into her mouth to keep her from crying for help. Then he pushed her roughly to the floor and, ordering Josie to keep an eye on her while he fetched his mount from the stable, Wesley started for the door.

A suddenly panicky Josie ran after him, clutching at his sleeve and whining, "But, Wesley. Whatever shall we tell Rafe?"

Shaking off his wife's encroaching hand with an impatient motion, he snickered and said, "You'll think of something, Josie. You always do." Upon voicing that confident statement, Wesley ran from the room.

Moments later, a dazed and befuddled Caitlan was hauled—none too gently—across the saddle in front of Wesley. He gave a command and the horse bolted forward, galloping off into the night toward some unknown destination. The saddle horn dug mercilessly into Caitlan's side with each jolting step the animal took, but she would soon learn that this discomfort was mild in comparison to that which Wesley had in mind for her.

Caitlan lost all concept of time during the uncomfortable ride, therefore, she had no idea how far they had traveled or where they were when Wesley finally reined in his mount and dragged her to the ground. She knew only that she was cold and miserably tired and that every muscle in her body ached from being bounced on the back of his horse for miles on end. Hatred burned in her breast and, knowing there was nothing she could do in her disadvantageous position, Caitlan utilized the only resource available to her by kicking out at her tormentor. She knew her efforts had been successful when she heard his coarse oath and had a brief glimpse of him sprawled face-first in the dirt at her feet.

Caitlan's triumph proved short-lived, however. The enraged man clambered to his feet and, whirling, gave her a dose of her own medicine. She did not try to get up; she realized that Wesley would only knock her down again if she did so. Caitlan lay with her back to him, biting back the painful tears that stung her eyes, for she was determined that this spineless weasel would not make her cry. As she lay with her cheek pressed against the cold ground, Caitlan became aware of Wesley's labored breathing and, curious as to what he was doing—and more so, what he was planning to do to her—she tried to twist around toward him.

After considerable effort, Caitlan managed to wiggle around to face Wesley only to find that her efforts had been in vain. The moon was obscured by a thick covering of clouds, making it impossible for her to determine what he was about. Eventually, she made out his small shadow in the darkness as he straightened from completing his task. In the next moment, Caitlan heard a noise that sounded very much like that of the creaky hinges on an unoiled door.

Then Wesley's hands were on her again, dragging her—though she protested, kicking and struggling all the while—toward the place that had made that ominous sound. Despite his diminutive size, Wesley proved to be the stronger of the two as he jerked Caitlan to her feet and twirled her around so that her back was to him.

Caitlan felt her courage waning. Indeed, she was terrified by the fear of the unknown. But all too soon, she would come to learn the precise depths of Wesley's hatred of her and her family.

Caitlan heard Wesley's demented chuckle an instant before he thrust his fist into her back and pushed her forward. Her heart verily leaped into her throat as Caitlan realized that she was being propelled toward an opening in the ground. With her hands bound behind her, she was helpless to try to protect herself from—what was certain to be—a bone-breaking fall. An hysterical scream exploded in Caitlan's head as she fell forward into the black abyss. She heard the sound of rending material as her cloak became entangled on some object, then gave way, and a split-second later, she landed with a painful thud against the cold, straw-covered earth.

Somewhere in the murky darkness above her, a sarcastic

voice bid her a fond farewell. Then the creaky door was sealed shut over her and, while an ill-abused Caitlan slipped into blessed unconsciousness, her fiendish persecutor climbed atop his horse and rode away.

Chapter Seventeen

❧❀❧

Rafe paced up and down the length of sidewalk before the jewelry store, his boots tapping out an impatient rhythm against the wooden planks. He had arrived in Baton Rouge by half past ten and gone straightaway to the hotel to wash away the dust of the trail, change from his riding clothes into more suitable attire, and soothe his parched throat. Therefore, by the time he had made his way around to Cogan's Jewelry Store, the noon hour had been upon him. In fact, Rafe had just crossed a busy thoroughfare and stepped up onto the sidewalk, his hand outstretched toward the door latch when the shopkeeper had shot the bolt and hung a "Closed for Lunch" sign in the window.

Despite Rafe's pleading expressions and anxious hand gestures, the jewelry store owner had remained adamant in his resolve to see that his habitual store hours were maintained. Giving his aged head a regretful shake, he had turned away to disappear inside the store. Thus frustrated, Rafe had been left to cool his heels while the shop owner had gone off to partake of his midday meal.

Rafe pounded up and down the walkway for what seemed like an eternity before he came up short and, glaring at the "Closed" sign, shook his head in dismay. Vaguely wondering

how the man could possibly run a profitable business if he
insisted on being gone half the day, Rafe snatched his watch
from his vest pocket and glanced down at the time. With a
begrudging sigh, he saw that the storekeeper had barely been
away a quarter of an hour. Resigning himself to a lengthy
sojourn, he snapped the watch lid closed and returned the
timepiece to his pocket. Then folding his arms across his chest,
Rafe leaned back against the tethering post and settled down
to await the man's return.

At precisely two minutes before the hour, Mr. Cogan reap-
peared at the window to remove the sign and unlock the door.
The sound of the bolt being released caught Rafe's attention
just as a trio of young ladies passed in front of him. Doffing
his hat in gentlemanly deference to them, he entered the shop
amid their girlish titters and the tinkling of the shop bell that
hung above the door.

Before Rafe had a chance to address the store owner, the
elderly man said, "I'm sorry to have kept you waitin', young
fella, but my missus has an ornery streak, I'm afraid. If I'm
more than two or three minutes late for dinner, she's apt to
throw it out. She's a quirky thing all right is my Hattie, but
that's her way. She's been like that for nigh on thirty years,
so I guess there's no use tryin' to get her to change her ways
now. I can't tell you the number of sales I've missed on account
of her being so contrary," Harvey Cogan murmured with a
sorry shake of his head. Settling in behind the glass display
case, he smiled at Rafe and said, "But enough of my troubles.
How can I help you?"

Pulling a small leather pouch from his coat pocket, Rafe
shook the contents out onto the counter and said, "I was wondering if you could tell me anything about this tiepin."

"Let me have a look," the jeweler said, taking out his wire-
rimmed spectacles and securing the end pieces over his ears.
Mr. Cogan laid the twinkling diamond and ruby pin in the
palm of his hand and studied it carefully for several moments,
turning it this way and that to observe the bauble at various
angles. Eventually, he lifted his suspicious gaze to Rafe and
mumbled an evasive, "Could be."

Rafe, sensing that months of painstakingly searching the
countryside for the gem's owner was about to pay off, tried

not to appear overzealous as he asked, "Do you know who it belongs to?"

"Not so fast, young fella." The shopkeeper's eyes narrowed and his fist closed around the tiepin in an instinctive gesture. "First, suppose you tell me how it is you happen to have this fancy gewgaw in your possession."

Rafe understood the man's implied meaning; the shopkeeper no doubt suspected him of some underhanded dealings. Knowing full well that the jeweler's answer depended on his own willingness to cooperate, Rafe ultimately decided that a half-truth would suffice and said, "I found it. You see, I've been looking for the owner for quite some time now, so I might restore the pin to him. I figured that—considering its unique design and all—if I asked around, I'd eventually happen across someone who recognized it. I must have inquired at every jewelry store between here and St. Louis, but so far, I haven't had any luck. I suppose I'll just have to keep looking." Rafe heaved his shoulders, obviously discouraged that what had started out as a promising interview had gone sour.

"Maybe not" came Mr. Cogan's unexpected reply, ignoring the hand Rafe extended toward the pin. Having taken Rafe's measure while he tendered his explanation, and fancying himself to be an excellent judge of character, the shopkeeper tossed the costly gem into Rafe's open palm. Deciding that the tall man with the purposeful expression could be trusted, Harvey Cogan removed his glasses and laid them on the counter, saying, "Fact is, I can most likely tell you everything you'd like to know."

"Oh, why is that?"

"Because you're lookin' at the man who made it, that's why. It's been more than twenty years, but I'm not likely to forget a gaudy piece like this," he advised Rafe. Scratching his chin, Mr. Cogan said, "It was Mrs. Carter up in Pointe Coupee Parish that commissioned the pin. It was to be an anniversary gift for Mr. Carter, only the scalawag up and ran off with a neighbor's wife the very day Mrs. Carter had planned to give it to him. She had arranged a huge party, invited half the parish, as I recall."

"Are you telling me this tiepin belongs to John Carter, formerly of the Foxborough Hall Plantation?"

"Well, yes . . . and no" was the jeweler's obscure answer. The tinkling of the shop bell momentarily drew Mr. Cogan's attention away from Rafe. Nodding at the customer who had just entered the store, he said, "I'll be with you in a moment, Mrs. Fletcher." To Rafe, he said, "You see, Mrs. Carter never had the opportunity to give the gem to her husband. Instead, she gave it to her son . . . John. Are you acquainted with the Carters?"

"Somewhat," Rafe murmured, bouncing the JC-shaped pin in his palm in a contemplative motion. "I wasn't aware there were two sons though."

"There's not," Mr. Cogan said, going on to explain, "There was only young John, named for his father. The lad couldn't have been more than sixteen when Mr. Carter abandoned the family. As you might expect, he took it hard . . . started actin' crazylike. You never knew how he might act when he passed you on the street. One time, he'd treat you like you was a long lost friend, and the next, as if he'd never seen you before. He refused to go by John after his pa up and left the way he did, and took to callin' himself after his mama's surname. You most likely know him as Wesley Carter."

Rafe straightened as if jolted by a lightning bolt. "Wesley?" came his hoarse whisper.

"Yes. He stops in now and again when he's in the city. In fact, I've seen him wearin' that very pin on more than one occasion." The man grunted and said, "I always thought it peculiar that, considerin' how he hated his pa and all, it didn't keep him from sportin' that showy tiepin. But then, Wesley has always shown an unnatural disposition toward fancy duds and such. If you want, I'll make sure the tiepin is returned to him next time he comes into town," Mr. Cogan offered, suddenly wary of the darkling look flashing in the stranger's blue gaze.

"What? No, thank you," Rafe replied, feeling uneasy with the knowledge that he had unwittingly left Caitlan with the very monster he had been searching for all these months. His mien grew positively grim as he added, "Considering the pains I've taken to track him down, I believe I'd like to see Mr. Wesley Carter's expression when I hand this over to him . . . in person," Rafe said with a menacing growl, returning the tiepin to its pouch and drawing the leather straps taut. Tucking the container in his pocket, he extended his hand toward the befuddled jeweler and said, "Thanks for your trouble. You've been very helpful."

"No trouble. I was happy to be of service, young fella," the shopkeeper returned, shaking Rafe's hand. Thinking he might turn the situation to his advantage before the angry-looking man took his leave, Mr. Cogan suggested, "Could I interest you in some trifle for a lady friend before you go? Perhaps some eardrops? I have a lovely pair of emerald—"

"No, thank you." Rafe cut the man short. "Actually, I'm in a bit of a hurry. Another time perhaps," he said with an abrupt gesture. Wheeling about, he promptly exited the jewelry store, leaving a disappointed jeweler in his wake.

Upon learning that Wesley Carter was the murdering, thieving bastard he had been scouring the countryside for all these months, Rafe had gone directly to the local authorities to report his findings. He had done so under the misguided expectation that the sheriff would see that justice was swiftly served. Less than half-an-hour later, however, Rafe had emerged from the sheriff's office sorely disappointed and more frustrated than ever.

As luck would have it, it happened that the sheriff was a longtime acquaintance of Wesley's and took exception to a virtual stranger waltzing into his office and casting aspersions on his friend's good name. Furthermore, Rafe had been informed by the indignant peace officer that, if he insisted on making these ridiculous allegations, he would have to file formal charges with the district marshall since Pointe Coupee Parish and Foxborough Hall were out of the sheriff's jurisdiction.

When Rafe had coolly inquired as to the district marshall's whereabouts, the sheriff had taken the utmost satisfaction in telling Rafe that the law officer had ridden over to Zachary to tend to some domestic squabble. Normally, the marshall would not trouble himself with such a trifling matter, the smug sheriff had assured Rafe, but seeing as how the local constable had fallen ill with the typhus, Marshall Lowry had been left with no choice in the matter. After all, someone had to see that the law was upheld.

Rafe had been about to inform the lazy upstart law officer that it was a pity he did not emulate his superior's example when he had thought better of it and bit back the retort. Nothing constructive would come of bantering insults with the sheriff, had been Rafe's level-headed rationalization. Besides, he had further reasoned, it was entirely possible that he might end up in jail himself on some trumped-up charge if he provoked the short-tempered man. Even though he would have derived considerable personal satisfaction in putting the sheriff in his place, Rafe had decided that his purpose would be better served if he made an unscheduled trip to Zachary. In a voice fairly dripping with sarcasm, he had thanked the sheriff for his time and taken his leave of the insufferable man.

Once on the street, Rafe swallowed his bitter disappointment at not being able to return immediately to Foxborough Hall and confront the wily Wesley. Now that he had concrete evidence linking his brother-in-law to his friends' murders, Rafe was not about to jeopardize this opportunity to see that Wesley was held accountable for his ghastly crimes. He only hoped that Caitlan had taken his advice and found activities that took her away from the mansion . . . and Wesley . . . for much of the day. Thus resolved to find Marshall Lowry and have his say before returning to hold Kettie in his arms, Rafe collected his belongings from the hotel. He did not bother to change into riding clothes, but merely climbed atop Wanderer and set out for Zachary.

He ran his quarry to ground a few hours later at the local tavern in Zachary as the marshall was sitting down to a late supper. When the innkeeper brought the law officer word that a newcomer was asking after him, Marshall Lowry graciously invited Rafe to join him in his private chamber. Unlike the haughty sheriff in Baton Rouge, the marshall took Rafe seriously and listened intently while Rafe aired his rather extensive list of complaints. Occasionally, the peace officer would interrupt to ask Rafe to clarify a point that he found confusing, but when he was done listening to Rafe's amazing narrative, Marshall Lowry was convinced that this was a case that warranted further investigation. In fact, he vowed he would set out for Foxborough Hall at first light and conduct a personal inquiry into the matter.

Relieved by the marshall's promise, Rafe polished off the remaining morsels on his plate and washed them down with a lengthy draft of wine. He took his host by surprise, however, when he stood up from the table and strode over to snatch his cloak from a peg on the wall. Turning toward the marshall, he said, "I'm afraid I can't wait until morning. You see, I left a very special lady under Wesley's protection, and . . . well, considering what I've learned today, I think you can understand why I'm eager to get back to make sure she's all right.

"God help Wesley if she isn't," Rafe added in a forbidding undertone.

"Reconsider, man." Marshall Lowry tossed his napkin onto his empty plate and stood to confront his grim-faced companion. "That's sleet you hear pelting the window. It's not a fit night for traveling. Surely a few hours won't make a difference one way or another. Wait and ride along with me in the morning" came the marshall's logical suggestion.

"But that's where you're wrong, Marshall," Rafe said, shrugging his broad shoulders into his overcoat. "I'm familiar with Wesley Carter's brutal methods. A few hours can make *all* the difference. I pray to God I'm not too late already."

Upon uttering that portentous statement, Rafe walked straightaway to the stables. Tossing an extra coin to the stable boy who had seen that Wanderer received a proper brushing and a heaping bag of oats, Rafe saddled and mounted the horse. Gathering his coat as tightly about his chin as possible to protect himself from the icy pellets that awaited him outside, Rafe directed the animal through the open stable door and horse and rider galloped off into the night.

Caitlan became vaguely aware of some faraway noise, not unlike the soft pattering of raindrops against a rooftop. Many a lonely night that same soothing sound had lulled her to sleep in the attic room at Tuttle's Boarding House. But as Caitlan stirred against the hard, unyielding surface, she quickly came to realize that, as much as she despised the tiny chamber that had served as her jail for so many years, she preferred it over the cold, black hole in which she presently awakened.

As Caitlan gradually regained consciousness, the events of
the evening flooded her memory in painful detail. The last
thing she remembered was hearing Wesley's taunting laughter
floating down from above her in the night. Caitlan shivered at
the thought; then came a frightening discovery . . . it was not
only the memory of Wesley that made her tremble; she was
truly cold. The dampness of the earthen floor had seeped
through her clothing and chilled her to the bone.

Theorizing that she would be warmer if she were not lying
flat against the cold surface, Caitlan tried to wriggle to a sitting
position. That was her first mistake; the instant Caitlan moved,
she was paralyzed by a blinding flash of pain. The sensation
was so acute that it took Caitlan's breath away. Yet, at the
same time, it was so widespread in nature that she needed
several moments to pinpoint the precise location of the more
severe spasms. An impromptu self-examination revealed that
the worst of her injuries appeared to be her left shoulder, her
right knee, and her head . . . all of which throbbed mercilessly
at the slightest provocation.

A sense of relief washed over Caitlan when she determined
that she had not suffered any broken bones, nor did she appear
to have lost any blood to speak of. As Caitlan concluded this
mental checklist, she blew a grateful sigh and pressed her cheek
against the cold floor. As she lay there, shivering and struggling
to gather her wits about her, Madame Griselda's words came
sneaking into her thoughts.

What was it the woman had said? Caitlan crinkled her brow
and tried to summon the fortune-teller's exact words.

"There is one who wishes you much harm."

Well, Caitlan now knew the identity of her forewarned nemesis, however, there still remained one very large nagging mystery . . . why? Why had Wesley done all those reprehensible
things?

"I sense blackness all about you . . . and coldness," Madame Griselda had also said.

The woman had been right about that, too, Caitlan realized
with a hollow shiver and adjured herself to think warm
thoughts. Thus inspired, she imagined herself all safe and
warm, snuggled up in her bed at home above the tearoom . . .
cradled in a protective embrace by a pair of muscular arms.

These ruminations quite naturally led Caitlan to recall another portion of the soothsayer's eerie words.

"You must have trust in the one you love. Think of him . . . only of him . . . for he loves you truly and only he can save you . . ."

Caitlan prayed that Madame Griselda's predictions concerning Rafe might also prove as accurate. Though she had no idea how much time had passed since Wesley had entombed her in this underground prison, she was fairly certain that her prophesied champion had not yet returned from his business trip to Baton Rouge. In fact—a begrudging thought wormed its way inside her aching head—he was most likely sleeping peacefully in a comfortable feather bed at the finest hotel the city had to offer while the very scoundrel he had gone in search of continued his reign of terror at Foxborough Hall.

Resigning herself to her fate . . . rescue—if and when it came—was still several hours away, Caitlan gave a dejected whimper and slumped against the floor. After a moment or two of indulging herself in this manner, however, she experienced a resurgence of spirit. Deciding that—since she appeared doomed to while away an undetermined length of time in this pitch-black, miserably cold dungeon—she might as well channel all her frustration toward some worthwhile pursuit, Caitlan began to rub her wrists back and forth in an effort to loosen the knot that bound her hands together.

She continued in this fashion for a long while, the thoughts of a blazing fire, a hot bath, and a steaming cup of tea spurring her on. By this time, Caitlan had come to speculate as to her whereabouts. Most likely, considering Wesley's unnatural hatred of her family, he had locked her inside the Thistledown root cellar. Assuming she was correct, she had to give the man credit for his genius. It was the perfect hiding place . . . a run-down, ramshackle plantation, with no one for miles around to hear her cries for help—providing, of course, she could free herself of that nauseating gag.

The calculating Wesley had not counted on one important thing, however. Rafe. Rafe would move heaven and earth to find her, of that Caitlan was certain. And God help poor, stupid Wesley if he was foolhardy enough to get in Rafe's way.

As the relentless peppering of frozen rain continued to pelt the surface above her, another faint sound penetrated Caitlan's deep concentration. Whereas the drumming of sleet against the door had imbued her with a sense of tranquillity, this noise filled Caitlan with terror, thereby fulfilling the last—and perhaps most horrifying—of Madame Griselda's prophecies.

RATS!!

Caitlan had no way of knowing how many of the detestable creatures shared the black pit with her. She was certain of only one thing . . . she had to find a way out of the root cellar without delay!

Sensing that one of the rodents was just beyond her head, and fearing that it might entangle itself in her hair at any moment, Caitlan screamed and jerked away from the animal. Though the wadded handkerchief absorbed most of her frightened cry, the muffled sound served to frighten the vermin away. Hearing the skittering of tiny rodent feet across the dirt floor, Caitlan heaved a tearful sigh; she realized that the horrid creatures would momentarily return to terrorize her.

A feeling of desperation washed over her and, impervious to the pain that sluiced throughout her being, Caitlan somehow managed to pull herself to a sitting position. Bracing her shoulders against the wall, she dragged her legs around in front of her and sat poised, ready to strike at the first sign of trouble. She remained on guard for the longest time, her legs growing stiff and sore from being constantly held in the cramped position. While she sat, Caitlan continued to twist her hands against the knotted sash until—barely believing it herself—the material at last gave way.

Wriggling free of her bonds, Caitlan wrenched the gag from her mouth and gulped down a mouthful of stale, albeit welcome, air. Knowing there was a short staircase nearby, she reached out with tentative fingers to grope in the darkness for her only possible route of escape. Eventually, she happened upon a length of wood and, thus armed with a slat from a broken crate, her search became more intrepid. At last, she heard the clunking sound of wood against wood. Summoning all her strength, Caitlan dragged her bruised and aching body over to the steps.

Sitting on the bottom step, she pushed herself up to the next one, and so on, until her head bumped against the closed door.

Then Caitlan heaved with all her might, but from her first effort, she knew that further attempts would be futile. She would be better served if she saved her strength; the door would not budge. Wesley had obviously weighted the portal with some heavy object; it was steadfast. There was nothing she could do . . . but wait and pray.

Disheartened by her discovery, and feeling suddenly drained of all energy, Caitlan yawned and her head drooped forward onto her chest. At that moment, she heard the telltale scampering of little feet across the floor underneath her, and she jerked awake. Green eyes snapped open to peer into the darkness, her ears quirked in the direction of the noise, and she gripped the wooden slat—its jagged edge pointing outward—with a meaningful air. Caitlan blinked back the fearful tears that stung her eyes and gave her arm a vicious pinch when she felt herself growing drowsy again.

She would not . . . must not . . . sleep. She would not think about the rats, or the blockaded door, or how Rafe would go about finding her, or—worse—what would become of her if no one ever found her. Instead, Caitlan resolved to do that which Madame Griselda had told her she must do from the very beginning. She would think of Rafe . . . only of Rafe, for only he could save her.

A saddle-weary traveler rode past the Thistledown Plantation an hour before dawn the following morning. There had been many times during the journey from Zachary when Rafe had been tempted to seek shelter and a warm bed for the night. But he had resisted, pausing only now and again to give Wanderer a much-deserved rest, then pressing onward through the night . . . driven by a twofold purpose.

Rafe was itching to confront his weasel-faced brother-in-law, to watch Wesley squirm and attempt to explain away the mountain of charges that Rafe had brought against him. But even more intense was his desire to see for himself that Caitlan was all right. He longed to bury his face in the shimmery softness of her hair and to hear her trill of laughter when she scolded him for worrying over her needlessly. More importantly, Rafe yearned to hold her against him, to cradle her in his arms and let her kiss away this uneasy feeling that had plagued him the livelong night.

His thoughts thus preoccupied, Rafe was to be forgiven the barely civil greeting he gave the stable hand when he jumped down from Wanderer upon arriving at Foxborough Hall. Muttering some offhand instructions as to the care and feeding of the overworked animal, Rafe tossed the reins to the stable boy and trudged off toward the mansion. He was a little less gruff when he encountered Mandy just outside the kitchen door a moment later. Nevertheless, he declined the cook's tempting invitation to sit down to a hot cup of coffee and marched straightaway into the house and up the wide staircase to Caitlan's room.

Thirty seconds later, Rafe, a wild look flashing in his blue eyes, kicked open the door of the master bedchamber at the opposite end of the hallway. Mindful of the chaotic scene that erupted within the room—the abrupt splintering of the chamber door had taken the slumbering couple within completely unawares—Rafe braced himself on the threshold and surveyed the room. A wishful sneer curled Rafe's upper lip as he observed Wesley frantically groping for the gun on the bedside table.

Rafe's initial instinct was to put a bullet through the miserable bastard's head and have done with it. But realizing there were still too many unanswered questions, he put personal vengeance aside and strode into the room. Heedless of his sister's hysterical shrieks as she snatched the counterpane up to her chin, Rafe stepped up and over the foot of the bed and pinned Wesley to the mattress. Drawing his six-shooter from the holster that was strapped to his thigh, Rafe knelt down and placed the gun barrel under his brother-in-law's quivering chin.

"Where is she, you son of a bitch? What have you done with Kettie?"

"What? I'm sure I don't know what the devil you're talking about" came Wesley's remarkably cool response.

"Liar," Rafe drawled, his tone even more threatening than his expression. "Tell me before I give in to this overwhelming desire to make my sister a widow."

"No!" Josie screamed, scrambling to her knees and clutching at Rafe's arm. "Leave him alone, Rafe! Wesley hasn't done anything to Katie. She left yesterday morning just after you did.''

"What?'' Rafe blurted, obviously jolted by Josie's stunning pronouncement. The gun never wavered from its target, however, nor did his intimidating countenance falter when Rafe averted his shrewd gaze to study his sister's face. Eventually, those forbidding eyes returned to regard Wesley and, wrenching his arm free of Josie's encroaching hand, he said, "I don't believe you.''

"But . . . but it's true, Rafe. I . . . I swear,'' Josie stammered, sitting back and twisting the ribbons on her nightdress between nervous fingers. "Don't you trust me? Don't you believe me, your very own sister . . . flesh and blood? I wouldn't lie to you. Katie left yesterday just like I said. She said you would understand, that she simply had to get back to Vicksburg to tend to her dress shop. She said to tell you that she'd . . . see you . . . there and . . . '' Josie's voice tapered off when she saw the savage glint in her brother's eyes.

"That won't wash this time, sister dear,'' Rafe growled, digging his knee into Wesley's stomach to discourage him from attempting to retrieve the weapon that lay just inches from the little man's fingertips. Then grabbing hold of his sister's wrist, Rafe jerked her toward him until their faces were but a hairsbreadth apart and seethed between clenched teeth, "I *trusted* you to deliver a letter to Kettie seven years ago, and I *believed* you when you told me she was dead. I'm not likely to do either again.''

"No, you're wrong,'' Josie squeaked, more fearful of her husband's murderous glare than of Rafe's cruel grip. "I'm telling you the truth.''

"Shut up, Josie!'' Rafe spat in disgust and shoved her sideways into the headboard. "What do you take me for . . . a fool? Kettie doesn't run a dress shop, you simpleton, she owns a tearoom. I told you only that she had her own business and you stupidly assumed the rest.

"What was I supposed to think when I arrived in Vicksburg and Kettie wasn't there, Josie?'' Rafe settled his cold-blooded stare on his sister. "That she had been set upon by highwaymen and murdered or carried off?

"How can you be my sister and know nothing about me? I

love Kettie" came his throaty admission. "I've loved her for nearly fifteen years. Hell, I never stopped loving her even after you told me she was dead, Josie. Now that I've found her again, do you truly think I can be duped into believing another of your lies? Kettie's not in Vicksburg. She's here or somewhere close by, and I'll not rest until I've found her," Rafe vowed, grabbing a fistful of Wesley's nightshirt and jerking the hapless man toward him.

"No!" Josie screeched, lunging at her brother. "Leave him alone, Rafe!"

"Stay out of this, Josie," Rafe warned, shaking her off. "If I were you," he added in an ominous undertone, "I'd start praying that I don't take a buggy whip to you after I've settled matters with your lowlife husband here."

Noting that Josie appeared to be even more frightened of him than before, Rafe snickered and said, "You would do well to be wary of me, dear sister. You see, I'm on to you and Wesley. It's taken me long enough . . . too long," he added, regret clouding his fiery blue eyes. "I was unable to prevent him," Rafe leveled a scathing glare at Wesley, "and his demented band of cutthroats from butchering Ethan Meadows and his wife . . . and God only knows how many other poor souls. But one thing is certain, Wesley old boy, you won't be able to harm anyone else once your mangy hide is dangling from the end of a rope."

Vaguely aware of Josie's near-delirious reaction to his threat, Rafe pressed the gun barrel tightly against Wesley's plump chin and whispered, his tone deadly serious, "Of course, I'm fairly certain that a bullet would serve the purpose just as well and save a judge and jury a lot of wasted time. Now, where is she?"

Despite the fact that Rafe held him in an unrelenting grip and he was at a clear disadvantage, Wesley hissed, "Go to hell. You're just guessing, Rafe. You don't know anything."

"Could be," Rafe agreed, caressing the ivory-handled Colt revolver with a thoughtful gesture. "Then again, it could be I know enough to convince the district marshall to ride over here and conduct an official investigation," he drawled and watched Wesley—mentally if not physically—squirm.

"You're bluffing," Wesley seethed, the arrogance with

which he had made his boast, not quite reaching his eyes. Those beady, black orbs flickered with uncertainty.

"Am I? Perhaps you'll feel differently when Marshall Lowry arrives," Rafe taunted and, seeing the nervous beads of perspiration forming on Wesley's upper lip, added for good measure, "He should be here by noon. Where's Kettie?" he prompted, nudging Wesley with the gun.

Wesley, realizing that Rafe outmatched him by sheer brawn, decided that he had no choice but to rely on the cunning that had sustained him through the years and had, thus far, kept him one step ahead of the law . . . and a hangman's noose. Thinking he might be able to improve his circumstances if he could plant a seed of desperation in his adversary's mind, Wesley scoffed, "You may call out the militia for all I care, brother-in-law. It won't make a difference; your precious Katie will be long since dead before you find her . . . *if* you find her," he added with a maniacal snicker.

Unfortunately for Wesley, he underestimated his brother-in-law's mettle. Though Rafe was visibly distraught by Wesley's dismal revelation, rather than throwing him off balance, he was imbued with a sense of primitive fury that promptly rendered him incapable of rational thought. For Rafe's head presently whirled with a single, unconscionable image, that of Kettie—*his* Kettie—being brutalized by this pathetic little worm of a man.

The room verily reverberated as a guttural cry of pure rage was torn from Rafe's lips. "You bastard!" he roared, shoving Wesley back and burying his bald head in the pillows. Jabbing his fist into the protesting man's throat, Rafe positioned the deadly revolver under Wesley's left eye, and he possessed both the look and sound of a man gone truly mad when he cried, "By God in heaven, this is one murder you won't get away with, Wesley! Prepare to join your colleagues in hell." With this ominous threat, Rafe leaned close and drew back the pistol's hammer.

Upon hearing that heart-stopping clicking-sound, Josie panicked. Without thinking, she hurled herself at her brother and began pummeling his face and chest with vicious blows.

"*No!*" she sobbed. "Stop it, Rafe! Don't you dare hurt Wesley. Leave him alone! Get out. Get out of my house!"

came Josie's hysterical ravings. Then glancing over Rafe's shoulder at the open doorway, Josie saw one of the house servants—his face frozen in gape-faced bewilderment—on the threshold. "Joseph!" she yelled at the stunned man. "My brother's gone mad. Run over to Melville and fetch Sheriff Gladstone before he murders us all."

Rafe, his sister's delirious attack having served to pall his rampaging passions, flung away from the couple in disgust. Returning the revolver to its holster with a savage punch, he whirled and shouted after the fleeing servant, "You better be quick about it. I just might change my mind and tear the bastard apart with my bare hands."

Marshall Lowry had arrived in the early afternoon to find the Foxborough Hall household in a virtual uproar and immediately took charge. After quieting a thoroughly disgruntled Rafe, the marshall had sequestered the brooding man in the library while he went about questioning the suspects. Josie and Wesley had been subjected to lengthy, albeit separate, interrogations during which the marshall noted several discrepancies in their stories. Thus, Marshall Lowry had determined that, coupled with the evidence Rafe had given him, he had sufficient cause to take Wesley into custody.

Rafe presently sat slumped in a chair in the library, staring blankly at the life-size self-tribute of Wesley that hung over the mantelpiece. Following the emotional leave-taking of both Sheriff Gladstone and Marshall Lowry—with their hapless prisoner in manacles—Rafe had begun a room-by-room search of the huge mansion on the off chance he might find some clue that would lead him to Caitlan's whereabouts. His persistent detective-work eventually led him to the library, and Rafe knew he was on to something the moment he pushed open the chamber door to find his sister instructing two servants to take her husband's portrait down and burn it.

"No! Leave it," Rafe had countermanded Josie's order. Coming into the room, he had dismissed the domestics with a wave of his hand, saying, "Go on about your business. I'd like a word with my sister . . . in private."

"What do you want now, Rafe? Haven't you done enough damage? And how dare you bully my servants about. You have

no authority here. In fact, I want you to leave immediately,''
she had screeched at him, and would have flounced from the
room had Rafe not caught her wrist and jerked her around to
face him.

"I want Kettie. I think you know where she is.''

"No, I don't. And even if I did, I wouldn't tell you simply
because you've been so mean to me. Kettie!'' Josie had
spewed. "Is that all you think about . . . care about?'' she had
whined. "What about me . . . your own sister? Don't you care
about what happens to me?''

Rafe had glared down into the once beautiful face that had
long since grown ugly from greed and a false sense of self-
worth, a wrinkled face that looked years older than it actually
was. As his eyes had traveled down the onetime shapely figure
that had become plump from childbearing and neglect, Rafe
knew he should have felt pity for this pathetic creature, but he
had not. He had felt only disgust. And in that moment, Rafe
had realized something else. He did not give a tinker's damn
for what might become of his self-centered sibling. After all,
had it not been for Josie's meddling, he and Kettie would have
been together years ago. Indeed, his only concern was for
Kettie.

With an oath, Rafe had pushed Josie away from him and
spat, "You don't need me to worry about you. That's all you've
ever thought about, isn't it . . . yourself? Well, now you have
just cause, dear sister. For if Wesley is remanded over for trial,
you may very well be tried as an accomplice to all his crimes,
with one exception. If Kettie dies, you won't answer to the
law . . . you'll answer to me!'' he had snarled, a deadly glint
flashing in his eyes. "Think on that if you will. Now, get out
of here. I can't stand the sight of you." With that, Rafe had
propelled his sister across the threshold and slammed the door
in her horrified face.

Following Josie's departure, Rafe had stalked over to a tray
laden with crystal decanters and poured himself a brimming
glass of whiskey. His hand had trembled noticeably when he
lifted the drink to his lips; his thoughts had returned to Caitlan.
Thus distracted, he had slammed the glass down onto the library
desk and whirled toward the door, determined to scour the
countryside until he found some trace of her.

Rafe had started for the stables no less than a dozen times already, but each time he had vacillated. He had changed his mind this time as well and dropped into a chair in utter despair. The sad fact was, he hadn't the slightest clue as to where to begin his search. And though a willy-nilly romp about the parish might serve to assuage his own guilt-feelings and sense of uselessness, Rafe knew in his heart that it would be of little help to Caitlan. Besides, the sheriff had already sent his deputies off to inquire if anyone on the neighboring plantations had seen Wesley with a woman fitting Caitlan's description. Still, Rafe could not just sit idly by. He had to do something!

As he sat there, staring up at his brother-in-law's smug likeness, Rafe felt suddenly outraged. In a fit of helpless frustration, he grabbed his whiskey glass from the desk and hurled it at Wesley's portrait. As the goblet shattered into a thousand pieces and the amber-colored liquid splattered against the canvas, Rafe fell back into his chair and buried his face in his hands.

"Bastard!" He choked on the sob that swelled in his throat. As tears of anguish filled his eyes, Rafe shoved his hands through his hair in a desperate motion and groaned, "Aw, Kettie, what has he done to you? Where are you, darlin'?"

"The tinker-lady said you'd know how to find Katie, Uncle Rafe," said a small voice at his side.

Startled by the interruption, Rafe jerked his head up. Glancing sideways, he discovered his nephew watching him with a curious expression. "What? What did you say, P.J.?"

But P.J., his eyes wandering over the drenched portrait of his father, did not answer Rafe's question, saying instead, "You broke one of Mama's glasses. She won't like that."

"Never mind that now, P.J.," Rafe said, pulling the child over to stand in front of him. "What was that you said about a tinker-lady and Kettie?"

"Oh, I don't remember all the lady said," the child informed his disappointed uncle. "Only that part. When will Katie be comin' back, Uncle Rafe? I miss her. She bought this for me." P.J. proudly showed off the wooden musical pipe Caitlan had purchased from the tinker.

"I don't know, son. I wish I knew," Rafe said with a gloomy sigh. "I miss her, too."

"Those men that came here today . . . they took Papa away, didn't they?" came P.J.'s unexpected query. "Daniel said they took Papa away because he did bad things. He said if I didn't give him my pipe those men would come and take me away, too. But they won't, will they, Uncle Rafe?"

Rafe's lips parted in a tolerant smile and, lifting the boy onto his lap, he said, "No, P.J. Don't let your brother bully you into parting with your new toy. No one is going to take you away."

P.J. mulled this over in his child's mind for a moment, but rather than reassuring him, he seemed more confused. Looking up into his uncle's face, he said, "But I don't understand. Papa took Katie away last night, and she didn't come back, and now he—"

"What!" Rafe exclaimed, squeezing the boy's arm. Seeing his nephew's painful grimace, Rafe relaxed his grip and said in a cajoling voice, "You like Kettie, don't you, P.J.?"

"Uh huh."

"Then you must think *real* hard and tell me everything you remember about last night. It's important, P.J. You might be able to help me find Kettie. You'd like me to bring her back, wouldn't you?" Seeing the child's eager nod, Rafe added, his tone imploring, "Then you must tell me . . . what did you see?"

P.J. considered his uncle's grave face, and detecting a sense of urgency in Rafe's expression, he lowered his voice to a conspiratorial whisper and said, "You promise you won't tell Mama or Miss Pendleton, 'cause they'll be angry if they find out I was up so late."

"I promise."

"Well, I couldn't sleep 'cause I kept worryin' about Daniel tryin' to steal my new pipe," he explained. "So, I got out of bed to look and see if it was still in the hidin' place where I put it. That was when I saw Papa out the window."

"Which window? Can you show me?"

"Sure!" The child hopped down from Rafe's lap and skipped toward the library door, motioning his uncle to follow him.

Several minutes later, amid curious stares from the governess and the maid who was tidying the children's room, Rafe knelt down beside P.J. at the nursery window. "Okay, P.J. What did you see?" Rafe prompted.

Directing his gaze out the spotless glass, P.J. said, "Papa brought his horse up from the stable and went inside the library. When he came back out a little while later, he had Katie with him. Papa had hold of her real hard." P.J. winced, as if he knew firsthand what it was like to suffer his father's wrathful disposition. "She acted like she didn't want to go with him, Uncle Rafe, but Papa insisted. He pushed Katie up on his horse, then climbed up after her, and they rode off that way." P.J. pointed toward the distant horizon.

"Are you sure?" Rafe prodded, a glimmer of hope beginning to take hold of his heart.

"Uh huh," P.J. said, turning away from the embrasure to look at his uncle, his visage serious. "You said it was important, Uncle Rafe. I wouldn't lie to you. Are you going to find Katie now?"

"Yes, I am," Rafe said. Hugging the little boy to him, he murmured a grateful, "Thank you, P.J. You've been a big help. I believe I know where your papa might have taken her."

Indeed, Rafe cursed himself for not thinking of it sooner. Knowing Wesley's perverse mind, the miserable cur would have undoubtedly considered it a fitting irony for Caitlan to perish at the very place that had served as a haven to her most of her life. Rafe likewise understood his brother-in-law's demented sense of vengeance insofar as the Webber family was concerned. Caitlan would not have been granted a swift and painless death . . . that was not Wesley's style. That son of a bitch would have condemned her to die slowly, horribly.

Ravaged by this torturous thought, Rafe gave an anguished moan and stood up. Praying that he was not too late, that she would still be alive when he found her, Rafe bolted from the nursery. Within minutes, he was astride Wanderer and riding hell-bent for leather toward the deserted Thistledown Plantation.

Rafe blew a heavyhearted sigh and leaned against the deteriorated door facing of the once grand manse. He had forgotten just how big the Thistledown plantation house was. Rafe had spent more than an hour in which he explored every nook and cranny of the great rambling mansion, only to come up empty-handed. It did not appear to him that anyone had been inside the dilapidated house in months.

Glancing heavenward, he mentally calculated the amount of daylight available to him and promptly decided he better get on with his search. He had checked the stable upon his arrival and, with the house out of the way, that left only the row of slave cabins behind the barn. With a growing sense of dread, Rafe pushed away from the door—the spurt of optimism he had experienced after his talk with P.J. having fizzled considerably—and walked around the end of the house to the path that led to the slave quarters.

When Rafe emerged from the last cabin a half-hour later, his visage was more desolate than ever. With his shoulders slumped in defeat and feeling like an utter failure—like he had let Caitlan down—he wandered over to where he had tethered his horse beside the barn. Though he was loath to do so, Rafe mounted the animal, preparing to head back to Foxborough Hall. But as he settled himself in the saddle and wheeled the animal about, a brilliant splash of color caught his eye. Seized by a nagging sense of familiarity, Rafe climbed down from Wanderer and went to investigate.

Kneeling down beside the root cellar door that had been covered over with rocks, tree branches, and other heavy debris, Rafe reached out to pluck the scrap of royal blue material from where it had caught on a rusty hinge. His heart lurched when he recognized the fabric . . . it was from the cloak he had given Caitlan as a Christmas present. With a strangled oath and, berating himself as a fool for not having thought to investigate the cellar when he first rode up to the plantation, Rafe flew into action.

One by one, each obstacle that blockaded the doorway was flung aside until the only thing keeping Rafe from knowing what awaited him inside that black hole was a padlock. Without hesitating, Rafe drew his gun and, taking careful aim . . . fired. The deafening explosion caused his horse to shy away from the sound, and the last refrains of the blast were still echoing about the barnyard when Rafe wrenched the door open and clambered down the cellar steps.

Rafe squinted in an effort to help his eyes adjust to the

darkened pit . . . and then he saw her. She lay unconscious against the far wall, clutching—what appeared to be—a broken and bloodied wooden slat in her fist. An anguished sob rose in his throat when he discovered the reason she had armed herself with the makeshift weapon; the carcasses of at least three dead rats lay strewn about the cellar floor. As he looked on, compassion and anger sluicing through him for the horror she must have suffered, Rafe saw another of the disgusting rodents scurry across the floor toward Caitlan.

With an embittered cry, Rafe lunged forward and, with a vicious kick, hurled the unlucky animal against the opposite wall. As the lifeless vermin fell with a thud to the dirt floor, Rafe knelt beside Caitlan.

"Kettie," he whispered, his anxious gaze sweeping over her. "Kettie, darlin'. It's Rafe." He reached out in a tentative gesture—fearful of what he might find, that he had come too late, after all, that she was already . . . dead—and brushed his hand across her forehead.

This action served to fill him with a sense of dread; she was stone cold. Beside himself with despair, Rafe dragged her deathly still body into his arms and cradled Caitlan to him. As he rocked her gently in his powerful embrace, warming her body with his, tears of sorrow welled in the blue eyes.

Thinking the worst, but not yet willing to believe that he had truly lost her, Rafe buried his face in her neck, his plaintive murmurings ricocheting off the four cellar walls, "No! It cannot be. Not after all we've gone through to be together. You can't leave me now, sweet pea. Not now."

Rafe remained thus distracted for several long moments and when it became apparent that her limp and lifeless body could not be revived, he drove his fist into the wall and his primal cry of outraged frustration rumbled up and out the open doorway. Then as Rafe started to pull away from Caitlan, a miracle happened. It was the slightest of movements, but he felt her stir in his arms. As he stared down at her, his expression a mixture of disbelief and unexampled joy, Caitlan lifted her hand and touched her fingertips to his tearstained cheek.

Chapter Eighteen

❦

Caitlan gave a contented whimper and nestled farther down under the covers in the roomy bed. Her efforts to wriggle onto her side brought a painful moan to her lips, however, causing her eyes to flutter open. Gazing about the dimly lit room in sleepy wonder, it took her a moment to recognize her surroundings as the bedchamber she had occupied at Foxborough Hall. In that fleeting instant, all the horrors of the past twenty-four hours flooded her being, and she bristled with anxiety. Glancing at the foot of the bed, as if she fully expected to find Wesley's evil face leering down at her, Caitlan was understandably relieved to find only the soft shadows of lamplight flickering there.

As the cobwebs gradually cleared from her drowsy head, Caitlan became aware of a faint sensation. Looking down the length of her arm, she saw a hand protectively entwined in hers. Caitlan directed her misty gaze upward to where the hulking giant of a man sat slumped in sleep in a chair beside her bed, and her lips parted in a loving smile . . . Rafe. Knowing that she could rest easy with the knowledge that he safeguarded her, Caitlan closed her eyes and drifted off to sleep once more.

When she next awakened, it was to find a strange—albeit

kindly—masculine face peering into hers. As it turned out, the man was the local doctor that Rafe had summoned to look after her. Caitlan lay quietly while the physician conducted his medical examination and was relieved when the man favored her with a reassuring smile. Interpreting his sunny countenance to mean that her injuries were not so very serious, Caitlan relaxed.

After a time, the man said, "You're a very lucky lady, Miss Webber. Mr. Bradrick has told me all about the ordeal you suffered. I'm Dr. Smithfield. I asked Mr. Bradrick to wait outside while I examined you," he explained. "Shall I fetch him now or would you prefer to hear what I have to say alone?"

"No, tell me, please," Caitlan said, vaguely disturbed by something in the doctor's eyes.

"As near as I can tell, you're going to be fine" came his encouraging prognosis. "You've got a badly wrenched knee and a dislocated shoulder which I'll put back in place before I go." He smiled knowingly when he saw Caitlan's tenuous face at the prospect of this painful procedure. Patting her hand, he said, "There now, don't get all worked up thinking about it. Granted, it will hurt like the dickens for a while afterward, but nothing like the pain you're experiencing now, I fancy. You'll be much more comfortable," he assured her, adding, "Mostly, you're suffering from exposure . . . being out in the cold. But a few days of resting in bed and Mandy's hot soup should fix you up as good as new in no time," the doctor informed her, rolling up his shirtsleeves and eyeing her shoulder with purpose.

After the painful procedure had been completed and Caitlan lay back against the pillow, gasping for breath, she felt a sudden wave of nausea wash over her. Later, as she wiped her face with the cool washcloth the doctor extended toward her, Caitlan offered him an apologetic smile as she watched him carry away the basin that he had but moments earlier thrust under her chin.

"I'm sorry, Doctor," Caitlan mumbled, an embarrassed flush spreading across her face.

"Don't give it a second thought, dear." The physician offered her an understanding smile. "After all, this sort of thing is quite common among women in your condition. Now, about the baby—"

"Baby!" Caitlan exclaimed, her hands instinctively flying to her stomach.

"Yes. You didn't know?" Dr. Smithfield raised a surprised eyebrow, obviously thinking this singularly peculiar.

"No, I . . . uh . . . " Caitlan splayed her hands in a helpless gesture. "I didn't know."

"Well, it should be fine, too," he said in a fatherly tone. "But just to be on the safe side, check in with your regular doctor when you get home. Now, you get some rest, young lady. I'll see if I can persuade that big strapping fella that's pounding up and down the hallway outside to wait a while before he comes in to see you." With a doubtful wag of his head, he mumbled, "Something tells me I'll be wasting my breath."

His hand on the doorknob, Dr. Smithfield put Caitlan's raging fears to rest by saying, "Don't you fret now. I'll leave it up to you to tell him what's ailing you."

Understanding his implied meaning, Caitlan offered him a grateful smile, saying, "Thank you . . . for everything."

The door had no sooner closed behind the departing physician than it swung wide again to admit Rafe. He approached the bed with caution at first, but upon finding Caitlan wide awake, he abandoned his tentative demeanor and came full into the room. As Rafe stood gazing down at her, his expression reflecting the feelings that wrenched his heart, he discovered that he could not speak. Oh, his head was full of words right enough, but unfortunately they had all jumbled together in a mass of emotional confusion the moment he saw Caitlan smiling up at him. In short, Rafe did not know where to begin.

Caitlan, sensing his turmoil, stretched out her hand to him, saying simply, "Hold me."

Rafe did not hesitate then, but sat down on the edge of the bed beside her. Very carefully, he drew Caitlan into his arms and gathered her against him to breathe in her soft fragrance.

"Are you all right?" he asked, when he could at last find his tongue.

"Yes, Rafe," Caitlan assured him and, feeling a warm glow creep over her with the secret knowledge that she was pregnant with his child, she smiled to herself. To Rafe, she said, "I'm fine, just a few aches and pains is all."

Upon hearing this, Rafe blew a heartfelt sigh of relief and said, "My God, Kettie. I thought I'd lost you forever this time. Can you forgive me, darlin'?"

"Forgive you?" Caitlan repeated, pulling away to scrutinize his anguished face. "Oh, my love," she whispered, stroking his cheek with her fingertips. "There is nothing to forgive, so stop torturing yourself. This was not your fault. You had no way of knowing it was Wesley. Indeed, had I not chanced upon the tiepin in his portrait, I daresay none of this would have happened," she cooed, letting her hand stray to smooth the hair at his temple.

"The portrait?" Rafe murmured with a thoughtful frown. "So, that's why Josie told her servants to take it down and burn it. It's a good thing I stopped her. That's another piece of evidence we can use against Wesley."

Caitlan, pulling Rafe near, pressed a kiss against his pensive mouth before asking, "Why did he do all those horrible things?"

"Kettie," Rafe adjured. "Are you sure you're up to this? Perhaps we should wait—"

"No, I want to—need to—know now."

With an understanding nod, Rafe settled Caitlan back against the pillows and began by saying, "Evidently, my brother-in-law suffers from an overdeveloped sense of greed . . . he did it for the money. According to Josie—"

"Josie?" Caitlan exclaimed.

"Yes, I experienced much the same reaction when I learned she had agreed to cooperate," Rafe drawled, leaning across her to rest his hand against the mattress. Crossing one leg over the other, he explained, "Apparently, once I made it plain to my dear sister that she could be tried as an accomplice to all of Wesley's crimes—and very likely go to jail or worse—she sang like a bird."

"Tell me everything."

"Well, honey. Like I said, Wesley did it for the money. I guess it all started back when his father ran off with your mama. He never got over it . . . the gossip, and the sidelong looks from people, and the hushed whispers. Something inside him must have snapped. And, since he couldn't get back at the ones responsible for making him a local laughingstock, he took his hostility out on everyone else . . . especially your family, dar-lin'.''

''What do you mean?''

Taking Caitlan's hand in his, Rafe gave the delicate appen-dage a reassuring squeeze before saying, ''Brendan didn't just happen into a duel with Page Wilkerson, Kettie. He was goaded into it. Wesley knew that he himself could never best Brendan in a fair fight, so he paid the best shot in the parish to do his dirty work for him. It's my guess that Wesley suspected another blow like this would drive your father over the edge . . . which it did. Didn't you say it was after Brendan's death that Law-rence took to gambling?''

Caitlan gave a dull nod, thoroughly numbed to learn the precise extent of Wesley's sinister doings.

''And if that hadn't served the purpose, I'm fairly certain Wesley would have been at the ready with some other dastardly plot'' came Rafe's offhand comment.

His narrative was interrupted then by a knock at the door and, while he went to answer the summons, Caitlan had a moment to absorb all he had told her thus far. Noticing her ashen pallor when he returned to the bed, carrying the dinner tray Mandy had sent up to them, Rafe decided she had heard enough for one afternoon. Setting the tray on the bedside table, he lifted the covers from the dishes and could not help but grin when he saw the bowl of gruel and cup of spiced tea that were to be Caitlan's meager repast. Deciding his own meal could wait, Rafe dipped the spoon into the bowl of pungent-smelling broth and brought the utensil to Caitlan's lips.

''What is it?'' she asked, eyeing the foul-smelling concoc-tion with a suspicious look.

''I'm not sure'' came his truthful reply. ''It smells like that awful stuff you spoon-fed me for days on end when I was laid up at the boardinghouse.'' Then the irony of the situation hitting him squarely between the eyes, Rafe gave a whoop of laughter and said, ''Now, this is poetic justice, wouldn't you say, Ket-tie? Me finally getting even with you for smearing me all over with those smelly ointments and making me drink that awful-tasting broth you brewed up. Drink this down, young lady. It will help make you strong again.'' Rafe taunted Caitlan with the very argument she had used on him time and again when she had served as his nursemaid.

"Later," Caitlan said, pushing aside the hand that held the unappetizing spoon under her nose. "I want to hear more about Wesley."

From the set of her jaw, Rafe realized they were at an impasse. Scratching his chin, he decided to strike a compromise with his headstrong miss. "How about this . . . I'll tell you what I know, if you promise to drink down every drop in this bowl."

From the dubious look on Caitlan's pretty face, it was obvious she believed that Rafe had gotten the better end of the bargain. With a conciliatory shrug, she opened her mouth and accepted the spoonful of soup without demure.

Swallowing, she grimaced and said, "Go on. How else did Wesley plot against my family?"

"He had Page Wilkerson act as his agent in buying Thistledown from your father," Rafe explained, easing himself onto the mattress once more. "That's why the place is in the shape it's in, Kettie. I suppose that was Wesley's way of getting back at your father—letting Thistledown go to ruin—seeing as how he took such pride in that plantation."

"And yet he did not cavil at bringing many of Thistledown's furnishings into his own home," Caitlan offered, her expression bitter. "Have you seen the library, Rafe? It is exactly as Papa kept it."

"I know, honey," Rafe murmured, giving her arm a sympathetic pat. Setting the empty bowl aside, he shrugged and said, "There's never been any rhyme or reason to Wesley's evildoings. I suppose that, by surrounding himself with such extravagance, it made him feel as if he were someone of consequence, even though you and I know Wesley for what he truly is."

"But how could he afford all this?" Caitlan made a sweeping gesture of the room with her uninjured arm.

"Oh, a variety of ways. He sold the remainder of Thistledown's furnishings, as well as the slaves and whatever else he could find. But mostly my brother-in-law came by his ill-gotten gains by murdering and stealing from others," Rafe said, his countenance growing grim. "You see, Wesley felt no great affection for Foxborough Hall after his father left. He was an indifferent planter at best, but he'd grown accustomed to a certain way of life. Oh, he tried to make a go of the plantation while his mother was alive, but after she died, he gave up the farce and devoted himself to the cultivation of his criminal activities instead.

"From what I gather from my sister, Wesley preferred to let hirelings—like Sam Rawlings—commit the actual crimes. Believe it or not," he scoffed, "Wesley was the brains behind the operation. He would select the victims, get to know them, then plan when and where the pigeon would be plucked, as it were. But on occasion, Wesley would ride along so that he could be in on the kill. I don't know why. Perhaps he derived some sort of perverse thrill from watching people die. I suppose one would have to enjoy it, in a manner of speaking, in order to make a livelihood in such a ruthless manner.

"In any event, as it turns out, I suppose—if Ethan and his wife had to die—it was fortunate Wesley chose that night to accompany Rawlings. I might never have made the connection otherwise; it's that gaudy tiepin that led to Wesley's undoing. Without that, he'd still be out there, butchering innocent people." Rafe's voice tapered off and a contemplative frown creased his brow as he said, "You know, honey. It's kind of ironic."

"What is?" Caitlan murmured, pulling him down beside her.

With her head nuzzling his shoulder, Rafe pressed a kiss against her brow. Then twirling a russet-tinged tendril between his fingertips, he touched the curl to his lips and explained, "That tiepin didn't even belong to Wesley. It was his father's. I think it's fitting justice that the man who was, in effect, responsible for creating this detestable monster is the same one that will ultimately send him to the gallows."

Neither of them spoke for the longest time after Rafe concluded his bone-chilling narrative. Caitlan was merely content to lay upon the bed with Rafe's arm wrapped securely about her and revel in his nearness. Eventually, however, a nagging thought occurred to her, prompting her to ask, "What will happen to Josie?"

Rafe hunched his shoulders in an indifferent gesture and

said, "I don't know. And, at the moment, I don't much care. I haven't told you everything, sweet pea."

"What?" Caitlan demanded, twisting around to get a better look at his face.

"It was Josie who conspired—along with Wesley—to keep us apart all these years. Even the first time, when I left because I lost my nerve about asking you to marry me, it was Josie who kept filling my head with doubts. She said you were too young, that I needed to establish myself before I took a wife, that we had plenty of time. . . . Anyway, I guess it was partly my fault because I was foolhardy enough to listen to her prattle."

Rafe saw Caitlan's sorrowful expression and looked away, unable to endure the sad look that glistened in her eyes. Clearing his throat, he continued, "Come to find out, Wesley had told Josie that if you and I ever married, he would throw her out . . . bag and baggage. He told her that he'd sooner bear the shame of a divorce than have a Webber as a married relation. That's how you came to receive this, sweet pea." Rafe reached into his pocket and withdrew the letter he had taken from her dresser back in Vicksburg.

"How did you—"

"I'll explain later. The important thing is that you believe me when I tell you this letter was *never* intended for you, but for some other encroaching female who had designs on me at the time. When father became ill and I was called home, I wrote two letters and gave them to Josie to dispatch for me," he explained, his watchful gaze never leaving her face. "At first, I thought I was to blame . . . that I had inadvertently put the letters in the wrong envelopes. But as I came to understand the extent of my sister's deceit, I realized what truly happened. Josie deliberately switched the letters. You must believe me, darlin'. I never dreamed she would do such a thing, else I never would have entrusted the letters to her.

"I promise you, sweetheart," Rafe caressed her cheek with his knuckles and Caitlan was persuaded to meet his turbulent gaze, "your letter was penned by the hand of an ardent suitor."

Knowing that he would not rest until she put his mind at ease, Caitlan snuggled against him, saying, "I believe you,

Rafe. And I suppose it was Josie who made up that wretched story about me being dead.''

Rafe nodded. "That was the only way she could make sure I didn't try to contact you again. Unfortunately, it worked.''

"But how could she do that to you . . . her own brother?''

"What can I say? Josie thinks only of herself. Our happiness didn't mean anything to her.''

Caitlan, feeling suddenly cold, gave an uncontrollable shiver and burrowed against Rafe. Her tone was imploring when she said, "I don't want to stay here any longer, surrounded by so much hate and deception. When can we go home, Rafe?''

Rafe, fondling her hair with gentle, loving strokes, said as if pacifying a small child, "Just as soon as the doctor says you're fit to travel. Go to sleep now, love," he cajoled. "I won't leave you alone again. I'll be here when you waken.''

The couple arrived in Vicksburg a week later to find the city abuzz with the news . . . Mississippi had seceded from the Union. Though talk of secession had been in the air for months, even years, Caitlan had never paid much heed to it. But now, as she sat at her kitchen table—while Essie flitted about the room preparing refreshments for them—her gaze settled on Rafe's pensive face, and she was given every reason to abhor the dreaded word. She knew that look, and as Essie brought the coffeepot and a plate of freshly baked cookies to the table, Caitlan found herself wondering just how long it would be before he left again.

All too soon, she would have the answer to that nagging question.

The steady pounding of rain against the windowpane awakened Rafe just before daybreak and, rolling to his side, he reached out to caress his bedmate's rigid back. Chuckling to himself, he thought it was just like Kettie to remain vexed at him even while she slept. If he knew her, she was probably dreaming of all the terrible things she would like to do to him before he left. Rafe's gaze grew warm as it wandered across the shapely curves beneath the bedclothes and, with a roguish grin, he thought to himself that there were a couple of things he wouldn't mind doing before he left either.

Suiting his actions to his lustful musings, Rafe reached underneath the bedclothes and, with a gentle, loving touch, began to stroke her arm. His fondlings grew more intimate, however, as he scooted closer to press the length of his hard physique against her softer curves. But as inquisitive fingers concluded their carefree gamboling atop the now-stiffened peaks of her breasts and pressed farther downward, bent upon wreaking havoc of a purely sensual nature, Rafe made a puzzling discovery. It was as his hand fluttered across Caitlan's customarily flat belly that he felt something was different.

As Rafe continued to gently finger the tiny bulge, a thoughtful frown wrinkled his forehead. Then suddenly he knew and, snatching his hand away, he bolted upward in the bed.

"Don't stop now," a drowsy voice murmured in the dreary semidarkness.

Rafe, his head still reeling with the joyful realization that he was going to be a father—that Caitlan was carrying *his* child—could not immediately find his voice. His elation gradually gave way to irritation and, dragging Caitlan around to face him, his tone was harsh when he demanded, "Why didn't you tell me, Kettie?"

Caitlan, realizing that he had unwittingly discovered her secret, heard not only the accusation in his stern voice but the hurt as well. Rolling onto her back, she stared up into that brooding face for a long moment before she found the courage to reply.

Touching her hand to his brow, she blew a nervous breath and explained, "Because you're going away, Rafe. I know you have told me that you'll come back as soon as you've made some business arrangements in St. Louis and New Orleans. And I do want you to come back, truly I do . . . but because you want to . . . because you want *me*. Not because you feel obligated about the baby."

"Aw hell, Kettie," Rafe groaned, an impatient glint flaring in his blue eyes. "What can I do to make you understand? I love you, honey. The fact that you're carrying my baby . . . *our* baby," he rubbed his hand along her stomach, "only makes me love and want you all the more."

"Then . . . then *why* must you go?" Caitlan blurted the question she had vowed not to ask.

His amorous mood having fizzled, Rafe rolled away from her to sit on the edge of the bed. Running his fingers through his hair in a restless motion, his voice was full of frustration when he said, "I've already explained, Kettie. Three other states besides Mississippi have seceded and, from the looks of things, Georgia and Louisiana should follow suit any day now. There's a war brewing. I don't know when, but it will be with us before you know it. I've already stayed a week longer than I should have."

Bending forward to retrieve his discarded clothing from the bedside chair, he started to dress, saying, "Now, I have no way of knowing how things will turn out, but I'm not going to sit idly by and take a chance that I'll lose everything I've worked for just because the warmongers want to stir up trouble and the politicians who run things can't see eye to eye. I intend to do my damndest to make sure we've got something to make a life with when the smoke clears," he said, shoving his foot into his boot with a determined grunt.

"But . . . what if there is a war as you say? What will happen to us then? Will you fight?"

"I don't know, Kettie. That's a decision I'll have to make when the time comes" came his honest, albeit vague, answer.

Standing, he shrugged his broad shoulders into his coat and turned to look at her. When he beheld Caitlan's glum expression, Rafe stepped around the bed and bent to kiss her goodbye.

"There," he murmured, gazing at her with loving eyes and stroking the shimmery blanket of brown-and-russet tendrils that fell across her milky-white shoulder. "That will have to keep you until I get back, sweet pea. And I will be back."

Caitlan watched him turn and stride toward the bedchamber door—that self-assured swagger that set him apart from the rest—and held her breath, half hoping he would change his mind, yet knowing in her heart he could not. This was something he had to do. Rafe would be back . . . he had promised her as much. She must believe him, trust him. Still, there persisted that nagging sense of doubt that always took hold of her heart whenever they parted.

Upon hearing the click of the door as Rafe swung it closed behind him, Caitlan flung herself onto her side and clasped his pillow to her breast, feeling miserable and lonely . . . missing him already.

It was a prodigiously downhearted expression that fashioned Caitlan's pretty face later that morning as she wended her way through the tearoom. She had gone down to the kitchen shortly following Rafe's departure, but it had been obvious from the outset that her thoughts were not on cooking this day.

First, Caitlan had burned a pan of biscuits, then horribly mutilated a chicken that had been destined for the frying pan, but—thanks to her hapless efforts—had been rendered fit only for stewing. The final straw had come, however, when she set fire to a dishcloth as she bent to remove a pie from the oven. Essie had just straightened from wiping up the puddle of milk that Caitlan had spilled earlier when she saw the flaming cloth. Jerking the rag out of Caitlan's hands, Essie had tossed the dishcloth into the sink and whirled to thrust a dismissive finger at the door.

Thus, having been tossed out of her own kitchen, Caitlan had returned to the house proper.

As she strolled among the tables, checking for soiled table-cloths, tattered menus, and whatnot, she happened upon the previous day's issue of the *Daily Whig*. With an offhand shrug, she sat down at a nearby table and began to peruse the news-paper. A particularly amusing article had just brought a smile to her lips when the sound of a steamboat whistle in the distance infiltrated her thoughts. The sound sliced through her heart like a sharp knife and, consequently, Caitlan's lighthearted mien vanished as quickly as it had appeared. Tossing the tabloid aside, she decided she might as well go upstairs and see if she could find something worthwhile to do.

As Caitlan stepped into the corridor, she was distracted by a knocking at the front door. A puzzled look knit her brow as she stepped toward the portal; the tearoom did not open for another hour or more. It was on her lips to apprise the visitors of this very thing, but when Caitlan pulled the door open, her prearranged speech promptly sputtered on her tongue.

"Hi, Kitty!" exclaimed a familiar voice.

"Becky?!" came Caitlan's startled gasp.

Thoroughly taken by surprise as she was, Caitlan could do

little more than stare in dumbfounded fascination at the tiny arms that stretched out toward her. Once her initial shock subsided, however, she gathered the little girl in her arms and hugged Becky to her. Pressing a kiss to the child's forehead, Caitlan gave a shaky laugh as Becky returned the gesture by pressing a wet kiss against her cheek. Caitlan's head was awhirl with a thousand questions. Thus, she directed her confused gaze at the young woman who remained standing on the porch. But before Caitlan could put a voice to even one of her nagging questions, Becky commanded her full attention.

"Kitty!" Becky trilled, jumping up and down in Caitlan's arms.

"Yes, honey. I know. I'm happy to see you, too," Caitlan murmured in loving tones.

"No, *kitty*," Becky repeated, pointing down the long corridor to where Beau had just sauntered in from the backyard. "Down," the little girl demanded, squirming in Caitlan's arms.

Caitlan immediately lowered Becky to the floor and watched for a moment as the little girl toddled down the hallway. She gave a half smile of understanding as she observed the lazy tabby—obviously sensing trouble was afoot—scamper into a nearby dining-room. Then as little Becky gurgled happily and gave chase, Caitlan turned to Miss Pendleton.

"How—"

"Mr. Bradrick made the arrangements before he left Foxborough Hall, Miss Webber," the woman explained. "He asked me to go to New Orleans and get Becky from the convent and bring her here. He also hired me to stay on as her governess. I . . . I hope that's all right with you, ma'am," Miss Pendleton ventured, worried by Caitlan's confounded mien.

"What?" Caitlan mumbled, a vague expression darkening her pretty features. Then giving herself a mental shake, Caitlan offered the woman a reassuring smile, saying, "Of course, it's all right, Miss Pendleton. Please, come in." She moved aside and beckoned the governess across the threshold.

"Thank you, Miss Webber." The young woman offered her a grateful smile as she stepped inside. "I had no idea Mr. Bradrick would spring such a surprise on you. I thought he would surely give you advance warning about Becky and me coming to live with you.''

"Oh, Mr. Bradrick is full of surprises all right," Caitlan said with a chuckle, a hint of a smile dancing in her eyes.

"That reminds me," Miss Pendleton said, reaching inside her reticule and withdrawing a small parcel. "Becky had a chance to visit with her daddy for a while before we left the riverboat. He asked me to give this to you," she explained, handing the package to Caitlan.

Caitlan wasted little time in opening the present. She had no idea what she might find, but considering her subsequent bewildered expression, she had not expected to find a diamond and emerald ring—the very one Rafe had given Harriet as payment for his boardinghouse account—twinkling up at her in the hazy morning light. Her heart gave a joyful lurch as she understood the implied meaning of this very special gift.

Glancing out the open door, Caitlan had an impulsive thought and, turning toward the governess, said, "Miss Pendleton? Has the *Magnolia Princess* left yet?"

"No, ma'am. Although, Mr. Bradrick said they would be pulling out soon."

Upon hearing this hopeful news, Caitlan bolted across the threshold and scurried down the tearoom steps. Heedless of Miss Pendleton's admonishing shout that she would "catch her death of cold" without her cloak, Caitlan sprinted through the gate and across the thoroughfare. She was out of breath by the time she arrived at the top of Washington Street and paused to peer down at the Vicksburg landing. Despite her winded condition, she nearly cried aloud when she saw that the *Princess* was still there. Lifting her skirts so as not to risk losing her footing and thereby take a tumble down the treacherously steep hill, Caitlan made her way carefully down the street.

She saw Rafe, standing on the deck of the riverboat—conversing with one of the crew members—as she neared the landing. Clutching the ring box to her bosom with one hand, she lifted the other above her head and waved at him in an effort to get his attention. Her side was splitting and her knee throbbing from her unprecedented race from the tearoom, but Caitlan did not care about that now. There was something of the utmost importance she had to tell him before he left. Indeed, she could not let Rafe leave again without telling him.

It appeared, however, that her impassioned declaration might have to wait; as Caitlan stepped up onto the wharf, she heard the steamboat whistle blasting out to all who could hear the news of its impending departure. With a sinking heart, Caitlan saw that the workmen had started to haul the gangplank away from the pier.

Rushing forward, Caitlan shouted Rafe's name. Unfortunately, her throaty summons was drowned out by yet another shrill cry of the riverboat whistle. Not one to be easily frustrated, she waited until the echoing shriek died away, then waving her arms above her head, she called his name again.

This time Rafe heard her. Wheeling away from the deckhand, he saw her . . . this wildly emotional young woman, standing on the wharf, frantically trying to get his attention. Barking out a command for the crewmen to lower the bridge once more, Rafe ran down the gangplank toward her.

They met in the middle. Indeed, Caitlan nearly toppled him when she flung herself against his broad chest.

Stunned by the force of her affectionate—not to mention very public—display, Rafe wrapped his arms around her and held Caitlan to him. His expression was incredulous when he said, "Kettie, what the—"

"You *are* coming back!" she cried, breathless and near tears. Rafe gave a hearty chuckle and with a ponderous shake of his head, pulled her even tighter. "Of course, I am, darlin'. I've been telling you that for days now. What made you finally believe me?"

"Becky," Caitlan explained. "You brought her to live with me. You . . . you wouldn't do that if you weren't coming back. You love her too much."

"I love you, too," he reminded her, nuzzling her chin with his nose.

"And then there is this," she said, proffering the ring box in her trembling hand. "How . . . however did you get it back from Harriet?"

"Don't look at me like that . . . I didn't steal it." Then giving this statement some thought, he scratched his beard and said, "Then, again, I suppose you might say I did. You see, honey.

Do you remember the day old prissy-faced Penelope accused you of taking the ring from Harriet's room? Well, I'm the one who took it. I happened by her room and saw it lying on the floor outside her door, not in her trinket box like she said. So, I figured that, if she couldn't take any better care of the ring than that, she didn't deserve to keep it.'' He saw Caitlan's reproachful look and hastily added, ''Now, before you go climbing up on your high horse and start quoting the scriptures or some such at me, I want you to know that I have since repaid the redoubtable Miss Tuttle for her services . . . in full.

''The truth of the matter is, I never intended for Harriet to keep the ring anyway. I only gave it to her to pacify her for a time.'' Looking at Caitlan, his blue eyes deepened with desire and there was an emotional catch in his voice when he said, ''I've always had other plans for this ring. You will marry me, won't you, Kettie?''

''Yes, yes! Of course, I'll marry you!'' came Caitlan's happy reply. Her fingers were shaking visibly as she took the ring from the box and handed it to Rafe, whispering, ''Put it on.''

Rafe slipped the ring onto Caitlan's finger and embraced her once more. As he stood there, holding his love against his heart on this cold and dreary Mississippi morning, Rafe had never felt more at peace. His contented expression changed to one of puzzlement, however, when he heard Caitlan's plaintive sob against his chest.

Pulling away to look at her, he caressed her tear-streaked face with his thumb and said, ''What is it, sweet pea?''

Caitlan, too, had never felt more contented or more loved. Reading the encouragement in his eyes, she whispered, ''I . . . I love you.''

''Aw hell, Kettie.'' Rafe blew a heady sigh. ''I know that. It sure is good to hear you say it though.'' He touched his lips to her cheek and his breath was warm and thrilling when he murmured against her ear, ''Say it again.''

''I love—''

The remainder of her impassioned declaration was silenced by the impatient cry of the steamboat whistle. Rafe, however, ignored the shrill summons and swept Caitlan into his arms.

This would be an embrace that neither of them would soon forget. Caitlan's long-suffering feelings of doubt, loneliness, and insecurity were swept away on a tidal wave of passion as Rafe's lips descended upon hers. They were quickly supplanted with more frightening emotions, however. Feelings that made her tremble with their intensity. Feelings such as longing, yearning . . . and most overwhelmingly of all . . . love. This was a kiss that would seal their destiny forever and bind them together in spirit even when they were miles apart.

When the insistent shriek of the riverboat whistle at last commanded Rafe's attention, Caitlan did not cavil when he pulled away, but went willingly from his arms. Standing on tiptoe, she kissed him once more and stepped away from the gangplank. Wrapping her arms about her waist, Caitlan turned and walked a little way up the steep incline before she thought to turn and wave farewell. Her heart swelled with love as she saw Rafe standing on the deck; she could feel the heat of his gaze caressing her even from that great distance.

When Caitlan turned away from the river, there was a livelier bounce to her step as she trudged up the hill toward the tearoom. A soft rain had begun to fall, but Caitlan barely noticed as the drizzling pellets saturated her thin blouse. Her thoughts were of Becky and the baby that grew inside her, but mostly they were of Rafe. Just like so many times in the past, he had left again. And like the meetings and separations that had gone before, this encounter had been just as bittersweet. But the next time would be different; the next time Rafe came home it would be for good. She would see to that. And of this thing Caitlan was certain . . . Rafe would come home again.

AUTHOR'S NOTE

I welcome letters from my readers.
Please feel free to drop me a note
at the following address:

Luanne Walden
P.O. Box 299
South Point, Ohio 45680